THEIR PATHS WERE DESTINED TO CROSS . . .

"I have given you every warning!" he thundered.

"And I would rather die than be raped by a beast like you!" Elise retorted in torn anguish.

"Rape?"

To her amazement, Bryan Stede went dead-still, then laughed—but he did not release his hold on her.

"Duchess, my last intent this night is to rape you. Were I to want a woman, it would be one who was warm and winsome, not one with the cold, black heart of a thief!"

He meant his words. Never in his life had he desired to take a woman by force. Since he had been a youth, women had come to him. From peasant girls to high-born ladies, they had come to him. Warm and giving, wanting to be wanted. Never could he imagine stooping to force. There would be no pleasure in it.

Especially not with this woman. A born beauty, yet carrying the ring he knew to be King Henry's. Pleading innocence, pleading rank, yet clearly holding the evidence against her.

No, the thought of rape had never entered his head.

Nor had he truly thought, even vaguely, of wanting her . . . until now . . .

* * *

Raves for *Blue Heaven, Black Night*

"A sweeping tale of medieval life . . . Sensual, adventurous, and stormy romance!"

—*Romantic Times*

"A web of hatred, passion, and intrigue . . ."

—*Baker and Taylor*

Raves for Shannon Drake

"[A writer of] engrossing, sexy historical romance!"

—*Publishers Weekly*

"Shannon Drake knows how to tell a story that captures the imagination."

—*Romantic Times*

"A writer of incredible talent!"

—*Affaire de Coeur*

BLUE HEAVEN, BLACK NIGHT
SHANNON DRAKE

ZEBRA BOOKS
KENSINGTON PUBLISHING CORP.

ZEBRA BOOKS are published by

Kensington Publishing Corp.
850 Third Avenue
New York, NY 10022

First Zebra Books Printing: September, 1995

Printed in the United States of America
10 9 8 7 6 5 4 3

*For Liza Dawson
and Meg Blackstone—
wonderful editors, and very
special people to have
as friends!*

THE LEGEND

Fulk the Black, Count of Anjou, was descended from Rollo, the great Viking who had laid claim to Normandy. He was a warrior, fierce and hard like his forebears, tenacious and determined.

One winter he waged battle against Ranulf, a viscount of his territory. From dawn to dusk he sent his men against Ranulf's castle, in a fury to drag it down. Flaming arrows flew over the ramparts with no mercy; battering rams were taken again and again to the gates. At last, Ranulf's castle went up in flames, the gates were breached, and Fulk, riding upon his magnificent warhorse with his naked sword, tore about the courtyard to do battle with his rebellious viscount.

But Ranulf was already dead; the scene was one of death and destruction, flame and smoke. Fulk hurried to the donjon of the castle, in search of whatever treasure might be had.

It was there that he first saw Melusine. She stood upon the staircase, mindless of the flames that rose around her. Fulk could not move when he saw her; he stood transfixed. Her hair appeared as a sea of flame, red and gold; her eyes were a turmoil of blue and green, like clashing waves glittering beneath a high sun; her skin was flawless and her form was both slender and sensual; never in all his travels had he seen a woman of such uncanny beauty.

As he stared at her, he heard the distant rumble of thunder; the day outside grew dark and the sky roiled with black clouds and the promise of a storm. And yet she, *she* seemed to glow, surrounded by an unearthly light, in a mist of magic, haunting him, holding him, bending his will, as a smith might bend steel . . .

Yet the eyes that stared down upon him bore him hatred; they blazed with the fires that razed the castle. Fulk could not care for her hatred; he had become possessed by her great beauty, and he wanted her more than dreams of heaven, more than riches or land, more than his life, or his soul.

She screamed when he approached her; she cursed him and reviled him. But she had invaded him, body and mind, and he did as his forebears would have done—he raped her.

Yet it was not enough; it did not cure him of the longing, of the need to know her, possess her as she did him. He learned that her name was Melusine, but he could not fathom her race, or from whence she had come. He had learned only her name— and that fire would not burn her, though it encircled her, that the birds would cease to sing when she entered the courtyard, that even the breeze would fall silent.

He could not let her go. And he, proud warrior, begged her to love him, as he loved her. To give her love to him joyously.

Melusine agreed, but marriage would be her price. It seemed a small price, as he would gladly have sworn his soul to the devil to possess her fully. She could bring him no lands, no power, no dowry—and yet Fulk agreed. He took her for his bride. As she had promised, she came to him, night after night. Like warm scented oil her body caressed his, like a tempestuous wind, she aroused him to a fever of desire that made him forget all else. He fell ever more deeply beneath her spell.

But Fulk was a strong man, and he came to know that he was possessed, for never would she answer his questions, never would she tell him who she was, or where had been the place of her birth. Fulk's bishops were horrified by his obsession; they claimed to know that Melusine was the daughter of Satan himself—a fact verified, they said, by the fact that she refused to remain at mass when it came time for the eucharist to be celebrated.

Count Fulk, therefore, had her seized one sabbath when she would have vacated the church. Strong knights grappled to restrain her. She screamed a scream so loud and shrill, it chilled all who heard its echo. Then she disappeared; the knights held nothing, and a cloud of smoke rose to waft away out a window, and the beautiful Melusine was never seen again.

But she had left Fulk two children, and from her children descended one Geoffrey, Count of Anjou, soon to be known as Geoffrey "planta genet," from the sprig of bloom he wore to battle. Geoffrey married Mathilda, heiress to the Crown of England, a granddaughter of William the Conqueror. From these two sprang the royal Plantagenets, Henry II, Richard the Lion-Heart, John . . . and a dynasty of heirs, both legal—and natural.

But the "devil" legend was never to leave the Plantagenets. They were a brood with passionate tempers, quick to love, quick to hate.

"From the devil they have come," said one saintly bishop of the time, "and to the devil must they pay their dues."

PART 1

"THE KING IS DEAD . . ."

PROLOGUE

The rider was gaining upon her. With each thundering moment that passed, she heard the relentless pounding of the destrier's sure hoofbeats come closer and closer.

Her own mount was sweating, gasping for each tremulous breath that quivered through flank muscles straining to maintain the insane gallop over the mud and through the forest. Elise could feel the animal working furiously beneath her, the great shoulders flexing . . . contracting . . .

Elise chanced a backward glance as the wind whipped about her in the darkness of the night, blinding her with loosened strands of her own hair. Her heart suddenly seemed to stop— then to thud more loudly than even the sound of the destrier's hooves behind her . . .

He was almost upon her. The mare hadn't a chance of escaping the pursuit of the experienced warhorse.

And she hadn't a prayer against the dark knight who rode the midnight-black stallion. She had seen him mount the horse. He was even taller than Richard the Lion-Heart, as broad of shoulder, as lean of hip.

"No!" Elise gasped, leaning against her mare's neck to encourage greater speed. *No, no, no!* she added silently. *I will not be caught and butchered. I will fight. I will fight. I will fight until I draw my last breath . . .*

Dear God, what had happened? Where were the men who should have been about the castle? Who should have heard the screams of the guards?

Oh, merciful Christ in heaven! What had happened?

Just an hour ago she had plodded slowly along this same path to reach the castle. To say her last good-byes, to cry, to pray for Henry II of England . . .

And now she was racing insanely away in terror, pursued by the lowest of thieves, the most cold-blooded of murderers.

"Halt, coward!" she heard the dark horseman command harshly. His voice was deep and strong, sure and arrogant against the night. Elise pressed her knees more tightly against the mare. *Run, Sabra, run!* she prayed silently. *Run as you have never run!*

"Halt! Desecrater of the dead!"

She heard the words, but they made no sense. *He* was the murderer! He was the thief! The lowest snake of the earth to attack the dead.

The dead King of England.

"I'll slit you from throat to belly!" the dark knight roared out.

Panic whipped through her like the relentless wind, riddling and racing through her blood, making her quiver as she tried to hold hard to the reins. She turned again. The destrier was pulling beside her mare. She could see him, the dark rider.

His hair was as black as the ebony sky. His face was ruthlessly handsome. His lips were taut and grim. His chin was as strong and firm as the stone of the castle.

His eyes . . . she couldn't tell their color. But they burned with a dark fury beneath sharply arched brows . . .

He wore no mail, no armor. Not even a cloak. Only a dark tunic that whipped in a frenzy about him with the force of the wind and ride.

His arm, muscled and powerful, reached out.

"No!" Elise shrieked, and she brought her small whip down upon him with all the strength that she could muster.

"Bitch of Satan!" he thundered, and reached for her again.

This time she could not stop him. His arm swept around her, and his hand clamped about her waist like an iron manacle. She screamed and gasped as she was lifted from the mare. Then she was thrashing in earnest as she was thrown roughly over the flanks of the destrier, and the air was knocked from her.

Her dagger! She needed her dagger! But it was caught in the pocket of her skirt, and she could neither twist nor move. All she could do was flop against the massive, silken flanks of the mighty animal and pray that she did not fall beneath its lethal hooves.

The dark knight reined in sharply; she was shoved to the ground. A rush of air escaped her as she fell hard. For a moment she was too stunned to move.

Then instinct took over. She tried to roll, but she was tangled in her cloak. She could only gasp again as he straddled her, seeking her wrists and pinning them to the ground.

Her breasts heaved with fear as she tried to twist again. She tossed her head, and clamped her teeth into his arm. A grunt of pain grated from his lips, but he jerked her hands higher, leaving her with no part of his flesh to bite.

"Where are your accomplices, bitch?" he demanded harshly. Vaguely she realized that he spoke to her in French, the common courtly language from Hadrian's wall to the borders of Spain since the days of the Conqueror. The words were natural, fluent, but they bore a trace of accent. They had not been his first language.

"Tell me now, or as God is my witness, I will strip the flesh from your body inch by inch until you do!"

Still struggling wildly, Elise lashed out in return, choosing to shout in English—language more guttural, more crude.

"I have no accomplices—and I am no thief! You are the thief, you are the murderer! Let me go, whoreson! Help! Help! Oh, help me someone. Help me!"

She was stunned into silence as the back of his hand cut across her cheek. She clamped her teeth so that she would not cry out with the pain. And she saw his face more clearly.

His eyes were not dark at all. They were blue. Sapphire blue. On fire, burning deeply into her. His cheekbones were high, his forehead broad, his nose long and slender. His face was bronzed deeply by the sun; rugged from exposure. She took all this in with the thought, *How I hate this man! Loathe him. Is he a murderer? The thief? He must be. He followed behind me. He assailed me.*

"You robbed the dead. Henry of England."

"No!"

"Then I shall find nothing of his upon you?"

"No!" she shrieked. "I'm not a thief, I'm—"

She cut off quickly. She could never tell the secret of what she was. This man would never believe her.

And he still might be the murderer himself.

"Can't you see, fool? I carry nothing of the king's—" She broke off again, trying to hide her sudden panic. Because she did hold something that had belonged to the king. Oh, dear God. No, he would never find it.

Or would he?

She closed her eyes, berating herself viciously for her own stupidity.

"We shall see, madam," he told her, his voice a deadly hiss, "if you can prove your innocence."

Her eyes flew open and met his. They were ruthlessly determined. "I am the Duchess of Montoui!" she declared heatedly. "And I demand that you let me up this instant!"

His eyes narrowed. "I don't care if you're the Queen of France! I intend to discover what you have done with what you stole."

"Touch me, and I'll see your head on the block!"

"I doubt that, Duchess."

He released her arms and sat up, staring at her as he crossed his arms over his chest. "We're going to take a ride back to the castle. I suggest you be ready to talk by the time we reach it."

Swiftly, arrogantly, he rose, then strode to retrieve the reins of his destrier.

Just as swiftly, Elise slipped her hand beneath the folds of her cloak and delved into her pocket. Her fingers gripped tightly around her pearl-handled dagger.

She would have to wait until he turned. Wait until he made another move toward her. And she would have to strike swiftly and surely.

Wait . . .

And as she waited, she knit her brow in confusion. *What had happened?* Who was this man? A knight from the castle—or one of the thieves, thinking that she might have taken something before he had robbed the body?

He had to be a thief. A murderer. No knight could behave so despicably.

Dear God, here she was in mortal terror, hoping to drive her dagger into a man's heart.

And not long ago, the night had been one of dull and dragging misery. She had come because she loved the man she was being accused of robbing . . .

1

July, 1189
The Castle of Chinon Province of Anjou

The rain had become a miserable drizzle. It had long ago soaked through Elise's cloak, a plain garment of woven wool, but best for the pilgrimage she made tonight. The hood dipped well over her features and hid the luxurious length of her red and gold curls, which might—at a time such as this—have given certain men pause.

A time such as this . . .

The dull pounding of the raindrops that struck upon the pommel of her horse's saddle seemed like tiny hammer blows against her heart.

The king was dead. Henry II—by the grace of God King of England, Duke of Normandy, and Count of Anjou—was dead.

And for all that he had been—beautiful, courageous, triumphant . . . or cruel, old, and beaten—Elise had loved him with a simple, blind devotion few other women could have given.

She had understood him as few women could; she had known him, and she had eagerly studied all that she could about him.

Henry, the grandson of another Henry—the youngest child of William the Conqueror—had been born the heir to Anjou—and Normandy. His father had fought to give him Normandy; his mother had fought to give him England. She had failed, and Henry had battled long and hard against Stephen of England to win that inheritance at Stephen's death. Through Eleanor of

Aquitaine, he had obtained those vast holdings in southern France. He had not just been the King of England; he had been a European ruler of the greatest dimensions. For Normandy, Aquitaine, Anjou, and Maine, he had owed fealty to the French king—but Henry had been the ruler, indisputably. Until the young King of France, Philip Augustus, and Henry's own sons, chaffing at the stern bit he kept upon them, had teamed together to stand against him.

Henry . . . known far and wide for his famous Plantagenet temper, for his long argument with Thomas à Becket—and for being the cause of the murder of that man. Henry Plantagenet—quicksilver. A man of energy and power, always moving, always ready to battle back against all odds.

But this time, he had lost. Death had been the victor.

Elise closed her eyes in fervent prayer. How she had loved him! She could only ask God that history record all the good he had done. Even in his quarrel with Becket—it had become personal, yes, but Henry had sought to give justice to the people. To make murder a crime whether it be perpetrated by a layman or a member of the clergy. Henry *had* been a man of the law! He had created wonderful courts, and a system of justice that would long outlive him. He had obliterated trial by ordeal, brought witnesses into his courts. He had been a friend to his people.

And now he was dead. For months he had been battling the young King of France and Richard—his own heir. Battle after battle, town after town. Richard and Philip had finally forced him to sign a document with humbling demands, and he had died, a once great king, now a broken man.

Elise had come to mourn him, because to her, he had been all things. She had dearly, dearly loved him.

She traveled with only one companion, Isabel, a young maid in her service. It was assuredly dangerous for her to do so, for although she had left all vestments of finery behind her, cutthroats and thieves might travel her same route in search of easy prey. But she was adept with her dagger, and too dispirited to give thought to her own peril. As her horse plodded monotonously through the endless mud and endless drizzle, the blanket of depression weighed ever more heavily upon her. From Montoui, Elise's small duchy in a fertile valley bordered by Aquitaine, Anjou—and lands under the direct rule of Philip of France—it was a fifty-mile ride to Chinon. For the most part the roads were good, Roman roads kept passable by the constant movement of churchmen, emissaries, pilgrims—and Henry's perpetual energy and travel throughout his domains. But good roads could mean added danger, and Elise had spent part of the journey slipping into seldom-used paths that had been muddy and treacherous. It had been a long ride and they had traveled hard, galloping half the distance. Their speed was slowed, now, only by the onslaught of the miserable rain.

An owl screeched suddenly from the nearby forest, and her horse halted of its own accord.

"It's the castle, my lady," Isabel said nervously, drawing beside her. "We've reached it." Isabel was very tired—and scared. Elise shouldn't have brought her, she thought belatedly. Isabel was a gentle spirit who did not like adventure of any sort. But Elise had reasoned that Isabel was young, her own age, and would not mind the swift pace at which she'd had to move. Elise sighed; it was too late to change things now. She should have left Isabel home, and she should have come alone. But she knew she would have never evaded other loving servants at Montoui had she attempted to leave completely unattended.

Elise narrowed her eyes against the night. The moon was pale in the rain-dark sky, but indeed, they could see before them the high stone walls of the castle. Chinon. One of Henry's castles, a place where he had come in illness after his meeting with Philip and Richard. Chinon, with high walls of stone, a large castle, a defensive castle, stretching across the landscape in the night like a fortress.

Light gleamed from narrow archer's slits, but that light hazed with the misty glow of a moon half-obscured by clouds and made the castle appear as if it were an eerie silhouette cut out of the night.

"Come," Elise said to her uneasy young maid, "I see a bridge ahead." She nudged her horse forward again.

"Milady, are you quite sure that this venture is wise? The castle will abound with the king's knights—"

"Yes! This venture is necessary!" Elise snapped. She was in no mood to tolerate outspoken criticism from a servant. But as the words left her mouth, she relented. She encouraged her household to take pride in themselves; her servants were taught to read and write—and to reason.

And reason certainly did decree that they were upon a fool's errand.

I only wish to see him. I must see him. I owe him this last respect . . .

"Isabel," she said more kindly, "these men will be in deep mourning. And they will be honorable men. They are those knights who remained at his side when all was dark, and all those without loyalty or devotion deserted to join Richard and Philip Augustus of France. You'll see," she added more positively than she was feeling, "we will be treated with the proper respect."

"Humph!" Isabel sniffed, but her mistress's temper was sharp this night, so she gave no further argument.

Isabel's palfrey shied away from the narrow bridge leading to the main gates. They were challenged by a guard whose thundering bellow caused Elise's spirited mare to rear in snorting fear.

"Halt—In the name of the Crown! State your business here, or turn about."

Elise fought to calm her prancing mare, despising the awkward sidesaddle she had chosen for the journey.

"I am Elise de Bois, Duchess of Montoui!" she called out with sharp and ringing authority. "I have come to pay my final respects to Henry of England, my liege king and overlord!"

There was a rustling about behind the gates. Elise gave a sigh of relief when they cranked open the gates to admit her. She led her horse over the remainder of the bridge with Isabel close behind her.

A weary, tattered guard met her at the dank entrance to the castle. Beneath his armor he was thin; his features pinched. Elise felt a surge of compassion for the man. Henry's loyal followers had brought him here with few supplies; the son he had warred against for so long and the King of France had been on his heels. And Henry had just signed the humiliating truce with the pair before his death. These men had probably had little food and little sleep for weeks. Perhaps months.

The tired, sallow-faced guard surveyed her with interest. "I do not know you, milady. Nor do I know of the duchy of Montoui."

"It is a small duchy," Elise said flatly. "But if you do not know me, sir, then call your superior, for I am the Duchess of Montoui, and have traveled a miserable road to reach my king."

"They are all at mass—" the guard began to murmur.

"For sweet Jesu's sake!" Elise cried irritably. "We are two women alone. What harm do you think we bring a dead king!"

The guard stepped back. Like most of the aristocracy, Elise had learned the manner of one who was to be obeyed.

"I can see no harm to a dead man," the guard muttered.

Elise slipped unassisted from her mare.

"Then tell me the way to the king. My maid will await me."

"John Goodwin!" the guard called out sharply, drawing from the shadows a second armored man. "This is the Lady Elise de Bois, to pray for Henry of England. Her maid may bide here, and I will keep an eye upon the horses at the bridge. You will escort her to the chamber."

The man nodded, turned, and led her into the castle's interior. They came first to the gatehouse, the room beyond the draw-bridge where sharp steel spikes lined each side of the wall; should the gate ever be breached in battle, a lever could be sprung to send the spikes soaring inward, impaling the first rush of invaders.

Chinon was a castle planned for battle. The walls were high and thick and guarded by numerous towers. It was very dark and damp this night. The smell of the tallow candles was harsh and acrid upon the air. They passed no one as they came from the gatehouse to the open, outer ward, and then past a wooden fence to the inner yard and moved on to the donjon, or keep. Elise gazed about herself a little unhappily. She did not like Chinon. It seemed barren tonight. True, she walked through the defenses and not the living quarters, but there seemed to be nothing whatsoever elegant or even warm about Chinon. There was only cold stone, harsh and strong—and unwelcoming.

Inside the keep, she was led past the spiral of worn stone stairs that should have led to the living quarters. Elise raised a brow and paused to question the knight who escorted her. She did not know Chinon; she had never been here before. But she knew that Henry liked to keep his quarters on the second floor, right above the guards and weaponry.

"Where do you take me, sir? Should the king not be laid out in his chamber?"

"The king is upon this floor, milady," the guard said sorrowfully. "He was, in life, too ill and pained to be brought up the stairs. And in death . . . this floor is the coolest, milady."

Elise said nothing more. She understood all too well the need to protect the body from decay.

A short time later they stood before a door, and she at last saw other signs of life. Two tired soldiers flanked either side of the entrance to the death chamber.

"The Lady Elise de Bois to see the king," her escort said stiffly. "See that she is undisturbed in her prayers."

The knights nodded and parted. Elise placed her hand upon the heavy wooden door and pushed. With a small groan and screech, it moved inward and she entered the chamber and closed the door behind her.

For a moment she merely stood there, bracing herself against the solid oak. And she stared upon the aged and wasted figure laid out—at peace at last—between four posts set with thick candles that burned staunchly against the dampness of the night.

Gone was the Plantagenet glory. The body was that of a man, old before his true time, ravaged by illness and sorrow. The cheeks were deeply sunken in death, the face furrowed with lines, the lips drooping. He lay with his crown upon his head, his sword and scepter by his side, yet he looked too pathetic to have ever been a proud and arrogant king.

Unwittingly, Elise brought her knuckles to her mouth and bit down upon them. She felt no pain as she tried to subdue the cry of loss that rose within her.

Suddenly she rushed to his body and dropped to her knees at its side. Though his hand was bloated with decay and stiff with death, she gripped it, and her hot tears bathed it with love.

She didn't know how long she knelt there, numb with loss, but at last her silent tears ran dry and she stared tenderly upon the ravaged face once more, adjusting a strand of the graying hair upon his forehead.

Once he had been beautiful. Vital. Every inch a king. Henry Plantagenet had been a man of medium stature and height, but well sinewed, strong and agile from constant days in the saddle. He had been a man sometimes autocratic and rude, vain and demanding—and given to wild tempers. But where he had walked, the force of life had always followed. Vibrant, determined, stubborn, and proud. He was an impassioned king—and despite all else he was just and respected for his mind, for his wit, for his knowledge. He had been an astonishing linguist; his lands had encompassed several tongues, and he had been well acquainted with them all: the Provencale French of his southern regions, the Norman French of the north continent and the English court, the Anglo-Saxon of his English people, and the Latin that was known throughout Christendom. He had even known the language of the Welsh, and the Gaelic of the wild Scots. His mind, like his body, had moved like quicksilver.

And when he smiled, a ray of the sun came down; he smiled as a king.

Elise would never forget the first time she had seen him. Or remembered seeing him. She had been about four years old when he rode up to the castle at Montoui.

He had ridden with few retainers, but still she had been awed at the sight of him. His cape of royal blue was fringed with ermine fur. It flowed behind him as he sat his horse in splendor; a rider born to the saddle.

And his hair . . . red and gold . . . had reflected the light of the sun.

She had thought he might be God at first. Surely he was a king above kings.

From the castle keep where she threw pebbles into a puddle, she had run through the banqueting hall, up the steep stairwell, and into her mother's chambers.

"God has come, milady mother! God has come!"

Her mother had laughed gaily, the sound of a brook splashing in springtime.

" 'Tis not God, poppet. 'Tis our liege Lord Henry, Duke of Aquitaine and Normandy, Count of Anjou and Maine, and King of England!"

Many times when important visitors came, she was sent away with her nurse, but it was not so that day. The man who had come, the great man, the *king,* had come to see her. She was ecstatic with joy, and happy to crawl upon his lap, delighted to display before him both her manners and her wit. It was a happy occasion, for her mother and her father, the Duke and Duchess of Montoui, smiled with the greatest pleasure as the king laughed and commended them upon the beauty of their child.

That same year, another royal visitor had come to the small court at Montoui.

Her parents had not been so happy then. Elise asked her mother why she was so frightened; Marie de Bois paled, then denied her fear.

"I am not frightened. It is just that the queen is a very great lady, powerful in her own right . . ."

Marie de Bois, who had never had a quarrel with Eleanor of

Aquitaine, was quite justifiably nervous. Henry II had begun an affair with Rosamund Clifford that was to have disastrous consequences. Eleanor and Henry were separated, and the king's eldest two sons, Henry and Richard—embittered already by the lack of freedom and trust given them by Henry—had rallied to their mother's side in open defiance of their father.

Now Eleanor was to appear at Montoui. And Montoui had divided loyalties. It lay between Anjou and Aquitaine; the latter was Eleanor's birthright, and the rebellious Richard had been proclaimed Duke of Aquitaine, while Anjou was indisputably Henry's.

Montoui could not remain neutral territory for long in the battle of king and queen and princes. By feudal custom, Henry, through his own European holdings, was the overlord of the dukes of Montoui.

Elise was too young at the time to understand all the intricacies of the Angevin empire, or the feuding that had split apart a family, but just as she had been in awe of Henry, she was in awe of Eleanor.

The queen was older than the king, but just as splendid, and just as beautiful. Elise had heard the tales about her. She had once been married to the King of France—before she had been married to Henry, of course—and she had ridden like an Amazon warrioress along with him to the Holy Land, leading her own army on the Crusade.

She was tall and regal and lovely and elegant—and very smart. She quizzed Elise relentlessly, and seemed pleased with all the answers she received. She gave Elise a sweetmeat that was accepted with eager pleasure by chubby little hands.

But then she had been sent from the room.

"You do well by this child," the queen told the Duke and Duchess of Montoui. "She has his courage and his wit, and you guide both well."

"I don't know what you mean, Your Grace—" Elise's mother began.

"Please, Marie!" The queen seemed both pained and amused.

"As well as his wit, she carries his banner! Hair that is gold and fire! Fear not—I seek no revenge. I wanted only to see her and assure myself that she was indeed his. She shall always have my protection. God knows, I hold no rancor toward Geoffrey Fitzroy—and have always protected him. 'Tis a fair pity, I assure you, but at times I must admit that Henry's bastard would make the better heir to the throne. Henry and Richard are rash and impetuous, and John is as trustworthy as a snake in the grass."

The queen's eyes, lovely and sparkling, fell upon Elise once more. "She is a beautiful child. Stunning, and bright. I am pleased to have seen her."

Elise was told to bow to the queen. Then she was hastily taken from the room, but not before she had begun to wonder what a "bastard" was.

The cook's son, three years older than she, was glad to tell her what a bastard was. But though he taunted and teased her, Elise was assured that she was not a bastard. Beautiful Marie de Bois was her mother, and William de Bois, Duke of Montoui, was her father.

But as the years passed, the King of England continued to visit.

Elise was sorry to hear that Henry had imprisoned Eleanor, his queen. She had liked the queen very much, but even a child knew not to challenge the order of such a powerful ruler, and so she said nothing.

As she grew, she was allowed to ride with him.

"You know, Lady Elise," he told her on her tenth birthday after he had presented her with an expertly trained falcon, "that you are your parents' sole heir. You will one day be the Duchess of Montoui."

"Yes, I know, Your Grace," Elise said proudly. She had been told at an early age that Marie could bear no more children, and that she must take her duties very seriously. Montoui was small, but her lands were fertile. And Marie had modeled her court after that of Eleanor of Aquitaine; the most learned historians and poets and scholars of the day were made welcome. Musicians were invited for a month and stayed for a year. The castle was not cold and miserable and drafty as most, but hung lavishly with warming tapestries, with clean rushes always upon the floor. Duke William had gone on crusade to the Holy Land with Louis of France—and Eleanor of Aquitaine, when she had been his queen—and had brought many of the amenities of the East home with him: Persian rugs and draperies of silk and goldware and porcelain and marble and silver . . .

"You must learn to understand the world very well, my girl. You are too precious to be . . ." Henry paused for some seconds.

"To be what, Your Grace?"

"A pawn," he said softly. "Come—we return to the castle!"

From that day forward, Elise found her education comprehensive. She learned all the boundaries of England and Europe and the East; she learned who the powerful princes were, and what lands were fading into obscurity.

On her fifteenth birthday, she saw the king again. It was a rare occasion, for by that time, young Henry had died, and Richard had sided with Philip, the young King of France, in a furious battle against his father.

Eleanor was still locked within her prison, and Elise was still mourning the death of her father. William de Bois, Duke of Montoui, had sickened and died of a wound to his shoulder, incurred during a battle for his overlord against Richard.

The king was melancholy. He had grown old.

But Elise sensed that he found a haven with her. He brought none of his knights when he visited Montoui; it was as if he escaped from battle and pain and bitterness.

Elise was glad to be with him, especially that day. She had learned all that she might to please, and since her father's death, she had managed her estates brilliantly. Marie had considered her old enough to take full responsibility for her inheritance, and Elise had proven herself responsible. She balanced the household accounts, dealt with the head of the castle guard, encouraged her villeins to greater efficiency in the fields, and kept Montoui in a productive state of internal peace.

And she had studied very hard. She had mastered English and Latin, and much, much more. At fifteen, she had grown tall and straight and shapely—a stunningly beautiful young woman. She had learned to despise the general lot of womankind, to abhor the system that decreed women to be vassals—bought and sold for their wealth and lands by fathers and husbands.

But she had also learned the wiles and cajolery of her sex.

"Mother says that I am more than of age to marry," she told the king as they rode. "She has suggested the Duke of Touraine, but I feel that such an alliance would be a grave mistake." She did not tell Henry that she despised the Duke of Touraine for being a dandified fop who never sat straight in his saddle; she used cool logic. "His loyalty to the Angevin empire is questionable; he has too often in the past been in the company of the King of France."

"You are quite right!" the king cried passionately. "No, you shall not be the wife of such a man. Nay, you shall not marry at all until I have chosen for you. Ah, the pity, the price of it!" He spat. "With his legitimate heirs, a man must sell for the highest bid and the best alliance; not with you shall I do that, my little Elise."

And so she learned that day that she was a bastard. The king's bastard.

No one knew, he assured her. He had loved her true mother, a young peasant girl from nearby Bordeaux. She had been gentle and kind and sweet, and as she weakened toward death after the ordeal of childbirth, she had asked Henry one boon. Her child was to be raised by nobility, but spared the stain of bastardy . . .

So she had been brought to the childless Duke and Duchess of Montoui, and been given the gift of legitimacy.

Elise had been stunned. Unsure. All her life she had dearly

loved her father and mother, and now she was learning that the noble William was not her father at all . . .

She was the king's bastard.

"I have taken much from you, with a truth I should have kept silent," Henry told her astutely. "Ah, my pet, I am so sorry. But perhaps I can give you much in return. I will give what I could not give my legitimate daughters. I will give you your freedom, and your duchy. For a woman, that is a great gift. *You* will choose your own husband, my daughter. And you will rule your own lands. But bear in mind, daughter, that it is only by deception that Montoui can be yours. If your true birth were known, the country would abound with *'legally* related' wolves to claim Montoui. While I live, no one would dare assault you, but should something happen to me—"

"Please! Let's not speak of such a thing, Your Grace!"

She could not bring herself to call him "Father."

"Sire," she asked him, "did you truly love my mother?" Elise was no fool. She had heard of the king's many conquests—not the least of whom was the fair Rosamund Clifford, dead, too, these many years now, some said poisoned by the queen's hand. But the queen had already been incarcerated while Rosamund lay dying, and Elise could not believe that Eleanor had hired a murderer.

"Aye, that I did. I was very much in love when you were conceived." Henry lifted his hand and showed her the small sapphire ring he wore upon his smallest finger. "She gave me this when we first loved together. I have worn it since."

Marie, Duchess of Montoui, died the next year. Henry was fiercely engaged in his war with Philip and Richard, but he managed to come to the castle.

He looked horrible. Old and dissipated.

But Elise knew now that she loved him no matter what sense of betrayal she had felt at learning that she was a bastard. He was her father. Her heart went out to him.

"Father," she asked him, when they were alone, "is there no

way that you can make peace with Richard? Perhaps, if you were to free the queen—"

"Never!" Henry railed. "It was she who set my sons against me! Nay Richard will come to heel! He is an arrogant young pup . . ."

The king raved on. Richard was an insolent young pup; Henry had asked so little of him. And Eleanor was as dangerous as a black widow.

Elise felt she understood a large part of Henry's problems—problems that had made the great warrior king old and bitter and garrulous.

He had been hurt as only a father can be hurt by a son. He was judging his son as a boy, but Richard Plantagenet, already the "Lion-Heart," was not a boy asking for a new steed or bow. He was a hulking man in his prime. And Eleanor . . .

Well, Elise could well believe that the queen could be dangerous. But she also believed that Eleanor still loved Henry.

His line of thought had followed hers.

"Eleanor," he murmured, and Elise knew that his mind had wandered to thoughts of his wife. He glanced her way, and for a moment his smile was young. "I saw her once when she was the French king's wife. Old Louis. Yes, Louis should have been a monk. He was no match for Eleanor. She was dazzling then, the brightest flame of Christendom, perhaps. She had more wit and strategy in her little finger than Louis had in his entire flaccid frame. How I wanted her! And Aquitaine, of course. We created the Angevin empire, she and I. And she has never broken. Jailed all these years and she is a proud and wily old fox! Always plotting and planning! She is a queen, my Eleanor, that she is . . ."

Henry paused a moment and stared piercingly at his daughter. "But you see, my child, that she sits in prison—as she has for almost twelve years! Follow her example in pride and spirit, but should you marry, be warned! Don't turn your sons from their father."

With the change in him, Elise suddenly forgot protocol and

threw her arms around him. "I shall never do so, Father, for I am in love!"

"In love, eh? With whom?"

"Sir Percy Montagu, Father. He is a knight who serves you well. And I know that his father has approved our match; he will soon ask for my hand."

Henry laughed. "Ah, and well. I know of young Montagu, yes. I would have approved a more prestigious match for you, but—"

"But you promised that I might marry where I loved!"

"That I did."

"And, Father, I will retain ownership of my lands."

"Good! You have paid heed to your tutors."

"Yes, it can be done quite legally."

"When young Percy asks for you, send him to me. I will approve the marriage, if that is what you seek."

Elise tried to hide her glee.

"Thank you, sire," she told Henry gravely. But in her heart, she was pitying her father, and envying herself.

I have learned so much from you, Father, she thought a little sadly. *I will always know that a man—or a woman—must not use a child as a pawn in battle. I will know that my children are as much my husband's blood as my own, and that to injure a parent whom they love is to injure them.*

I will not fall prey to a man with a roving eye—such as yours. When I say that I love, I will do so, with my whole heart and purpose, forever.

As I love Percy, and Percy loves me.

Lands and titles will mean nothing to the two of us; we will protect ourselves from the way of the world with the blanket of our own truths and sincerity.

Her roving thoughts ceased as Henry cleared his throat and caught her attention.

"Elise . . . I . . ."

"What is it, sire?"

"Nothing. I . . ."

He had not said it for so long. To anyone. Life had become too bitter for King Henry II of England, Count of Anjou, Duke of Normandy. The words faltered on his tongue. But then he said them.

"I love you, daughter."

"And I love *you* . . . *Father* . . ."

It had been the last time she had seen him alive.

"Oh, Henry," Elise whispered, tears forming in her eyes again. "It was so very bad for you. If only you had learned to speak to your legitimate son as you spoke to me."

She had heard about the end—the truce he had been forced to sign with Richard and Philip. He had been stripped of his pride, of everything. A lifetime of success had been turned to failure.

And then he had died. Died, after discovering that his youngest son had been among the men to desert him at the end. Prince John—John Lackland, as they called him, since all had been parceled out to his older brothers before him.

They were a nest of vultures.

They were her half brothers.

A shiver rippled through Elise. Thank God no one knew. Almost no one.

Eleanor knew. And Richard would surely release Eleanor from her prison of sixteen years immediately.

Elise clenched her eyes tightly together. She could not believe that Eleanor would betray her. Eleanor had once promised to protect her. She was safe then, or so she fervently hoped.

Richard would be crowned King of England.

But Richard would bear her no malice. After her father— William de Bois, that was—died, Henry would allow no other knights from her duchy to fight with him. Henry had, in truth, granted her all his royal care.

Elise flicked at her lashes and stared at the shriveled face of Henry the II. A new wave of tears filled her eyes.

"It ended with sorrow, Your Grace, but know this: you did give to me—so much. So very much. And I did love you. I love you now. I will love you all the days to come in my life. And I will be happy, Father. You left me that. I will arrange my own betrothal to Percy Montagu. We will rule our lands together, and live in peace and harmony with one another. I will have learned from you, Father."

Percy. Elise thought of him now with longing. Tall and slender and golden, his mahogany eyes so ready to mirror compassion and caring—and laughter. If she could but be with him now.

Soon. The war was over. The majority of Henry's men had gone north into Normandy after Henry had decided to come south with only a few retainers for his last confrontation. Percy would be in Normandy now, horrified to hear of the king's death. But Richard could not punish honorable warriors who had fought for the crowned king; and even if Percy were to be stripped of his lands and wealth, she wouldn't care in the least. She had Montoui. And the small, neutral duchy had an army of five hundred strong to defend her borders.

Oh, Father!

She clenched his cold hand and felt the bite of metal.

Elise smiled wistfully as she looked upon the small emerald ring on his little finger. Her mother's sapphire.

She bit her lip suddenly, then drew the ring from the bony finger. "I hope you don't mind, Father. It is all that I might ever have of both of you. I never saw her, and now you too are gone."

She smiled then, and slipped the sapphire into her bodice. Henry would have understood. And he wouldn't have begrudged her the ring that meant so much to her.

Then Elise forgot the ring, for she realized with horror that she hadn't said a single prayer for him.

Henry was in dire need of prayer!

It was rumored that he had denied God his soul when he had fled before Richard after LeMans—the city of his birth—had been burned over his head.

Elise folded her hands together and bent her head in fervent supplication.

"Our Father, who art in heaven . . ."

11

He stood upon the ramparts of the castle, staring eastwardly. The dreary rain had at last ceased, and the night breeze lifted his cloak and had whipped it about him.

He was a proud and formidable figure, tall and still in the night. His was a true knight's form, hard and trim from constant battle in his king's behalf.

He might have been a king himself. He was tall enough to stare the Lion-Heart in the eyes. And like the Lion-Heart, he was proven in both tournaments and battle. A more fierce warrior did not exist, nor one with greater cunning and skill. For all his sinewed size, there was a feline grace about him. He could dodge a double-headed ax with ease, leap above the swipe of a sword with the grace of an acrobat. He knew that he was feared and respected, but the knowledge gave him no great pleasure.

No single strength could have changed the tide of war.

He had ridden with Henry for three years. And in that time, he had always matched his voice against the king. He had never backed down, despite the king's famed temper; yet Henry had never banished him from his company, no matter how fierce the argument. It was Henry who had dubbed him the "Black Knight," the Rogue, the Falcon. All in affection, for he had always known his plainspoken and somewhat unorthodox warrior to be completely loyal—to both his king and to his own conscience.

He stared out upon the night now, but without really seeing it. Blue eyes so deep that they often appeared to be indigo or black were even darker still with his brooding. The rain-soaked breeze grew wilder, but he was heedless of the wind. Indeed, it felt good. It seemed to cleanse him.

He had grown so tired of the eternal bloodshed.

And now he was left to wonder: For what?

The king is dead; long live the king. Richard would be crowned King of England. It was right; Richard the Lion-Heart was the legal heir.

There was a movement upon the ramparts, the click of boots against stone. Always a warrior, Bryan Stede spun about, instantly alert, his knife in his hand, poised to parry a blow.

A deep chuckle sounded from the dark pit of the nearest tower, and Bryan relaxed, grinning, as he realized that he was being interrupted by a friend.

"Sheathe your knife, Bryan!" William Marshal said, striding toward him. "God knows, you could be defending your life soon enough."

Bryan slipped the knife back into the strap about his ankle and leaned against the stone of the castle as he watched his friend come closer. There were few men he respected as he did Marshal. Many called him "the Arab," as he was a swarthy man with a thin beak for a nose, but whatever his background, he was an Englishman to the core. He was also one of the best fighters alive; before becoming Henry's right-hand man, Marshal had traveled from province to province, besting anyone who cared to challenge him in a tournament.

"If I am to be defending my life, friend Marshal, so shall you. I met Richard on the battlefield; we came to an impasse, and both bowed out, but you unhorsed him!"

Marshal shrugged. "Who is to say which of us he would rather draw and quarter? 'Tis true I might have killed Richard, but he was unarmed when he charged across that bridge. He met you in fair battle—and could not kill you. It can't do much for that great pride of his to know that either of us might have dealt his deathblow."

Bryan Stede laughed, and the sound was only slightly bitter.

"I guess we have to face it, Marshal. Tomorrow we shall see if Richard cares to give his father his last respects. After that, he shall be the king. Lawfully. And we shall be worth less than the ground he walks upon."

Marshal grimaced, then grinned.

"I couldn't have changed a thing, Bryan."

"No, neither could I."

They stared out at the night in companionable silence for a moment. At last Marshal asked, "Are you afraid to face Richard, Bryan?"

"No," Bryan said flatly. "His father was the rightful King of England." He paused a moment, studying the stars that were breaking through the darkness of the night. "It should never have come to warfare between those two, Marshal. It all seems so petty now. But I cannot ask the new king to pardon me for fighting for the old. To my mind, it was right. Richard is welcome to strip me of what little I have, but I will not beg that he forgive me for following my conscience."

"Nor I," said Marshal. Then he laughed softly. "Hell, shall I remind the man that I could have killed him, but instead held my blow."

"And thank God that you did," Bryan muttered, suddenly fierce. "Could you imagine Prince John King of England?"

Marshal sobered hastily. "No, I could not. I still believe that Henry might be with us still had he not seen John's name at the top of the list of traitors who left him at Le Mans."

Again both men were silent, thinking of the dead king. Poor Henry! To lead such an illustrious life and to be brought so low at death, hounded to his grave by his sons.

He had been in such pain at the end. Garrulous and miserable.

But Bryan Stede had grown to love his monarch. Henry had been no elegant fop. He had lived in the saddle; he had forged his realm. He had possessed cunning and courage and bold determination until the end. Life had broken him—not death.

"There is one bright spot to all this," Marshal said.

"And that is?"

"Eleanor. I'm willing to bet that Richard's first action will be to order his mother released from her prison."

"That's true," Bryan mused. "Marshal?"

"Aye?"

"What do you think she will be like after fifteen years in prison? God's blood, she must be almost seventy now."

Marshal laughed. "I can tell you what Eleanor will be like. Bright and alert and raring to go. Sorry—despite the fact that he jailed her all those years—that Henry is dead, but grateful that she lived to see Richard king. She'll be his greatest asset, Bryan. She'll rally the people behind him."

Bryan grinned, agreeing with Will Marshal.

He had argued openly with the king about Eleanor, time and time again. And any time that he had been in England, he had made a point of visiting the queen. He had never denied to Henry that he had done so.

"The sad spot is that I shall lose my heiress," Marshal said grimly.

"Isabel de Clare?"

Marshal nodded. "Henry promised her to me in front of witnesses, but I have no claim upon paper. I doubt that it would matter. Richard will be taking from me, not giving." Marshal sighed. "I would have been one of the most powerful landowners in the country."

"I doubt not that I shall lose Gwyneth," Bryan said with far more lightness than he was feeling.

"Perhaps not. Everyone knows that you and the lady . . . have consorted," Marshal consoled his friend. "I have never seen the lady Isabel de Clare."

"Then you are the better off, my friend. I know fully all that I will be losing—the beautiful widow, and all her beautiful land."

"True. Ah, well, we can travel to the tournaments together."

"Yes, I suppose."

The weight of the night seemed to settle over Bryan. There was a dull pain in his heart for Henry, and a dull acceptance of his future. The loss hurt.

He didn't know if he had ever been in love with Gwyneth, but he had enjoyed her cheerful company. He had enjoyed even more the prospects of her land. Marriage was a political affair—and in Henry's arrangements for his chief supporters, Bryan had come out well. Not only would he have become the ruler of a powerful province, but he would have acquired a winsome and attractive bride. And a home.

No man could deny the craving for land, Bryan thought. Only a fool could lose such riches and not be bitter.

No matter what the loss, he would not hang his head before Richard. He had supported Henry because he chose to; that he would never deny.

He might not acquire his lands, but he *would* maintain his pride, and his own self-esteem.

"I hope that Richard arrives soon," Marshal said dryly. "Then we will be able at last to see the king buried. Our duty will be at an end. And I, for one, will welcome a night of freedom. I intend to consume a gourd of wine, and dive into a real bed with the cleanest young wench I can find with a taste for a silver coin."

Bryan Stede idly raised a brow at his friend, then returned his stare to the night beyond the castle.

"You know that you will serve Richard, Marshal, just as you served Henry."

"I'd say the same of you, friend, except that we shan't know much of what the future will bring—until we find out the depths of the grudges Richard bears us. 'Tis more than likely that we shall be sent packing—if we manage to stay alive!"

"I daresay that we will stay alive," Bryan said dryly. "It wouldn't much become our new king to slay—"

He broke off abruptly as an agonized scream pierced through the darkness of the night like the honed edge of a blade. For a bare fraction of a second, the two knights stared at each other in stunned surprise and wonder. Then they moved with toned agility, racing toward the tower from whence the scream had come.

* * *

Elise had truly attempted to pray, but words became a meaningless monologue within her mind. Her pain was a dull pounding that sounded in her ears and seemed to envelop her, leaving her to feel listless and adrift.

But Henry needed prayer so badly! she reminded herself.

She wet her lips to begin again out loud, but she never spoke. A sound had come to her from outside the heavy door; not a loud sound, and nothing that she could instantly place, like the creak of armor or the natural fall of a footstep.

The sound was something quiet and muffled; she would have missed it had she been whispering aloud.

As it was, she felt a chill settle over her, like the coming of a sudden snowstorm. Rivulets of ice seemed to trickle down her spine, and she went dead-still, barely breathing, to listen again.

She bolted to her feet as she heard further, furtive sounds. Sounds of a strangled moan, of . . . something heavy . . . like a man . . . falling upon the stone floor behind the door.

And then the door itself began to creak.

In sudden panic, Elise spun about, searching out a refuge. A group of tapestries hung against the north wall, near the heavy door, and she raced toward the first, diving behind its shelter just as the oak banged hard against stone and a group of dark-clad men rushed into the chamber.

"Hurry!" hissed a rough and grating voice.

"Get the scabbard!" commanded another abrasive tenor. "Look at the jewels in the handle—"

"Gape later, you idiot! Work fast now!"

The order had been issued in the first, gravelly tone. Flattened against the wall, Elise bit down hard upon her lip, torn between terror and fury. How dare they! Henry was dead. Henry the *king* was dead, and these . . . these . . . filthy dung were daring to rob him in death.

Oh, if he were alive you would not be so bold or so foolish! she thought. *He would skewer you, impale your heads upon poles to rot, feed you limb by limb to the wolves.* But Henry wasn't alive. And it seemed that these robbers were as free as the wind to defile him as they chose.

How many of them were there? Elise wondered, remembering that *she* was alive, and dearly wanted to remain so. Inching her slender form carefully, she moved to the edge of the tapestry and peered beyond it. Thank God that the room was shrouded in darkness and shadow, and that only the candles about the bier gave light.

She could not manage a full view of the room, but there were at least four men within the room, possibly five. They were all clothed in dark tunics and dark hose, and they resembled the vultures that they were. As she watched, sickened and angry, they stripped all the finery from the room, casting it into even greater darkness as they knocked over the candles to steal the brass-and-gold-inlaid sconces.

"The body!" someone hissed.

Not even the king's lean and decaying form was to be left sacrosanct. He was tossed and turned about, his crown taken, his boots, his remaining rings, his belt, even his shirt. Elise almost cried out as the thieves finished with their macabre task—and allowed the body to fall upon the floor with a pathetic, dull thud.

"Hurry! Someone is coming!"

"A guard! He must be killed!"

One of the dark-clad figures pulled a knife from his belt and slipped back outside the door. A second later, Elise heard a sharp, anguished scream, one that ended abruptly with death's gurgle.

The door was charged open once more; no more care was being given to quiet or stealth.

"Let's be gone! That knight died like a squealing pig. They'll be on us like a plague of locusts now!" cried the murderer, racing back into the room.

"Move! Grab the tapestries, and we'll be gone!"

The tapestries. Elise heard the words like a death toll. Terror chilled her; she was cold as she had never known cold before. It possessed and constricted her limbs, her heart, her throat . . .

as one of the figures began a sure stride straight toward her hiding place.

No! she thought, and to her salvation rose the burning heat of pure fury. Buzzards, vultures, filth, dung! They had ravaged her father's defenseless body; they had murdered honorable and faithful men. They were *not* going to murder her!

Like lightning she moved, reaching beneath her cloak for the pearl-embedded dagger at her girdle. Her fingers clasped around it, firm and steady, and as the tapestry was ripped from the wall, she was ready.

A scream issued from her throat, not of fear, but of rage. Like a catapult she flew from the wall, hand raised high against the dark form who was stunned from his task of ripping treasure from the wall. He didn't have time to think—in fact, he could have barely had time to realize that a harpy was descending upon him with deadly intent.

Elise hurtled herself and the knife upon him with a furious vengeance. She felt the sickening crunch as her blade found flesh, and she heard the man's astonished bellow. But she couldn't worry about much else. She jerked her knife from his staggering form, aware that he was sorely wounded, but not mortally so. When he finished staggering, he would come for her.

As would the other men. The dark vultures.

She spun about and practically flew toward the door, racing beyond it, and, with a mad burst of strength, slammed it behind her. It would not take them long; at best it would give her a few extra seconds.

She almost tripped over the crumpled form of a dead guard as she started to run again, and as she slowed to watch her footing, her heart seemed to catch in her throat. There were four crumpled heaps upon the stone, massive men, warriors all, murdered by stealth.

The sound of the oak door to the death chamber scraping open once more set Elise to flying once again, running so quickly that her slippered feet barely seemed to touch the floor. The dark corridors, strangely shadowed by low, glowing torches, appeared as if they stretched and curved forever, one mist-shrouded hallway leading to another. Elise's heart took on a thunderous beat; she could hear her own breathing, laborious and shallow.

She had to keep running. There were guards at the castle's entrance. If she could reach them, she would be safe. But when at long last a dark corridor broadened and led to the entrance, there were no guards about—at least, not to be seen immediately.

She stumbled upon their bodies as she spun about in confusion. Not wishing to believe what her eyes told her, she knelt by the man who had challenged her earlier.

"Sir! Good sir!"

She moved him to tap gently at his cheek, praying that he was not dead, but perhaps unconscious.

She recoiled in horror as she saw his eyes. Wide open; death-glazed. The neck and front of his tunic and armor were stained crimson.

His throat had been slit from behind.

"Oh, God, dear God!" Elise exclaimed in horror, springing to her feet. The thieves were truly without mercy. Practitioners of treachery and cowardice, cold-blooded and despicable murderers.

And they would add her to their list of victims if she didn't hurry, she reminded herself as the echo of pounding footsteps followed after her like the deadly snarls of a hungry wolf from the depths of a cavern.

Isabel! she thought in sudden panic and remorse. Where was her companion, her maid? Elise looked beyond the massive bodies of the soldiers so easily crumpled by the slit of a slender vein. Against the cold stone northern wall lay another crumpled form. Small, truly pathetic and . . . broken.

Bile rose in her throat as a sick and heated fury filled her limbs with the strength of rage. How dearly she would love to see the men who killed from behind and slay a woman to meet their just rewards. Burning upon a stake would be far too merciful a death for such as these. They should be hanged until half dead, disemboweled, then drawn and quartered.

"Here! This way!"

The shout, coming so close upon her heels, stunned Elise into rapid movement. She looked out into the night. Her horse, a beautiful Arabian bred from those brought back from the first Crusade, awaited her upon a grass spit before the drawbridge.

Isabel's horse awaited a rider, too.

But there would be no one to mount the gray palfrey. It was a bitter thought to Elise as she raced beneath the moonlight to the animal poised in lovely silhouette. She hiked the skirt of her drab tunic into one hand and clasped the pommel of her saddle with the other, leaping upon the mare with a smooth and supple grace. Shouts were ringing in her ears once more as she balanced upon the awkward sidesaddle and nudged the mare into a startled, full-speed gallop.

"Christ in heaven! Have you ever seen such atrocity!"

Marshal and Bryan had reached the king's chamber; behind them stood the remainder of the king's men.

They all stood in stunned and stricken silence.

Bryan did not reply immediately to his friend's horrified observation. He looked about the room with a quick eye, feeling a heat like a rage of fire grow within him.

Atrocity? Yes. Beyond comprehension, beyond description.

The room had been stripped bare.

As had Henry.

In death, the king had received his greatest indignity.

But Bryan's anger went beyond the irreverent indecency done to his king. It encompassed the horrible waste and total disrespect of human life.

The guards . . .

They had been his friends. Men who had fought valiantly beside him. Proud men, brave men. Men with vast loyalty who had clung to their beliefs and their king despite all odds, with their heads raised high.

"They must be caught."

He spoke so low that his voice shouldn't have been heard, yet it was. Clearly. And the dark and deadly threat within it made even his own men feel as if they had been struck by chills and shivers, and thank God that they were not among the thieves who might receive vengeance at this man's hands.

Having spoken, Bryan spun about sharply upon a heel to shout out orders. "Templer, Hayden—see to the king. Prine, Douglas, Le Clare—comb the ramparts. Norman, arrange a party to comb the castle. Leave no stones unturned. Joshua, take the surrounding fields. Marshal—"

"I'll take the north woods."

"And I the south."

He broke off suddenly, having heard something. "The entry!" he shouted suddenly, and his strides took him from the chamber before the others could think to move.

Bryan heard the echo of his footfalls, eerie against the stone walls of the castle, as he raced along the corridors. The torches set upon the wall did little to ease the somber darkness or the dank chill; they but added to the treacherous shadows along the way. But Bryan gave no thought to a sudden attack. Those responsible for this assault had no stomach to meet a warrior upon even footing; they were like serpents, striking the unwary from the dark. And never, not even in battle, had he felt such a blind fury, such a determination that justice be met, that an enemy should meet the cold steel of his sword.

He paused at the entryway, his outraged fury renewed as he came upon two more bodies. He paused to close the eyes of a young knight, then stood once more, staring out to the night.

Something had alerted him to the entry. Some sound. But now . . .

It was then that he saw the rider beneath the moonlight, in a clear silhouette, rising in a breakneck gallop from the valley beyond the bridge. He planted his gloved hands upon his hips with a cold and deadly intent. "My destrier!" he roared as men pounded along the corridors behind him.

A second later he heard the clash of his great destrier's hooves upon the stone. He sprang upon the horse and the stallion pranced and clattered to the bridge.

"Sir!" called Jacob Norman. "Wait but a moment. We will ride with you!"

Upon his destrier, Bryan could clearly see the hill that rose from the valley beyond the bridge. The rider had halted, and turned back to stare at the castle.

Under the startling glow of the full moon, Bryan thought grimly, it was probably most obvious that he was coming in chase . . .

The distant horse reared and spun, and tore into another gallop up the hill.

"Nay!" Bryan answered his soldier. "I haven't a moment, and I chase but one. Follow the orders I have given. It appears that they have scattered. I want them all!"

With his final commands shouted out over his retreating shoulder, Bryan gave his stallion free reign. The great horse tore over the drawbridge, threatening to render the heavy timbers to splinters beneath its powerful hooves.

The wind whipped around Bryan. The cold of the night embraced him and fed his fury. He had lived half his life in the saddle, and now he was as one with the huge beast bred for courage, speed, and war. He felt as if he flew in the darkness; the great heart of the stallion pounded along with his own, and from the vast ripple of muscle beneath his thighs, he drew strength into his own.

The hooves of the warhorse seemed to consume the valley, tearing up huge chunks of earth as it raced up the hill. Thick forests laced the countryside, with few trails passable for horses. Although the rider had disappeared into the denseness of the dark forest, Bryan had little difficulty following his quarry. The panicked rider had left signs behind: broken branches, ravaged dirt, and brush. In another five minutes of hard riding, Bryan saw the rider again, breaking into a clearing.

"Halt, *coward!*" he thundered out, his rage exploding with the release of his words. "Halt, you! Desecrater of the dead! I'll slit you throat to belly!"

The superior stamina of his destrier was evident now against the other horse, a smaller animal, but one of great beauty, Bryan noted vaguely. An Arabian mare, if he wasn't mistaken. Probably stolen, taken in a thievery as despicable as this.

Feeling him close, the rider of the Arabian turned in the saddle. Bryan was stunned to see that it was a woman. As fine and graceful as the horse . . .

Despite the ebony of the sky, the rain-cleansed moon gave him a sudden and brilliant picture of the girl. She was swathed in a nondescript cloak, but strands of red and gold hair escaped from the cowl to frame her delicate features like the rays of a magnificent sunset. Her eyes were wide in her face, and for a moment he saw them, too, with a crystal clarity. Not quite blue, not quite green, but a stunning shade of aqua . . . or turquoise, and set beneath high arching brows, brows that were honey-colored, like her eyelashes, lashes that were thick and rich and long, that formed alluring crescents over cheeks that seemed kissed by roses.

With a stern mental jolt he reminded himself that she was a thief—worse than most, she had robbed the dead.

And created more dead. She had probably used her beauty to stun and murder. All the more despicable . . .

Looking at her, they had first been robbed of their senses, and then of their lives. Startled, as he had been, caught off guard, and then slain.

Such beauty, such treachery. But it would not work with him. He could close his eyes easily to her beauty, for beauty was often cheap. And when it encased a black heart, he could be totally cold, and totally impartial. Totally just.

In an icy calm fury, he bore down upon her once more, reaching out to grasp for her arm. She brought a riding whip down upon his hand with an astounding vigor.

"Bitch of Satan!" he growled heatedly, reaching for her again. This time he caught her. She was light for his strength; he was accustomed to unhorsing warriors in full armor. He dragged her without faltering from her mare and tossed her slender form over the pommel of his saddle as he reigned in his destrier.

Once the giant horse had come to a halt, he gave her a firm shove, sending her sprawling to the ground. He stared at her with sharp, impassive eyes, then saw that she, even now, breathless and stunned, was trying to escape him, rolling from the still hooves of the destrier, but finding herself entangled in the cape.

Bryan threw his right leg over the horse and leaped to the ground, pouncing upon her before she could gain her footing. He straddled over her form and secured her flailing arms. She sank her teeth into his arm; he barely felt the pain, but he jerked her hands higher above her head to avoid her vengeful bite.

"Where are your accomplices, bitch?" he grated out. "Tell me now, or as God is my witness, I will strip the flesh from your body inch by inch until you do!"

She was still struggling against him, a tempest of fury and energy. "I have no accomplices!" she spat out. "And I am no thief! You are the thief! You are the murderer! Let me go, whoreson. Help! Help! Oh, help me, someone! Help . . ."

Bryan felt as if, somewhere deep inside his heart, something broke. Something that cried out in anguish and fury against the treachery and pain of the night. Her cry made him feel as if his blood burned within his veins. She cried for help, she cried for mercy—and she had given none.

He clasped her wrists with one hand, and drew the back of the other hard across her cheek.

"You robbed the dead!" He hissed coldly as her stunned eyes met his. "Henry of England! You were seen!"

"No!"

"Then I shall find nothing of his upon you?"

"No! I am not a thief, I'm—" She stopped suddenly, then continued. "Can't you see, fool? I carry nothing of the king's—"

Her voice broke suddenly once again, and a look of alarm flashed through her turquoise eyes, and her lashes fell like lush fans to cover them for a second. When they opened, they were clear again, bright with indignity and anger.

A consummate actress, Bryan thought. Quickly disguising true emotion with a fine show of outrage. But she hadn't been quite quick enough. Before the treacherous shade of her lashes had fallen, he had seen the truth in her eyes. He had frightened her. It was probable that she did hold some property of the king's upon her.

Her eyes fell closed once more; her body was stiff beneath his.

Bryan's lips curved in a grim semblance of a smile.

"We shall see, madam," he hissed, his voice even more of a threat than his tense grip upon her, "if you can prove your innocence."

Her brilliant eyes flew open to challenge his. "I am the Duchess of Montoui! And I demand that you let me up this instant!"

Montoui? He'd never heard of it. Yet no duchess went around as poorly clothed as his captive—not that it mattered at the moment who she was. Had the Virgin Mary perpetrated the deeds at the castle, his fury could not have been abated.

"I don't care if you're the Queen of France! I intend to discover what you have done with your booty."

Her body went more rigid beneath his; he felt her attempt to curl her nails to gouge his hand.

"Touch me, and I'll see your head on the block!"

"I doubt that . . . Duchess," he mocked, fighting hard to control his temper against her imperious tone. It was very difficult to remind himself that he was a knight, and not a judge and jury. If Henry had accomplished anything, it was to give law to England. He was not an executioner. Had she been a man, he could challenge and fight, he could have slain her. But as it was, she deserved the death sentence. But he had no right to decree it.

He released her wrist and crossed his arms over his chest, staring harshly upon her as his thighs continued to imprison her to the ground. "We're going back to the castle," he told her. "I suggest you be ready to talk by the time we reach it."

Swiftly, contemptuously, he rose, striding to retrieve the reins of his destrier.

He turned back to her. She still lay upon the ground, just as he had left her, except that she had her arms hugged about her chest.

"Up, Duchess," he said.

Her eyes met his, wide and shadowed and suddenly . . . hurt? Or perhaps frightened?

"I'm winded," she murmured, "and I'm caught in my cloak. If you would help me?"

Impatiently, Bryan reached down to drag her to her feet. But once he had clasped her left hand, she sprang to her feet with an astounding ease, raising her right hand high into the air. The moonlight caught and reflected the shiny blade of her dagger just as it caught and reflected the hatred and venom in her now crystal clear and sharply narrowed eyes.

She wasn't frightened at all; she was in a murderous rage.

And she encompassed surprising strength and expertise in her deceptively slender form.

Only his greater strength and war-trained reflexes saved him from the well-directed blow of her dagger. His arm bolted upward to capture hers, forcing her to drop the dagger. She cried out in startled pain as he jerked her hand, twisting her arm behind her back.

He couldn't help but delight in her shiver when he whispered against the nape of her neck, "No, Duchess of thieves and murderers, I will not be your next victim. But if harlots and thieves believe in God, I suggest you start praying. For, at the castle, I guarantee that you will be my victim—and that you will pay dearly for this night."

III

A cloud fell over the moon as he spoke the words, casting them into an almost total darkness. The wind picked up in sudden and chilling gusts.

She felt his whisper, and his hands upon her, like icy fingers of doom. And his presence. His towering form, his muscular form emitting a furious heat.

"Duchess?" His voice mocked her, and sent new ice shivers streaming along her spine. How she hated the sound of his voice. Deep, husky, autocratic, ever-condescending.

But at least he hadn't wrested the dagger from her hand and stabbed her—as she had intended to do to him. Her dagger lay harmlessly upon the ground. Her wrist still chafed, but she was too aware of him.

She could feel the strength that emanated from him as he stood close behind her. He was sinewed like the steel of a blade, as staunch as an oak, and as threatening as a hungry wolf. Like the darkness, he was all around her, and like the sudden, bitter wind, he could buffet her as he so chose.

She had made a horrible mistake in attempting to stab him.

His fingers vised around her arm like talons. "Let's go, milady—before the rain." He spanned her waist with the long splay of his fingers and set her high upon the back of the destrier. She stared at him as he gathered the reins to mount behind her. She had never seen anything quite like his expression before: totally impassive, chiseled from the hardness of rock. The deep, midnight-blue of his eyes offered no chance of mercy; he had judged and condemned her.

"Who are you?" she demanded suddenly. If he was not one of the thieves, then he had to be one of her father's knights.

"Sir Bryan Stede, Duchess," he told her grimly. "Henry's man to the end."

Henry's man. Then he really would return her to the castle. And one of the knights who knew her would be at Chinon, someone who knew that the king had made many journeys to the province of Montoui.

Yet, she wondered, what good would that do if they decided to search her? They would discover Henry's ring, and they would assume that she was among the thieves. After what had occurred, no one, from peasant to royalty, would be beyond the wrath of the forces of Chinon. She couldn't allow herself to be searched; it was that simple. She would have to bear herself with such dignity that none would dare to touch her. She had learned a great deal about autocratic authority; she was, after all, Henry's daughter. She could generally command obedience with a cool gaze and soft statement. No one had ever dared touch her with the least disrespect.

Until tonight.

Until this ill-bred stone-and-steel facsimile of a knight.

Elise lifted her chin regally and offered him a dry smile that matched his for mockery. "Then, Sir Stede, let's do hurry for the castle. Surely there will be an authority there who will make you pay dearly for what you have wrought this night! When it is proven just who I am, Sir Stede, you—"

"Duchess," he said, cutting her short, "I have already informed you that even if you were the Queen of France you would find no mercy if you proved to be a thief."

She wanted to make a sharp retort; she could not, for all that escaped her lips was a startled gasp as he nudged the giant stallion into movement and she was left to grasp at its thick mane for balance. The animal bolted into a run, throwing her hard against the knight's chest.

She ground her teeth together as the harsh wind whipped about her face, tearing the cowl of her cape from her head, and releasing her hair with a stinging fury. A grunt behind her told her that at least her hair was also tangling about his face—and his discomfort gave her great pleasure. She felt as if she rode a storm, and knew not when the maelstrom would end, or if she would ever find a peaceful shelter again.

It was so dark, so very dark, and growing colder by the minute. How did the massive horse know where it ran at its breakneck speed? Surely it would lose its footing and plummet them to a sure death.

But the man behind her seemed unconcerned. He leaned hard against her, low with the horse, as if he were accustomed to these wild rides. Perhaps he was. But she was not, and her thoughts became nothing but a monotonous prayer. Let it end, let it end, oh, please, God, let it end.

Just when she was certain she couldn't possibly be more miserable, the darkness of the night sky was rent into a brilliant glow with a streak of jagged lightning. A scream caught in Elise's throat, but to her amazement, the destrier didn't bolt or falter. He just kept racing through the night.

The thunderclap that followed the lightning was deafening, but still the horse portrayed no signs of nervousness. Elise kept silent, wondering how the castle could now be so far away. Where were they? Had the dark knight really chased her so far?

Suddenly, as if an ocean had opened upon them, the rain began. It wasn't the drizzle that had accompanied Elise to Chinon; it was a cold and vicious deluge, so forceful that at last the destrier slowed his gait, and the dark knight swore beneath his breath. Instinctively, Elise bowed low against the heavy neck of the destrier, trying to duck the savage beating of the wind and water. Her cloak and tunic were soaked. She was damp and cold to the bone, no longer able to control her shivering.

The knight swore softly again, spoke to the horse, and turned about, finding a little-used and overgrown trail that appeared to go straight into the foliage.

Something struck hard upon Elise's shoulder and she emitted a startled cry. She twisted upon the mount, searching out the dark eyes of the unchivalrous knight.

"Fool!" she accused him. "There will be no vengeance for either of us if you don't seek shelter from this—"

"I am seeking shelter!" he bellowed out in return as the rain was made more bitter with a driving pellet of hailstones. "Get your head down!" he commanded, using one gloved hand to push her back around and press her face low to the horse's neck.

She felt him move against her again, and she was shielded from the storm by the breadth of his chest as his back took the punishment of the hail.

It still seemed as if they plodded miserably along forever. But at last Elise saw a break in the trees and heavy foliage, and by straining her eyes against the rain and the wind, she could make out the outline of a small building. A few seconds later they were upon it, and she could see that it was a hunter's cottage, built of timber and roofed with thatch. There was no fire burning within, no hint of light, and Elise realized with a sinking heart that the cottage had probably been built by the knights who had come to Chinon with Henry, built by them to give them a place of rest on the days when they foraged far into the forest for game to feed the retinue at the castle. She would be alone in the cottage with Sir Bryan Stede.

"Come!"

She gazed down to see that he had already leaped from the horse and now reached out his arms to assist her down. She ignored his arms, but when she attempted to dismount from the horse on her own, her sodden cape became hooked upon the pommel, and she would have fallen had he not been there to catch her.

For a moment she stood shivering; she could barely move her fingers, they had been cramped in a death grip upon the destrier's mane for so long. But she felt a sturdy shove upon her back, forcing her toward the narrow door of the cottage. "Get inside!"

Another hailstone fell hard upon her shoulder, and Elise needed no further urging. She raced to the door of the cottage, flinging it inward, and stepping beneath the shelter of the roof. She turned back to see that the dark knight was leading his horse around the corner of the cottage.

Now! she told herself. Now was her chance to escape. The hailstorm and the wind were merciless, but it would be far better to take her chances with the weather than with the menacing and insolent Sir Stede.

She had to run. It was her only chance.

Elise stared out into the darkness of the storm, took a deep breath, and pulled her soaked cowl over her head and low over her forehead once more. Then she left the doorway behind and bolted out into the clearing.

Her shoes sank and then slipped within the mud, and she stumbled and fell before she had gotten halfway to the sanctuary of the trees. She struggled back to her feet and started to run again. Another bolt of lightning struck, right in front of her, filling the sky with an awesome light and the air with a horrific screech as a tree was struck. Elise screamed as thunder followed almost instantaneously after the lightning, seeming to shatter the earth itself with the force of its explosive boom. The trees and foliage, she realized belatedly, offered her no shelter, only certain death.

But before she could turn back, she found herself hurtled back into the mud, and then encaptured in a cruel grip. One moment she was on the ground, the next she was in the air. Bryan Stede had no difficulty walking through the slick mud. His strides were long and efficient. He might have carried a length of cloth rather than the weight of a woman. He didn't even glance at her as he returned her across the distance of the clearing to the cottage.

But she could see him. The line of his lip was so compressed that it appeared to be no more than a white slash across his darkly tanned features. His jaw was hardened to a solid square, and a vein ticked furiously against the corded column of his throat. His eyes had grown so dark again that they appeared like the black, bottomless pits of hell.

He kicked open the cottage door with his foot and Elise bit back a scream of terror as he slammed it behind him in the same fashion. The tension in his hold betrayed the depths of his anger, all the more acute to her senses as they were pitched into the total darkness of the cottage. He was furious enough to rip her limb from limb, she was certain, and in the blackness, she felt as if he would readily do so.

But he did not. He set her down, shoving her away from himself. Elise stood dead-still, stunned by her release, and blinded to even the shadow of his movement. But suddenly a spark of light showed through the darkness, and she realized that the cottage had been supplied with flint, and a fireplace.

With the ease of a man who had spent years in the field, Bryan quickly had a fire burning. Its glow filled the cottage with soft light and warmth. Elise blinked against the sudden light, and quickly surveyed the cottage. It was well kept, and well supplied. On one side of the fireplace was a large trunk; on the other was a long trestle table, flanked by parallel benches. In the opposite corner of the room were two low-framed beds, spread with heavy wool blankets.

Clean rushes graced the floor, and Elise knew instinctively that her first impression had been right. The knights had built and supplied the cottage, and used it frequently when hunting game in the forest.

But although she could see now and the fire quickly began to burn with high, warming flames, Elise did not feel in the least warmed—or secure. Her soaked and muddied garments clung to her and continued to chill her, as did the proximity of the man she had spent long hours trying to escape.

At last he turned from the fire. There was nothing in the least reassuring about his stone-hard features. His midnight eyes swept over her from head to foot, and Elise wondered suddenly why she had found the lightning at all frightening.

She should have kept running.

He stood, still watching her with that cold gaze, and cast off his own soaked mantle. He turned his back to her to drape it over a bench near the fire, but when she shuffled a foot to shift her stance, he turned back upon her with an uncanny speed.

Elise lifted her chin and met his gaze silently.

He spoke at last. "You are either a complete fool, Duchess, or truly desperate. Are you so anxious to find a quick death in the storm?"

"I am not anxious for death at all," Elise replied coolly, intentionally refraining from offering the courtesy of a title.

He took a seat upon the bench to remove his boots, keeping his eyes upon her as he performed the task.

"Yet you claim that you are not guilty of theft or murder?"

"I am not guilty of anything—except for offering my prayers for the dead."

"Then why try to escape me, when to do so would mean death?"

"Not necessarily."

He emitted a curt oath, tossing one boot across the room with a sudden fury that almost made her jump. But she was determined that she would show him no sign that he could frighten her, and so she followed the fall of his boot, then returned her eyes to his with a cool disdain.

"Do you deny that you were intent upon murdering me?" Bryan demanded.

"No, I do not deny it," Elise replied without faltering. "I assumed you were one of the thieves—"

"You tried to stab me after you knew that I could not be a thief."

"I am still not sure that it is not you who is the thief and murderer!" Elise exclaimed furiously. "You certainly do not behave like a knight. You have the courtly manner of a large boar!"

To Elise's surprise, Stede laughed. "Nay, madam, we are in no court, and therefore I see no use for 'courtly' manners. If you think to find my judgment less severe because you are a woman, I am sorry, you are mistaken."

"Sir Stede," Elise enunciated carefully, "I expect very little from you, as it appears to me that you surely sit upon whatever mind you might have. I am not a thief—"

"Aye, yes, so you've said. You're the Duchess of Montoui.

Then tell me, Duchess, why were you racing from the castle? Why didn't you halt when I demanded you do so?"

Elise sighed with a great show of impatience, but none of her mannerisms or words seemed to have the slightest effect upon him. "I came to the castle this evening to offer my prayers for King Henry. It was while I was at prayer that I heard sounds in the hallway. I hid within the chamber, then fled—"

"You escaped these thieves when full-grown men fell to their treachery?"

Elise grated her teeth together at the hard skepticism in his voice. "I hid behind a tapestry. When one of the cutthroats would have discovered me, I attacked him with the advantage of surprise, and then ran."

"You . . . attacked a man . . . and came out of the battle unscathed?"

"There was no battle. I attacked first, and as he staggered with the surprise, I ran."

"That's a fair defense you have woven," Stede murmured, yet from the indigo glare that still burned upon her, she could tell nothing of his thoughts. Careless of her presence, he rose and stripped off his woven wool hose, draping them, too, upon the table near the hearth to dry. For a moment he might have forgotten Elise's presence; he pulled off his gloves and cast his heavy scabbard upon the planked table, then stood with his face toward the fire as he warmed his hands.

Stripped down to nothing but his thigh-length tunic, he was even more formidable than he had been swathed in his dark cloak. Elise had never seen a man appear more threatening by simple virtue of his masculinity. A knit shirt clung tightly to his arms beneath the sleeveless tunic, yet the material clearly enhanced the sizable muscles that rippled with his slightest movement. His shoulders appeared very broad, his waist very narrow. He was clearly a man who lived hard, practiced daily with his weapons, and kept his physique as attuned as his senses in the pursuit of staying alive upon the field. His legs, now bared, were long, and shapely and oak-hard, evenly flecked with a wealth of short dark hair to match the raven's black upon his head. Inadvertently, Elise shivered. She was tall for a woman, yet she felt his size keenly. His hands could eclipse her own; if he chose, he could wrap his fingers around her throat and snuff out her life with the closing of a fist . . .

He turned back to her suddenly and his indigo eyes swept over her form with little expression.

"You are dripping wet," he said.

"What an astute observation, Sir Stede," Elise replied with thick-laced sarcasm. He gave little sign that he had noted her tone, yet she sensed that something tightened further about his hard features. She was a fool to taunt him, she realized, and wondered why she did so. But she didn't really want to look closely at the answer. She was terrified, and taking the offensive might keep her from falling full prey to that terror . . .

"One would assume," he said lightly, "that any woman with sense would not need to have such an observation pointed out. If you were to take off your cloak, you would not be so wet—or so cold."

She was loath to give up her cloak. Outside the rain still fell with a vengeance, and the wind blew viciously. But . . . rain always came to an end . . . eventually. And she was still near the door. If he were to . . .

Were to what?

He would hardly pass out right before her. No stone would fall from heaven to knock him out. And running blindly would not help her; he knew the terrain, and he was swift as well as strong. If she ran again, she would have to be sure of escape.

Reluctantly, she removed her sodden cloak and walked slowly forward to spread it out upon the table near his. She felt his eyes upon her all the while, and she drew out the task. But eventually she knew that she had to turn and confront him once more, and again, he made no pretense that he wasn't inspecting her thoroughly, but again, she could read no emotion from her eyes or his tight but impassive expression.

He moved back a step from the fire, bowing low with what

she was certain had to be further mockery, and ushering her toward the warmth of the fire. She did not like the idea of her back being toward him, but she forced herself to step forward, placing her slender fingers toward the fire and allowing the flames to warm them from numbness.

Elise heard the crackle of the kindling and logs and the savage whip of the wind outside the cottage walls. But deeper than the fury of the night was the silence that reigned between them. He said nothing to her, and as the minutes passed in an endless progression, she came closer and closer to screaming in an agony of apprehension. Although he said nothing, she knew that he hovered close behind her. Very close. She sensed the rise and fall of his breathing, felt that his heart thundered above her own with menace, and that the vibrant heat of his body would shortly overwhelm the faltering bravado to which she clung in fevered desperation.

His hand clamped suddenly upon her shoulder, and she had to draw blood upon her lip to keep from crying out. "Come, Duchess, sit," he told her politely, and as he spoke, he drew one of the benches behind her, then pressed her down to it.

"Thank you," Elise murmured regally, wishing that she might have stood all night rather than feel his burning touch upon her. But she knew that she was not to be spared his interrogation, or his proximity, and that her only hope was in maintaining such a great dignity that he would have to respect her noble birth.

"Your story is a good one, Duchess," he drawled at last, and the whisper of his voice so near her earlobe almost caused her to jump. He leaned upon the bench, not touching her, but with his arms on either side of her, like bars. "Very good. But don't you think it might be more plausible to believe that you are one of a band of thieves? How easy for you to lead the chase in one direction, while your accomplices disappear in another. And how easy for you to plead innocence. When apprehended, you are a woman alone. And one surely capable of winding men about her finger with the wide eyes of naiveté."

Elise stiffened her spine against his tone. "I have told you,

Stede, that I am the Duchess of Montoui. I have no need to join with thieves."

"Or murderers?"

"Or murderers."

"You are quite adept with a dagger."

"Yes."

"Is that perhaps the newest of courtly feminine pursuits?"

"No, Sir Stede. But I am a duchess in my own right; I rule my own lands. In such circumstances, it is wise for a woman to know something of self-defense."

"Ah. Why is it that I have not heard of this Montoui?"

"Perhaps because you are grossly ignorant."

He did not move; he did not snap out a reply. But she sensed a tightening in the banded muscles of the arms that were a cage on either side of her, just as she felt a constriction of the broad chest that hovered not the width of his thumb behind her. And a strange heat, as if lightning had sizzled suddenly at her back, assailing the entire length of her spine.

"Your tongue, Duchess, is as sharp and honed as your dagger. And you strike with it just as quickly—and foolishly."

She said nothing, and forced herself not to tremble when he straightened and touched her, his long-fingered and calloused hands oddly and frighteningly gentle as they picked up the length of her hair to spread it about her shoulders.

Elise clenched down hard upon her teeth as he persisted silently with the task, drawing from her hair the pins that had fallen awkwardly during the night. It was a simple and courteous enough service, yet she wanted to scream at the false intimacy of it. No matter how gentle his fingers, she could feel the contained power of his hands, and the contradiction of his soothing motion to his stinging words was a bitter play upon her senses.

If it were Percy . . .

She closed her eyes for a moment, thinking sickly of the knight she loved. If only Percy had been with the king at Chinon! She would not be suffering this indignity now. Percy was all that a knight should be: brave upon the field, yet tender and sensitive in the hall. Percy could speak with the sweetest words; he spent his leisure time with the troubadours, composing ballads for her. There was nothing rock-hard and impenetrable about Percy, as there was about this knight. Percy was slim and more of a height with her. He was gallant and kind, and his eyes were a warm golden-brown, and his mouth continually turned to a wistful smile that held no mockery. He was gallant and steadfast, and he always fell to his knees when he returned to her, kissing her hand with reverence. He kept her atop a pedestal, and though they had exchanged exciting kisses that made her long for more, Percy would not dream of dishonoring her before marriage.

Thank the Virgin Mary, Elise thought with a moment's irony, that her natural mother and Henry had vowed to keep her birth secret—and to give her as a daughter to William and Marie de Bois. Percy often claimed that the king had been a licentious old man. And he believed in the old "Melusine legend"—that Satan's blood ran in the Plantagenets. If Percy had known that Henry's blood ran in her veins, and that she was a bastard, as well, he would surely not have offered her such tender care, finding fault with the troubadours if their lyrics proved to be too bawdy for her maiden's ears . . .

Offered her tender care! *Admit it,* she warned herself in a moment of truth; Percy might still love her, but he would never marry her if he knew that she was the king's bastard. For all that she loved him, Elise also knew him. Percy believed deeply in legalities, as well as in bloodlines. In a well-ordered society, man was born to his class, and the feudal system was the way of the world. Family lines should be painstakingly charted, and bad blood must be excluded.

Bastards—especially Henry's!—did not fit into Percy's view of the well-ordered world.

Elise had often argued with him; William the Conqueror had been a bastard. The royalty of England were the descendants of a bastard. But Percy was adamant in his beliefs. He knew what had come to the English royalty: bloodshed between father and son. God did not sanction a bastard.

It was a sore spot between them, but Elise wisely kept her own council. Man was not created to be perfect; Percy was far more so than most, and so she was willing to accept him, and love him, despite what she, naturally, believed to be faulty thinking.

Shrewdly, Elise knew that there was a far more important consideration Henry had probably taken in mind when determining to keep her birth a secret. Montoui. While he lived, she could never lose it. But after his death, were it known that she was not the legal issue of William de Bois, there might be many ready to stake a claim to the duchy. Distant cousins of Duke William could spring up like mushrooms in a forest, ready to do battle for the duchy. Cousins who, no matter how distant, could trace their bloodlines to the de Bois family, and therefore prove themselves the legal heirs.

She was the daughter of a king, yet she had every reason to be grateful that the fact was not known. Every reason to protect the secret of her birth. The two most important factors in her life were involved: her duchy, the land she ruled and loved; and, even more important to her happiness, the *man* she loved.

Oh, Percy! she thought wistfully. *Were you just here, this wretched steel-bound nighthawk would not dare to accuse and defame me! He would have you to reckon with, my love.*

If only it were Percy who touched her so, she would have relaxed in sweet oblivion, savoring the solicitous ministrations of such a masculine touch . . .

Bryan allowed himself a bitter smile as he loosed and laid out the girl's hair. He could feel the stiffness of her back, and knew that his touch made her acutely uncomfortable. Yet he needed her on edge, for only then could he hope to disarm her—and get to the truth. The workings of the night were still a deep pain that knifed and delved into him, and each time he closed his eyes, he could see afresh the dishonored body of the king, and the sightless eyes of his dead friends.

And if all had been brought to such a state by the trickery of a woman, then that woman was going to pay.

She was, he thought, perfect for the role of thief's accomplice. The hair he touched was as beautiful as the firelight, flaming gold one second, red the next. As it dried with the warmth from the flames, it became soft within his hands, like a golden skein of the purest silk from the Orient, or endless waves of fire. It fell with a rich and luxurious length down her back, almost to her thighs. It almost brushed the floor as she sat.

And her eyes, those startling turquoise eyes, framed by the deeply contrasting, dark honey lashes. They could wear a guise of sweetest and most outraged indignity. Had he not seen her run—had he not almost become the victim of her viciously raised dagger—he could have readily guessed her innocent.

Her face was flawlessly constructed with lovely high cheek-bones, full, wine-red lips, and a pink-tinged, ivory complexion. She could well be a child of some noble line, yet no well-bred lady would hearken into the night alone.

He was also well aware that her beauty encased the temper of a shrew and the tongue of a viper. She had been more than ready to murder him. Perhaps that was the deciding factor with him now. She had tried to stab him, and she had spoken to him in such condescending tones that it had taken the greatest willpower to prevent himself from cuffing her against one of her elegant cheeks and sending her sprawling against the wall.

That would have left her with no question as to the extent of "courtly gallantry" he was willing to go.

"So," he murmured softly, "you are the Duchess of Montoui. And you traveled cross-country by yourself to offer your prayers at the bier of our King Henry."

"Yes," she said stiffly.

"Why should you do such a thing?"

"What?"

Bryan kept smiling. At last he seemed to have found a chink in the armor of her story.

"Why?" Bryan repeated. "Why should you have come to

pray at the castle, when you might have offered masses at your own? Are you perhaps a relative of the king?"

She did not hear the taunt in his voice. She heard only the truth, and quickly and breathlessly denied it.

"No!"

"Then why should a duchess in her own right set upon such a perilous journey?"

"Because . . . I . . . I . . ."

"Because you are a vile liar!"

"No!" Elise jumped to her feet in a spurt of fury that was as hot as the blazing fire. "I tell you, Stede, that you will suffer for this night! I have friends in high places, and I will see that you are disarmed and dishonored! I will see you sweat in a dungeon, and perhaps I shall even have the ultimate pleasure of seeing your fool head depart from your body! You can see that I am no thief! Do I carry a tapestry? Or the king's scabbard? Fool—"

In ultimate frustration and fury, Elise raised her arms high in the air, shifting the material of her unadorned tunic across her breast.

To her horror, the ring, her mother's ring, the one she had taken from her father's finger, fell to the floor.

Spinning and whirling with a shrill clang upon the planks, then laying still between her feet.

She met Stede's eyes with horror, and saw within their indigo depths a rage unlike anything she had ever known.

She gave up all pretense of dignity as he stepped toward her, and screamed out her terror as his no-longer-gentle fingers bolted out to clamp around her shoulder.

In desperation she fought, flinging her hand hard across his face, digging at his cheek with her nails. He seemed not to feel the pain, nor did he falter as she kicked and lashed and bit at him.

"Let's see what else you're trying to hide, Duchess."

The long fingers she had known to be powerful closed about the neckline of her tunic. She grabbed at his hands, but her strength was nothing to combat his. The next thing she heard was a rendering tear as he ripped the tunic from her neck to the floor, and dispassionately wrenched it from her.

IV

Clothed only in the thinnest of linen shifts, Elise felt her face flame crimson with fury and outrage.

Instinct made her grab desperately for her garment, even as a spew of oaths that would have done a full-blown warrior proud poured heatedly from her lips.

"Bastard! Dung! Son of a diseased bitch! Spawn of a whore—"

Elise clawed furiously at the fist that held her wool tunic, but Stede caught her wrists with his free hand and sent the remnants of the woolen tunic flying across the room to land in a heap at the far corner. In dismay Elise paused to stare up at her tormentor. Indigo eyes that fired with condemnation returned her scrutiny harshly; his jaw was set in rock-bound determination.

He stooped to retrieve the ring, making her gasp and curse him anew as she was dragged along with him.

"Nothing of the king's?" he demanded.

"Wait!" Elise sputtered. "You don't understand—"

"Aye, but I do understand. I've understood all along."

"No—"

He rose again, jerking her up. "The shift, milady."

"What?"

He released her, walking around the bench once more to sit expectantly upon it, arms crossed over his chest as he assessed her with cold and calculating eyes.

"You heard me, Duchess. The shift. Now you can take it off yourself, or I can do it for you. I'm afraid that my way is a little rough, so if you wish to retain at least one garment in one piece, I suggest you do it yourself."

"You must be a lunatic!" Elise hissed, trembling with sudden shock. This could not be happening, not to her. She had been cherished by her parents, a favorite of the king's—and she was loved and respected by her people. She issued orders in a soft tone and they were instantly obeyed; her knights rallied to her side in any crises, ready to lay down their lives for her protection . . .

And now this . . . beast of the night . . . was treating her with more contempt than he would a common scullery maid.

And she was allowing him to do so. He was edging beneath her skin and stripping away more than her clothing; he was robbing her of the dignity and nobility carefully crafted throughout her entire life . . .

"A lunatic?" he repeated dryly. "Perhaps, the moon is full, and one might easily say that soul-deep fury borders upon lunacy." His voice had almost been pleasant for a moment, a husky velvet that would have stood well in Eleanor's once-famed court. But then it changed again, became as cutting and rigid as steel.

"The shift . . . milady."

Elise lifted her chin and willed a spark of lightning to straighten her spine and proudly square her shoulders.

"You are no honorable knight, Sir Stede," she told him with her coolest hauteur. "No knight would thus treat a lady—"

"But you are no lady, Duchess," Stede broke in unhurriedly. "No lady would speak with such a sharp and vile tongue."

"Anyone would speak with a vile tongue when beset upon by a vile creature!"

He smiled, and she did not at all like his smile. "I'm waiting, Duchess."

"Then you've a long wait, sir, for I've no intention of stripping before you like a common trull."

He shrugged, as if the matter were entirely her choice, but then he began to rise. From experience, Elise could not doubt his intent, or his capability to carry out any threat. Dignity was lost to the wind again as she stamped her foot with frustrated fury upon the ground.

"Wait!" she commanded, but there was far more plea to her voice than she would have wished. But he paused, hands upon his hips, a brow arched, as he gave her a chance to speak further.

"Sir," she began, deciding that a quiet beseechment might best serve her now no matter how she loathed extending even the least of courtesy to the man. "Surely you must see how gravely you have already compromised my position! You tarnish my reputation by holding me here even as this storm rages, you have done me the greatest indignity already by leaving me so ill clad as it is, yet now you would have me naked to the core so that any honorable man would . . . would . . ."

"Would what, Duchess?" he queried politely.

Another flood of crimson washed to her cheeks. Why was she stammering so? The situation was obvious.

"You compromise my position!" she flared, her temper rising despite herself. And with the words out, she realized that her position might become truly compromised. Bryan Stede was proving himself to be even more uncouth than she had first imagined, if that was possible. It was clear that every word she spoke convinced him more thoroughly that she was a thief. And now he was holding evidence that she had taken something from the king. If he believed her to be nothing more than a common thief and a harlot, then he might engage in any dishonorable action . . .

"Duchess," he said evenly, "you compromised your own position—when you saw fit to join in murder and thievery."

"May the devil take you!" Elise grated, knotting her fingers into the palms of her hands and trying not to attack him foolishly in an insane frustration. "I tell you—"

He held up the king's sapphire, allowing it to gleam in the firelight.

"This ring," he said thickly, "belonged to Henry Plantagenet. He wore it upon his small finger, day and night, as long as I can remember." For a moment his eyes were upon the brilliant stone, and they were dark and clouded with memory. Then they were upon her, as sharp and glittering as the stone.

"The shift, Duchess."

"I swear to you that I carry nothing else—"

"You swore to me that you carried nothing to begin with."

It was a foolish gesture, a desperate gesture, but Elise was desperate. She ran. Skirting the bench, she made a mad dash for the door that led into the night. She touched the hard oak, and grabbed wildly for the handle. The door began to open.

But just as it began to veer inward, he flew to close it with a reverberating slam. Elise felt herself vised about the middle, and wrenched crudely to the ground. She started to roll, but he came after her quickly, moving with the swift ease of a cat with a cornered mouse.

"Leave me be!" she screamed out in fear and fury as she rolled herself into a corner and he planted a foot on either side of her waist. "Leave me—"

He started to lower himself, his legs straddled around her to imprison her once more with his body. The elemental warning that had sent her running to begin with kept Elise fighting. As she saw his towering form about to eclipse her, she began to kick with all her strength.

A sharp, whistling intake of breath and a growl of pain rewarded her efforts, but her feeling of victory was quickly dashed by the sound of the rising wind. Pain did not deter the man from action. He braced himself coldly around her, catching her still-flying arms, and restraining them at her side for a moment as he took a deep breath, and stared at her with such a furious hatred burning from the indigo fire of his eyes that she quickly regretted her rash actions.

She was amazed as he slowly released her, warning her with those eyes all the time not to move as he eased himself to his haunches, keeping the bulk of his weight off her.

"Duchess," he said slowly, "don't move again. I would enjoy an excuse to snap your 'noble' neck, so if you are wise, you will not give me one. You try my manners, milady, but I promise you that, by this point, a goodly portion of your 'courtly' knights would have readily beaten you black and blue. I have refrained from abuse, I have sought only to restrain you. Be still, and cease goading me, for every man—no matter how 'noble'—has a breaking point."

Tears were coming to her eyes, tears of pure panic. In a matter of seconds she would be crying like a small child, and she had no intention of doing so before this man.

"Restraint! Abuse!" she protested, her fingers itching to strike out for his stone-and-ice features. "I have merely fought being abducted! You ravaged me to the ground from my horse, carted me about at your whim, and have abused me. You—"

"I did nothing but catch a thief!"

"Bastard—" The itch in her hand became too much. She struck out at him, but was denied even the pleasure of affording him that small pain. He was too quick. He caught her arm even as it sailed toward him, and the ice smile that touched his lips as he replaced her arm at her side was so chilling that she did not dare move again.

She held herself perfectly still, watching his eyes, and trying not to tremble. But when his hands fell upon the bodice of her shift, she could no longer lie still. She clawed at them and writhed in a furious effort to dislodge him from her person.

"Damn you, bitch! Little fool—"

She cried out as he snatched back her wrists again, his grip so cruel that her tears rose and sparkled.

"I have given you every warning!" he thundered.

"And I would rather die than be raped by a beast like you!" Elise retorted in torn anguish.

"Rape?"

To her amazement, Bryan Stede went dead-still, then laughed—but he did not release his hold as he pulled her hands above her hair and bonded them together with just one of his own.

"Duchess, my last intent this night is to rape you. Were I to want a woman, it would be one who was warm and winsome, not one with the cold, black heart of a thief!"

He meant his words; yes, he meant them. Never in his life had he desired to take a woman by force. Since he had been a youth, women had come to him. From peasant serving girls to high-born ladies, they had come to him. Warm, glad, and giving. Women, he had learned, often yearned for the pleasures of the bed with as much passion as men. They longed to be taught, to please, to be pleased. Gwyneth was such a one. Lovely, long-legged, and lusty. Ready to embrace him with a sultry heat and promise . . .

And Gwyneth came with lands and wealth.

It had been a long time since he had had Gwyneth. A long time since he had felt her sweet warmth and met her knowing eyes . . .

It was equally true that he might never see her again. If Richard decided to punish those who had stood fast by his father, Sir Bryan Stede could quickly forget Gwyneth and her titles and land, and turn his efforts once more to the bounty that could be earned at tournaments.

But even so, he knew, there would still be women. Warm and giving, wanting to be wanted. Never could he imagine stooping to force. There would be no pleasure in it.

Especially not when he despised the woman as he despised this one. A born beauty, yet carrying the ring he knew to be Henry's. Pleading innocence, pleading rank, yet clearly holding the evidence . . .

No, the thought of rape had never entered his head.

Nor had he truly thought, even vaguely, of wanting her . . . until now.

And now . . .

Now he glanced at the wealth of red and gold curls tangling their length about them both. At the luminous turquoise eyes. He thought of how she had appeared before the fire, breathing heavily, full, rounded breasts heaving, her bared shoulders gleaming like alabaster. He thought of the feel of her flesh, like silk, the fine fragility of her bones, the long, wickedly lean shape of her legs.

Yes, he could want her. The pulse that grew within his groin was sure proof. He could want her with a passion that filled his limbs with fire, his blood with aching desire. She was as beautiful as a dream of Avalon. And it had been a long time since he had held any maid. With the last battles, with Henry's pitiable death . . . it had been almost a month.

He could want her, he reminded himself with a sudden fury, but he would not. He would not want a cunning bitch who had surely been part of foul murder and theft . . .

Elise went as still as he for a moment, watching the dark emotions roil further clouds across his tense features. She bit her inner lip, scarcely daring to breathe, and praying that his words were true. Then the ignominy of her position once more assailed her, and she was infuriated anew that she had been brought so low as to be tossed about and scrutinized by a man she would love to see boiled alive.

"Get off—"

"Not quite yet, Duchess. Not quite yet."

"No!"

She screamed, but could do nothing as he at last caught the fabric of her shift at the bodice and ripped apart its length. And thrashing beneath him for her freedom did little good. All she managed to do was bare more of her skin as the shift slipped from her writhing body.

And then, to her horror, she felt his hand moving over her.

Thoroughly.

Quickly.

His broad, calloused palm skimmed over her breasts to search beneath her arms. He shifted his weight, rolling beside her. Then his hand skimmed again with a chilling efficiency, touching her belly and hips, then sliding lower.

"No!" Elise raged once more as she felt his fingers upon the intimate and tender flesh of her inner thighs. She thrashed against his grip, bending, trying to kick again, but he checkmated each of her moves with one of his own, wedging his knee between hers to force them apart, and sliding his fingers along her thigh once more until he came to the golden triangle at the juncture.

Elise screamed with rage to no avail. She felt him touch her where she had never been touched before, and the invasion of her feminine privacy was an affront she would never forget. Just as being so entirely helpless was an indignity that would never leave her. She could not free her wrists, could not fight the strength of the muscled thigh that held her own apart, leaving his hand and eyes free to travel and invade where they would. She closed her eyes as a trembling seized her. She had never felt anything as acutely as she felt him. The weight of his sinewed leg, the dispassionate touch of his brief but determined search. *So help me God in heaven!* she swore silently. *I will kill this man!* But her vow meant little at the moment; it was nothing more than a ray of hope to sustain her.

Then, just as surely as he had held her, he left her, rising to his feet in one smooth motion. She heard him as he strode toward the corner of the room. For a moment Elise was dazed; the tremors of shock and black fury refused to leave her. She opened her eyes slowly and saw that he stood above her once more, a blanket in his hands. He tossed it upon her with a careless disdain.

"I will kill you for this myself one day," she told him, meeting his eyes as she pulled the blanket to her chin.

He shrugged. "I would suggest, milady, that you do it soon. Thieves oft hang for far less than you have stolen. Should a court of law decide to go gently, as you are a woman, you will still be incarcerated within a strong tower."

He turned his back upon her and returned to the fire, sitting upon the bench and warming his hands.

Elise realized that he had discarded her for the moment—as if she were garbage. Stripped her, searched her, and discarded her. If only she still had her dagger, she would gladly suffer the consequences to pierce through his skin just once and draw the blood of his black heart.

As she lay, still stunned and seething, he rose, and, as if he were alone, bent over the trunk by the left of the fire to forage through it.

Evidently, the cottage was oft and well supplied. From the

trunk she saw that he drew a large drinking gourd and a leather-wrapped parcel. Still ignoring her, he sat back upon the bench and drank heartily from the gourd.

Elise chewed upon her lip, then looked from him to the door with such fierce longing that he must have sensed what was in her heart and riveted his eyes to her once more. She jumped when she heard him speak, turning to stare at him again with a scathing hatred.

"Don't try it again, Duchess. I have decided to leave your judgment to the law, but truly, you weary me. If I have to come for you one more time, I will bind you hand and foot and gag you, too, to spare the ears the blade of your tongue."

"You have decided to leave my judgment to the law?" Elise retorted in an angry demand, fighting tears once more. "Is that why you chose to grapple and strip . . . and search me?"

She was trying so very hard not to burst into tears, but still a huskiness caught in her throat, and the moisture glistened in her eyes, making the turquoise as stunningly brilliant as a perfectly cut stone. She was not seeking compassion, but somehow she saw that she had struck a chord within the dark knight.

"Milady," he said gently, and without the usual mockery he held in his tone when he addressed her as "Duchess," "this night I have seen much. I have seen the body of a dead monarch stripped and desecrated, I have seen old and loyal friends lie in pools of their own blood, with their sightless eyes staring hard upon me. And I have seen your eyes upon me, too, filled with venom and hatred—and the acute desire to skewer me through. I have seen you cry that you are innocent, that you are the Duchess of Montoui, fresh from prayers for the dead. Yet while you cried your outrage and innocence, the evidence of your lie fell to the floor at your feet, concealed upon your person. Yes, therefore I stripped and searched you. But I have done you no harm. It was, perhaps, a kindness. Or would you have rather found yourself before a quickly formed jury of peers, then stripped and searched? You speak of dishonor, milady. At least here we are alone. Whatever decision is reached upon for your future when we return to the castle of Chinon, you will know that you will not be inspected so again—before a multitude of others."

Elise felt her teeth begin to chatter. After all this, could there possibly be more to befall her? No, she would welcome the thought of Chinon. There would be those there who knew that she had been Henry's friend . . .

But would they care? Would they all believe that she might have robbed the king, especially when this man could produce evidence? Evidence that they had all seen upon the king when they had cleansed and dressed his body and readied it for burial.

She lowered her head. She had to escape. Once she was free from this man and back at Montoui, there was nothing that anyone could prove against her. Her own forces were five hundred strong; and should Bryan Stede persist in his pursuit, it would be only his word against her own. And she would plead her case straight to Eleanor of Aquitaine, and Eleanor would understand.

And Elise could at last find revenge against this man . . .

It was a beautiful dream, one that salved the rage of humiliation that still burned within her.

But it was only a dream. Unless she could get away from him.

There was the horrible possibility that she would be judged guilty by the nobles at Chinon and find herself suffering some terrible punishment before anyone could step in to save her.

The blood drained from her face as she realized suddenly that she was staring down at his bare feet and that he was once more towering over her. A little cry escaped her as he bent down and scooped her, blanket and all, into his arms. She could not prevent the alarm from leaping into her eyes as she met his.

"I apologize, Duchess," he said more softly than she would have expected, "but I do not trust you."

She found herself deposited upon the rear corner bed, far from the door. But although he had been far from solicitous, he had not handled her roughly, and Elise watched him as he walked back to the bench with speculation brewing within narrowed eyes.

He was many things, she decided, primarily rude, but although he hadn't the tender and courtly mannerisms that graced

Percy's little finger, he wasn't a cruel man. If she had realized from the start that he was not one of the thieves in pursuit to silence her into eternity, she would have turned to him and begged his protection. If she hadn't been so terrified and fought him so foolishly, he would have probably believed her.

Instead, it had come to this.

This night of degradation she would never forgive or forget . . .

If only she hadn't tried to stab him—

Or if only she had succeeded!

But that was all in the past. If she didn't drag her wits about her quickly, she stood in good stead of finding herself in an even worse situation. If she could only swallow her anger and her pride, just long enough to save herself!

She thought dryly of Henry, her father. There had been a time when he had been the greatest knight and king of Christendom. He had possessed skill and daring and strength and had ruled his lands so justly that he had come to be known as "Henry, the Lawgiver." But for all his vast strengths, he had always had a weakness for women. A pretty face and ample figure could easily attract his attention; a winsome smile could take his heart, if only for a brief spell.

All she needed was a brief spell.

And she didn't need to take the dark knight's heart. All she had to do was soften it from steel, and pray that somewhere in his soul a core of mercy and chivalry did exist.

Elise became aware that he was watching her in return, and she allowed her lashes to fall farther, shielding the sharp cunning in her eyes as she laid her plans.

To Bryan it appeared that she had at last been subdued, and it was not without a certain exhausted gratitude that he saw her so. He had enjoyed but an hour's sleep since the king's death, and his weariness was sinking into his bones.

But there was something about her huddled form that also made him feel irritatingly guilty. She was huddled with her feet beneath her, the blanket clenched tight to her breast with long, delicate fingers. But above those fingers he could see the high swell of her firm breasts, and the smooth, ivory column of her throat. Her head was slightly lowered, so he could not see the luminous turquoise pools beneath the rich honey lashes, but he did note the purity of her bone structure. Her hair, almost thoroughly dry now, fell about her in a lush cascade, and he would be hard put whether to name the color sunrise or sunset. Copper burned within it, and the most glorious gold. And as he stared at her, he could not help but wonder how it would feel to be completely entangled within that skein of gold, knowing its silken caress with the whole of his body as well as his fingers.

From such thoughts it was natural to think back just minutes, when he had held her beneath him. Natural to remember that all of her flesh was purest ivory, without blemish; that her breasts tempted a man to touch and taste, like firm, ripe fruit, budding high and proud, their crests like the beautiful, enticing color of a dew-morning rose. Her waist was narrow, curving like that of the ancient Roman's Venus to flair into a tantalizing bounty . . . that her belly dipped low between them until ivory flesh was shadowed by the mystique of a lush triangle of deepest honey and copper and gold. . . . Her legs were made to entwine with a man's, long and soft to touch, yet shapely.

Not even Gwyneth, the woman he would wed, could match this girl for sheer perfection.

Bryan took another long drink from the leather gourd of wine, feeling the heat well up within him. He studied the girl openly, yet it seemed not to matter, for she kept her eyes—discreetly? nervously? furiously?—lowered.

She was a thief, at best, he reminded himself dryly. Possibly a harlot, probably a murderess.

But he couldn't keep his senses from coming acutely alive, and he admitted with a dry shrug that he couldn't remember wanting a woman as he wanted this one. He was young, and vibrantly healthy. And, as tired as he was, his warrior's body was reminding him that his desires were healthy at the best of times, and lately, he had been on a long stretch of deprivation.

Yet, as he had told her, he would never think to force himself on a woman—not even one of her treacherous nature.

He closed his eyes and swallowed down a long draft of the wine. It was irritating, annoying—and painful. But natural, he assumed. Even if she was all that she might be—thief, harlot, murderess—he was contemplating a softening of his judgment, merely an appeasement of an elemental desire.

Still, beneath the shelter of the blanket, she looked both woebegone and proud. With her hair tangled and flowing about her, she might easily have been the heroine of a legend. The Lady of the Lake, perhaps; Guinevere, torn between two lovers.

Lost in misery . . .

Bryan shrugged and a grin tugged at his lips. Damn, but he was tired. Surely that was the only reason such fancy played upon his mind. But he was not God; nor was he a king, nor even the magistrate of a court of law. He held no power of life or death except in battle, and his battle with her was over. The storm still raged, shrilling through the cracks and crevices of the cottage. They would not travel again that night, and as he was her jailer, he was responsible for her care.

He rose and walked over to her. She did not raise her eyes until he offered the gourd to her. She stared at him suspiciously, as if doubting he might wish to see to her welfare in the least. Something about the still haughty cynicism in her stunning eyes touched a core within him, eliciting both a tenderness and a new anger. Yes, he had treated her roughly, crudely. But she had been the one fleeing the castle. She had pleaded innocence, then proved herself to be a liar with a ring. If she wanted courtly manners, she should have behaved in a courtly fashion.

"It's wine," he said brusquely. "No poison, Duchess. I drank from it myself."

He was startled when she suddenly began to tremble, then moistened her lips with the pink tip of her tongue. "Thank you," she whispered, taking the gourd and sipping the wine.

He was tempted to move away from her; she was betraying

her fear of him, and that feminine weakness brought forth the surge of desire to protect.

She needed no protection . . .

But he could not back down himself, and so he watched her as she drank the wine. She took a long sip, then coughed, and stared at him once more with startled eyes.

Bryan couldn't prevent a spurt of good-natured laughter. "Duchess, I assure you the brew is nothing but wine. But it is a local variety, quite potent, and not nearly as smooth as some to the palate. But it will not harm you."

Her eyes lingered upon him a moment, a mist of emerald-blue light. Then her lashes lowered once again, and she took another long swallow of the wine.

When she finished that time, she handed the gourd back to him and kept her eyes upon his with level intent. She spoke quietly.

"You are wrong about me, Sir Stede," she said softly.

"How so?" he heard himself ask.

"I took the ring from Henry, yes. But nothing else. And I was not with those who robbed him so irreverently and murdered his guards."

Elise forced herself to sit calmly, and to keep her eyes upon him as she spoke. His left brow raised in skepticism, but he did not dispute her, and she wondered if she had not at last found the chink in his armor. He turned from her and walked back to the fire, staring at it with his hands clasped idly behind his back.

"Despite the fact you tried to kill me," he said at last, "I would like to believe your story. I am not fond of public executions, or of seeing people locked away from the light of day for the remainder of their lives. But your story makes no sense. Why travel on such a night to pray at the bier of the king? Richard will come—he will have to. But who else? Eleanor has been locked away. John turned traitor. The king's bastard, Geoffrey Fitzroy, is expected, but no one else. Henry's body must be interred. And under circumstances such as these, only those who were with him at the end are expected to care for him here. Masses will be said throughout his lands.

"Yet you came, the king was robbed, and fine men were murdered. Then you ran from me as if I were the devil, and attempted to end my life with your dagger. I find that you carry the king's ring. You still tell me that you came only to pray, and took only the sapphire ring. But there is no reason for me to believe you. Tell me why I should, and I will try."

How she wished she could throw the gourd at his ruggedly handsome and arrogant features and tell him that she didn't give a tinker's damn if he believed her or not! But she had to care, because only by disarming him could she hope to escape him.

"The matter . . . was personal," she whispered, careful to make her words broken and breathy.

He turned from the fire and stared at her sharply, and for a moment she almost panicked, thinking he had realized just how personal it had been. But he arched that annoyingly superior brow once again and said quietly, "Such a reply left as is could easily cover many a deception."

Elise closed her eyes briefly, allowing her mind to spin. The truth; she could tell him the truth. She could take the chance that he would behave honorably and hold her secret . . .

She almost laughed aloud at herself with the irony of her thoughts. Honorably? Stede could never behave so. He had already proven himself to be one of the most ruthless and callous men she had ever had the distinct displeasure of meeting.

A hollowness settled over her, helping to calm her. No, no matter what lie she had to tell, or what deception she had to play, she could not tell him the truth. He might well cry it out to the world, and laughingly embellish upon his evening with the "king's bastard daughter." He could too easily be believed; people might begin to see the resemblance she bore to her father . . .

Her dream of her life with Percy would be shattered, her heart warned her. But it was her mind rather than her heart that convinced her that a lie, no matter how ridiculous and shameful, would better suffice than the truth. Henry was dead; Richard was coming to the throne. The scales of power among the nobles and soldiers would be swaying precariously. If someone wished to wrest Montoui from her, this would be the time to strike. And although her forces were strong, there were always those that were stronger. If the truth of her birth were known, Montoui could be pitched into bloody warfare; hundreds could die; the homes and farms could be burned to the ground, and the animals slaughtered by the attackers, leaving the people of the now rich duchy to starve when summer faded to winter . . .

She had to lie.

She had to manage to manipulate Stede. He had the strength of his sex; she must use the alluring guile of her own.

She had often managed to manipulate her father, and Henry had been the king. She could sway Percy to her whims with a soft smile and sweet whisper. Why not this knight?

Why not, indeed.

It seemed her only choice. And if it worked the way she planned, she would be free. If not . . . it would spread a different rumor. Elise smiled secretively. Her lie would be far more demeaning than the truth, but a demeaning deception would be the thing that saved her. And if Stede spread that rumor . . .

No one would believe him. Her chaste affair with Percy and her moral standards were too well known.

There was a way out. She had to play her role with sweet, feminine artistry . . .

V

She lifted her chin, yet allowed herself to tremble once more. "Sir. Stede, by what I have suffered at your hands so far, I hardly find you to be a man in whom I would care to confide." Elise fluttered her lashes prettily and took another long sip of the wine. It was an extremely potent drink, fruity and dry. She had been drinking wine and ale all her life, but this . . . this . . . was nice. It filled her with warmth. And with courage. False courage, she was aware, but desperately needed, nevertheless.

For a moment he was caught, caught by the firelight playing upon the wealth of her hair, by the soft whisper of her voice, by the plea within it.

"Milady, if you can say something that will clear you of the deed, please do so."

It was working! Like every other man, he could be veered from his course and led by the nose with little more than the effort of a false smile. Exuberance and warmth and a feeling of power swept through Elise and she determined to play her act. She stood, sweeping her blanket along with her chastely, yet swiftly assuring herself that a calf was innocently bared.

"I would gladly speak to you, Sir Stede! I would have spoken to you from the first had you not behaved so . . . crudely."

She said the last with such an aching hurt in her tone that she almost believed herself. And though Stede stood with an elbow rested upon the rough mantel, his ever-raised cryptic brow still high, she saw that his eyes were opaque, shrewd still as they appraised her, but perhaps betraying the shadow of doubt.

He did not bow down to apologize, but from him, the response was almost as gratifying.

"Milady, you know full well why I acted as I did."

"You were angry, yes, and . . . understandably so." She had to turn from him to utter such a fantastic lie, but even her swift shift to stare into the fire with her head bowed low was to her credit. He was silent for several seconds, then reminded her, "Duchess, you have yet to say anything that sheds light upon the situation."

She braced herself for the climax of her performance, stiffening her spine beneath the blanket and casting back her head so that the profile of her chin was high.

"I would rather die a thousand deaths, Sir Stede, than reveal my true reasons for being where I was known!"

That much was true. And she would rather die than have the real reason known. But the lie she was about to tell would surely suffice; and should it ever spread, it would not be believed.

She expected that he would swear to silence, but his voice was a soft drawl as he warned her, "Duchess, it is possible that you will die."

She felt him come near her, but he merely swept the gourd from her hand and drew from it as he straddled the bench, then opened the leather-bound satchel he had taken from the trunk. She heard a loud crunch and turned to see that he had bitten into a large, very fresh and very red apple.

His eyes were upon hers—expectantly.

"This cottage is very well supplied!" she exclaimed, just managing to keep the irritation from her voice.

"Yes, it is," he replied pleasantly, sweeping his hand to arc the room in the firelight. "With Richard always at our heels, we dug in immediately at Chinon. I built this place with Marshal—and two of the men who died tonight. We kept food and wine aplenty at all times, as the hunting to feed the army was important, and so was sanctuary, should we find ourselves caught in demon weather such as this night's storm. Apple?"

He tossed the fruit toward her. Elise, instantly aware that she would lose her blanket if she reflexively caught it, smiled sweetly, and allowed it to bounce to the floor.

Not that she had anything at all left to hide from the man. But she would assure herself that he would never touch her again—unless it was to her design.

Still smiling, she lowered herself gracefully with her blanket about her and retrieved the apple.

"We have all night, Duchess," he told her quietly.

Elise turned toward the fire once more, holding her apple. For a second she felt absurdly hot, as if the fire burned within her. The flames leaped and crackled and the room spun. She stared at the apple in her hand, then bit into it, and for some absurd reason she thought of the Bible, and of Eve, taking that first bite of fruit that led to original sin . . .

She shouldn't have drunk so much of the wine, she realized. It had given her strength, but now it was numbing her mind, and creating a world of shadows when she needed so badly to make every play correctly. Needed to convince this man that she had known Henry well, and had reason to secrete away a single small treasure.

"I was his mistress," she blurted out suddenly.

She heard the startled intake of breath that followed her brash statement, and then she heard an utter silence. She longed to turn to see the effect of her words upon the man, but if she did anything other than hang her head in feigned disgrace, she would lose the impact of her shamed appeal.

"Mistress!"

The single word was like a whip against the wind.

"Aye," Elise whispered, trembling.

"Henry was far too ill—"

"At the end, yes," Elise murmured. "At the very end. And . . . and I had not seen him in months . . . but . . ."

At last she allowed herself to spin around, and she slid gracefully to her knees at his feet, imploring him with eyes as vast and brilliant as a crystal sea. She placed her hand tentatively, delicately, upon his thigh in gentle supplication, and fought not to withdraw it as the heat seemed to burn her. And then she was struggling not to smile, for she felt the quick shudder her touch elicited, and was pleased that she had judged the foolish weaknesses of the male so accurately. "Sir Stede, I have trusted you with my life to say these words, for should this truth be known, I would be forever tarnished and ruined. But I loved Henry, as God is my witness, I loved him! The ring had a special import between us; I did not think that he would grudge it to me!"

Her speech was good, she knew. Passionate, and ringing with a certain sincerity. There was much that was true within it.

He stared at her, and his jaw stopped its movement over the apple piece he chewed. His eyes narrowed, as dark and dusky as the midnight-blue of the storm-filled sky. Then he touched her, smoothing her hair from her temple to her neck. Elise curved her lips into a slight smile that she hoped was enchanting and instinctively nuzzled the silken softness of her cheek against the rough texture of his palm—as a kitten sought warmth and sympathy on a cold night, so would she. Surely even ruthless knights knew that children, small animals, and young women craved gentle care and chivalrous protection!

With a sudden movement he tossed the apple into the fire to hold her head to his with both hands.

"Henry's *mistress?* " he repeated in a husky demand, and in it, Elise could read a multitude of his rapid-fire thoughts. He had softened, melted like steel in the craftsman's blaze. She was no longer a murderer; no longer despicable. And he was experiencing a certain regret for having labeled her so and treated her so roughly . . .

Not half so much regret as you will feel when I am free and you discover that I am capable of avenging the wrongs done against me, she thought.

His face lowered toward her. She felt again the strength in his hands, yet it was a trembling strength, and the touch more a caress than an imprisonment.

"You . . . *loved* . . . the king?"

There was a strange inflection upon the word, but it did not alarm Elise, as she assumed he was merely assuring himself that her emotion was real.

"Passionately," she replied, meeting his heated indigo stare.

But Bryan Stede was not, at the moment, in the least concerned with emotions—or with the king he had so faithfully served.

He was thinking only that the girl was no innocent maid; that if she had known a lover's touch and been long deprived, she would need feel such a touch again.

And that the heat of the fire that roared behind him seemed to have become a part of him, ripping, tearing, consuming his blood, consuming his mind and his thoughts. The wind that whipped furiously beyond the cottage walls fanned and fed the fire until it was a storm that burned heated and blue and golden and red. Anger, desire, passion, and loss . . . all exploded within him. He had to have her. The weeks of tension and warfare, exhaustion and deprivation were overcome by the simplicity of that fire; the basic need of the warrior and the male within him clamored as wildly as the wind for the succor of an interlude of physical pleasure and forgetfulness.

"Duchess . . . the king is dead."

"I . . . I know . . ." she murmured in sudden confusion. "And I . . . I believe that you loved him, as I did, and that is why I beg that you not drag me back as a thief and—"

"Nay, lady, I will not drag you back as a thief."

"Thank you, Sir Stede, thank you—" Elise began, but she cut off as he stood abruptly, his hands sliding to her shoulders to bring her to him. She saw that the indigo of his eyes had burned to a smoldering flame, and that his features were again tense, with a pulse ticking against the hard corded muscle of his neck.

"Nay, lady, I will not drag you back as a thief. I will give us the tempest of this night, and we will fill the voids within one another as the rain rages past."

"What . . . ?" Elise murmured, her confusion growing ever vaster, until she at last recognized the blue flame burning ever more intensely in his eyes.

Desire. Naked, elemental desire.

He was not thinking of her as a kitten, or as a child. Nor was he thinking she needed sympathy or protection . . .

"Sir Stede!" she protested, fighting the web of the wine and the spinning room and the hot steel touch of his hands upon her. "I was Henry's mistress—not a common harlot—"

He laughed. "I take you for nothing common, Duchess, believe me!"

Elise stared at him with wide eyes, her position suddenly coming threateningly clear to her. Whereas she had assumed herself the spider spinning the web, she was suddenly the fly caught within it. She had sauntered boldly forward, and too late realized that she had fallen into the entanglement of his strength.

You have played the fool! she raged silently to herself. Her mind raced for the words to remind him that he took no woman by force, yet in the fire of his eyes she knew he thought not of force, just of passion, and that he believed she would welcome his tempest in her loneliness and loss . . .

Dismay, and a sense of belated wisdom, came to her. She was so accustomed to being in control. She had known her father well, and she knew Percy well. With them, she could tease, she could cajole; she could take a game as far as she so pleased—and still call a halt that would be instantly obeyed. But Stede was no admiring gallant. He would never allow a woman to play a game, to tempt a man and walk away.

But he would not force her! She had to think, and speak quickly, convince him that she made a plea for his sympathy and nothing else . . .

She opened her mouth, but the time for words had passed. She was mesmerized, her eyes locked with his. Then she no longer saw the fire, for she felt it as his mouth seared down upon hers.

She didn't know if it was pleasure or pain; she was only aware that it was the greatest shock her body had known. Too stunned to protest, she felt only sensation breaking through the fog of her confusion and dismay. He was the sensation. The sound of his heartbeat against her breast thundered like the night, and the steel of his body was not cold at all, but molten, enveloping her with his heat. His mouth was firm upon hers, and its demand was hungering, but persuasive. The brush of his cheek was slightly rough, and the stroke of his tongue against her lips was, again, pure fire. He invaded her mouth fully, and the sheer masculinity of him was such that she was overpowered before she could rally her wits to fight. Deeper and deeper he kissed her, until she was clinging to him not to fall, until the breath was taken from her body, until all spun about her until there was nothing but the roaring fire and the raging wind.

It was a kiss, she tried to tell herself, somewhere in the misted regions of her mind. Nothing more than a kiss. She could not allow herself to believe . . . to accept . . . that she had made a mockery of her determined plan to win him sweetly to her cause—with no repercussions. It was still just a kiss . . .

How often had she been like this with Percy—glad to play, glad to test her power? How often had they broken off, laughing, Percy swearing that he could not guard her honor were she to tempt him so? But just as she wondered with growing excitement herself what it would be like to allow him to love her further, she knew that he would step back, breathing heavily, his heart racing, and vow that they would have to marry soon. She was the one in control, and despite amusement and wonder, Percy knew that she would not have him until they were legally wed. A kiss, to tempt and beckon, but that was all. They had shared so many kisses . . .

But never like this. Never this rage of heat and smoldering fire. Never this power that sent the world spinning and reeling to the tempest of the storm. Percy had never been steel, overwhelming, breaking down barriers, commanding her will.

Only a kiss . . . to taunt and beckon. To make a man want more, to enchant him. So that when he stepped away, he would fall all over himself, forgetting all but to be gallant and to please . . .

A kiss . . . no more.

But this was not Percy; it was Bryan Stede. Swept into his spiral of hunger, she could not combat the force of his arms, she could not twist away from his lips . . . could not fight the mercurial heat of his invading tongue. She clung to him merely not to fall . . . yet she realized with a shivering fatality that it would seem that she beckoned him ever onward.

His hands moved upon her shoulders and the blanket fell to the floor. When he drew his body from hers, she was clothed only in the lustrous length of her hair, which fell like silk upon the velvet of her skin. Her eyes beheld his, wide and dazed, and he fell ever more into a trap of legend and myth, beauty and fantasy. Tendrils of red and gold wisped about her fine features, and waved over her breasts. They fell like a cloak to feather sweetly along her hips and thighs. The perfection of her form again swept over his senses; the high, rose-crested breasts, the narrow waist, invitingly curved hips, and long lean flanks—all in unmarred ivory . . .

"Nothing common . . ." he said softly, and again stepped toward her.

His words were like an awakening clap of thunder, and Elise instinctively stepped backward, stretching out her hand in reflexive self-defense.

She doubted bitterly that he had noticed; he was upon her again so quickly, sweeping her into his arms as if she were no more than air.

"Stede!" she at last gasped out, yet she still could not struggle from the spider web of strength that held her, and the shock of the response she had elicited continued to numb her wits, no matter how she fought to clear them. "Stede!" She brought her hands against his chest, but it was like pressing against armor. His urgent stride brought them quickly to the low-framed bed of goose feathers, and she no sooner felt that softness beneath her back than she felt his hardness atop her. He still wore his dark tunic, yet it seemed to grant no barrier between them; his length burned against her as his sinewed weight kept her easily captive.

"Stede!" Elise began again, but his fingers threaded through the sides of her hair, and she had but a brief glimpse of the intense desire burning darkly in his eyes before his mouth once more claimed hers.

Again there was the shock, rippling like bolt after bolt of lightning throughout her. And the air . . . the scent that came to her, not perfumed, but musky, clean, but threateningly male. Her teeth were parted by the hungry force of his assault; she hadn't even the power to work her jaw as his tongue leisurely delved into the deepest recesses of her mouth, leaving her with no choice but to parry with her own . . .

Desperate instinct brought her hands against him, but she could find no hold with which to wedge them apart. It was all so fast . . .

So smooth, so swift . . .

This was not what I intended! she shrieked inwardly, but she couldn't speak, for he had effectively silenced her; she couldn't strike out at him, for now her arms were trapped by his. She tried to kick him, but when she raised her leg, she found that she had abetted him all the more, for his weight wedged fully between her thighs, and his tunic was pulled high upon his hips, leaving her position far more perilous . . .

Darkness seemed to fall around her. A darkness lightened only by a single torch of flaming fire. The rush of the wind was all about her, robbing her of all else but the moment, and the storm of sensation. Somewhere, in that darkness, she knew that he was the fire, the only light that could come to her now. Muscled steel and burning flesh. Lips that demanded and scorched, hands that began to play upon her, running along her body, to stroke her breast, to find her thigh, and gently force it to accommodate his form. She felt his touch, an intimate caress. Light, but as experienced as the firmly persuasive kiss that continued to imprison her in silence. Then she felt the force of his body, the power of his male sex as he began to shift against her . . .

Steel, she thought, near hysteria. This was truly steel. Heated, strong, alive . . . and pulsing with life and demand. For a moment primal fear stilled all else. He would kill her; tear her asunder; rip her apart with the strength of his blade . . .

Something else came to her. Would he know that she hadn't been Henry's mistress, or could he be deceived? Could a man be deceived—

Fire! Streaking into her, piercing with a full and potent accuracy that was white lightning, rendering her slender form to stunned shudders as the lightning filled and filled her. A sensation of burning, exploding pain that was so great, Elise at last managed to tear from his passionate kiss, inadvertently burying her head against his shoulder to draw blood from her lower lip to keep from screaming out. The wind was a part of her, piercing into her, raging throughout her. Ceasing, like the eye of the storm, then slowly whistling, rising, buffeting to a tempest once more. Elise tried desperately to keep her tears in check.

Stede! How she despised him, and now . . . now he was a part of her, inside her. He knew her more intimately than she had known intimate could be; he claimed her inside and out. He was part of her, and with each of his powerful strokes, he filled her ever farther, taking her so thoroughly that this possession would forever be a brand upon her, and she knew she would never forget him or these moments of tempest as long as she lived . . .

The pain subsided, but not the feeling of fire. She was shocked that her body should so give to his, that although her heart and mind had not truly assimilated what had happened, her body had instinctively adjusted to primal ritual. She clung to him, her nails digging into the shoulder of his tunic, but her form moved to the heated rhythm of his, absorbing his masculinity. She was not going to die, or be torn apart. And . . .

There was promise about it, promise in the flames, in the roar of the wind. Something . . . if she just reached for it. Something that was sweet, that filled her senses along with his intimate touch. Something that promised of starlight and beauty, and a soaring ride acrest the wind. If she allowed it . . .

No! This was not Percy! It was Stede, and for all his lean, muscled splendor, he was a beast of the night. Now he had taken everything from her and she was left to cringe against him as he imprinted his will upon her for all eternity. Stroking, holding, touching . . . and then . . .

Groaning, low and guttural, and falling hard against her.

Flooding her with himself, even as he left her . . .

The winds died; the glow of the fire ceased.

Elise bit into her lip again, and when she strained swiftly to curl away from him, he allowed her.

Rage roiled within her now. Rage and bitterness. She wanted nothing more than to be away from the man whose damp and powerful form still lingered far too near. She wanted to cry and scream and rail against God, and it was all the more bitter that she couldn't allow herself to do so, for she was still his prisoner. If she remained perfectly silent, and played out this final role, he might at least free her, or she might still escape . . .

She felt him shift again, raising upon an elbow to rest his head upon a hand. And stare at her. And completely eradicate her last hope with his first words.

"Henry's mistress, eh?"

She cringed.

"Henry's *mistress,* and the *Duchess* of Montoui?" He laughed aloud. "Aye, milady! And I am King of the Night Wind! What do you take me for, Duchess! An inexperienced idiot?"

The tone was soft and pleasant—so soft and pleasant that the taunting mockery within it drove her nearly mad. She spun about, and her rage spewed forth.

"An idiot? Oh, no, Sir Stede! I take you for an arrogant bastard and an unmitigated liar! Your honor is as false as your tongue. Vulture, snake, most vile of beasts—"

"Speaking of tongues," he interrupted her harshly, and she saw the dangerous narrowing of his now clear indigo eyes, "yours, milady, will definitely be your downfall. How did I lie?"

"That you can ask!" Elise shrilled, trying to pull her hair from beneath his form, then meeting his steady gaze with the furious clash of her own. "Rape! You wouldn't think of it! Force—you wouldn't use it—"

His free hand bolted out to catch her chin, threatening to

crush the fragile bone. "Duchess, you came to me—on your knees, I might remind you. You didn't resist."

"Resist!" The tears at last stung her eyes, but rage kept them from falling. "How could one resist you! You came after me like a stallion at rut, abusing and tormenting and brutalizing—"

"Hold your tongue, Duchess, I warn you!" he thundered. His eyes simmered to a dangerous black, and his expression darkened. "You were not abused, tormented, or brutalized. Had you not lied to me, I could have eased the pain. Yet, had you not lied to me, we would never have reached such a point. I am sorry for your pain, but it is quite natural—I hear."

"You hear? Oh, God! So help me, Stede, there will come a day when I will cut you in pieces, feed you to the wolves . . ."

He stared at her as her harangue continued, his jaw hardening. The virago now spewing venom upon him was a far cry from the seductive maid who had knelt so sweetly at his feet. She had proved herself to be a liar once more, yet he was overcome with guilt, and irritated that he should be, furious that she had put him in such a position. His knowledge of her circumstance had come far too late for him possibly to withdraw and leave her intact, and so all that passed was of her own making. She hadn't cried out, and hadn't given way to tears, and somehow that, too, worked upon his sense of guilt, perhaps because he had to admire the courage that kept her fighting, just as he could not regret that he had possessed her—in fact, had been the first to do so. Without meaning to give, she had been a sea of sensuality. She had brought the storm of his emotions to a sheltered harbor of satisfaction, eased his tensions, received his fever and his seed.

And now become a harpy once more. Just when his physical gratification had combined with his long stretch of lack of sleep to bring him to total exhaustion.

"Stop!" he snapped. "I've had all I'm going to take from a lying, conniving little thief!"

She did stop speaking; she drew in a sharp intake of breath, and her cheeks paled as the brilliant fury faded from her eyes.

"I . . . I am not a thief . . ."

The words were barely a whisper, touching a chord of pity within his heart. Whatever he said to her, he keenly felt his own part in her misery, and although he could not change what had been, he was sorry for her. And she was still beautiful. More so now, as she tried to draw her hair about her to cover herself, like tattered remnants of her pride and innocence.

"Don't fear, Duchess, I have no intention of seeing your pretty neck severed—now. Your soft, sweet speech has too en-amored me. I'll see to your welfare, just as your 'lover'—the king—would have done."

"What?" Elise gasped out, then followed his meaning. "I'd rather lose my head a hundred times than endure such a—"

"Bestial rutting?" he supplied with polite and cryptic sarcasm.

". . . with you again. A most decent description!" Elise lashed out in quick anger.

His quick laughter did little to ease her anger or dismay. " 'Tis the first complaint I've ever had," he told her, grinning easily. "But I doubt that you should describe it so for long. Since I was unaware that you fought me, it would surely be true heaven to bed you when you felt the true heat of passion. I doubt, too, milady thief, that it would take you long to learn the heights of passion and desire. You were created to grace a man's pleasure, sweetly sensual even when the bedding was all a lie."

She stared at him for a moment as if he were truly insane, then heard the grate of her nails against the bedding. "I swear to you, Stede, as God in heaven is my witness, I'll—"

"I know, I know," he said, the strong sting of exasperation and impatience deep in his voice, "you'll skin me alive, feed me to the wolves, and so on. But for now, Duchess, I suggest you shut your mouth—or take a strong chance of finding a gag about it. I wish to get some sleep."

She was silent for a second, again giving him that stare that labeled him a lunatic.

"Just like that?"

"What?"

"You're going to go to sleep just like that? You abducted me, threw me about, ravaged my person, and ruined my life—and you're going to go to sleep?"

"Precisely."

"Son of a—"

He moved like lightning, clamping a hand over her mouth, and leaning dangerously near once more. "I warn you, and I warn you, Duchess, yet you persist in testing me! One more word, a scream, a cry, a whisper, and the tatters of your shift can quickly become a gag and bounds. Or . . ."

Elise stared wide-eyed and belligerently into the dusky orbs of indigo, noticing that when he stopped speaking to grin wickedly, his smile could change his countenance. His birthright had been a handsome set of features; the years had added power and ruggedness. Yet when he smiled, there was a hint of youth about him, and Elise was bitterly certain that many a maiden would find him devastating beyond measure. His physique, she well knew, could not be more finely honed or muscled; and his arresting height and dark blue eyes could surely draw tremors of fear upon a battlefield, as well as tremors of longing from the smitten hearts of women . . .

"Or . . ."—His grin broadened, and she felt a disturbing flutter within her own heart— ". . . if you are so determined to keep me from sleep, I would not wish to waste the time."

Elise felt her breasts suddenly swell firm against the expanse of his chest; they both felt the rose crests instinctively harden as he pressed his chest against her. Even through the fabric that covered the rippling muscles of his chest, she felt the flesh with her own. Her cheeks reddened with horror as he shifted and used his hand to slide between them, finding the fullness of her breast and the tempting peak of the betraying nipple to massage each gently. His palm, calloused and rough, moved with a disturbing tenderness, and even as she sank into a sea of helpless outrage and humiliation, she felt that touch throughout her. Her body suddenly seemed empty without him; a hint of the fire scorched through her in little ripples . . .

He laughed again and rolled from her. "Go to sleep, Duchess, before I have a chance to set myself up for more lectures on brutality."

It was too much. Even knowing she would lose, Elise was ready for battle. She spun about, managing to bring her palm in cracking contact with his cheek. His laughter died as he gripped her arm, twisting it to force her to her back once more. "I'll try to understand that one, Duchess. But you are too late now for protest and indignity; too late to avoid my eyes on your nudity; and too late to begrudge my touch on that which I have already had. Go to sleep, and leave me in peace. I promise I will care for you as well as any king, and I will save you from the gallows or sword."

"I would rather die—" Elise whispered, her defenses draining as her strength gave out.

"No—I also promised that you would not. In the years to come, you will know that your life is far more valuable than any consort between a man and a woman. Rest, little vixen. It will all look better in the morning. And don't try to escape me. I wake with the rustle of the wind."

He lay down beside her once more, keeping an arm about her waist, and pulling her close. Elise heard only the now soft crackle of the fire, and the gentle whisper of the dying wind.

"I assure you, Stede, that I will never be a consort of yours! Not even should hell below freeze. I will shortly be another's *wife;* and you will be called to answer for this abominable outrage—"

"Shut up, Duchess . . ."

The voice held deep and husky warning. Elise closed her eyes and pursed her lips tightly together. *No more impotent threats!* she told herself. *Wait . . . wait . . .*

Seconds passed, and then long minutes, during which she felt nothing but misery. Then she heard his deep, even breathing and she chanced twisting her head to see his face.

His eyes were closed; his features relaxed. She bit her lip, willing herself to remain still.

Not yet. . . . Not yet . . .

She was sure he did wake with the breeze, his senses acutely attuned from the moment he opened his eyes. But he was truly exhausted. He had dozed so quickly. If she just gave him time to fall into a deep, deep sleep . . .

She closed her eyes again, now willing time to pass quickly. She hated his touch upon her; the hand so casually upon her bare waist, the arm that draped against the edge of her breast. She hated that he lay beside her so easily when she felt so vulnerably naked; she hated that he assumed such an intimacy with her.

And she hated that he had been inside her, hated that she felt his mark within and upon her still.

Hated his strength, and his power, and the masculinity that had so overwhelmed her.

Hated the fact that this night had changed her so.

She had been the fool, all along. Life had sheltered her; Henry had nurtured her to believe herself powerful.

Tonight she had learned she could be defenseless, that all her wiles had led her to enter a battle with the weapons of a child . . .

She had expected him to behave like a man. And he had. But she had not realized that there were certain men who could not be goaded or beguiled—except to their own means.

It was a hard lesson. Bitter and hard. And the seeds of vengeance would still simmer and grow within her. Prayerfully, when she did meet Stede again, she would know fully well the man she was up against. Never would she underestimate such a man again.

Elise's thoughts raced through her mind again and again as she waited. Waited until the fire burned low in the hearth, and the wind gave up its hold on even a whisper.

Then she slipped carefully from beneath the hold of his arm. Waited again. Slid her weight slowly from the bed.

Still he slept.

If she hadn't hated him so, she could have felt a sympathy for the exhausted lines of his face, only now beginning to ease. She might have admired the warrior's frame, at ease, but still so vital. If . . .

She came upon the remnants of her tattered shift and tunic, and she wanted to scream aloud. They were proof of the night, just as the male scent of him that still lingered about her, as the life fluid that clung to her thighs, as the memory still burning betwixt aching joints that ached as if they had been torn asunder . . .

She could not scream. Her hurt and fury would have to be taken with her; at another time and in another place she could find privacy to vent her rage and lick her wounds.

Her clothing was almost useless, but she slipped quickly into it. Her cloak, at least, was encompassing, and only a little damp now. As she swirled it about her, she noted Stede's hose and boots, and his cloak. On impulse, she picked them up, nervously watching him all the while.

His mantle . . . it was laid upon the table near hers. She took that, too, and glanced longingly at his sword. What a lovely thought to imagine she might slide it through his gullet—or hack off the surging, invading steel of his masculinity!

She didn't touch the sword. Experience had taught her to stay as far from him as possible.

It was a pity, too, that he hadn't bothered to doff his tunic and shirt. She would have loved to have left him as stripped and vulnerable as she had been. But . . . at least he would have to see his way back barefoot and on foot.

She glanced at his form once again, feeling another sweep of fury ride over her so hotly that she began to tremble. No . . . he hadn't even bothered to remove his tunic . . . she had been the one to be totally stripped and vulnerable. Stede . . . Stede had merely been in a fevered hurry!

Swift sport had been his only concern, and when that had been achieved, he'd had the despicable arrogance to turn to her and tell her that she had not resisted.

Her eyes looked longingly to his sword; but a heated argument within her own mind at last convinced her that she would rather leave him alive than risk awakening him if she should falter in either her aim or resolve.

Just as she was about to leave, something glinted, a streak of blue fire from the bench, catching and crystallizing the glow of a low-burning ember.

It was the ring.

Her father's sapphire ring.

She strode quickly to it and picked it up, slipping it onto her middle finger. The fit was loose, but it would stay.

She had paid a high price for the ring, a very high price. Bitterness welled within her, but she was not about to leave it behind now.

She watched Stede as she opened the door carefully, and barely breathed as she closed it behind her. Then she gnawed at her lip as she hurried around back and found his massive destrier beneath the cottage overhang, protected from the storm by the shelter of an enclave.

Could she control the massive warhorse? she wondered desperately. She would have to . . .

Thankfully, the horse was still bridled. His saddle had been removed, but she would rather try her luck without it anyway. She would cling low to him, giving her commands with her thighs and heels, and hopefully convincing him that she was in complete control.

Elise whispered soothingly to the stallion, gripped the bundle of clothing she had taken, and breathed a prayer as she dug hard at his mane to swing herself over his back.

She made it. She nudged her heels into the stallion's flanks, and to her joy, he responded.

Without gazing at the hunter's cottage again, she turned and rode into the night.

VI

July 7, 1189
The Palace at Winchester England

Freedom . . .

For a moment Eleanor of Aquitaine closed her eyes and savored the sound of the words within her mind.

She was free. Henry was dead, and she was free. After sixteen years of imprisonment, she was free.

"Your Majesty, are you—"

Eleanor opened her eyes and smiled softly upon her jailer. He was a squat fellow of thirty or so who looked much older, heavy-jowled, florid, and half bald. But he was a decent man. His heart and conscience were good. He had been given no direct orders to open her door, but he was doing so, and perhaps taking a risk upon his own head. In all the manors and castles where she had been kept over the past decade and a half, he had been the kindest keeper.

And he had just hurried in to tell her that news had reached him that King Henry II of England was dead.

"I am fine, milord."

"If you care to leave—to hurry to London, for surely it is there that Richard will go—I will make arrangements."

"Nay, nay, good sir. I shall wait here—for, surely, Richard will send someone for me. I thank you for your concern, and for the kindness you have shown me. Now, if I might impose upon your hospitality a bit longer—"

"Of course, Your Majesty! But of course!"

"And milord," Eleanor added, a smile again curving her lips, "if you wouldn't mind . . . well, I would that you would close that door for me again, for right now I would prefer to be alone."

"Oh, yes, yes, Your Majesty. Of course . . ."

The door closed quietly. Eleanor closed her eyes once more, then turned and walked to the rear of the chamber. Upon the wall was a tarnished silver mirror, beautifully wrought. Will Marshal had brought it to her. . . . What was it now? Two years ago? Three? Time was lost so easily.

Time. Sixteen years she had been a prisoner! It was so easy to lose track of a year or two.

She opened her eyes wide and smiled at the old woman who returned her stare.

"You are free," she told her reflection. "Free—and nigh upon seventy years old. Your youth is gone; Henry is dead, and, admit it, Eleanor, Henry was your youth . . ."

Her eyes suddenly looked sad and weary. The eyes of an old woman. Because Henry was dead. She could still remember the day when he had ridden to claim her. She had been a decade older than he, and quite in control of her own future at the time, but he had come to claim her nevertheless. His speeches had not been of love, but of dynasties, and yet she had known how badly he had wanted her. As a woman. When she had still been married to Louis of France, Henry's eyes had followed her, coveted her . . .

He had been her knight gallant. Handsome, beautifully strong, fierce, and proud. His gold and copper hair a flame of glory in the breeze. How she had loved him. How she had longed for him. His ambition had been great, his vitality enormous. Between them, their empire could stretch from Scotland to Toulouse. The Angevin empire. *They* were ambitious; *they* were strong; she was in love and there was a lifetime to be shared in burning triumph . . .

"Ah, Eleanor!" she told the old woman who faced her. "You love him just a little bit still. He could be cold and brutal, selfish and cunning, but seldom has there been such a king as Henry! He lived upon his horse and by his sword, and never could I bemoan his lack of courage!"

And now, Henry was dead. She was free.

What would an old woman do with such freedom? The lines about her eyes were as numerous as the roads to a market; her once luxuriant hair was almost entirely gray. But . . .

A spark returned to her eyes and a smile came to her lips as she straightened her shoulders and spine. She was really quite remarkable for a woman her age.

Certainly, Eleanor, it is remarkable that you are alive at all.

Her smile went deeper and she patted at the coif of her hair. *An old woman, yes, that you might be. But the most remarkable woman of your day. The richest heiress in Christendom, wife of two kings.* She had known envy and scandal, passion and love, bitterness and pain. But she had lived. Ah, yes, she had lived. She and Henry had brought London alive; she had brought poetry and grace to England, just as Henry had brought law and justice . . .

And the world was once again waiting for her . . .

Richard was going to need her. The English people had always loved her. They would rally to her now. She would pave the way for Richard's coronation.

Then there would be John to look after. Eleanor sighed as she thought of her youngest son. She had often wondered if she was an unnatural mother, because she knew his faults so clearly. He was sneaky, conniving, and self-serving. He would surely be a thorn in his brother's side.

But perhaps it was hard to live in the shadow of such a brother. Despite the fact that Richard had his own dark secrets to endure, he was the picture of a king. No one could doubt him in combat and courage, while John . . .

John. What could be said? John would be the first to run

from danger. The first to cower. The first to claim victory and prowess by the blood of others.

Henry, how did we whelp such a pup? Eleanor wondered.

He was her son, and, yes, she was not enough the unnatural mother not to care for him. She would have her hands full. Richard on the one, John on the other.

And Geoffrey . . . Henry's bastard. She could never forget Geoffrey Fitzroy. She didn't want to forget Geoffrey. She had lost two of her own sons. William, and then Henry . . .

Geoffrey Fitzroy. She thanked God that he accepted his bastardy! He was bright and powerful and cunning—more cool of head than Richard, not untrustworthy like John. Pity he hadn't been born to her . . .

But they would get on fine. Geoffrey—she would see to it—would climb his ladder of ambition with the Church. She would help him all that she could. They understood each other.

Ah, life! So much to do. And then there was the girl.

Eleanor smiled. She loved her daughters so dearly. It was easy to extend that love to the precocious little creature who had so enchanted her! Elise was no longer a child, but surely she had grown to be a lovely woman.

She, too, would fall beneath Eleanor's powerful wing. There would be court again, poetry again, music again! Politics spoken of politely and wittily; monks and clerics would be welcome, the greatest theologians of the day. Literature could flourish . . .

Freedom . . .

Such a beautiful word.

Eleanor suddenly spun from the mirror and whirled about on her toes, clapping her hands together. A bone made a slight creak, but it only caused her to smile.

She paused before the mirror once again, laughing at herself. The lines seemed to fade a bit, with her eyes sparkling so. Her features were pleasant; she had dignity, and grace. Beauty might fade, but the vestiges could remain within the heart. She could walk proudly on Richard's arm. She didn't need to be afraid to meet the people. "Yes, Eleanor, you are old. But freedom is precious at any age. It is an elixir of youth . . ."

"And though you are old, you are still Eleanor of Aquitaine. Queen of England. Still proud, still straight. Still vital!"

"Still alive!"

You know the world. Marriages, alliances, warfare, and law— they are all your training, your life.

And they are yours once more.

Oh, Henry, it hurts. No matter how bitter the past, a part of me lies with you now. You were my knight gallant, once, and still are in dreams. Yet you and I fought; I paid my dues with these past sixteen years; you pay yours now with your death.

And I am alive and free . . .

Once, she had been stunning. She was, at the very least, still regal. Wise—she had already lived more than a lifetime. And they needed her. They *needed* her.

She would be there for them all.

Eleanor walked more sedately and sat down upon her narrow bunk. She began to stretch and flex her fingers, as if she already tested her power.

Soon . . .

Soon, now, they would come for her. Who would Richard send? Perhaps William Marshal. Perhaps de Roche . . .

Perhaps young Bryan Stede. Henry's men—but loyal men. And her men, too. Just as they had loved their sovereign, they had loved their queen—and never denied their love.

Yes, it was likely that they would all make their peace with Richard. And it was likely he would send one of them to her.

She would be waiting.

And she would be ready.

She was, after all, a very young seventy. And she had so much more to give.

VII

Chinon

William Marshal had spent the better part of his night in a futile search for the thieves. When he hadn't had his mind filled with his heartsick and harried task, his thoughts had been even worse. He had worried himself to a nearly frantic point wondering what had happened to Bryan Stede.

The morning had brought further turmoil, but by the time the sun was high in the sky and midday approached, he was atop the ramparts again, scanning the countryside once more for a sign of his friend.

At long last he discovered the lone figure, barefoot and shivering, limp down the hill toward the castle of Chinon. For a moment his brow furrowed in puzzlement, and then a grin tugged at his lips.

It was Bryan. God be praised! It was Bryan, returning alone, without his destrier, without his boots.

Anxiously, William strode to the nearest turret and hurried down the winding steps. Guards sprang to attention as he continued his brisk walk to the entryway and bridge, but he waved aside their confused questions and offers to serve as he walked on past them and crossed over the other side.

He stopped atop the crest just before the landscape dipped into a valley.

Bryan Stede was still hobbling along, swearing with a vengeance beneath his breath. As William watched, Bryan paused with a particularly vicious oath, and balanced on one foot to pluck a thorn carefully from the other.

"Gods . . . balls!" The knight swore vehemently, and William—his vast sense of relief combining with his amusement at his friend's condition—laughed out loud. He had seen his tall and formidable friend receive many a battle wound without a flinch; burrs and stickers were proving to be an Achilles' heel.

Bryan glanced at him with a piercing stare that would have sent shivers racing down the spine of a less courageous man. Then, seeing that the offender to his sensibilities was William Marshal, he scowled and turned his attention back to his foot.

"Damnable burrs!" he grumbled. "Feels as if I've walked over a field of nails!"

William chuckled again. He was so pleased to be seeing Bryan. He had tried to assure himself that it was the storm that had kept his friend out for the night, but concern had tugged at his thoughts anyway, and he hadn't been quite able to subdue his fears that Stede had met with an enemy, and had been left dead or dying upon a lonely road beneath the onslaught of the weather.

It was such a blessed relief to see him alive—and well—except for the small matter of a few annoying splinters.

Will clapped Bryan warmly on the shoulder, demanding, "Where have you been all the night? I must admit that I feared you had met your end at the hands of the enemy."

"I sought shelter from the storm," Bryan said briefly. Then he asked anxiously, "Were any of the thieves caught, Will?"

"No, but we'll discuss that along the way. Come, my friend," William said. He placed a comradely arm about Bryan's shoulder and indicated the castle. "You can soak your feet in a bucket of nice hot water, and tell me why one of the most powerful knights in Christendom is limping along—minus shoes, cloak, and horse!"

Bryan gingerly placed weight upon his sore foot once more and followed William's lead, glancing questioningly at the other man. "Not one of the thieves was found?" he asked sharply.

"Not one, but the answer to the riddle of their disappearance has been discovered. There are subterranean passages beneath the castle. They lead to the village. Those who manned this fortress before we came to it swore they did not know of the existence of the passages. There was no reason not to believe them. But it seems that the thieves have eluded us—and you as well?"

Bryan didn't reply immediately. He narrowed his eyes against the afternoon sun and stared at the castle, then asked, "William, have you knowledge of a small duchy known as Montoui?"

Startled by the question, William stopped walking and turned to stare at Bryan more searchingly. "Montoui?" he answered at last. "Why, yes, certainly, I know of it."

"You do?"

William was surprised by the dismay in Stede's voice. "We are not at all far from Montoui. A day's ride with no encumbrances."

"Damn!" Stede muttered.

"Why?" William demanded.

"Never mind," Bryan muttered. Then he added explosively, "Why have I never heard of this bloody place?"

William shrugged. "It is small, and not oft in the path of an army, as it has been neutral territory since the old duke died. Henry decreed it so and Philip and Richard respected his wishes."

Bryan was glaring at him sharply. "Since the old duke died . . ." he repeated slowly. "So who rules this duchy now? And if it's so small, how is that you know of it?"

"It is ruled by the young duchess, old Will's daughter, of course. And I know of it for I traveled there many times with Henry."

"With Henry?"

"Dammit! Stede, you're starting to sound like one of those parrots at the bazaars in the Holy Land. I have been to Montoui many times with Henry."

"Then why haven't I?" Bryan demanded blankly.

William Marshal's brow furrowed. Then he shrugged. "Last

year when we went, you had returned to England to check of Henry's affairs with the archbishop. The year before that, I believe you had been sent to escort Prince John someplace. And I believe that the year before that—"

Bryan lifted a hand in the air. "Enough, enough, Marshal! I'm following the line of thought quite well." He started hobbling toward the castle once more and William hurried to catch up with him.

"Why all these questions, Stede?"

Stede spun about once more, his usually laconic expression now one that was a cross between a scowl and disbelieving confusion.

"This . . . duchess—what is her name?"

"Elise—Lady Elise de Bois."

"Damn!" Bryan swore. "William, can you describe this lady for me?"

"Elise?" Will Marshal's face broke into a broad grin. "She is absolutely charming. As lovely and vital as a sunrise. As—"

"Dispense with the poetry, I beg you!" Bryan groaned.

"Well . . ." William grimaced, thinking. "She is a tall woman, slender, yet shapely. Her eyes are the color of the seas, a shade between blue and green. And her hair . . . is like a sunset, perhaps. It is not gold, it is not red, but, again, a shade between the two. Her voice is as soft as the morning lark's—"

"Oh, God's blood, it is!" Bryan growled low in definitive interruption. "She shrills just like a screaming peahen!"

It was Marshal's turn to be taken by surprise. "Elise? But you just told me—"

"I met up with your 'charming' chatelaine of Montoui last evening," Bryan said dryly. "She has the claws of a cat, and the tongue of a viper. And she's just about as fragile as a black widow—"

"Whoa! My friend, you've lost me! Where did you meet up with Elise when you left here to chase a thief—"

" 'Charming' Lady Elise was the thief."

"Elise? I don't believe it! Montoui is small, but rich—and

thriving. Her land is the most fertile for miles, her cattle and sheep fatten overnight, and the old duke brought back a fortune in gold and gems and ivory from the Crusade!"

"I hate to rattle your ivory tower, my friend, but the lady carried property of the king's."

"Did she, now?" Marshal demanded, startled.

"I tell you this confidentially," Bryan said, suddenly grave, "for I would not see her prosecuted. But, yes, she had upon her the sapphire Henry wore on his small finger. And I know it was upon him, for I saw it when he was placed upon the bier."

"The sapphire . . ." Marshal muttered, further puzzled. He scratched his head in deep contemplation, then shook it. "Makes little sense that I can see. But you are right about the sapphire; he always wore it. Yet Elise de Bois would have little use for the sum that it could draw—even if it were substantial."

"Perhaps she was an accomplice—leading a chase to draw us from the true direction of the others."

"Elise? I doubt such a thing. But I am glad you have not brought her back, for there are others who might not, and in my heart I can not believe her guilty."

"How well do you know this girl?" Bryan demanded, annoyed with William's apparent enthrallment with the object of his disgust, especially since Marshal had had little time for enchantment in his days. He had always been busy with tournaments and battle; he enjoyed a willing woman who would share his bed, but he was not much for courtly games or poetry. The king had promised him Isabel de Clare, reputedly one of the loveliest—as well as richest—heiresses available, and not even of his unknown future bride had he ever spoken so whimsically.

Marshal lifted his shoulders and allowed them to fall. "I know her fairly well, and not at all. Henry visited Montoui once a year for almost twenty years—"

"Twenty years!"

"You forget"—Marshal laughed—"that I have a decade over you, Sir Stede. Yes, I went to Montoui with Henry once a year since I came into his service. He told me it was a trip he had been making for years before that, so I would safely say twenty years."

"The devil take me!" Bryan gasped.

"Looks as if he already has. Or was it the Lady Elise?"

Bryan shot William a hostile glance, but refrained from a heated reply. "The lady helped herself to my horse and boots, yes," he said shortly.

"It must have been quite a meeting."

"Yes, it was. Tell me, do you know anything else of this woman?"

"Only that Montoui is solely hers. Oh, yes, it is rumored that she will marry Sir Percy Montagu. Her own choice."

"Montagu . . ."

"I know. I don't care for the man myself. Courteous, pleasant—but slippery. He does hold quite an attraction for the ladies, though. Years ago there was a scandal with Countess Marie of Bari; seems young Percy sowed his oats with little discretion as to the marital status of conquests. But, of course, to enter into marriage himself, he had always let it be known that he intended to be very discriminating. And," Marshal added with a shrug, "Percy is reputed to be charming and charismatic to the ladies. Elise discouraged any interest from possible suitors until she met young Percy, so apparently her marriage will be one for love. The de Bois family line is impeccable, so she meets Sir Percy's vision of marital material perfectly."

"Humph!" Bryan muttered. So she was to marry, he thought. Good for her—and Sir Percy Montagu. It should be a relief to him that the lady abhorred him and was determined to pursue her own affairs. After last night, she might easily have chosen to throw herself upon his honor and demand that he marry her. Which he would do. . . . In fact, knowing now that she was the Duchess of Montoui, he would have gone to her himself with such a proposal after last night. He considered the entire situation completely her own fault, but he had still been responsible for changing her "virginal" status. That he still considered her to be a liar and a thief could not change that responsibility.

Bryan shrugged to himself. She had made it blatantly clear that she despised him and wanted no part of him. She was going to marry Percy Montagu. He should be pleased to let her be.

His own future still hung on the winds of change. If he'd been honor-bound to go to Elise de Bois, he would have lost the hope that Richard would decide to honor his father's debts; there would have been no Gwyneth, and no vast lands in England to become his.

Yes, it was a relief . . .

But it was also annoying to think of Percy Montagu with the girl. Montagu was too slippery to deserve such a . . .

Conniving liar? They would have been a perfect match.

No, because liar that she might be, the lady was stunning. She had been cast and molded to a pleasing perfection . . .

She was also a screaming virago. Maybe they did deserve each other.

He smiled to himself suddenly, amused by his possessive feelings. *Maybe I am a bit of a primitive beast,* he thought. *I feel as if I would like to hack Percy's hands off were he to touch her, and he is apparently her choice.*

Bryan frowned suddenly, thinking of Marshal's apparent infatuation with the girl. It seemed Marshal had never seen or heard her in a rage.

She reminded him of someone when she cursed. The words she used, the inflections. He shook his head, damned if he knew who he was thinking about. The memory was there, but totally elusive. Bryan gave himself a little jolt; he realized that Will had been talking as they walked, and that he hadn't really heard a word.

"Stede, are you listening to me?"

"Oh, aye. Sorry, Marshal."

"Percy does have his good points. Never faltered in battle. Henry was quite fond of him." Marshal paused a moment, then queried, "So you and Elise tangled—heatedly, I assume, since you have just come home barefoot and unhorsed. But I shouldn't worry about the ring—we didn't catch one of the murdering thieves, and all that was stolen is lost to us." He hesitated. "Bryan, there are many who believe it was Henry's own attendants who robbed him—servants who feared they would receive nothing. But whether he was robbed by familiars or strangers, it matters little now. And to bring an accusation against Elise could damage her incredibly."

"I intended to tell no one but you," Bryan said.

"Then it seems that the matter is closed."

"Closed?" Bryan queried. He shook his head. "I cannot allow it to be closed, Will. She was in the castle when the thieves were, she carried Henry's ring, and she tried very vehemently to stab me. She lied to me; I think the only truth she gave me all night was her name. I don't know what I believe anymore—except that at worst, she could be a murderess, and at best, she is hiding some grave secret."

Will paused, urging Bryan to stop and listen to his words. "Bryan, I can promise you this: Elise was very fond of Henry. She would never have done the least irreverence to his earthly remains. Believe me, she could not have been among the thieves."

Bryan stared at Will, wondering for a moment if he should explain himself to his friend. Then he became impatient with his own sense of anger, and guilt. He would say no more. Not even to Will. He ground his teeth together, still trying to decide if she could really be as innocent as Will claimed. He just didn't know. But for the moment, it seemed he might as well give her the benefit of the doubt. "All right," he told Will. "The ring is forgotten." It wasn't forgotten; he wouldn't forget it until he had discovered what secret lurked so strongly within Elise de Bois that it had driven her to her knees at his feet, rather than allowing her to speak the truth.

"Well," said Will, "this solves one dilemma."

"And what is that?"

"The young serving wench we have now as a guest. We found her among the . . . bodies of the slain guards. Her throat had been slit, but we found her breathing, and Henry's chief physician treated her immediately. She lives—seems the fools didn't bother enough with her to kill her—but she has not been conscious or coherent, and we have been at a loss to know from whence she might have come. That riddle is now clear. The maid must be a servant to Elise de Bois."

"Quite probably," Bryan muttered uncomfortably.

"We will send a rider to Montoui to inform the duchess that her woman lives. When the maid is well enough to travel, perhaps you would like to escort her to Montoui."

"Lord, no!" Bryan began, and a smile tugged slowly at his lips. "Yes, Marshal, perhaps I shall."

It would be quite interesting to see how his little virago would behave if they came face to face once again. Would she be ready to admit their acquaintance, and more?

It was possible she would have her archers upon the castle walls, ready to greet him.

"Fool that man is!" Marshal laughed. "Always ready to meet the devil. But you have a greater devil to deal with than any woman at this time."

"I have?"

"The Lion-Heart has arrived."

"Richard is here? Damn, Marshal! Why didn't you tell me? How have things gone? At least I see that you are still alive and walking. What stand is he taking with us?"

"Not a bad one," William replied, clapping Bryan upon the shoulder and urging him toward the castle once again. "Oh, he raved and ranted to me, and claimed that he would have taken me had he had his armor. But he took no great exception when I reminded him that a king need learn the lesson not to ride without armor, and that I did deflect my blow. You know Richard. He huffed and puffed and put on a great show. But then he embraced me and said that I had been a loyal man to his father. He expected us both to put the past behind and look to the future of the crown."

Bryan mulled over the information in his mind, quickly forgetting the night that had passed as his thoughts turned to Richard Plantagenet. The Lion-Heart seemed to be behaving with commendable good sense, and with an honor and wisdom that could do credit to his reign. He clenched his fists tightly before talking again to Marshal.

"Did he speak to you . . . of rewards promised by Henry?"

"Aye, that he did."

"And?"

"And . . ." Marshal's sallow features were brightened by a broad grin. "He seemed doubtful at first that Henry should have promised me such great riches, but when he learned that many had heard the king's words, he was ready to acquiesce. Isabel de Clare is to be mine. I am to be the Earl of Pembroke. All those lands will be mine!"

"Damn, but the best of luck to you, my friend!" Bryan exclaimed with the greatest sincerity. "Well . . . then it seems that I will see to my own fate shortly, then, doesn't it?"

Marshal laughed. "Aye, Sir Stede, it does seem that 'tis your turn to meet with the devil!"

Bryan halted with visible annoyance just before the entrance to Chinon.

"What is it?" Marshal inquired.

"I'll flay that little 'charmer' of yours if I do come across her again," Bryan replied irritably. His eyes were upon the men who lined the ramparts and stood guard alongside those who wore Henry's badge. At least forty men walked the ramparts, half of them Richard's. They were still clad in mail and armor— very proud now to carry Richard's lion crest upon their shields along with their own family symbols. These were the warriors Bryan had fought in Henry's long battle against his son and the King of France. Foes to be turned to friends. But men who had once longed to see his downfall, who would still feel a bitter rancor toward him now . . .

And he was going to have to pass them all minus hose and shoes, mantle and horse.

"Damn her!" he hissed. Then he swept past Marshal with his spine straight and his hands upon his hips. And he passed by the Lion-Heart's knights with such a towering power that none noticed that the well-respected warrior was embarrassingly lacking in dress.

But he knew. And even as he gritted his teeth to meet the Lion-Heart, he was thinking once more that he would love to take a horsewhip to her well-curved derrière.

Bryan had barely passed through the gatehouse when he heard Richard's thunderous voice hailing him. He winced, thinking that the "Lion-Heart" did indeed summon with a roar. He squared his shoulders and stopped, standing straight as he watched the new King of England and ruler of half of continental Europe approach him.

Whatever ill might be said of Richard, no one could deny the fine figure he cut with his stature. He was tall, perhaps a half inch shorter than Bryan, but then Bryan was among the tallest men of his day. He was muscular to the extreme, having spent his days at joust and battle since he had been a lad not full grown. Richard was a true Plantagenet; his eyes were sometimes a stormy gray, sometimes as blue as the sky, and, at rare moments of peace, they could be aqua like the Mediterranean Sea. His hair was wheat-gold, bleached by the sun; his beard betrayed many streaks of a blazing red. Where Richard walked, the ground shuddered. Yet for all that he had battled Henry so long, Bryan knew Richard to be a man of character—with principle. Bryan did not flinch at the approach that would have intimidated a lesser man.

"Stede! You have taken your time to make an appearance! And bootless, no less. Good Lord, where have you spent the night?"

"Chasing thieves, sire."

"And being robbed yourself, so it appears."

"Yes," Bryan answered simply.

Richard raised a brow to him, but made no further comment on the subject. Rather, he indicated the doorway to the keep and urged Bryan toward it. "Let us be alone to speak. We have much to discuss."

He started to precede Bryan to the keep, then paused, spinning back so suddenly that Bryan was forced to leap backward to avoid a collision with the king.

"Stede! Do you solemnly swear that you accept me as your sovereign? We have battled long and hard, you and I, but I respect the loyalty you gave my father, and would have it for my own."

"Henry is dead, Richard," Bryan said wearily. "While he lived, I could never pay you homage. Now you are the king, the rightful king, ruler of all his domains. Yes . . . now I pay you all the homage I did give him."

"Kneel, Sir Stede, and swear me fealty."

Bryan did so. Richard quickly bade him to rise. Then he nodded briefly and headed toward the keep. A fire had been drawn in the great lower chamber, but still Chinon, beloved by Henry, left Bryan cold. The great banqueting hall was sparsely furnished. Table and chairs were curiously bland, with no artistry of carving. They were serviceable, and nothing more.

Richard went to the head of the table and sat, kicking out a chair by its feet so that Bryan might take it for his use.

"Sit, Stede," Richard commanded. Then he grinned. "I never could abide your height!"

"There is little difference—"

"I am accustomed to gazing down at other men." Richard raised a hand; a servant came quickly from the shadows with wine and set it between them. Richard waved the servant away and poured out a chalice for each of them.

Bryan raised his chalice. "To a long and prosperous reign, King Richard."

The two drank. Then Richard banged down his chalice. Suddenly he was on his feet again, pacing the room restlessly, and reminding Bryan of his father.

"They are already saying that my father began to bleed when I paid my respects to his earthly remains. What do you think of that, Stede?"

"I think that many things will be said," Bryan told him bluntly.

"Damn!" Richard swore, pounding a fist upon the table and staring at Bryan with a fire blazing in his eyes. "I did not know that he was so ill when we battled last. . . . Will history revile me, or revere me, Stede?"

"I'm sure, Your Grace, that that remains to be seen."

Richard laughed suddenly. "You'll never really kneel before me, will you, Stede? Or before any man. Ah, well, I was not so much to blame. My brother John actually began this battle years ago before his death. Father himself caused it. He loved to grant us all his titles, to dole out his domains, but he never wanted to relinquish the least bit of his power. We were to be puppets, nothing more. And when we sought to rule, he was of the mind that we were still children to be bullied about by him. He had my brother crowned king during his lifetime, but he wouldn't allow him to govern a duchy. But young Henry died and I was left heir—and left to battle Father." He paused again. "I never wished to see him die so broken, Stede."

Bryan looked straight at Richard and shrugged. "The news that your brother John betrayed him is what killed your father, so the physicians say."

"Uh . . ." Richard murmured darkly, walking around the table to take a seat again. "John—I've no idea where the boy is. Have you seen him?"

"Not since he disappeared after the battle at Le Mans."

Richard drank deeply of his wine and leaned back broodingly in his chair. "No doubt he is in hiding, having heard that I do not reward traitors. But, God's blood! Doesn't the young fool realize that I am his brother?" Richard sighed. "He is my blood, and he is my heir. May God help me make him fit for a throne!"

"Amen," Bryan murmured, earning a scowl from Richard.

"I have inherited all of my father's responsibilities," he told Bryan, "and I mean to uphold them—almost all. No doubt, Stede, you will tell me, as Marshal did, that my father promised you a great heiress?"

Bryan shrugged, determined that Richard would not taunt him. He would not play games. Gwyneth would be his, aye or nay.

"He did. He promised that I would have the Lady Gwyneth of Cornwall."

Richard raised a brow. "A great heiress, indeed."

"Yes," Bryan said simply.

"Well . . ." Richard began. Then he broke off suddenly in laughter. "Stede, I cannot promise one of the greatest heiresses in Christendom to a bootless man!" He smiled. "I'm not saying that I will not reward your long and loyal service to my father. But I've work for you. I must remain on the Continent to receive homage as overlord from all my European barons. But I wish my mother released; she will be my regent until I can come to England. You and Marshal will see to her release—and to her travel, for I want her seen by the people across the countryside. The majority of the people loved her; they will be glad to forgive my sins and recognize me when they see her." He paused. "I've also another errand. We've a servant here who belongs to the Duchess of Montoui. You will see to that journey, and you will see that Elise is brought here, quickly, for my father to be interred at the Abbey of Fontevrault, as he desired. Oh—and I believe I will have the duchess accompany you and Marshal. Mother might well need a nobly born attendant."

Bryan was startled by Richard's words; Henry should be buried with all haste. Richard was willing to wait for the attendance of the Duchess of Montoui. Why?

Perhaps, Richard was hoping John would make an appearance by then, Bryan reflected. Whichever, Richard had almost promised that Gwyneth and her lands would be his, so it did not seem an appropriate time to question his monarch. But what was it about Elise de Bois? Temptress, vixen, thief—what was she?

Bryan closed his eyes quickly, annoyed that he could not forget her or put her from his thoughts. But he couldn't deny it; he had wanted to see her again—watch her reactions to him—and Richard was ordering him to do so.

"And then, Stede," Richard was continuing, his voice growing richly impassioned as he slammed his fist against the table again, "it will be time to prepare for the Crusade! Henry vowed to join Philip in the holy quest to regain Jerusalem and our Christian shrines in the East. My father can no longer do so; it is my destiny, and one that I am eager to fulfill! You will ride at my side, then, Bryan Stede."

"Aye, Your Grace, I will ride at your side," Bryan answered. Why not? He had known that the infidels had taken Jerusalem—all of Christendom had been talking of little else. Knights were God's warriors; the Crusades were the holiest battles to be fought, for they were fought for His glory.

The East promised adventure and learning; Bryan would enjoy the change. If all went well, he would leave behind a loving wife, vast lands, and resources, and return to find that he had an heir as well.

"Go find some boots, Stede!" Richard commanded suddenly. "You must be ready shortly to ride for Montoui!"

Bryan nodded briefly and rose, heading for the door. Richard called him back and he paused. Richard was rising, and coming toward him.

"Stede, you will be rewarded. Do you trust my word?"

"Aye, Lion-Heart. That I do."

Richard smiled. Their pact had been made.

Ah, Montoui! Never had home looked so beautiful to Elise, resting in the valley amid the red and gold colors of the sinking sun!

High atop the last hill that rose before her own lands, Elise paused, taking a deep breath as she stared down upon her castle, her town, her duchy. From her vantage point, she could see the entirety of the stone wall that surrounded the town, which consisted of numerous homes, the mill, the smithy, the Church of the Madonna, the workshops for the potters, the tinsmiths, goldsmiths, and craftsmen of all varieties. Beyond the wall that promised safety for her people in times of battle were the farmlands and the fields, fertile acres where grain and corn and wheat and greens were grown, where sheep and cattle grazed and grew fat. And beyond the farmlands were the forests, alive with game, wild boars and wild birds, and deer in abundance.

And beyond the walled town itself rose the castle of Montoui. Moated and tall, it shined with a white brilliance at dusk. Elise's castle was an octagon with eight tall towers, seven to house guests and her men-at-arms, the eighth being the family donjon where her own apartments lay. Home—a place that was warm and beautiful. Bustling and alive. Fires would be burning, meat would be roasting; the tapestries would warm the walls and fresh rushes would be strewn all about the great banqueting hall. Above the banqueting hall her own chamber would await her, the windows facing the east for the morning sun, her bed, draped in silk, covered with elegant linens and furs. Home. She had reached it at last. It had seemed to take her forever to travel the long miles.

She hadn't been about to return to her duchy tattered and ragged, and so she had taken back roads until she had come across a toothless and aging crone in the forest. The old woman had been glad to exchange a coarse wool tunic for the fine pair of men's boots Elise had offered her. And she had been amazed when Elise had thrown the well-woven hose and striking mantle into the bargain.

Elise had been only too pleased to rid herself of Bryan Stede's property, and to find that she no longer had to clutch her cloak tightly about herself to remain respectably clad.

At the outer wall to the town, men-at-arms challenged her, then rushed forward to greet and escort her. She forced a smile to her lips, called cheerful greetings in return, and waved them aside.

"All is well, my fine sirs! I have returned unscathed!"

"But milady—"

The call came from Sir Columbard, Captain of the Guard, but Elise still managed to evade him.

"Sir Columbard! I am frightfully exhausted. I will beg your leave for a later time!"

She rode quickly through the one main street of the town that led to the castle drawbridge. Clattering over it, she hurried to give the destrier's reins to a stableboy as soon as she passed the tower entrance and came into the outer ward.

But though she had quite easily raised a hand in greeting to her villeins and freemen and had ridden past, she could not deny her stableboy, Wat, his anxious words of welcome.

"Milady! Bless God that ye've come safely home! Since your mare returned—"

"Sabra returned?" Elise asked quickly.

"Aye, 'fore dawn, she did! I cared for her well, milady, I promise you, but my hands were shaking, I was so afrighted for you—"

"Thank you, Wat, for caring for Sabra, and for worrying so. But I am home now, and safe. But so weary!"

Elise smiled at the earnest young boy, and started to hurry past him.

"Milady! Wait—"

She had to pretend that she hadn't heard him. If she didn't find the privacy of her chamber soon, and sink into a steaming bath, she was going to start screaming like a lunatic, and then crying her eyes out like a child.

Only in privacy could she allow herself to vent to her feelings of rage and frustration.

Five guards in Montoui's colors of blue and gold warmed their hands at an open fire that burned before the door to the main keep and banqueting hall. They straightened and rushed to kneel at her feet as she hurried toward the hall.

"Milady!"

"Thank the blessed Lord!"

"We've searched for you in shifts e'er since—"

"Please! Dear sirs! Rise. I am well and safe. Just so eager for rest that I beg you to excuse me!"

With a smile and her chin tilted high, she hurried past them, ignoring their calls in her wake. Whatever business was pressing could wait.

In moments, she would be free to rant and rave and shiver and shake as she chose, with none to witness such unseemly conduct . . .

She had managed to pass by the guards with no explanation, but within the banqueting hall—with its warm, welcoming fire and comfortable tapestries—she found Michael de Neuve, her father's steward and then her own, waiting for her.

De Neuve had fought with William de Bois as the knight's squire; he had gone on crusade with his duke to the Holy Lands to capture Jerusalem, then returned to retire from the field and run the castle. He loved Elise as he had her father, and now, though his face was lined with age and his shoulders were beginning to stoop, his sense of responsibility was fierce.

"Milady! What has happened? I have worried myself ill since your horse returned this morning! And then when the messenger came about poor Isabel—"

"Hold, Michael, please!" Elise begged, feeling a throbbing headache begin to pound at her temples. "What is this about a messenger?"

"A rider came from Chinon not an hour ago, milady. He was surprised that you had not returned, and therefore I worried all the more! Isabel lives, though she is sorely injured. They shall return her here as soon as they might."

"Isabel lives?" Elise demanded, stunned and incredulous.

"Aye, milady, 'tis so—"

"Thank the Lord!" Elise murmured, suddenly overwhelmed with guilt. She had been so hurt, and then so furious, that she had forgotten to grieve for the maid. But Isabel lived. Her reckless behavior had not resulted in the death of another. There were things for which she had to be grateful . . .

"But, oh, milady! What happened?" Michael demanded.

"The king's body was set upon by thieves who murdered the guards. I was forced to run through the night, but I am here now. And that is the end of it, Michael."

"Thieves! Murderers! Oh, my lady! I knew I should never have agreed to such a foolish whim on your part. Isabel, almost butchered! And to think that it might have—"

"Michael—stop!" Elise commanded more harshly. "There was no one who could have dissuaded me from my pilgrimage! The king was kind to my parents, kind to me. I felt it my duty to go; nothing would have changed that. Now, Michael, where is this messenger?"

"Gone, already, milady. I offered all the hospitality of the castle, but as Richard is now at Chinon, he returned immediately. The man assured us that Isabel would be returned, and since a knight named Bryan Stede had seen you, he was quite convinced that you would return at your own speed. Lady Elise, whatever took you so long to return to us?"

"I stayed to the back roads, Michael."

"Back roads! More thieves and murderers and . . . oh, dearest Christ in heaven!" Michael began again, and as much as she loved the old man, Elise wanted to scream.

"Michael! I beg of you! I am sorely weary. I long only for a night's rest. And a bath. Summon Jeanne for me, if you will, please; I require a bath. Tell her that I must have hot water, and plenty of it."

"Aye, milady, aye," Michael murmured, shaking his head slightly. His duchess seldom displayed it but she possessed a temper that could make the devil pause. She was speaking to him courteously—the genteel etiquette of Marie de Bois had been instilled within her daughter through rigorous hours of training, but Michael knew Elise. Authority was in her tone now. Her chin was raised, her eyes were dangerously sparkling, and there was no doubt that the lady knew her place in life—and how to use it.

This was one of those occasions when the Lady Elise might well lose the regal composure for which she was well renowned. Michael chose wisely to turn quickly and hurry toward the kitchens to find Jeanne, his lady's maid.

From the great banqueting hall at Montoui a flight of wide

stone stairs led to the gallery and the richly furbished family quarters. Elise tried to walk calmly up the stairs, but as soon as Michael's footsteps faded toward the kitchens, she found herself running without ceremony. Upon reaching her door, she threw it violently open and slammed it behind her as if the devil were still after her.

He was not, she reminded herself. He had already caught her and . . .

I am home. In my own castle. I am the Duchess of Montoui and he will never ever have the power to touch me again. Here the power is all mine . . .

And it is all worthless! she thought with renewed dismay and fury. All of her life she had been trained to understand that she was the nobility. That she need only speak to be obeyed. That if she was fair and just, she would be served without question.

She had learned that the most powerful knight could be stalled with a winning smile. Henry had promised her that she would rule her own destiny.

And now . . . it was gone. Bryan Stede had taken away all of it. He had taught her that nobility meant little or nothing when a man decided that he wanted a woman; and worse, far worse, he had taught her that she could be completely powerless . . .

According to the messenger, Bryan Stede had "seen" her. So he had limped back to Chinon. Apparently, he knew for a fact who she was, and it still meant little to him. She had taken Henry's ring, which made her a thief, and therefore fair game for whatever he had done.

He had ruined her damned life, and all he had had to say was that he had "seen" her!

"Oh, God!" she moaned, leaning her head against the door. "Dear God, just let me forget him! Cleanse my mind of him before I go mad with the fury and humiliation . . ."

Her whispered entreaty broke off as there came a soft tapping at the door.

"Milady?"

Elise turned swiftly about and drew open the door. Jeanne bobbed a quick curtsy and moved out of the way. Several of the servants moved in quickly, bearing the heavy bronze tub. Several moved in quickly behind them, carrying huge buckets of steaming water. The bulky youths all blushed and offered her a welcome home, then hurried out of the chamber. Only Jeanne stayed behind.

Jeanne, Elise thought, grating her teeth together hard, was not going to be easy to evade. Jeanne's will matched the steel color of her graying hair. She was a slim woman, but by her competent manner, she might have been a stone tower. She was like a second mother, and Elise knew that Jeanne loved her with complete loyalty—and she was grateful for that love, and returned it. Like Michael, she had been with the household for decades. She had served Elise since the duchess had been eight years old.

She was not going to be put off by any regal airs, no matter how practiced or majestic.

The others were gone, the door had closed. Jeanne had stayed behind; her work-worn hands upon narrow hips, she scrutinized Elise quickly.

"You look all right, child. Where have you really been?"

"Making my way home," Elise replied crossly. "Jeanne . . . I do have the most horrible pounding in my head! I need no help—"

"You won't rid yourself of me that easily, Elise de Bois!" Jeanne stated firmly, moving with determination into the large and sumptuous chamber.

Once, the main chamber had belonged to her parents. It was appointed with a massive, postered bed. The draperies that hung about it were silk, brought back from the east when her father had gone on a Crusade. In the Holy Lands, William had found time to shop and barter. Persian rugs adorned the floors, and heavy tapestries adorned the walls. Fine cabinets, hewn by German master craftsmen, flanked either side of the archer's windows, and a twenty-foot-length wardrobe stretched along the left wall. At the foot of the bed were two Turkish trunks, one housing a supply of fine linen toweling, and one containing such an assortment of rose and herbal soaps and scented bath oils as to be decadent.

Jeanne, long accustomed to attending her mistress, hurried to the trunks and—ignoring the dangerous scowl upon Elise's face—began to gather an assortment of accoutrements for the bath. Jeanne placed linen towels and soaps upon the bed, then dug farther, and withdrew an empty vase that had once contained an Egyptian musk. She grimaced as she approached Elise, handing her the vase.

"What—" Elise began.

"Throw it," Jeanne advised, her dark eyes still brilliant despite her four decades.

"Throw it?"

"Aye—throw it! Hard—so that it will take strength! Make it shatter against the stone of the wall!"

Elise thought of quickly reprimanding her maid and ordering her from the room—not even Jeanne could disobey a direct order—but suddenly she laughed. It was a bitter sound, not a pleasant one, but it was, at least, laughter.

She accepted the empty vase and sent it flying against the wall with admirable power.

"Good!" Jeanne applauded the action. "Now, do you feel any better."

"Aye, I do," Elise admitted.

"The bath will help improve your disposition even more." Jeanne smiled. She took Elise's cloak, and, with a sigh, Elise stripped away her shoes and the rough woolen tunic and stepped into the water.

It was hot. So hot that it burned. But it stole away the tension in her muscles, and the mist that rose high above the tub helped to ease the pounding in her temples. She closed her eyes for a moment, then opened them to find Jeanne ready at her side with a cloth and a thick sliver of rose-scented soap.

"Thank you," Elise murmured, accepting both. Jeanne moved

away, taking a hard, straight-backed chair that gave an archer's view of the countryside beyond the castle. Elise glanced at her maid, then at the soap and cloth. Then she began scrubbing herself with fury. If she washed and washed, she could begin to wash away the memory of Bryan Stede.

"So," Jeanne said at last, "did you lose your heart to a thief, milady?"

Startled, Elise desisted with her furious scrubbing. "Don't be absurd, Jeanne!" she replied with annoyance.

Jeanne was silent for a moment, and then she sighed. "I am glad, milady. Yet you would not have been the first noble maid to leave the confines of her class and find love with a strapping young peasant. Nor the first to know the pain that such a foolish affair could bring."

"Have no fear," Elise said coolly, sinking beneath the water to wet her hair, then rising again. "I assure you, I have given my heart to Sir Percy, and it will belong to no other."

"Ahh . . ." Jeanne murmured. "Then you think that you will fool Percy?"

Elise closed her eyes once more and gritted her teeth together. "Jeanne, I do not wish to be queried, or annoyed. I am exhausted, and—"

"Elise! I am quite sure that I do try your patience! But you must bear with me—for my age, for the service I have rendered your family all these years. And for the future of Montoui."

"Montoui? Jeanne, whatever are you babbling on about?" Elise placed the cloth over her face with annoyance as she allowed the soap to linger upon her hair. If she could smell roses, she would not be plagued by the male and musky scent of the knight . . .

"Milady, you may fool an old man like Michael, and your guards dance to your tune, but I am a woman—an old one at that—and I have seen too much of life. You returned in clothing not your own, alone, on a horse that could only belong to a knight—or to a thief who had stolen it from a knight. There is a deep burning fury in your eyes, and you seek nothing but your own company. 'Tis been my experience that only one thing can cause this in a woman—and the one thing is a man."

"All right—I am angry with a man," Elise muffled out through the cloth.

"Were you raped, or seduced?"

"Jeanne!"

"Have me whipped, milady, the question still stands. I ask for your future, and because I love you."

How had she known? Elise wondered dismally. She might as well have worn a placard that decreed she had warmed the bed of that indigo-eyed devil! Would it all be so evident to Percy? What was she going to do? Tell him? She had to tell him. It would only be honorable. But what if Percy challenged Stede and swords were drawn? She could be responsible for the death of one of them.

Stede deserved to die. To be drawn and quartered, hanged, disemboweled, beheaded . . .

But what if it were Percy to die? She wouldn't be able to bear it . . .

What was she—crazy? She couldn't tell Percy!

"Is the man no one that you could marry, milady?" Jeanne asked softly.

"Marry!" Elise shrieked, at last pulling the cloth from her face to stare at Jeanne. "Never!"

"But if he raped you—"

"He didn't . . . exactly."

"No matter who he is, if he seduced you, he can be brought to the altar. Henry is gone now, of course, but surely Richard will prove to be just in his dealings—though God forgive him for hounding his father to his grave!—and you are the Duchess of powerful lands. 'Tis a pity that if you were an ordinary maid—"

"Jeanne! You do not comprehend this situation. I do not wish to marry this man! I hate him! I will marry Percy as I have planned. I am in love with Percy Montagu, as Percy is with me."

"Will he be so in love, I wonder, if you carry another man's

child? Or is that a possibility that has not crossed that shield
of anger you wear?"

Elise's silence assured her maid that her words were true.
Elise dipped back into the water, carefully rinsing the tangling
mass of her hair. She still felt Stede's touch upon her; more so
now, with Jeanne's words. Still silent, she started to scrub herself again.

"Elise, speak to me," Jeanne pleaded softly. "Tell me what
happened. Who was this man? How did—"

"Nay, Jeanne, stop! I will tell you no more than what you
have discerned. I cannot talk about it, and I will not! Rest content with what you believe, because I will say no more!" Elise
lathered the soap against her flesh with a greater fury.

"You cannot wash him away," Jeanne advised softly.

"Just his scent," Elise replied briefly.

Jeanne sighed softly. "It seems he made more of an impression upon you than you care to admit."

"Oh, he made quite an impression," Elise replied bitterly.

"Come out, little one. I will dress your hair, and we will talk.
I will question you no more, I promise. I will try to help you
see the future, since what is done is done."

Elise bit her lip. Perhaps it was best. Jeanne might well nag
at her like a mother hen, but she would never betray her confidence. And Elise knew she had to regain her poise and sort
out her thoughts before she did see Percy again.

"Aye," she said softly.

Jeanne was ready with a huge towel, and then with a soft
robe of caressing silk. In moments Elise was seated before her
dressing cabinet, facing the huge oval mirror of hammered silver. Jeanne began to comb the tangles from her great mass of
damp hair.

"I am certain that I do not carry his child," Elise said, suddenly quite calm. "The timing is not right."

"Are you sure?"

"Yes. And I would never marry such a man."

Jeanne at last lost her worried frown to laugh for a moment.

"Ah, Elise! Your fate has been a good one! Most ladies of noble birth are bartered to husbands they have never seen! No more than pawns upon the king's chessboard. Yet you say 'aye' or 'nay' with complete authority! Sometimes I worry about you because of this. The world is hard and brutal; it is oft easier to face when you have not been led to believe in your own mind."

"Nothing has changed!" Elise said vehemently. "Somehow, I will find a way to wreak vengeance upon that arrogant . . . bastard! And I will marry Percy!"

"What do you intend to do?" Jeanne queried softly.

"Lie," Elise murmured unhappily. "Oh, Jeanne! I don't know what to do! I love Percy because we are open with each other. We come together as equals. He respects my mind and my thoughts, and he has seen that I am capable and just and manage quite well what is mine. We talk, Jeanne. About everything. I've never lied to him . . ."

Her voice trailed away. She hadn't ever really lied to Percy; but she had never told him the truth about her birth. Henry had warned her to tell no one; she had respected his wishes.

But she wondered now if—in the back of her mind—she hadn't also known that Percy might not love her if he knew the truth. Bloodlines meant everything to Percy.

"We love each other," she murmured, and then she eyed Jeanne sharply through the mirror. "What would happen to me if I didn't lie?" she asked herself softly. Holding back the truth of her birth was one thing; she could think of it as a "vow" to Henry. But lying about herself, about something that had just happened . . .

"It would be noble, milady," Jeanne said dryly. "And stupid."

"You're right, aren't you?" Elise sighed. But what about the pretense she would have to assume? She had tried to pretend that she wasn't a virgin when she was, and had been caught. Now the time would come when she would have to pretend that she was a virgin when she wasn't. It all seemed an ungodly mess, and it was all Stede's fault.

Jeanne appeared to be reading her mind.

"There are ways to fool a man such as Percy, Elise," Jeanne said softly. "A scream upon the wedding night; a tiny vial of calf's blood—"

"Oh, Jeanne! It's so horribly unfair! I have never been so grateful for anything in life as my freedom—to love and marry where I would! To escape the fate of being bartered or manipulated for political reasons! My marriage was destined to be one of sharing, honesty, and trust. And now I am to begin it all with lies and deceit!"

She felt a jerk upon her hair, and frowned, then noted that Jeanne had absently left her to walk to the archer's slit of a window.

"What is it, Jeanne?"

Jeanne turned around with her dark eyes wide and alarmed.

"Think, then, what you will say quickly, milady Elise, for he rides this way."

"Percy!" Elise cried out, flying from the chair to rush to the window.

"Aye! See his standard upon the hill? He comes this way now!"

Elise's heart began to pound; a thunder to join that which remained in her head.

No . . . it was too soon. She was not ready to greet him. It hadn't even been a night since . . .

"I will need my tunic with the ermine-lined neck, please, Jeanne. And the white headdress, I believe. It goes well with the flowing sleeves."

"Aye, milady," Jeanne murmured miserably. Elise was standing straight; her chin was high. There was no quiver to her lip, nor tremor to her voice.

She was calm, and poised. And regal.

Jeanne had never felt more proud of her young mistress.

And yet she was frightened of the folly of youth. Elise was so horrified at the thought of her lie, and so passionately furious. Would she give herself away?

Don't! Jeanne wanted to tell the girl. *Forget your vengeance*

*against this other man, forget it completely, if you wish to wed
Percy in happiness.* Men could behave so strangely. Percy might
well love her, but he would be furious and hurt—and he would
feel betrayed. And though men might wander where they would,
even a great heiress lost half her value when she lost her vir-
ginity.

Elise adjusted a golden girdle low upon her hips. "I am as-
suming Michael has alerted the kitchen that Percy is arriving.
I believe he comes with a retinue of . . . I counted five men.
Does that sound right?"

"Yes, milady."

"See that we have a fine Bordeaux wine with which to greet
them. They will be thirsty from the road."

"Aye, milady," Jeanne murmured.

Elise left the room, resplendent with the beauty nature had
bestowed upon her, and with the elegance of her fur-trimmed
white silk. She was majestic. And she was a duchess of a rich
land.

Percy loved her. It was true, too, that men even married old,
ugly women to possess their land.

And Elise was clever and quick. Very mature for her age—as
a duchess must be. She had kindness and mercy, and a touch
of steel when the need arose. Her people loved her; she knew
how to speak without saying a thing when the need arose, how
to command, and how to reward. Surely, she would handle herself well with Sir Percy.

But Jeanne had an uncomfortable feeling in her bones. She
would do all that Elise had asked . . .

Then she would await her mistress in this chamber. She would
be there, in case her regal and poised charge needed a shoulder
to cry upon when the audience was gone and she was allowed
to be what she was—a young girl, stunned, furious, bewildered.
And very hurt.

Jeanne felt a little shudder rake through her. What if things
did not go well with Percy?

Elise was so very angry. Furious to the depths of the soul.

Jeanne wondered with a miserable shiver just where that streak of blazing anger might take her proud and reckless young mistress.

VIII

Elise moved down the stairway with a decorum that belied her thundering heart. She wished that there was no one about—none of her own guard, none of Percy's retinue. She would have loved to have raced down the stairs and throw herself into his arms, begging that he hold her and give her all his gentleness and tenderness and ease her mind of the confusion and pain that filled her.

But there were people about—a household full of servants, and a great hall full of knights. And a duchess did not pelt down stairs like a child, ignore her other guests, and shame a man such as Percy.

"Milady!"

It was Percy who hailed her, striding from the fire to greet her, his eyes flashing with his pleasure as he bowed low over her hand, then tenderly took it in his own to lead her to the fire and the others. "Lady Elise, you know Sir Granville, Sir Keaton, and Sir Guie. I give you Lord Fairview, and Sir Daiton."

Elise inclined her head to each man in turn. "I welcome you to Montoui." She glanced at Percy, containing her longing to be alone. "Has Michael seen to your comforts?"

"Aye, milady!" It was Sir Guy Granville who answered her. He was an older, battle-scarred knight who had ridden with her father, and a man of whom she was quite fond. "We have been given a fine cup of wine"—he raised his chalice—"and promised a fine feast. Your hospitality is a welcome embrace indeed after the days we have spent in the saddle."

Elise smiled. "I am happy to give comfort to such brave men."

" 'Tis time for comfort all around!"

Elise returned her gaze to Percy with upraised brows. She saw a sense of excitement in his deep hazel eyes, in the grin that split his handsome features. More than ever she wished she might spin into his arms and share his happiness. He looked wonderful. Tall and slim as always, almost gaunt, but so endearing.

"What are you saying, Percy?" she asked softly.

"Ah, milady!" He gripped both her hands and bent to kiss her palms. "The rumors that reached us as we rode were the best! Richard is *honoring* those who clung fast to his father! Those who turned traitor—either to himself or to his father—are being stripped of their titles and lands. Those who were loyal and fast—be it to himself or to Henry—are being richly rewarded."

"That's wonderful!" Elise exclaimed, now understanding Percy's excitement. He would benefit richly from the service he had given Henry. They needn't fear anything, no reprisals . . .

Lord Fairview, a young and solid man, though not much taller than Elise, stepped into the conversation. " 'Tis said that Richard will give his father's two strongest supporters half of England. Isabel de Clare, the Earl of Pembroke's daughter, will be given to William Marshal. He will then be one of the most powerful nobles in England. And it is said that Gwyneth of Cornwall shall be given to Sir Bryan Stede, which will give him almost as much land as Will Marshal. He will be wealthy beyond measure, and his titles would fill out page after page of parchment."

Elise was glad that she stood at the head of the table by the fire; she could reach out and grip the back of the duke's chair with its elaborately engraved coat of arms.

The wave of emotion that had washed over her had been so strong, it had seemed that she had been bathed in a white, shattering light that had stolen the breath from her lungs, the substance from her bones. Then anger, molten and hot, gave her strength again.

Stede! The man responsible for all her torment was to be given one of the richest heiresses in England. Was there no justice?

"Of course," Percy was continuing for Granville, "nothing is sure, as yet. All that we have heard is rumor. We are on our way from Normandy now to Chinon, to give homage to Richard. And then . . ."—Percy chuckled softly as he allowed his voice to trail away—". . . then we shall see where we all stand beneath the Lion-Heart!"

Elise smiled weakly. Thank God they were all here! She could not be alone with Percy now!

But it became immediately obvious that Percy wanted nothing more than to be alone with her.

"Elise," he said hastily, "I need to have a word with you in private. I'm sure these knights will readily understand—"

"Percy!" Elise protested with light but forced laughter. "How can I leave my guests—"

"Milady!" Sir Granville interrupted with a deep laugh. "We are fine with the fire and the wine. Again, we thank you for the hospitality. Go where you will, yet return to us quickly, for it has been a long time since our eyes have been so appeased!"

Well said, gallant knight, Elise thought. But then her anger grew again. Yes, well said. These men knew the codes of knighthood. They could boldly speak the flowery words that made life so pleasant. Sir Stede was little more than an armored barbarian . . .

Well said—but exactly what she didn't need at the moment.

"Elise?" Percy urged her.

They were all looking at her. Of course, it was only normal that two young lovers would want a few minutes alone. She had no choice. If she protested further, Percy would surely know that something was wrong.

If only she could stay here by the fire. There was a certain safety in the presence of others. She would say nothing to Percy, and he would travel on to see Richard now, giving her time to think.

"Elise?" Percy prodded her gently again. His hand was upon hers with perfect etiquette. "The night is beautiful. A walk along the castle ramparts beneath the stars will ease your mind of problems, and I can advise you . . ."

She forced her lips to curl into a smile, and graciously excused herself. They left the hall through the spiral staircase that led up three floors to ramparts.

She felt his fingers upon hers. Long and tapering, they were. Percy's was a slender hand for a warrior; he always fought with a sword rather than an ax or lance. His strength was in agility, and she loved him for what he was—more gentle, more refined, than the average man of the day. He was a whispering breeze, whereas a man like Stede was thunder and the wind, she thought bitterly.

They climbed until they were beneath the stars . . . and alone, as the guards had withdrawn discreetly to the towers.

"Ah . . . Elise . . . !"

She was startled as Percy suddenly pulled her into his arms. She stared into his sparkling eyes, then caught her breath as his lips came down to touch upon hers, softly . . . reverently.

Yet the feeling she had always cherished refused to come. There was no excitement in her blood, no magnificent wonder. All she could remember was Stede, the fire and the hunger in his touch, so different from this touch of a gentle breeze.

It was the guilt that plagued her! Robbing her of even the comfort his touch should give. She was too upset to allow her love to flow. Upset, suddenly frightened, and shamed.

But she did not resist his kiss. Her mind was flying, touching the stars. She had to stay calm, and poised—and say nothing. Let him travel on to Richard so that she could have the time she so desperately needed.

"Elise! Elise!"

He drew his lips from hers and enveloped her against his frame. "I have dreamed of you nightly, my love. And now, hold-

ing you, feeling the softness of your form! Our dear king is
dead, but our world is also at last at peace!" He pulled away
from her suddenly, holding her by her shoulders as he stared
into her eyes.

He wanted her to say something, she knew. To proclaim her
love for him. She felt so . . . horrible. As if by touching her he
could tell that another man had known her.

"Percy . . ." His name came out as a whisper. It was just as
well; it sounded as if her emotion for him had robbed her of
audible speech. She swallowed. "Percy, I have missed you . . .
so." Why? she wondered. Why was she plagued by this belief
that he would know? She had scrubbed and bathed away Stede's
touch from her flesh, but Jeanne had been right; she had not
been able to remove it from her soul.

"Oh, Elise!" Percy held her tightly again, cherishing her, then
pulled slightly away, still holding her hands. "Elise, is your
chaplain at the castle?"

"Brother Sebastian?" she queried, trying to catch up with his
words as her conscience continued to hound her. "Yes, I believe
that he is surely near. He does not care to travel, you know;
lately, he has grown as fat as a waddling duck—"

"Then let's be married tonight!"

"Tonight?" Elise echoed with horror.

"Aye, tonight! Henry gave you permission to marry where
you would. But now Richard is our suzerain. You are landed
gentry, and I am not. Richard has been generous, but what if
he finds an objection to our marriage? If the deed is done, there
will be little that he can say."

Tonight? Elise thought swiftly. *Yes, marry him tonight!* Let
it be done, and when she was his wife, she would lovingly find
some way to explain to him why she had not come to him
entirely chaste . . .

Yes, tonight . . . her future would be sealed.

She closed her eyes. A cold trickle of shivers swept through
her. She could not. She would destroy all that set the two of
them above time and the world. Even if she deceived Percy, she

would live in terror, wondering each time they lay together if she would conceive a child with him, or if she had perhaps done so before she had become his wife . . .

If he found her in a lie, it would be finished. The magic of a marriage upon equal footing, an alliance of choice and love. She could bear a child with raven-black hair, and Percy could turn from her and go wandering the world. Or, worse still, cast her from him.

"Elise!" He shook her shoulders. "Speak to me!"

She pulled gently away from him and turned to stare out at the night. Strange, how she had dreamed of pitting Percy against Bryan Stede for vengeance. And now . . . now she could not want such a thing. Percy could die, and she would not be able to live with such pain and guilt and loss.

But neither could she blithely marry Percy.

"My love," she said softly, facing the stars and wondering how the night could mock her with such beauty, "I . . . think that it would be a serious mistake to marry tonight."

"Why?" Percy demanded. She heard the mistrust and confusion in his voice.

Deceiving Percy was so very hard when it came to . . . this. She felt tension riddle her body just as she tried to speak lightly and reasonably. "Because of Richard, Percy. He will expect us to ask his blessing—and permission. If we ignore him, we could well suffer for years and years to come."

Percy was silent. She didn't dare turn to look at him.

At last he spoke. "I don't believe you, Elise. Why should Richard care about an unlanded knight and the Duchess of a small spit of land that buffers him from the French King's domains?"

"Because he is Richard," Elise said flatly. "As proud and arrogant as his father."

Again Percy was silent. She felt him move behind her, and for her life, she could not ease her body from the rigidity that seized it when she felt his arms encircle her waist.

"What is wrong with you?" he demanded crisply.

She closed her eyes. She thought of the summer day when she had met him, here at Montoui, in Henry's service. She thought of the long talks they had shared late at night before the fire under the respectful eyes of the guards; she thought of the way he had always known when she was having a problem, deciding a grievance between two of her people, worrying about the harvest, or an illness that had affected the livestock.

He always knew. It was part of why she had come to love him so dearly. He was caring and sensitive. Always willing to listen; to respect her mind, and her decisions—even to learn from her.

"Wrong?" she murmured, stalling for time.

"Elise, I know you well, my love."

A certain strength returned to her. Percy did love her. It was possible that she had conceived a child, but very unlikely. And was the loss of her maidenhood such a great thing then compared with the love of a lifetime? She had to get past the guilt—especially when the guilt shouldn't have been hers!—and say something.

"Percy, I love you. And we will marry soon. But I cannot marry you tonight."

She felt him move behind her, and again she felt caressed and warmed by his love.

"Why not, Elise? If we hesitate, all could be lost. Tell me why you are so distraught. Elise, I love you—no matter what!"

She turned to face him again, touching his cheek wonderingly for a moment with her knuckles. He caught her hand and kissed it fervently.

"Percy," she said softly, "I am distraught. Percy, I traveled to Chinon to pray for the king. I felt it my duty; he has always been so kind to me. Thieves robbed the body while I was there, and I was forced to run. It was a horrible night."

He moved away from her, quietly walking along the ramparts. "Who is it, Elise? I would know."

"What?" she asked immediately, frowning as she wondered quickly what she might have said to lead him to such a question.

"You're in love with another man. Who?"

"Oh, Percy, no, no!" She raced to him then, catching his arm, spinning him around. "No, Percy! I promise that I am not *in love with* another man—"

She paused, horrified by her emphasis on the words "in love with." She saw his eyes; the leap of flame to them, of query and of pain, and she knew there would be no going back. She had to tell him what had happened now; the truth would be far better than the things he might suspect.

"Tell me, Elise," he whispered painfully.

"I love you, Percy," she told him.

"I love you. Tell me."

"I did tell you. Thieves robbed the body of the king. I was there when it happened. I had to run. And so I ran. But I couldn't run fast enough and I was caught—"

He jerked from her so suddenly that she was stunned. His fingers gripped hard into her arms, his eyes were intense. His voice was barely a whisper, yet it was harsh and pained.

"You were caught and . . . raped . . . by a thief?"

She suddenly felt her head spinning. Was there a difference if one was raped by a thief—or seduced through one's own stupidity by a knight?

"Not . . . not by a thief . . ." she faltered.

"By one of the king's men?"

He was shouting. Percy was shouting at her. She had never seen him so angry, and it was terrible not to know if he was angry at her, or at the man who had wronged her. He had promised to love her no matter what—but at that moment, it would have been impossible to touch him. She was at a loss as to how to handle the situation. She turned around, grasping blindly for the stone wall.

Tears—tears always worked well with a gentle man. And, dear God! Didn't she deserve to cry? She loved this man, and she was on the verge of losing him through no fault of her own.

Elise allowed her shoulders to shake and a ragged sob to

escape her. Once they began to flow, there seemed to be no end to her tears.

At last, Percy came up behind her. "Elise, Elise . . ." His hands caressed her shoulders. "My love, you must tell me what happened. This is horrible. Against all the laws of man and God and chivalry. You were raped by one of the king's men?"

"I wasn't exactly . . . raped. It—"

"It wasn't exactly rape?" Percy interrupted, shooting back at Elise in a state of confusion. "Elise, either it was or wasn't! Were you brutally forced?"

"No . . . not exactly, but I didn't intend—"

"Oh, my God!" Percy grated out. His gentle tone was gone, and his touch became a painful one. "It wasn't exactly rape! What was it?"

"Percy . . . I . . ." What was it? She could barely answer that herself. "I . . . I was tricked . . . I—"

"Tricked . . . ! How?" Percy snarled.

"Percy, it is a long, complicated story. He didn't know who I was, I didn't know who he was—"

"What a wonderful reason to bed with a man!"

"Percy!" Elise protested, searching out his gold and hazel eyes. Where was the man she loved, who had vowed to love her no matter what? She didn't recognize him. And she had thought that she had known him so well!

"All this time, I have revered you and placed you upon a pedestal," he told her bitterly, "and I've often gone cold and wretched into the night! Now you tell me that upon meeting some other knight you fall like a harlot into his bed! Perhaps I've been the fool all along! Respecting you as the grand 'Lady Elise,' Duchess of Montoui! Did you laugh all along? I should have sensed in your kisses the female lust for more! Do you tell me of just one, or have there been many? Will I merely follow a long line?"

"Percy!"

Elise was so shocked she could only echo his name, and try to assimilate the horrible things he said to her.

"Oh, God!" he groaned, and, pushing her from him, he leaned against the ramparts, slamming a fist against them. She felt his pain then, as well as his anger. And she tried to tell herself that his anger was caused by that pain—that he would strike out at her because he was wounded, not because he had ceased to care. Nothing helped; his behavior was still a shock to her.

But then he pushed away from the stone and gripped her shoulders once again, his fingers biting into her flesh. And when she heard the tone of voice, she stiffened.

"Who was this man? I will not be laughed at should I meet up with him. Nor will I hear whispers behind my back. Or have they been whispering behind my back already? Did you fabricate this story of being caught, since I would surely know I held no virgin once we were wed?"

The shock faded, and became rage. She slapped him as hard as she could across the face.

He staggered backward, staring at her incredulously. He brought his hand to his injured cheek, and his lips curled into a sardonic snarl. Percy, snarling. She had never seen such an ugly or threatening look upon his face; he was a different man.

He started to take a step toward her, and she realized that he meant to strike her in return. "Harlot, I should send you to your knees—"

"Come one step closer to me, Percy Montagu, and I will scream for my guards!" Elise snapped.

Apparently he believed her, for he paused, the snarl fading from his face. Once again he was just Percy, the man she had loved so dearly. Gentle and tender, capable of the sweetest poetry. How could he be so cruel?

She lifted her chin, trying to keep from trembling. "I cannot believe that you have said these things to me, Percy. As I vowed my love, so did you. If that love were true, you would not dishonor me so. No one has ever laughed behind your back, but had they, I would have hoped that your belief in me would have risen above any scorn. I could have married you this night, and possibly deceived you. But I did not."

Percy swallowed uncertainly. "Perhaps you could not have borne my anger had I found you out."

"Perhaps," Elise said coolly.

"Who was he?"

"Does it matter to you?"

"Yes, by God, it does!"

"Why? Do you intend to avenge my honor? Or do you intend to tell him that you passed me by—to maintain your own?"

"By God, Elise!" Percy swore savagely, clenching his fists at his side. "What happened?"

"I wonder if it really matters," Elise replied quietly. She turned away from him, placing her hands upon the cold stone of the castle wall. What had she expected from him? she wondered bitterly.

More than this! her heart cried out. How had she ever imagined she might explain it all reasonably? To Percy—of all men. With his sense of blood and right and wrong. Might she have said, "Henry was really my father, Percy, and so I stole his ring. I stole it because my mother, who was a Bordeaux peasant, scratched all that she had together to buy it for him. I didn't want that truth known—you can understand that, Percy, can't you?—and so I told the wrong lies to the wrong man?"

No. There was no way to explain such a thing to Percy. She had been blind to believe that she might. And yet it still hurt so badly; she couldn't believe that it was a man who claimed to love her, who she had believed she loved with all her heart, who was suddenly calling her a harlot. Percy had become as cold and rigid as the stone of the wall she touched. She had known him, yes. She had known all the good things about him: his love of poetry and music, his gentle side, his sense of honor and loyalty. She had also known he was the third son of a minor Norman baron; he had always been ambitious. Material things mattered to him, just as prestige among his peers mattered to him.

"What game do you play with me, Elise?" Percy demanded harshly. "You were 'tricked,' you say. Were you drugged or drunk? Or did you play a game with him, too? I know the ways of women well, milady duchess. The voice says no, the eyes say yes, and a man can be goaded just so far. Did you tempt him, Elise, saying no, meaning yes? Playing Jezebel with the same vigor as any common whore?"

Her nails scraped over the stone when she spun about to face him, her chin high, her eyes flashing.

"You have known many such women, sir?"

"Aye—"

"How many?"

"What difference does it make? I am a knight, I travel with the king, and I fight his battles. I am long on the road, sometimes weary and in need of comfort. And I am a man."

"And it seems to me, Percy, that you are a man far more 'used' than ever I shall be."

"What?"

"I'm quite certain that you heard me."

His hands balled into fists again at his sides; she saw him glance surreptitiously toward the closest tower. The guards are there, Percy, and they can be here in moments . . .

"God rest his soul, but this is Henry's fault for doting upon you so, Elise! A woman bears a man heirs; she must be chaste and loyal, for who would raise another's bastard?"

Elise smiled. "Montoui is mine, Percy. *My* child will be the rightful heir—no matter where I bed."

"Bitch!" Percy snapped suddenly. "And to think that I believed you to be the most pure, the most beautiful—the most devoted of women! You talk like a daughter of Satan!"

The desire to laugh was beginning to overwhelm her. Almost, Percy; I'm the daughter of Henry II. She did not speak.

"Perhaps you had best leave, Percy—before you find yourself tainted with my wickedness."

Percy turned from her this time, hesitating as he stared unseeingly out at the stars. There was a hurt and haunted look about his eyes when he at last faced her again.

"I am sorry, Elise."

"For what, Percy? The things you have said, or the way that they have gone?"

"I don't know, I don't know," he murmured, pressing his palm against his temple and closing his eyes. When they opened once more, there was a different look about them. He stepped toward her and she stiffened when he took her into his arms.

"Elise . . . I have desired you so very long . . ."

He drew back, then abruptly pulled away the headdress she had so carefully chosen. Her hair tumbled free, a streak of gold against the ebony sky. He threaded his fingers through it at the nape of her neck, gripping hard. "I have dreamed of having you . . . with your hair so, tangling about me, teasing my flesh. No other man should have had it so . . ."

"Percy, you are hurting me."

He didn't seem to hear her. "We could still be married. You would first have to seek shelter with a religious house where godly sisters might watch you until your time, until we are certain that there shall be no child."

"Percy, I will go nowhere. If you choose not to trust me in my own home, there would be nothing for which to wait."

"Elise, I offer you a chance for us—"

"Percy! Don't you understand! There is nothing that I seek if there is no trust! You don't really care what happened; all that matters to you is that I have somehow become tainted! Without the love, without the trust, I do not want the marriage! I do not need land, Percy—I have the land. I am the duchess. I—"

"Elise!" he interrupted her, and as she stared into his eyes, she realized that she had let her own temper fuel his. He was furious again as he continued: "You are a fool! Women marry where they are told! And, yes! You come to me tainted by another man, then claim you will still have your way! Have it so, then! But watch your step, my beauty. Richard the Lion-Heart is not the doting Henry; perhaps he will give you to an old and decaying man who will not care where a young wife has been!"

"Percy, you are hurting me! Let go of me!"

His grip eased; he closed his eyes tightly and shuddered.

"Elise, Elise, try to understand. I've wanted you so long. I've waited and waited for marriage, for our union to be honorable, and now I discover this. God help me, I believe I'm losing control of my mind. What was *mine* was taken, you understand?"

Elise shook her head, wanting to cry out, too hurt and angry and confused herself to do so. "No, Percy," she murmured, faltering for words as his touch became a gentle one again.

"I loved you, Elise. I loved you so very much."

Loved. So he no longer loved her now. And he was holding her, close to his body. She could feel his length, his warmth, his touch.

A touch that became halting, his fingers winding into her hair, arching her throat and bringing her eyes to his. The hazel seemed fevered, almost maddened. "Have me tonight, Elise," he urged her. "You gave yourself to a stranger; give yourself to me. I might be so beguiled as not to care—"

His lips descended cruelly upon hers, bruising with intensity. Elise fought the degrading onslaught with fury. This was not what she had wanted from him! She had craved sympathy and understanding, and the love he had vowed. All she had received was fury and punishment.

Elise emitted a furious sound from deep within her throat and managed to twist her head from his.

"Go, Percy! Leave me be, or I swear before heaven that I shall call the guards!"

"I will tell them that you're a harlot—"

"They serve Montoui, and they serve me. Is that it, Percy? You still abhor the fact that you cannot receive a virgin—but you would be the Duke of Montoui?"

She knew from his hesitation that it was so. Keeping her shoulders rigidly squared, she began walking briskly toward the stairs that would bring her back to the keep. "You needn't ride out at night, Percy. Montoui offers the hospitality of a meal and a night's rest to you and your fellows. You may tell them that I have been taken with a severe headache. It will not be far from the truth."

He did not reply to her. Elise heard only the stillness of the night as she hurried through the keep, and to the lower tower entrance to her chambers.

Jeanne started from where she had been dozing by the fire at the creak of a hinge.

The duchess had returned—quickly, it seemed.

Elise did not speak to Jeanne, but came to the fire herself, standing there silently as she warmed her hands.

Jeanne knew for a certainty that things had gone badly, that Elise had not been able to withhold the truth from Percy.

She will burst into tears, Jeanne thought. *Surely she will burst into tears, and perhaps it will be good, for she can cry away the sharpness of the pain.*

But Elise did not burst into tears. She stood before the fire for so long that it was Jeanne who could no longer bear the pain.

"Milady?"

"He was horrible, Jeanne. Arrogant, angry, and despicable. He said things to me that should have made me hate him. So why does it still feel as if my heart has been gouged out?"

"Oh, Elise," Jeanne murmured miserably. She wanted to go to the girl and comfort her; yet she stood too straight and proud to be offered comfort.

"I despise myself," Elise murmured almost curiously, "because I fear that I might still love him. I wonder if he has behaved as all men might. I just believed so much in our love . . ."

A sigh racked her slender frame. The white of her gown and the gold in her hair captured the flames of the fire and shimmered with an ethereal beauty.

Then suddenly she spun about, facing Jeanne with her eyes blazing.

"And he—Stede!—is to be rewarded with half of England!

One of the richest heiresses alive is to be given him. Titles and
lands and . . . oh! I will not let it happen! He has taken everything from me—and somehow, Jeanne, I swear it, I will take
everything from him!"

Jeanne tried to murmur something soothing, but she took a
step backward from her young mistress. She had never seen the
beautiful blue eyes blaze with such a fevered fury. Never seen
such tension and anger radiate from such a slender form . . .

She meant it. The Lady Elise was determined. No matter
what stood in her way, she was determined to destroy the knight
who had brought her to this moment.

"He will not have Gwyneth of Cornwall—no matter what I
have to do!"

Jeanne found herself seized by a fit of cold shivers. There
was a ruthless quality about Elise's voice that was terrifying.

"No matter what I have to do!" she repeated, and her eyes
narrowed to dangerous, glittering slits as she stared at the fire.

IX

"Riders, milady! Coming from the east!"

Elise struggled to waken as Jeanne burst into her chamber and threw open the draperies that closeted her bed. She had been awake most of the night, unable to sleep until dawn, and now she felt as if she were trying to emerge from a great fog.

"Oh, milady, do awaken! Come to the window!"

Elise urged her weary limbs from the bed. When her bare feet touched upon the cold stone of the floor, she was startled to full awareness, and hurried to the turret to stare out eastwardly.

They were still about three miles distant—a contingent of ten men in full armor. A pair of matching dappled grays, adorned with silks and feathers, drew a handsomely appointed litter.

Elise strained her eyes to study the men. The banners they carried were gold and red, and as they moved steadily closer, she began to make out the emblem.

It was that of a lion.

"They come from Richard," she said excitedly.

"Oh!" Jeanne exclaimed, clapping her hands together as she hovered behind Elise. "They return Isabel to us!"

"And more," Elise murmured uneasily. "You do not send ten men in full armor with emblems blazing beneath the sun just to return a servant . . ."

"What do you think they want?"

Elise frowned. "Not war—that is for certain. All know that

our garrison is five hundred strong. They come as an official emissary . . . I still don't understand—"

"Milady!" Jeanne chastised softly. "Even I understand! Richard sends his men so that you may swear homage to him."

"Perhaps," Elise murmured. As a "duchess," she should owe fealty to the French King for her lands, but since Montoui was so small it had always paid homage to the directly bordering Angevin lands. Therefore, she owed fealty to Richard now; Richard, in turn, owed fealty to Philip of France for his Continental holdings.

Elise should have been rushing to dress, she realized, but something was holding her to the window. The party kept moving forward, and the closer they came, the more compelled she felt to watch. There was something familiar about the leader.

How could there be? she wondered. He was in full armor; he wore a helmet and a visor, and a mantle of encompassing black over his chain mail. There was no way to recognize his features, or even the color of his hair . . .

Her heart seemed to stop and then thunder with a suffocating intensity.

It was him. She did not need to see his features to recognize the way he sat his horse, taller than those who rode with him. There was only one other man who sat a saddle so powerfully, and that man was Richard himself.

And it was not the Lion-Heart who rode. It had to be Stede.

"It is him!" she whispered aloud, the sound of her voice rigid with the fury that enveloped her. How dare he ride to her castle so brazenly! It was like a sacrilege. He had destroyed her life, and now he sought her hospitality as if it were he about to be crowned king, and no matter what the past, she owed him homage . . .

" 'Him'? Milady?"

She barely heard Jeanne's puzzled question. A flush of heat wrapped all around her; she felt as if she could gouge at the stone wall and tear it to pieces.

" 'Him'?" Jeanne persisted.

Still Elise ignored her, at last spinning from the archer's slit to confront her with blazing eyes. "I shall wear the blue with the fox trim, Jeanne. The headdress is quite high. And the golden earbobs and matching necklace Father brought back from Jerusalem. Hurry! They come closer and closer. The guards will halt them at the gate, but as they come from Richard, they will be allowed entrance. And it would not do to keep such an emissary waiting."

Jeanne lowered her eyes. "Aye, Lady Elise. We will hurry."

She left Elise at the window as she returned to the chamber to lay out the specified clothing. Him! So it was the man who had brought such grief to her lady, riding toward the castle as if he owned it! Jeanne decided there and then that the man should pay for his arrogance. But if she were going to seek revenge on her mistress's behalf, she would have to hurry.

"Milady?"

"Coming, Jeanne!"

Elise was ready at the main entrance to the great hall before the men entered. Only three came into the hall; Elise assumed that the others were soldiers who as yet had not earned titles or knighthood. They would, no doubt, be gaming now with her own off-duty guards.

Her heart beat hard as she watched the three men come toward her, removing their helmets and faceplates.

Bryan Stede wore a mocking smile, which increased her irritation to a state where she found it difficult to remain still and exude the pure air of icy nobility she intended. She stared at him coolly, with her head high, her dress portraying her wealth and importance. *You will not make me shiver or shake, Sir Stede,* she thought furiously, *nor goad me into childish temper. There will come a day when I strike vengeance, and you will be totally disarmed by then . . .*

But it was not Bryan who spoke to her first, and for a moment her anger melted away as Will Marshal stepped toward her, his dark countenance brilliant with the warmth of his smile.

"Milady Elise!"

He bent over her hand with a winning gallantry, all the more so, for Will Marshal was known for being the harshest of warriors, and not a gallant at all.

"Will!"

Elise hugged the man who had been Henry's most loyal warrior, his right-hand man for years, even when vehemently disagreeing with his monarch. She stood back to see that the third man in the party was Geoffrey Fitzroy.

She had met her half brother a number of times—and she liked him; he was proud, tall, and well built—and was resigned to his fate as a bastard.

She wondered if, had her own birth been known, she would have handled life as well as Geoffrey. He was twenty years her senior, and as he smiled at her now, she wondered uneasily if he knew of her relation. Worse still, she wondered if this gathering now meant that Richard knew.

"Duchess," Geoffrey murmured, stepping forward and courteously taking her hand, as Marshal had, to plant a brief kiss decorously upon it.

Elise exhaled a long-held sigh. They had come to return Isabel and remind her that Richard would now be king—nothing more. She glanced quickly to Bryan Stede. He stood several steps behind the other two men, watching her with amusement laced with something else.

A smoldering anger, such as her own?

She did not wait for him to approach her; if he touched her, she would scream. Gracefully, she indicated the fire beyond her and the trestles of the banqueting table.

"Welcome to Montoui, messires. May I offer you wine while you state your business?"

Will Marshal, who had known her since she was a child, was not about to stand upon ceremony. He slipped an arm about her shoulders as they approached the table. "Ah, Elise! How good it is to see you. You grow more beautiful daily! And it is quite a relief to see you so, for I was heartily worried when I learned that you had been present for a meeting with our thieves."

Chills swept along her spine. She longed to turn about and stare at Bryan Stede and demand to know what he had told these men. But she dared not, for fear of giving herself away. She held her back erect, wishing that Geoffrey and Bryan were ahead of them, and not behind them.

"Were the thieves apprehended?" she asked quietly.

"Alas, no!" Marshal said irritably. "Apparently they disappeared through subterranean tunnels within Chinon!" Will shook his head as if to whisk away the anger and unpleasantry, and then he chuckled. "And to think our friend—Stede, here—mistook you for a thief!"

She forced herself to laugh along with him, and as they had reached the table, she did turn to face Stede, murder in her eyes. "Vastly amusing, isn't it, Sir Stede."

"I found the night . . . intriguing," he said smoothly, setting his helmet upon the table.

"I almost split a gut when I saw this giant limping toward the castle! And Richard accosted him before we could get another pair of boots on his feet!"

Elise forced her lips to curl into a smile as she stared at Stede. "Ah, but meeting our new monarch bootless seems to have caused little harm. I hear that those who served Henry best are to receive the richest rewards."

" 'Tis true," Geoffrey said. "Seems my brother possesses some sense. Loyalty cannot be bought, but can be rewarded."

Stede was staring steadily upon her. Elise thought that at that moment she would have gladly sold her soul to the devil for a moment's strength to tear him to shreds. He had the audacity to stand there as if they had shared nothing more than a brief tussle and that all that had happened was that she had stolen his boots . . .

A feeling of heat crept over her again, and it had nothing to do with the fire burning in the grate. Thank God he had made no confessions regarding the night; they would all know . . .

And now, though Percy was gone, she could still cling to a certain amount of dignity. But it was galling. Each time she looked at him, she remembered his touch, and the heat seemed to set her ablaze, with fury, with weakness, with the desire to run away and pray that a cooling wind could rid her of memory . . .

No, she could not rid herself of the memory. Not until she had found a way to strip him as he had stripped her; rob him, violate him of something dear.

She would find her chance. If she played each scene with dignity. She could be a consummate actress when she chose, and she was determined to find a way to Eleanor, before Stede could receive his promised goods, to strip him of the lands and rank he desired.

"Ah!" she said politely, glad to see that Jeanne hurried in from the kitchen hallway with a silver tray bearing four goblets. "Here is wine, messires, so that you may wet travel-weary throats."

Jeanne bobbed before Will Marshal, who took the front cup; Geoffrey accepted the second with a murmur of thanks. Stede reached for the third cup, and Elise was both puzzled and annoyed when Jeanne staggered suddenly with the tray, almost dropping the goblets.

"Oh!" she cried out in distress, catching the veering goblet with her free hand. She handed it to Stede; it was not the one he had reached for.

"Sir Stede, forgive me," Jeanne pleaded.

" 'Tis nothing," he said lightly, smiling gently at the flustered Jeanne. Elise did not like to see his smile; it made him appear younger; it softened the severity of his features and made him look quite handsome. He had wasted no charm upon her, yet he was readily willing to forgive a servant when many a knight would have cuffed the offender.

Jeanne brought her the last goblet and Elise frowned curiously at her maid. Jeanne merely bobbed another little curtsy, then hurried out of the room.

"Ah . . . this certainly soothes the palate!" Marshal approved.

He drained his goblet and set it upon the table. "And now, milady, we will speak of the nature of our visit."

"We left your servant Isabel with the valet who greeted us when we entered."

Elise nodded. "Yes, Michael will see to her comfort and care. I was quite gratified to hear that she lived. But there is more, is there not? I assume you have come to ask that I swear homage as the Duchess of Montoui to Richard the Lion-Heart. Assuredly, Marshal, I shall do so. By God's decree, Henry is dead. Richard is then the legal heir, and I support the legal heir."

She noted that Bryan Stede was doing little of the speaking. Why was he along? she wondered. Merely to taunt her with his presence? Whether he spoke or not, she knew that he was there. Towering over both Geoffrey and Marshal, silent, dark and powerfully trim in his armor. She felt the threatening sting of his indigo eyes even when she did not meet them, and she felt tremors rack her limbs even as she stood straight. If only she could pummel him! But she could not, and so she had to live with the rage that consumed her until she could do him a different kind of harm . . .

Cunning can be more powerful than brawn, Sir Stede! she thought as she ignored him to continue to smile at Marshal.

"Then," said Marshal, unaware of the tumult that raced through her mind, "you will kneel to Richard's surrogate and swear allegiance?"

"Gladly," she agreed pleasantly, taking a step forward to seize Marshal's hand.

He chuckled. "Not I, Lady Elise! Bryan Stede wears the Lion-Heart's ring. It is to him you must bow."

Never! Elise thought, and yet she could ill afford to offend Richard.

"I fancy," Geoffrey offered a bit dryly, "that my brother considers Bryan his most effective counterpart. He is the only man Richard must face eye to eye."

Elise smiled and approached Bryan Stede, searching coldly for an expression in his deep blue eyes. They were enigmatic,

yet she felt the sense of a storm within him, and knew then that
he had come in anger. She had managed to humiliate him before
Richard by stealing the horse and boots of such a great knight.

She stretched her hand out toward him; he offered his own.
Even as she saw the lion engraved in gold upon the ring, she
remembered the touch of his hand. Sweeping over her. Intimately. The firm caress of the long fingers. The inescapable
heat . . .

Before he could act, she drew the ring from his finger and
spun gracefully from him, accosting Marshal with an innocent
laugh. "Do let me bow to you, dear Will! I remember your
friendship with our sovereign Henry so clearly; my allegiance
will be all the more heartfelt!"

Again, allowing no room for a reply, she grasped Will's fingers, slipped the ring on him, and sank lithely to the floor. "I,
Elise de Bois, Duchess of Montoui, do hereby pledge my loyalty
and allegiance to Richard Plantagenet."

She stood as quickly and gracefully as she had slid to the
floor. "Now, messires, I assume all is settled."

"Not quite," Marshal replied.

"Oh?"

"Richard has asked that you attend Henry's funeral."

A lump formed in her throat and for a moment she allowed
her eyes to fall to the ground. "Yes, of course I shall attend."

"We shall be your escort, of course." He paused. "There is
still more."

Elise raised her eyes curiously to Will. He smiled.

"King Richard also requests that you accompany us as we
journey to free the queen."

"Eleanor!" Elise exclaimed, startled.

"Aye—Eleanor. His first act will be to free his mother. He
will be held up here with business for several days." Will
paused, frowning distastefully. Then he said, "None of us has
seen Prince John since he deserted his father, and Richard is
determined to find him. But he also wants his mother freed
immediately. Then, he hopes that she will travel the land on his

behalf, so that the people will welcome him when he arrives upon English soil for his coronation."

Elise smiled slowly with true enthusiasm. Opportunity was reaching out to her! Richard had asked that she serve the very woman she was longing to see. It would be a long journey, though, she reminded herself. Henry, she knew, would be interred at Fontevrault Abbey, as he had requested during his lifetime. For all time, then, he could lie in his Angevin hills, not far from the castle where he died. After services, they would have to travel through Anjou and Normandy, and cross the English Channel before riding once again toward Winchester, where Eleanor was incarcerated.

Yes, it would be a long journey, with Stede at her side, so it seemed. But they would not be alone, and she would reach Eleanor.

"I shall be greatly pleased to accompany you to the queen! When do we leave?"

"With the dawn, milady. You will accompany us to Fontevrault, where we will put Henry to his final rest. And then we will be off for England."

"I shall be ready at dawn," Elise promised.

"Very good," Marshal approved. "If you'll excuse me, I'll see that the men are housed for the night."

"Michael will arrange accommodations," Elise murmured.

Marshal nodded and strode toward the door. Geoffrey followed him, and Elise waited for Stede to turn about and do so, too. He did not. Elise allowed her smile to slip from her features as she stared at him with undisguised hatred.

"Get out of here!" she hissed at him.

He shrugged and pulled out a chair, sitting easily despite his armor. "It does not take three men to arrange sleeping quarters for the night."

"I don't care what it takes. I want you away from me. Your arrogance is disgusting; you have no right to be here."

"I was ordered to be here."

"Ah, yes! By Richard."

Stede shrugged once again, yet she saw that there was nothing complacent about the fire in the indigo depths of his eyes.

"Richard intends to make me one of the most powerful men in England. That is not a bad reason to serve a legal king."

"That's right!" Elise exclaimed sarcastically. "Gwyneth of Cornwall and all her lands. You will be rich and powerful indeed, Sir Stede. Does it all mean that much to you?"

"Only a fool would turn down such wealth—and power—as you say."

"Only a fool," Elise replied dryly.

He lifted a dark brow cryptically. "You sound bitter, milady."

"Bitter, no. Furious, yes. You have no right to sit in my hall. No right to come into this room. You know how thoroughly I despise you!"

He laughed, and the sound was one of true amusement. "Would you have rather I announced to Richard that I dared not go near the Lady Elise, and she told me that she was experienced, yet I found myself deflowering her? That would have led to my explaining the situation, and telling him that you had robbed his father's corpse of a ring. Should I have done so?"

Elise did not answer the question. "You are a fool to taunt me, Sir Stede. You will find that although I have not the wealth or power of Gwyneth of Cornwall, I can extract a certain vengeance."

He rose, and started walking toward her. Elise discovered herself edging backward. She was in her own castle, yet his sheer strength was a menace that defied propriety, the staunch stone of her walls, and all five hundred of her men-at-arms.

"Take one more step," she hissed, "and I will scream for my guards."

"You may scream all you like, Duchess," he told her. "I will not be threatened by a lying, thieving woman."

There was a poker by the fire. Elise spun about and grabbed it menacingly. "And I will not be touched again by a barbaric rapist!"

" 'Twas hardly rape, Elise."

" 'Twas hardly anything else!"

He paused, yet she saw that it was only to laugh at her. "Do you hate me so because I did not fall to my knees to beg your pardon? Perhaps I should have come to you with a tear-stained face, begging your forgiveness and your hand in marriage? You would have loved that! Savored the opportunity to tell me that you despised me and would rather marry a crippled, aging peasant! But, of course, such words would have meant nothing, since you are so enamored of Sir Percy Montagu. I believe your judgment is a bit at fault, but I bear you no rancor." He swept her a mocking bow and murmured quite skeptically, "I wish you and young Percy long life and happiness."

She didn't move for a moment. Hate seemed to fill her so completely that she couldn't even breathe. She couldn't allow it to control her . . .

"Sir Percy is twice the man you can ever hope to be, Stede," she said coolly.

"What a pity. Tell me, have you told him of our . . . meeting?"

"It's none of your affair."

"What? Surely it is!" He mocked her, and she knew it. "I must prepare myself for the time when your future husband comes at me to avenge your honor!"

"I have prayed from the time we met, Stede, for God to strike you down dead!"

"Why bother with God? Send the manly Percy!"

He took another step toward her and she could see the laughter clearly in his features. For some absurd reason she imagined him with the vague Gwyneth of Cornwall: a woman eager to greet him, to feel his arms about her. She imagined him with his smile, harsh features made strong and handsome by tenderness. He was an experienced lover; Gwyneth would probably find great joy.

"One more step, Stede, and I swear I shall call the guards—and use this poker on your insolent face."

"Will you really?"

"Do you doubt my rightful hatred?"

"What I don't doubt," he said icily, a stern tension tightening his features and erasing his smile, "is that you are a temperamental vixen who has brought about her own downfall. You are the Duchess of Montoui; that is apparent to me now. And Will swears that the Duchess of Montoui is a lady of wealth, so I have come to believe that you were not an accomplice to the cutthroat thieves who so dishonored Henry. But you did steal the ring. We both know that. Why? It is a mystery, Duchess, an enigma I find that I cannot allow to elude me." Bryan paused, watching her, awaiting her reaction. Was there an honest reason she had stolen the ring? And if not, then what? It might mean something. Once, when the Viscount of Lien had died, his youngest son had carried his father's crest to a neighboring viscount—a signal that the father wished the younger son to inherit, and the viscount to engage in battle against the rightful heir.

Would Elise de Bois be involved in some such similar scheme?

She smiled at him, and her smile was both beautiful and bitter, sweetness and poison.

"If I am a mystery, Stede, it is a mystery that you will never unravel. If I am a temperamental vixen, keep clear of me. For I do despise you—and I despise all snakes and rats!" Her tone was rising at an alarming rate. His voice alone made her furious, and his words also touched off a new shaft of fear; he still wanted to know why she had taken the ring. Why she had lied . . .

Percy, she thought bitterly, was already lost. But she still had Montoui. And she would never chance losing it, just as she would never give Stede, of all men, the satisfaction of knowing the truth. She had lost far too much in her quest to give away her secret.

Would he never leave her be? How dare he stand before her, still issuing demands! Her hatred rose to a dizzying level; it drove her determination to be regal and calm completely from her mind, and she raised the poker against him, snarling, "Damn you, Stede!"

A sudden step brought him before her; she thought he intended to break her arm as he wrenched the poker from her. She was too startled by his swift movement to cry out, and then too unnerved by his touch. His eyes bore into hers as the poker fell and he jerked her close to him.

"Nay, damn you, Duchess!"

She felt the towering length of him against her like hot steel, and the instinct to fight was stronger than that to cry out for help.

"Stede, I promise you that you will bring about your own downfall! I will see you—"

"Tell me the truth of the matter!" he thundered in abrupt interruption. "Cease the tricks and lies and we can come to peace over the episode!"

"I will never tell you anything, Bryan Stede! You will let me go! This is my duchy . . . my castle! I am not at your mercy, and never will be again! Let go of me! I loathe you—"

She broke off sharply as his hold on her suddenly loosened. His bronzed features took on a ghastly gray color and he doubled over, clutching his stomach. To her amazement, he fell to the floor with a thunderous clash of chain mail and stone.

"Stede?" she inquired curiously, keeping her distance, but kneeling down beside him.

His head tilted toward her and she saw that his eyes were laced with agony; his features remained gray and twisted into a mask of intense pain. He whispered and she came near him to hear his words.

"If I live—"

"What is it?" she cried out, stunned. He couldn't be acting. No one could feign such a crippling torture.

She was unprepared as his trembling hand shot out, ripping away her headdress and lacing into her hair. She cried out as his vise grip brought her sprawling to the floor beside him.

"Murderous bitch!"

"What? I did nothing—"

"Twice . . . now. You tried . . . to stab me. Now . . . poison. God help me, if I live . . . you will pay . . ."

His eyes closed, glazing over. The grip upon her hair slowly relaxed. Stunned, Elise pulled away from him in desperate confusion. Was he really dead? It was what she had wanted, wasn't it? No! Not like this! She was not a murderess; she would never resort to poison . . .

It was strange to see him sprawled upon the cold stone of the castle floor, his great length and muscled breadth of shoulders rendered powerless. His body shook with a sudden convulsion and she stood, ready to tear for the door and call for Marshal.

She had not gone a step when she was jerked back by the hem of her gown. Again she found herself sprawling over his body. His eyes were open again, yet they were covered with a deathly glaze. "I will live . . . live to see . . . unholy bitch! I thought you would fight face . . . to face . . . I will . . . flay you within an inch of . . . life . . ."

"I did nothing to you!" Elise railed.

His eyes closed, but his hand was still clutched into a fist, tearing at the beautiful blue silk of her tunic. He appeared to be dying, and yet he used his strength to hold her. She felt the fire of him exuding into her, the muscles that crushed against her beneath the cruel bite of his mail. His lashes raised slowly and for a moment his eyes focused clearly upon her.

"Bitch . . . I will . . ."

His hold fell. She was free.

Elise scrambled to her feet, screaming. A moment later Marshal, Geoffrey, and two of her own guards were rushing into the room. Marshal was on his knees beside Bryan Stede, and Geoffrey was giving orders that a physician was to be found and brought immediately.

Elise felt as if she were in a dream as the physician arrived, gravely examined Bryan Stede, and asked if there were a chamber where he might be taken. She heard herself speak, saying that he might be brought up to the chamber adjoining hers, the room where she had slept as a child. It was not a vast chamber, but the bed in it was large and well aired; the windows also faced the east and brought in cool breezes. Family and special guests were usually offered the room, so she knew that the linens would be clean and fresh, and that the trunks within the chamber would offer extra towels and bedding should they be needed. The wardrobe might even carry some of her father's old nightgowns and short Norman tunics.

Will and Geoffrey carried him together with great but tender effort, and Elise could not pretend she did not witness the pain and anxiety in their features. *I did not poison him!* she wanted to cry out—but as yet, she had not been accused by them.

The physician ordered that a brew of curdling milk, moss, and a number of herbs be prepared. Elise was numb as she oversaw the execution of the foul-smelling concoction.

Hadn't she wanted this? she asked herself over and over. Hadn't she just told him how she longed to see him dead?

But not like this! She was not a coward, nor was she a murderess. And now . . . This would hang over her head like a cloud of the most degrading suspicion . . .

Elise carried the vile brew up the stairs herself; she was greeted at the chamber door by a worried Marshal. "Stay out, Elise, this is not pleasant. And the physician tells me that this"—he tapped the chalice with the curdled-milk mixture—"is to see that his insides are cleaned."

"Will—"

"We stopped at a farmhouse on the way here," Will said absently, more to himself than to Elise. "The physician says it is highly possible that rotten meat might have caused this."

Rotten meat! So at least Will did not suspect her of murder—yet. Dear God! She didn't even know what she felt anymore. She hated Stede—surely she hated him! But she couldn't wish such a death on him . . .

Yet if he lived . . . would he accuse her openly? He had held to his strength long enough to threaten her direly . . .

Tense and bewildered, Elise wandered back down the stairs. She sat, oblivious to time, as the men remained in the chamber above. At long last, Geoffrey Fitzroy came down the stairway and sank into a chair near hers.

"Geoffrey?"

He smiled at her gently. "He will live."

Elise did not know whether to feel relief or panic. "Thank God," she said softly, sure that Geoffrey would expect such a comment.

His eyes were on her with a tender bemusement and she flushed uneasily. "Shall I order something for you, Geoffrey? Are you hungry? I haven't paid any attention to the time—"

"Nay, Elise, I am not hungry." Geoffrey grimaced. "The physician gave Bryan that obnoxious brew in order to force him to be sick, and take the poison from his system. I shan't be hungry for a while."

"Oh," Elise murmured.

"You must see to your packing, Elise. Remember, our loyalty is to our new king now. Eleanor languishes in prison, and it will be a long journey of rough riding to free her quickly! A week through the Continent, perhaps, and days through the English countryside. At least."

"How can we leave now?"

Geoffrey chuckled. "Stede is a man of steel, dear Elise. A night's rest, and he shall be ready to go. Already he is swearing at the poor physician for the wretched sickness which has cured him!"

Elise managed a weak smile, but she could find little amusement at the thought. She could well imagine Bryan Stede swearing his head off, and the picture was not a pleasant one.

Geoffrey laughed, then hesitated a moment and Elise watched him, thinking that she liked him very much. His hair was graying, his features were weathered, and he was not yet forty; still there was a lot of Henry in this son. And more. Geoffrey possessed a gentle wisdom born of a precarious position in life; he was steadfast, honest, and loyal.

"Will you be pleased to be a companion to Eleanor in the days ahead?"

"Nothing could please me more," Elise replied softly.

Geoffrey drummed his fingers on the table, apparently idly. Then he spoke quietly once more. "Elise, I feel I should warn you of two things. I know that you are my sister, as does Richard."

She could not control the gasp that escaped her. She barely knew the Lion-Heart; she had seen him but once or twice. Geoffrey she had met several times in her father's company; they shared the taint of illegitimacy. She felt she could trust him, and she even felt that she could trust Richard. But if Richard and Geoffrey both knew, who else might? Not John—please, not John. Henry, who had loved him, hadn't trusted him. John Lackland, youngest of the legitimate Plantagenet brood . . . God had not created a man more conniving or selfish. If Prince John was in possession of this information, he could make her life a mockery . . .

Geoffrey reached across the table and drew his knuckles gently over her cheek. "Don't go so pale on me, sister. Richard is not such a monster, although I admit, he has shown me little courtesy. For all that I believe he did hound our father to his grave, he is not a man without honor. Look how he has seen to Henry's commitments with men like Stede and Marshal. Both men bested him, yet he shows them no rancor." Geoffrey paused. "Elise, I believe we were really sent here because Richard fully intends to keep your secret, and give you all his royal protection."

Elise lifted her hands, then dropped them. "If he keeps my secret, I will need no protection. Unless," she added softly, "John knows."

Geoffrey shook his head. "John, I'm certain, knows nothing. And I'm certain that he will not find out anything—from Richard, at least. Or me." He smiled.

Elise smiled slowly in return. "You know, Geoffrey, I think I like you a lot," she said. And she really did like this half brother of hers very much. She could remember how frequently he had traveled with Henry; the son who would receive so little in the way of rewards had always given Henry the greatest loyalty. She really didn't know him all that well; his visits with Henry had been sporadic. But she had seen him now and again all through her life, and so in a way, perhaps she did know him well. He could often be very quiet; he moved in the background, in the shadow of kings, and yet he watched and learned, and came to his own observations with intelligence and wit.

"I've a thing about blood," he said lightly. "Which brings me to my second warning."

"Oh?"

"Don't make an enemy of Bryan Stede."

"Why?" She hadn't meant to whisper; she had wanted to demand. "Surely," she added, giving strength to her voice, "the man has some scruples. He cannot call me out, and if he chose to wage a war—"

"Elise! Elise! Bryan Stede has many scruples! Too many. He was always willing to speak his mind to Henry; when he served Henry, he boldly defied Richard. You play games with a man you cannot best."

"What are you saying, Geoffrey? I did nothing to Stede." Did Geoffrey, too, believe that she would stoop to poisoning an enemy?

"I do not know what passed between you," Geoffrey said, "and I am accusing you of nothing. I am just warning you that he will seek until he finds that for which he searches. He suspects something about you, and not knowing what it is, he may well wonder that it isn't far worse than the truth. Perhaps you should tell him."

"Never! And why should I? He will marry Gwyneth and live far, far away from Montoui! He will be nowhere near me."

"Elise, you've a lot of Henry in you—too much, perhaps. I have seen your mind working like the gears that grind for a drawbridge. You've some kind of a grievance with the man, and you intend to harm him."

"I? What could I do?"

"The innocence is lovely, Elise, but I don't believe it."

"I despise the man, yet I swear to you, Geoffrey, I am glad that he did not die here today."

"Perhaps you should not be so glad," Geoffrey said, suddenly somber. "And believe me, I spent years learning from our father. It is possible to cripple a man—and never touch him—by the use of cunning and guile. You know exactly what I'm talking about. You always knew how to manipulate Henry—to your way of thinking. Bryan isn't Henry. I like him well, he is a friend of mine, a great friend. But he is tenacious, determined, and very strong, Elise, in mind and body. So whatever it is that has so inflamed your wrath, leave it be, Elise. Don't become his enemy."

"Why this warning, Geoffrey? Has Bryan Stede threatened something against me?"

"No."

"Then—?"

"I know you both; I felt the tension in the very air when you spoke earlier. From both of you, I could almost feel the sparks, like lightning. You are accustomed to command and having your way—so is he. I'm just warning you that he can be a very, very powerful adversary. I repeat, don't be his enemy.

Elise smiled sweetly and stood. "I'm not his enemy, Geoffrey," she lied blandly. "In fact, I shall go like a good duchess to see to his welfare."

"I wish I believed that."

She walked to the stairway, then turned back, pausing awkwardly for a moment.

"Geoffrey, I grew up virtually alone. I do not know how to say this, but I am glad to have you."

He smiled. "I could be your father, you know."

"But you're not. You're my brother, and I'm glad."

She hurried on up the stairs, blushing a bit at the sudden bond that had been drawn between them. Two royal bastards. Why not?

She rapped tentatively at the chamber door. It creaked open and Will Marshal greeted her. "He is much better, Elise."

Will's relief and pleasure were evident; Elise wished she could share the feeling. But at least she could be relieved that Stede had not accused her in front of others of attempted murder.

"May I see him?" she asked Will.

"Aye, and as you will be with him, I will join Geoffrey in a staunch cup of ale, if I might!"

"Of course, Will. As always, make my home your own. Call Michael; he will be glad to serve you."

"My thanks, Elise. Should he worsen again, the physician has gone to the kitchens."

Elise nodded. Marshal stepped past her and she nervously closed the door before approaching the bed.

They had stripped him of his armor and tunic. He lay upon his back, and though the covers had been drawn to his chest, the vast bronze strength of his shoulders was bare. His hair appeared as pitch against the white of the pillow; the clearcut severity of his features was enhanced by the softness of the bed.

She was almost afraid to approach him, but she did. His eyes had been closed; they flew open at her approach and his mouth formed into a hard line.

"Stede, I swear to you that I did not—"

"Cease with the lies! You will not hang, nor will your head lie upon the axman's block. I do not involve others in a petty battle with a woman."

"The devil take you, Stede!" Elise flared instantly. "I will never hang—Richard will not allow it. I tell you this only because it is true—"

"I don't believe you know how to speak the truth, Duchess. You so imbue facts with lies that you have no credibility. And Richard has no fondness for women; you needn't believe that he lives by chivalry alone."

"I am not—"

"Spare me!" He winced as he struggled to sit within the bed.

She would have been tempted to help him, except that even now, she didn't trust him if he could reach her. He looked angry enough to strangle her if he could just wind his fingers around her neck.

"I do not share Richard's complete contempt for your 'tender' sex," he continued, "but you are one woman I would gladly beat black and blue."

"You wouldn't dare touch me now—"

"Wouldn't I? Don't ever count on such a thing, milady Duchess!"

He was tired; weary and drawn with illness. His eyes were heavy-lidded as they fell upon her, yet she did not doubt the validity of his words for a moment. If anything, he seemed to offer his greatest danger when he was the quietest.

She threw up her arms and spun about in disgust. "You are not only a despicable bastard, Stede—you are a *stupid, despicable* bastard! I did not poison you!"

"Lady, you are a murderess at heart!"

"You, Stede, are a fool."

"Whatever . . . I am willing to let this drop. But keep clear of me, Duchess. For should you come too close, I may remember that you attempted to kill me twice."

"Pity I didn't succeed."

"Yes, isn't it?"

"May I remind you, Stede, that this is my castle?"

"Remind me of whatever you like. But no more tricks."

Elise would wonder later why she always lost control with him; now, she gave herself no time for thought. She flew back across the room like a wildcat and threw a searing cuff against his cheek. "You son-of-a-bitch! You assaulted and raped me and now tell me to stay away from you! I wish I had poisoned you! I would have done a thorough job of it and—"

He didn't get sick like normal men. Although his complexion was gray and strained, his grip was as sure as iron as he caught her arm and staggered from the bed to drag her close. He was naked, she thought dismally as she found herself grating her teeth as he crushed her irrevocably to his person. And she was trembling despite herself, hauntingly aware of his warmth and sinewed masculinity . . .

"You arrogant little bitch! Maybe it is time that you learned a lesson about playing games with men—"

"As God is my witness, Stede, I will scream!" Elise hissed.

She would have to, she thought, watching his face. The anger that flashed dark fire from his eyes was such that she thought he could readily snap her like a twig.

"You think to attack like a man, then scream like a woman."

"I have learned all the lessons I care to from you, Stede. And I will gladly use in combat whatever weapons are at my disposal."

He laughed suddenly, dryly, bitterly, and threw her none too gently from him before wincing, then hobbling back to the bed, with no thought of modesty.

"So we are engaged in combat, Duchess? I will remember that. And I will use whatever weapons are at my disposal, too, milady."

"And what is that supposed to mean?"

He turned his face wearily into his pillow and spoke harshly. "It means, Elise, that you have chosen battle. And you have set the rules; there are none. No code of honor or of chivalry. All is fair. And it means . . . that if you are not out of this chamber by the time I finish speaking, I will forget that this is your castle, and that you are a duchess, and remember only that you have tried to murder me—twice. Now, perhaps I am not prepared to do murder myself—yet—but I will gladly see that your tender flesh receives a good deal of pain by my hand and I will not care if you flood the duchy with your screams while I assure myself that you shall share my discomfort and pain."

"Bastard!" Elise hissed, deciding that an exit at this time might be the wisest move.

"Take care that you do not say the words so many times that you find yourself bearing one. Or would the noble Percy care, or even know, since you seem to be a mistress of deceit?"

Despite her respect for his strength, she found her feet carrying her toward him once again.

He spun about on the bed, eyes narrowed warningly.

"Elise! Have you never learned the art of retreat? I will give you no more warnings!"

She clenched her fists at her sides and forced herself to remain still.

"Enjoy the hospitality of the castle, Stede," she said coolly. And she spun gracefully about, exiting with all the dignity she could muster.

Once outside, she leaned heavily against the door.

She was quaking miserably, inside and out.

Composure! Why couldn't she maintain any around him? It was her only chance against him, and somehow, she had to win. Had to see that he was stripped of all that he desired.

He had taken it all from her. The dream, the illusion of love, and a life of beauty—all were as shattered as her innocence.

And now . . .

Now he was even convinced that she was a murderess.

Not a murderess, Stede, but a thief, yes. For I will keep my distance from you, but I will rob you as you have robbed me.

With that forceful thought in mind, she squared her shoulders and hurried to her own chamber, calling for Jeanne to help her pack.

PART II

"LONG LIVE THE KING!"

X

Henry's corpse was carried in state from the castle of Chinon, and through the narrow streets of the town. Across the bridge of the Vienne, sparkling peacefully beneath the sun. Through the forest, green and quiet, and at last to the abbey of Fontevrault. Bishop Bartholomew of Tours read the holy rites of burial beneath the high-domed roof of the granite abbey. The air was cool and fresh; Henry was at peace at last.

Richard was in attendance, as was Geoffrey Fitzroy. There was still no sign of Prince John Lackland.

Hiding from Richard's wrath, having heard that his brother was rewarding none of the traitors who had joined his ranks from his father's side, Bryan thought dryly as he watched the ceremony from his place beside Marshal. *Pity that his cunning doesn't extend to the knowledge that Richard will protect him as he might an errant schoolboy.*

But John Lackland was not his major concern at the moment—nor, to be honest, was Henry or the burial.

His eyes continued to fall upon Elise de Bois. Upon her knees on the abbey floor, she gave the appearance of the sweetest of saints. She wore white: a gown of shimmering silk, trimmed with white ermine. Beneath a gossamer headdress, her great wealth of hair spilled down her back like the rich and radiant burst of a sunrise. It was impossible not to be mesmerized by that hair, not to feel one's fingers itching to reach out and touch it, as a child would long to reach out for a sweetmeat.

Especially when one had a memory of it that had little to do with the mind, and everything to do with the senses. He had seen her clothed in nothing but that hair; he had felt its silky softness caress the rough contours of his own body.

She raised her head, and a stabbing sensation rippled through his body. Silent tears dampened her cheeks; her delicate features were drawn with pain. There was no denying that she had sincerely cared very deeply for Henry.

With her chin lifted, her hands clasped before her in prayer, she was indeed a glorious silhouette: slender, swanlike throat, lovely, delicate profile, high breasts, and a trim, graceful figure. The silk of her gown seemed to float about her. She might well have been an angel—had he not known she was far more a creature of hell than of heaven.

He tensed suddenly, grinding his teeth together as a cramp twisted its way through his abdomen. The day had been pure torture, with the aftereffects of the poison still in his system. With the renewed pain came renewed anger. It had shocked him that she could hate him so deeply as to poison him. And he knew he had been poisoned. Through the wine.

He had spoken of his knowledge to only one other; Marshal and the others believed that rotten meat had made him ill. But in his years of service he had, more often than he liked to remember, been the victim of bad food. This had been different. This had been a poison carefully administered . . . by Elise de Bois.

It made his fascination with her all the more galling. She was poison herself. Secretive, furtive—living out a major deception. He had wanted to see her again; now he wanted nothing more than to forget her. When he was near her, a part of him wanted to strangle her. Another part of him wanted to strip away her silk and fur and all vestiges of the world of nobility and chivalry and drag her into a bed of raw earth.

It was not the pain in his gut that caused him to clench his teeth a second time. It was the gnawing desire to know her again, and then sweep away her memory.

She despised him enough to kill him. He owed her nothing. Within two weeks, even barring bad weather, they would reach Eleanor; Elise would no longer be his concern. Shortly after that, Richard would have attended to all his affairs in his European holdings and he would arrive in London for his coronation.

As his duly crowned monarch, Richard would then settle with Bryan for all past services as promised.

There would be Gwyneth for a bride, and all her vast wealth and titles. Hard won, but prizes well worth winning for a man who craved land—and a home.

The monks finished a chant; Richard, Coeur de Lion spun about and exited the abbey. Bryan and Will Marshal exchanged dry glances and followed Richard from the abbey.

The sun was gleaming down upon his head, brilliantly enhancing the Plantagenet gold and copper of his thick crop of hair. He halted suddenly, causing his mantle to swing about him majestically as he spun about to encounter Bryan and Will.

"I trust you're ready to journey onward?"

"Aye, Your Grace," Will replied blandly.

"Hurry to my mother! She will act as my regent, and in my name she will have the power to release other prisoners—men held not for malicious crimes, but by the whim of Henry, or his administrators. That will set my reign off with a benign touch, don't you agree?"

"Aye," Bryan agreed. "A powerful man may well grant mercy."

Richard nodded, pleased with himself, pleased with Bryan's reply. "And while you travel with Eleanor, I give you something grave to think upon."

"What is that, Your Grace?" Bryan inquired curiously.

Richard slammed a fist into his palm. "Money! My good fellows! My father's and my battles have emptied England's coffers. I owe Philip of France the twenty thousand marks my father owed him—and I will need much, much more to raise an army and take it to the Holy Land." Richard paused, looking up and squinting at the noonday sun. From somewhere, a sparrow was chirping out a song. "I was but a lad when I heard that Saladin had taken Jerusalem with his army of infidels. I have dreamed since of a holy quest. And now, to fulfill my father's vows, I will set forth on that quest. But I will need money to do so!"

"We'll think about coinage, Richard," Bryan promised dryly.

"Think on it well, and remember—I would gladly sell London if I had but a buyer! I will raise the funds for my Holy Crusade!"

Marshal and Bryan glanced at each other, then nodded.

"And take care of the Lady Elise. I entrust her safety entirely to you. Remember that."

Startled, Bryan glanced into Richard's eyes. He had assumed at first that Richard was sending Elise de Bois to Eleanor on little more than whim; now he saw that even the Lion-Heart seemed to have a soft spot for the girl.

It was vastly irritating.

"We will protect her to the best of our abilities," Bryan replied blandly. "Yet, perhaps she should not accompany us. Marshal and I travel with but five other knights; there may be dangers along the way—"

"What dangers?" Richard interrupted impatiently. "We begin an era of peace. And I send her with the two most experienced knights in Christendom. She will be safe. Now, leave me. By God's grace, we shall meet shortly for my coronation!"

They were ready to leave Fontevrault. Their destriers were saddled; the horses were laden with supplies. A day's ride would take them to the Channel. With any luck, a few days' travel would bring them to England's shore, and a few more days would bring them to Eleanor.

Bryan and Marshal started for the horses, where the accompanying knights awaited them. Bryan halted with a sudden frown.

"How does the duchess travel? I see no form of conveyance—"

Will laughed. "She rides as we do."

"It is a distance we travel—"

"Don't worry, my friend. She rides as well as any man."

Bryan shrugged and mounted his own horse, so recently retrieved from the stalls at Montoui. "Where is she?"

"Taking her leave of Richard."

Bryan frowned as he glanced around to see that Richard was offering Elise his own mantle to cover her gown. It engulfed her, and something about the pretty scene was annoying. He glanced down at Will. "She rides with no lady's maid?"

"She is not alone. Joanna, wife of Sir Theo Baldwin, accompanies us, too." Will shrugged. "She is accustomed to following her husband about in battle, and neither woman should hinder our speed."

Women were always a hindrance in travel, Bryan thought, but he said nothing. He knew the Lady Joanna; she was a spirited, gray-haired matron, blunt and honest, and he liked her well. Better she than a simpering young maid, unaccustomed to the rigors of a hard ride.

"I leave the ladies to you, then, my friend," Bryan told Marshal, and Marshal laughed.

Bryan nudged his horse to the fore of the party, and raised an arm to Richard. Richard raised his hand high in return. Bryan noticed vaguely that Will helped Elise up onto her Arabian mare. He started out, setting the pace, a rugged one.

It was a beautiful day to travel, Bryan thought vaguely as he rode. It was full summer; the Angevin hills were lush with greenery, birds sang all around them, and wildflowers grew in profusion. The sun was hot, but the breeze was cool. They stayed upon the main roads, for Bryan had the journey planned. It was possible to reach the crossing near Eu in three days; with the women, it might well have taken seven. Bryan had determined that they would spend no more than four days on the Continent. They would bypass Richard's castles along the way—that at Le Mans, where Henry had been born, and certainly that at Rouen. They were not on a journey to be

entertained and pampered as Richard's messengers; they were
on a mission of urgency. Tonight they would seek simple shelter with the monks at the Abbey of St. John the Martyr, south
of La Ferté-Bernard.

Elise was silent as she rode; their speed was not conducive
to conversation, but had it been, she would still have chosen
quiet. She could not help notice the beauty of the summer day:
the deep grasses that grew over the sloping hills, the fervent
hunter's green of the forests. This was the heart of Henry's
lands; his Angevin domains. This was a beauty Henry had long
cherished. Henry was dead; his eyes were forever closed to the
beauty.

As the long hours passed, Elise sighed slightly and shuddered,
and a growing thirst drew her mind from grief. Mile after mile
they rode; Stede did not stop. Her throat was parched and she
ached from the hours in the atrociously uncomfortable sidesaddle. Misery made her think of Bryan, and thinking of him made
her ever more miserable. To stave her mind from both grief and
discomfort, she allowed herself to give free reign to revenge,
and she mulled over many a conversation in her mind in which
she found the right words to convince Eleanor of Aquitaine that
she must not allow Richard to reward Bryan Stede.

When the sun began to fall and her mare's steps started to
falter, Elise grew more and more annoyed with Bryan. Will,
perhaps sensing her thoughts, came up beside her.

"It will not be long," he promised. She tried to smile.

By dusk, they were still many miles away from their desti-
nation. Marshal rode forward to join Bryan. "Perhaps we should
stop and make other plans for the night," he suggested.

Bryan shook his head. "It isn't that much farther, Will."

Will shrugged. "Nay, but the terrain is rough for riding in
darkness."

Bryan glanced at Will. "Have we complaints?"

"No . . ."

"Then we will ride."

Elise was ready to fall out of her saddle by the time they

reached the Abbey of St. John the Martyr. Dear God! How could
a man ride so hard without thought or care for thirst or comfort?
But as they clattered into the abbey yard, Elise found Bryan
Stede's implacable gaze upon her, and she determined that she
would show no signs of exhaustion—or weakness. She met his
eyes coolly, then laughed radiantly at something Will Marshal
said—she didn't know what—as he came to help her from her
horse.

Henry, Elise quickly discovered, had been a patron to these
monks. Bryan knew the abbot well—it seemed, in fact, that they
were good friends. They were greeted warmly, applauded when
it was learned that they were to free the queen, and welcomed
for the night's rest. The abbey was small, but the summer harvest had been rich, and they were well fed with grapes and
greens, trout and river eel.

Throughout the meal, Elise occasionally felt Bryan's eyes
upon her. She ignored him and ate as one famished, which she
was.

The Lady Joanna was a pleasant enough companion; she reminded Elise of Jeanne. She was decades older than Elise, and
seemed not at all discouraged by the speed and conditions of
their journey, and so Elise decided that she could not be so very
tired.

But despite the hardness of her bed in the small, stark room
that she and Joanna were given to share, Elise slept almost instantly.

Dawn came with a shrill of birds, and a harsh rap upon the
door to the tiny cell-like room. Elise rubbed her eyes furiously,
and realized that the Lady Joanna was no longer sleeping in the
room.

The door was flung open without her having given a reply.
She instinctively drew the covers over her linen shift; Stede
stood there. He barely glanced at her. "Up, Elise, we ride soon,"
he said simply. Then the door was shut again with a sharp thud.

"Ride where you like!" she muttered beneath her breath,
longing to throw something after him.

But just then the Lady Joanna reappeared, bustling with energy, her cheery smile in place upon her plump cheeks. "There's boiled eggs and kidneys on the table, dear, and just beyond our window is the most delightful trickle of a stream! Hurry now, dear, for we must be off."

Elise smiled wanly and forced herself to crawl from the bed with a pretense of vigor. She rushed to the window. "A stream?" she queried.

"Right there. See?"

She did see. It was a narrow, babbling brook, leading to a lake beyond the abbey. Elise hesitated only a second, then leaped to the stonework window frame and smiled back at the Lady Joanna. "I'll be just a moment!"

Lady Joanna did not chastise her for crawling through the window in nothing but her shift. She laughed. "Aye, that I were young again! But, hurry, dear, lest a monk should come along! They're not all saints, you know."

Elise nodded, then hurried out.

It was barely dawn, but the sun was promising a sweet and wonderful warmth. Elise ran to the brook and hurtled her length against the rich grass on its bank, dipping her hands into the clear water, and joyously splashing it over her face. It was cold, but it felt wonderful. She dipped into it again and again, drinking deeply, splashing her face again and again. She was halfway drenched, she realized ruefully. The bracing water made her feel very alive—refreshed, young, eager—and strong. Whatever Stede could dole out, she could take. And she would think of some way to convince Eleanor in a charming way that Stede deserved nothing. *Nothing!*

With the cheerful thought in mind that she would prevail, she at last rose regretfully to her knees, then to her feet. She turned to run and sneak back in through her window, but when she would have moved, she froze instead.

He was there, between her and the window—watching her, and apparently not at all pleased to be doing so. His eyes met hers, traveled slowly to her feet, then rose upward again with no sign of emotion. "We are ready to leave," he told her. "You hold back the entire party—and you cast yourself into ridiculous danger."

"Danger—" she echoed.

He strode to her with air of annoyance, causing her to gasp as he clutched the fabric of her shift at the valley of her breasts. "You might as well be walking around naked!" he accused her. "And since your virtue is next to godliness . . ."

She could feel his fingers against her flesh; they brought a flush to her cheeks and an oath of fury to her lips.

"Let me go!" she told him, wrenching past him. Over her shoulder she added, "I did not expect to find a leering knight at my heels!"

He caught up to her, spinning her back around to face him. "You must learn that things are not always what you expect— Duchess. You will not wander around so again."

She said nothing, but lifted her chin to him. He released her with a little shove. "Get dressed—and get to the courtyard. Quickly."

On this, she did not disobey him, for she did not want to cause a delay in their journey. But she missed her meal in her haste, and as the morning passed, she was certain that her stomach growled audibly. She rode in misery once again, and more. Where he had touched her, her flesh continued to feel a heat. And her body, off and on, felt chills, and then a shuddering heat. All the more she determined that he would not lead life as he planned, with his arrogance rewarded. She would see that he was brought low.

Bryan rode with his sense of brooding tension increasing with the storm clouds that more and more covered the sky. He could not forget the sight of her, or the sound of her laughter when she had thought herself unobserved. He had been angry that she played with their time; more so because she had not realized that most men—even those promised to God—could be dangerous if provoked.

And, by God, she had been provocative! Hair spilling and

spilling about her like a red-gold extension of the sun, her shift so damp against her body that the firm roundness of her breasts had been clearly defined down to the deep and dusky rose of their peaks . . .

She is a curse upon me, he groaned in silence. *She despises me; my future lies elsewhere, yet she plagues my mind and body hour after hour.* She haunted him, possessed him . . .

The sky suddenly broke loose. Rain poured down upon them. They had reached the mountains, the roads were treacherous, and it seemed to Bryan that they crept along in sheer, chilling misery. But they could not halt, not for a summer rain. They had to keep their travel swift.

That night their accommodations were poor. They slept in a hunting lodge, all before one fire. Their meal had been tough fowl.

Another day of rain met them, another night at an abbey where they were able to bathe, and enjoy a fair meal once more. But the next morning held true to the sun, and by that night they neared Eu.

They came to a small village just south of Eu and near the port where several ferries crossed the Channel. Bryan decided they might as well stay the night. From the briskness of the air, it seemed that the rain would come soon. Tomorrow they would be ready to take to the sea.

Marshal rode to meet him at the front of the line. "There is a lodge here where I've stayed many a time. They've a room suitable for Elise and Joanna. We can sleep in the main room."

Bryan nodded his assent. "I know the place; I had it in mind myself." He called out the order to the other men. He swore softly as he saw the five armored warriors—as well as Will—stumble over one another to assist Elise de Bois.

Well, he would have no more of her. Let her poison another man's wine.

Dismounting from his horse, he threw the reins to a street urchin, telling the boy that all the horses were to be stabled.

Then, ignoring the hospitality of the tavern, he tossed his mantle over his shoulder and walked toward the sea.

He did not know how long he stared across the Channel, allowing himself to dream that he would, indeed, come to have a place to call home, when a scrape upon the earth alerted him to the fact that someone approached. Spinning about, he saw Marshal—equipped with a large skin of ale.

Bryan smiled broadly as he accepted the skin and drank thirstily. "Thanks, Will. The thought—and the ale—is well appreciated."

"Thought they might be. What have you been doing out here?"

Bryan laughed dryly. "Dreaming."

"Hmm. I've been wondering about my own fortune through the day."

"Nothing to wonder about, Will. You will shortly be Earl of Pembroke. Lord of Leinster—and God knows what else!"

"I know so little of women. I have heard that Isabel de Clare is very young, and very beautiful. I wonder how she will accept a battle-scarred and war-weary knight."

"She will shortly know you for the man you are, and that is all that you will need," Bryan advised. "Treat her as you do our fair duchess, and she will surely consider you gallant."

In the darkness of the night, Bryan felt Will's eyes suddenly sharp upon him. Had he spoken with unintended bitterness?

"Why the words of sarcasm, Bryan?"

"Was I sarcastic? I didn't mean to be so."

"You are hard on her, Bryan. You should solve your differences, for you are both favorites with Richard."

He shrugged. "What difference does it make? We will part ways after the coronation."

Will hesitated. Bryan could not see his features clearly in the darkness. "When I am with you both, it is strange. It seems as if thunder fills the room with all its portents of a storm."

"That's not so strange. I think a horsewhip would do her a world of good."

Will chuckled. "Well, you needn't worry. Gwyneth will need no horsewhips; she is sweet and compliant!" Will yawned and stretched. "I'm turning in for the night. Are you coming?"

"Soon. I like to watch the sea. It appears as if we'll have rain again tomorrow."

"A rough crossing."

"But we must make haste."

"Good night."

"Good night."

Will began the trudge from the shore toward the village, and Bryan wondered why he was still staring out at the misted sea. Something was rankling him. When Will had spoken of Gwyneth, he had experienced a strange foreboding. He had tried, when Henry lay dying and his future had loomed so dubiously before him, not to dream. Not to believe that he and Gwyneth might sanctify their relationship with marriage.

That he would not own vast lands within Cornwall, along the Dover coast. That he would not become the Earl of Wiltshire, and the Lord of Glyph County.

Now . . . it was all within his reach.

Yet, there was that foreboding.

Foolish, man! he told himself. Yet dreamers were fools, and having had none of his own, he could not stop himself from dreaming now of lands. Great wealth, gotten not through some ugly old hag, but through Gwyneth . . .

It was annoying not to be able to picture her clearly. Light, turquoise eyes kept replacing her. Hair like the sun, rather than like the night—

"Help! Oh! Helpppppppp . . ."

The sudden scream that pierced the darkness startled him and froze him to immobility, then sent him spinning and tearing toward the village. Halfway there, he paused, listening. Then he heard the scream again, coming from a dense thicket of seaside foliage.

He knew the sound of the voice. He had heard it railing against him often enough.

Crashing through the brush, he came upon her. She was furiously battling two assailants: one a youth, the other an older man. Both wore the tattered look of the poor. The older man was toothless; the boy carried a scar across his sullen, sharp-eyed face.

As Bryan came into the clearing, Elise kicked her way free from the boy, but the man awaited her, brandishing a rusted knife.

"Don't fight it, milady. We'll just ha' a bit o' sport and take our leave with a bit o' yer finery! Be nice like, now, ye hear, and ye'll not get hurt. I'd hate to slash up such fine flesh—"

Bryan stepped forward. "Touch her, and you'll die. She's a ward of Richard, Duke of Normandy, Aquitaine—and soon to be crowned King of England."

The boy started and stared at Bryan, focusing first upon his chest, then raising his eyes slowly. He had to realize that he was facing a knight in full health, full strength, and full armor. Yet he didn't seem to have any sense. "One o' him!" the boy cried out. "And two o' us, Tad!"

The older man laughed and made some sign to the boy. Bryan's eyes followed to the boy. Then the older man rushed him, brandishing the rusted knife upward toward his throat.

Bryan had little choice but to draw his sword hastily and slay the man before the rusted knife could slice his own flesh.

"Holy Mother! The devil himself!" the boy gasped out, backing up. "I'll not touch her. I'll run, I'll run . . ."

He was already running as Bryan dismissed him and furiously approached Elise.

She was gripping the torn mantle about her, yet as Bryan came near, she gazed at him with horror.

"You killed him!" she cried out, and yet it was, in her heart, as much with guilt as with accusation. If she hadn't felt so desperately that she needed fresh air, none of this would have happened. The man had been a thief; perhaps he had intended to kill her; still it pained her to know that his death lay at her feet.

"I'm sorry," Bryan rasped. "Should I have allowed him to slay me?"

"You didn't have to kill him! He is just old and poor!" she

exclaimed, determined that he would not know the true depth
of her feelings—or that she had known herself she was at fault.

He paused for several seconds, staring at her. His eyes glittered in the darkness.

"One should poison only knights who are young and in good
health. Is that it?"

"Believe what you like!" she snapped. Again, he was accusing her! Never would he believe that she had done him no physical harm. She stared down at the dead man, feeling ill. "This
was not necessary."

"No, it was not. I'm not fond of killing, Duchess. I have
done so—in battle. But murder is *your* game, not mine. What
are you doing out here? Your senseless behavior has caused me
to shed this blood!"

"Senseless behavior! I sought only fresh air—"

"Fresh air! You idiot! This man whose blood you cry over
intended to rape you."

Her face was bruised and smudged with dirt; her clothing,
the beautiful silk and the royal mantle, were ripped and muddied. Still she managed to draw herself to a regal stature and
her eyes caught a star fire and glittered their unique turquoise
as she faced him and spoke with dry sarcasm.

"It wouldn't be something that hadn't happened before."

"Wouldn't it? I think, Duchess, that you have still to see
just how ugly the world can be. Were it not for Richard, I
would be tempted to allow you your freedom to learn the true
meaning of the word." Bryan was surprised by the smooth
tenor of his voice. His anger was something that gnawed at
him, that heated and clawed his body, demanding that he act.
Somehow he controlled his temper. Somehow, he kept himself
from beating and strangling her—but just barely. He stepped
away from her just to make sure he wasn't tempted further to
do her bodily harm.

"Get back to the tavern. I will follow behind you. Richard
has asked us to assure your safety; therefore, I will. If you ever
need fresh air again, ask for an escort. If I ever find you alone

again, I will tie you hand and foot, and deposit you so before the queen. And don't, please don't, make the mistake of thinking that I threaten idly."

"I won't, Stede," she replied with no humility. "I will heed your warnings. I'd rather not be followed to Winchester by a trail of bloody corpses!"

She straightened her shoulders, drew the remains of the mantle about her, and strode regally past him.

His fingers itched to drag her back. His hands stretched toward her and knotted into fists.

He dropped them. When she turned back, his lips were curled into a grim and wicked smile.

The crossing was horrible. As many times as Bryan had sailed from the Normandy coast to the English shore, he couldn't remember a time when the sea had been more vicious.

The sky was a dead gray color, filled with dark clouds that churned and roiled and sporadically hurled cold sheets of rain upon them. Marshal had long since given way to nausea—as had the Lady Joanna and her husband—and spent the latter hours of the journey with his head bowed low over the rail. Bryan was sure that he would join his friend in his misery at any moment. Knights who could sever a head with no thought of distress were as sick as worm-ridden dogs.

Bryan hovered near Will Marshal, knowing he could do nothing to help, but hoping that his presence could lend sympathy, if nothing else. Will's knuckles were white against the railing, but he turned to Bryan with a grimace.

"You needn't watch over me, friend. This misery will, one way or another, come to an end. I'm an aging, battle-scarred knight. I'd rather you lend your support to the Lady Elise."

Bryan stiffened, his features hardening.

Will lifted a hand feebly in the wind. "She is my responsibility, yes. But if you offer me assistance as my friend, then I ask that you give that assistance to Elise."

Bryan shrugged. "As you wish, Will." Maybe the pitch and sway of the boat would have curbed her temper and softened her tone. He smiled grimly. It was not a kind thought, but he suddenly longed to see her laid low, stripped of pride and strength by the awesome power of the heavens and the sea.

Bryan stepped over a sprawled knight in search of Elise. He was quite certain that even the ferrymen felt the furor of the weather.

But not she . . .

She stood at the bow of the ship, tall and proud and straight, as if she greeted and embraced the tearing wind and the churning sea. Her eyes were brilliant, her cheeks were flushed with pleasure and excitement. She wore a woolen cloak, but she did not hug it about herself. The cowl was tossed back, her gold and copper hair flew and tossed with the wind, a part of it. Her lips were curled into a smile, her features, delicate as they were, tilted to the sky. Bryan thought with a shading of bitterness that she might have been an ancient priestess, a goddess of a cult, touched by dark magic.

His anger with her grew as he watched her. Had her skin paled, had her slender form been racked with agony, he could have felt empathy. He might have decided that it was a time to sue for peace between them.

Bryan sighed. There would never be peace between them. He refused to blame himself; she had lied to him with her every word. But he had taught her that her name and rank could mean nothing, and that she could be vulnerable to the whim of greater strength. It was a lesson for which she would never forgive him. For which, it seemed, she would even be willing to kill him.

And what difference did it make? he asked himself angrily. Yes, they would travel together with Eleanor while they awaited Richard's appearance, but then their paths would part. A marriage of wealth and power awaited him, and then the call of faraway ports and places. The Crusade awaited him. God's knights on their way to Christian battle under the banner of the Lion-Heart . . .

Bryan gritted his teeth. It would end soon. He had only to ignore her, to keep his distance politely.

But it still rankled him. Deeply. It was an irritation like a razor's edge to watch her stand tall, as if she absorbed the power of the maelstrom about her.

And it was a greater irritation to know that he wanted her still. No man with half a mind should want a woman who sought his life, no matter what her allure. Especially when he had a woman of sweet and gentle spirit awaiting him. But he did want Elise. He wanted to unravel the secret that lay behind it all. Maybe it was the secret that beguiled him so, that made her unique. Made his blood stir with raw desire each time he was near her, a desire that defied his own heart and mind. He wanted to hold and comfort her . . .

No! He longed only to break her body and soul, and keep her as a prized possession, under rein as his horse, polished and cared for as his sword and his armor.

Break her, and teach her that he was not a man who would tolerate her schemes, her treachery . . . her determination to see him laid low—or dead.

Perhaps then . . . then he could purge himself of her.

Leave it! Forget her, he warned himself.

Bryan turned on his heel to return to Marshal's side, a sharp oath escaping his tightened lips. England lay ahead. England, and the reign of Richard, Coeur de Lion.

Gwyneth . . .

Sweet and supple . . . and wealthy. Gwyneth would purge him of anger and dark desire . . .

The ship took an especially vicious twist within the sea. Bryan gripped the rail tightly, breathed deeply, and swallowed hard. One more lashing wave, and he would be every bit as sick as Marshal . . .

"Land, ho!" called out a sailor.

Land. England. The port of Minster. He would make it. He would make it . . .

Elise had never seen anything as intriguing as the English shore. Not so much the landscape—although she did love the hills with their rolling, grassy slopes, the harsh cliffs, and the forests that seemed to rise like sentinels in the background—but the people. They were everywhere! The port town was busy and bustling. Fishermen sold their yield, peasants hawked their produce, their hogs, their chickens, and every other imaginable ware. Balladeers strode leisurely along, clad in colorful rags, cheerfully grateful for any coin tossed their way.

For the most part, what Elise saw was poverty. The great manors were inland, and it was in these coastal towns where a new class was arising: the merchant class. Shops lined the streets. Shops where one could buy goods—at very dear prices—that came from all the provinces on the Continent. Sea power and the long centuries of the holy Crusades were bringing distant worlds together. Fine Oriental silks were available, Toledo steel, tableware wrought of silver and gold, brass candle sconces, and Persian rugs . . .

All for the peasants to see, the nobility to buy.

It was a strange world.

Elise found quickly that she was a curiosity herself. The people gaped with open amazement at their party: the armored knights upon their destriers; she in her finery. The town was abuzz with excitement from the moment they landed. And already the word was out; they had come to release the good Queen Eleanor from her years of bondage.

There were those, of course, who considered Eleanor a troublemaker and a foreigner. But to the majority of the people, she had long ago proved herself their queen. When she was young, her beauty had bewitched them. And now . . . now they remembered her dignity and her pride, her courage and her smile. She had loved England, and the people had known it. She had always been, in every aspect, a queen. The years could not tarnish or dim such a fact. The balladeers were singing of her, and even as the knights departed the ferry with their warhorses snorting from their time at sea, the people were calling out, "God save Richard, Coeur de Lion" "God bless Eleanor of Aquitaine! God bless our dowager queen!"

Elise smiled, because it was fun. Perhaps many of these people had sided against Richard when he fought their father, but the Lion-Heart was known throughout the Christian world and beyond for his great courage—and great heart. He was the uncontested heir to the throne. It seemed that they would welcome him heartily, with little encouragement needed.

The crowds waved to them and cheered as they moved through the town. Elise felt her heart go out to the women she saw. So many of them, not much older than she, were worn and drawn from the cares and labors of life. Children clung to their skirts, and even they looked worn and tired. They tried to touch her; tried to touch the silk and fur of her gown. Overcome with pity, Elise reached into her saddlebags and tossed coins to the throngs. The people did not scatter, but shouted even louder and thronged closer and closer, until the destriers and her own horse could barely move.

Suddenly she felt a wrenching grip upon her arm, and heard a shredding tear. Alarmed, Elise spun about to find that a bewhiskered old man had torn away the sleeve of her gown. His eyes were wild, and his grip was surprisingly fierce as he tried to drag her from the horse.

"No!" Elise shrieked out. "Please!"

" 'Tis silk! 'Tis silk!" the old man cried, and Elise realized with horror that he meant to take the clothing from her back.

The knights drew near, but insanity was breaking out. People no longer seemed to fear the huge hooves of the warhorses. Elise screamed, aware that she was about to slide from her horse. "No, please!" she cried again, catching at last the fevered eyes of the old man. For a minute shame filled his eyes, and Elise began to believe she had brought the situation under control.

She was never to know. At that moment, Bryan Stede came upon her. "Away!" he commanded the old man. He did not draw his sword, he did not attempt to strike any of the crowd, and yet they shrank away from him. Elise, too, wanted to shrink away. She knew that the indigo of his eyes could turn to the coal pits of hell; she knew him far too well. But at the moment, the fire and steel of his black-armored strength touched and terrified her even as it did the people.

"Fool!" He raged the one curt word to her, and then he had wrenched the reins from her hands. Her horse reared and bolted, and was next racing along behind his.

She heard a great thunder as the other knights broke into pounding gallops behind them. Tears stung her eyes as the wind whipped tendrils of her hair into them. But she was no longer frightened of Bryan Stede; she was furious. Was she always to find herself wrenched along by him? No, by God! She would never shrink or quail again, and he would learn that there were more ways to wield power than that of brute force!

It seemed forever, and yet she knew that it was only moments before they at last slowed their gait, then came to a halt. They had not left town, but they were at the far end of it, away from the pleasant, salt scent of the sea. A large, thatched-roof building stood before them, flanked by similar, wattle-and-daub structures. A weatherworn sign dangled from a wrought-iron pole; the sign proclaimed TAVERN.

The knights began to dismount as Bryan Stede issued orders. Where was Will Marshal? Elise wondered fleetingly.

Not where she needed him, she continued to muse bitterly as Stede approached and wrenched her ungraciously from the saddle. "We'll talk inside," he grated, his fingers banding around her arm. She was tempted to twist from him and dig long scratches into his cheeks with her fingernails, but she quickly thought better of the idea. He was not in a tolerant mood; she didn't think that even the witnesses about them could save her from his retaliation if he chose to strike in return.

Clinging to her pride, she accepted his hold and allowed him to escort her into the tavern. Where was the Lady Joanna? she wondered a little desperately. She would have kept Bryan's temper at bay.

It was a rough place. The main room consisted of little but a central fire and rows of hard-planked tables. Bryan left her warming her hands before the fire as he approached the tavern keeper, a hefty man wearing a large, grease-stained apron.

From the corner of her eye, Elise surveyed the other patrons of the establishment. Seafarers, they all appeared to be. Men with burned and leathered faces. But many of them wore a bright look of content within their eyes, and Elise smiled slightly. Yes, they should appear content. They had broken away from the lords and the lands that bound them to a life of continual labor; the sea, harsh mistress as she could be, was freeing them from lives of drudgery—on behalf of a self-serving overlord.

I am the nobility, she reminded herself. But she was a good ruler: just and merciful as Henry had taught her to be; kind as Marie and William de Bois had been. Montoui was a different province from most. Her people were well fed and well clothed. Yes, they worked for her, but they kept large portions of their crops; their labors were rewarded. Would it always be so? she wondered bitterly. As long as she lived. Once she had dreamed that she and Percy would raise their children with a sense of conscience. A deep pride in Montoui, but also a knowledge of the responsibility of all that pride should entail. But now . . .

Now, she would be alone. But she vowed then that as long as she lived, she would set the pattern for justice. She would always rule her tiny duchy wisely and well. Just as soon as . . . just as soon as this was over. This—her quest for vengeance.

For a moment, she felt a shiver inside of her, as if it touched her heart. She had been taught to be proud, but never spiteful or vengeful. She tried to tell herself that it was strictly "justice" she wanted—but it was more. She had never known such anger in her life. Elise knew that the Plantagenets—and she was one of them by blood—often hurt themselves in their furious efforts to right a personal wrong. But she couldn't help her feelings; Stede deserved to lose everything he so coveted. No matter how she craved it otherwise, she could not change her feelings. Stede had not only cost her Percy; he had stripped her of all illusion. She had not had complete control of her destiny, and she didn't think she could ever believe in love again. All that remained for her to do was to cling to her rank and her wits, and seek the vengeance—or justice—that Stede deserved.

"Do you wish to create more trouble?"

The hiss was grating against her ear. She turned from the fire to stare at Stede, startled. He touched the torn sleeve of her gown, and she twisted farther to see that the men in the public lodging were staring at her with speculative smiles.

Without a word Elise returned Stede's gaze. He took her arm again and led her through the main room to an adjacent ground-floor chamber.

Elise wrinkled her nose with distaste. There was a foul stench of unwashed humanity within the room. There were no mattresses, just rushes and blankets that she feared were vermin-laden.

"It's all that he's got," Stede told her dryly. "Except, of course, for the public room, and I assure you, the damsels who generally seek a night's rest here would offend you even further."

Elise said nothing. She walked to the latticed window to breathe clean air.

Stede was silent for a moment. When he did speak, his tone was one he might well use against a dangerously naughty child.

"I know you to be many things, Elise. Willful, dishonest, cunning. Proud to a fault. Eager to draw blood. Yet I always believed it was my blood you were eager to draw. I have already told you; I have no taste for wanton killing. You might have caused a riot today. Aye, you were always safe, milady—you had an escort of armored and armed men. It was those poor people who would have lain butchered. A cutthroat I will gladly slay on your behalf. But not a peasant, longing for what God has granted you."

Elise whirled around. "I sought only to give—"

"Then you are a fool, for that is not the way to give. Had we not been with you, you would have been robbed of every stitch upon your back. Raped and probably murdered. You have a penchant for putting yourself into such a position."

"Have I?" Elise inquired imperiously. "Then it is a penchant just acquired recently. I will remind you of a few things, Sir Stede. You are but a landless knight. I am the Duchess of Montoui. I am your superior, Stede. You take orders from me. And as to my penchant for trouble . . . well, I say again, what possible difference can it make? I should rather be taken by ten filthy peasants than to feel even the brush of your fingers again."

"Is that so?" Stede inquired politely.

"Aye, Sir Stede, it is."

He bowed to her—an extravagant, courtly bow.

"Your superiority, milady, is a theory we must put to the test one day."

Elise smiled sweetly. "I'm afraid that there will be no chance to do so, Stede. We will meet Eleanor, Richard will reach England, and we will part ways."

Stede smiled in return. It felt as if the chamber had been touched by a harsh winter frost. "Bear in mind, milady, that once Richard arrives, I shall be *your* superior."

"When you are wed to Gwyneth—and take on her titles?"

"Aye, when I am wed to Gwyneth."

Elise kept her sweet smile strained into her features. "The rewards you expect are still 'theory,' are they not, Sir Stede? Perhaps another theory that must be put to a test."

"Is it?" Stede replied, mildly interested. "Perhaps 'tis true—the future is always that which must be seen." He turned around, his hand upon the door. "I shall have a meal brought to you. I don't intend to fight a battle over you during supper. Should you need, anything during the night, I shall be asleep before your door."

"I don't wish to have you before my door—"

He laughed, looking at her once more. "A change of heart, Duchess? Do you wish to have me inside your chamber?"

"My heart shall never change, Stede," Elise said with frigid determination. "And you forget, the Lady Joanna—"

"The Lady Joanna is traveling on to Southampton with her husband. She has been of little use as a chaperone, it seems. Her heart is too good. Since you prefer I not be inside, I shall sleep before the door. God knows, I find you quite worthless myself, but Richard seems to think you are of some value. Therefore, I shall deliver you safely to Eleanor."

He stepped outside the door, a tall and formidable figure in the armor he wore so easily.

The door closed sharply; Elise could have sworn that wood splintered with the force.

But the cold remained.

Who was he, Elise raged silently, to do this to her? No one! No one of title or land. He was just a warrior. A battle-weary knight. A configuration of muscle and brawn who could wield a sword or a lance with deadly expertise . . .

He had touched her, he had destroyed her . . .

By God, she would do the same to him. Now, he had even sent the Lady Joanna away, and Elise had become so accustomed to her cheerful company. She would miss her sorely. And he'd had the gall to call her "worthless"!

Worthless? Lord, how the word rankled . . . and hurt. To him, she had been nothing more than a thief, and a configuration of feminine angles and curves. But he would learn. He would know that rank and wits could be every bit as powerful as steel and armor and brawn.

Elise wondered bleakly why she still wanted to sink to the floor and burst into tears. Maybe because he had been right. She had walked into danger. Last night. And again today. To Marshal, she could have admitted the error. Admitted she had a lot to learn. Begged pardon not for her wish to give, but for her lack of thoughtful judgment. To Marshal, yes—but not to Stede. Never to Stede.

She had never known an emotion as intense as that which she bore him. It was frightening.

But the die had been cast, and she felt she whirled in a maelstrom that was of her own making.

Like wind and fire, it roared out of control.

XI

July 15, 1189
The Palace at Winchester England

"Your Highness! They're here! Richard's messengers . . . they come for you!"

In an uncustomary gesture of emotion, Eleanor's jailer fell to his old knees before her. She smiled. She had seen the horses approaching the palace; she had seen the banners of Richard le Roi, Coeur de Lion. And at first sight of those banners, her heart had begun to fly.

She felt incredibly young for a woman of nigh on seventy years. Power, like a heated wine, had begun to warm her system. Joints that had ached moved with remarkable fluidity; her shoulders had squared, her spine . . . well, it had always been straight, but now . . . now it seemed actually to grow.

And why not? She was Eleanor of Aquitaine. Famed, notorious—but famed, nevertheless—the greatest heiress, lady, *queen* of her time. And she felt strong. The world was opening to her again. Her world. She had created the chivalry of the English court; she had been revered by poets from the East and the West . . .

And now . . . now she would reign as queen again. Not by marriage. But through Richard.

It was wonderful. She wanted to laugh and sing and cry out her joy to the heavens.

But she kept her smile small, her manner composed. Because she was Eleanor of Aquitaine.

"Do rise, dear sir," she told her jailer with quiet wit. "I'd not have you too crippled to allow my son's messenger's entry. And 'tis fairly certain they've had a long journey. Have we wine and food to offer?"

"Aye, Your Highness."

"Who comes?" Eleanor, with a grace that belied both her age and curiosity, turned toward the window once again. "Black armor . . . Stede! Richard has sent Bryan Stede. And I'd wager that Will Marshal is with him . . . Mother of God! How very considerate of Richard. I see that a woman rides with the knights!"

"If rumor holds true, Your Highness, the lady is Elise de Bois, Duchess of Montoui."

Eleanor's laughter was never loud or raucous; but now she did chuckle softly with pure delight. Her dearest son, Richard, eager for her happiness. He knew that she would long dearly to see the girl.

Her laughter ended with a soft sigh. There would be so much to do! The people must be rallied to Richard's cause, and then the nobles must be sorted and put into place for the new regime. Some punished, and some appeased. Some could ride the Lion's breath to fame and fortune.

And then there were the bastards. Geoffrey Fitzroy, Henry's natural son, had been raised in royal palaces along with her own; he had served Henry loyally as chancellor for years. She must not allow him to feel slighted; yet she must take care that he remembered his status as a bastard. And Elise . . .

Elise . . . a magnificent marriage, of course. In time. It was going to be fun to get reacquainted with the girl. She had been such a delightful child . . .

I am hungry for gossip, and hungry for life! Eleanor thought wryly. *Ah, yes, I am hungry to begin again . . .*

Queen of England. The title allowed her to play God to an extent, and Eleanor was far too much of a realist to consider such a thought as blasphemous. She would play God; she would be coercive and manipulative. She deserved to wield power far more than most people, because, if nothing else, her years had earned her a deep sense of responsibility, and the pain of her past had given her wisdom.

There was something about Eleanor of Aquitaine that kept one from seeing her as she really was, Elise mused curiously at first sight of the queen. In truth, she had aged. She was an old woman, slender to the point of gauntness. Her hair was graying, and her face betrayed her many years of both laughter and tears.

But when she moved, when she walked, when she smiled, and when she spoke, it was the age that became the illusion.

Eleanor was magnificent. Her presence filled the room. Her eyes were dark and yet brilliant and filled with vibrancy. She walked as if she floated on clouds, or sailed across a smooth sea. She had been imprisoned for sixteen years, but it appeared as if she had merely stepped from one stately court to another. She was so very regal, so very human, so perfectly lovely in speech and manner . . .

"Bryan! Will! How wonderfully gallant to see you upon your knees! But do get up. I am way too old to bend to kiss you, and I feel that I must!"

Elise, several paces behind the men, watched with a touch of rancor in her heart as Eleanor fondly embraced Bryan Stede, and then Will Marshal. It was as the queen gave Will a fervent hug that she glanced over his shoulder to see Elise. And then her beautiful smile, the smile that could strip away years, curled into her lips once more.

"Elise . . . ! Will, step aside so that I might see the child."

Grinning, Will did as he was told. Eleanor approached Elise and took both her hands in a strong grip. "How nice of you to come, Elise, and be with me now. It has been a long time since

I have had another woman with whom to converse!" Eleanor released Elise's hands and turned back to Bryan and Will.

"Now, tell me—how is Richard?"

"Hale and hearty," Will assured her immediately. "And handling his affairs quite admirably, yet it seemed his greatest urgency was to see you freed, Your Grace."

Eleanor nodded, pleased. "And Prince John?"

Bryan shrugged, but the motion was eloquent in itself. "Richard is looking for him now." He hesitated. "John disappeared after we were forced to flee from Le Mans."

Eleanor's gaze lowered momentarily. "For that I've great pity for Henry, God rest his soul. The place of his birth burned over his head; his favorite son turned traitor at the end. Marshal, how did Henry die?"

Marshal appeared uncomfortable. "In great misery, Your Grace. Illness, and an internal infection, overcame him. He could find no rest, you see. Had he been able to stop and nurse the ulcer, he might well have lived."

The queen's eyes were sad. "Believe me, messires, when I tell you I am sorry for the pain of his death, although his death frees me. Henry was a great man, greater than I believe history will record him. He cared for law and his people when it was not necessary to do so, but he brought about his own downfall. He tried to rob Richard of his lands so that he might bestow them on John. I don't think he ever realized that his sons had grown up—and were of his blood." She sighed. "So . . . he is looking for John. I hope he finds him quickly, and deals with him carefully. John has always coveted what was Richard's. And Richard, like Henry, when he holds power, can be overly generous with it." She shook her head gravely, but then she was smiling quickly again, and turning to Will. "I've heard you'll not be traveling with me now, Will Marshal. It is amazing, is it not, how words can so quickly fly? But it's my understanding that Henry promised you the hand of Isabel de Clare, and that Richard has upheld that promise. And you will go to claim her now."

Marshal laughed. "It seems that words do travel quickly. And it is true." His laughter faded, and his expression became slightly wistful. "Have you ever met the Lady Isabel, Your Highness?"

Eleanor chuckled softly. "She was but a toddling child when I was incarcerated. But—rumor again—she is young and lovely. And excessively rich. You'll find out soon enough. And if you would flatter me, William, call me by my given name when we are alone like this. Bryan never hesitates to do so!"

The queen's eyes fastened quickly upon Bryan Stede. "So you, Sir Stede, are to be my escort as we travel the countryside as Richard's entourage of goodwill!"

"A duty that is the greatest pleasure," Bryan replied graciously. "Richard has commanded that I stay with you until he arrives for his coronation, after which, in due time, he plans to join Philip of France for the Crusade planned by Philip and Henry right before his death."

"You are anxious for the Crusade?"

Bryan hesitated, then smiled. "I, like Richard, have been most eager to see you free."

Elise held back, keeping her silence. It was irritating beyond measure to see the queen's pleasure in him. *Don't be taken by this dark knight!* she wanted to cry out. *He is hard and ruthless and not at all what he seems . . .*

She did not cry out. Her time would come.

Servants came into the antechamber, carrying wine and trays filled with fresh breads, hard-boiled eggs, and a variety of cheeses. Whatever Eleanor had suffered in the past was to be rectified; her jailer had become her host. The servants scurried to please.

"I should so love to enjoy this repast in the garden!" Eleanor exclaimed softly. "Aged wine—and friendships that have become vintage through the years! Elise! Come walk with me. How tall you are, my dear! When last I saw you, I believe that you barely came to my knee." The queen, with the servants hurrying behind her, led the way out to the gardens, and to a wrought-iron table set between a trellis of roses—her delight with life apparent. She continued to chat, as if sixteen years of imprisonment had never taken place. A perfectly gracious hostess, she kindly waved the servants away and poured wine for them all. "Bryan, did you take the time to see Gwyneth?"

"Nay, Eleanor. We came straight to you."

"I'm flattered! But sorry that you shall be kept apart. 'Tis time you two took your vows."

Bryan laughed easily, which further annoyed Elise. "You must remember, Eleanor, that Henry promised me the lands and titles."

"I cannot believe that Richard would not honor his father's bequests!"

"Nay, I believe that he will." He lifted his hands lightly, palms up. "I don't know why he hesitates."

"Perhaps I do," Eleanor murmured. "I believe he might well be thinking of a way to make your fortunes even greater. When Richard chooses to give, he does so generously."

Bryan laughed. "Your Grace, I will pray that you know your son well."

"I do know Richard well. At this moment, he will be worrying about the empty state of his inherited purse! That is one we must begin to think upon, my children!"

Eleanor's sharp dark eyes turned suddenly to Elise. "And what of you, Elise? I have not lost any of my faculties—thanks be to God—and therefore my addition remains excellent. Why haven't you married?"

Elise froze at the question, but it didn't matter. Bryan Stede stepped in to answer mockingly for her. "The Lady Elise is deeply in love, Your Majesty! She intends to marry the man of her choice—Sir Percy Montagu."

"Sir Percy . . ." Eleanor frowned thoughtfully. "I'm afraid I do not know him—or of him."

Elise sipped her wine and forced her lips into a sweet smile. She had no intention of correcting Bryan Stede. "I'm sure that you will know him soon, Your Majesty," she said smoothly.

"Ah, love . . . I remember it well!" Eleanor chuckled softly. "And I am ever more flattered that you have all come to me!" She stood, setting her goblet firmly upon the table. "Bryan, Will, I leave you to plan the days ahead. Elise will come with me to pack so that, come tomorrow, we may be on the road bright and early."

The men, awkward in their armor, nevertheless jumped to their feet. Eleanor rewarded them with a benign smile, and reached out a hand to Elise. "You must refresh my mind on fashion, child. The blue jays have not much cared how I appeared before them."

Elise was touched when she saw the queen's small chamber within the palace. It was sparse and bare. A single window allowed light into the room.

Eleanor noticed that Elise's gaze quickly took in the circumstances. "Sunlight is beautiful, is it not? One can learn to cling to the sunlight, and to the blue of a spring sky." She paused suddenly, reflecting on the past. "There were many times when I was confined to this chamber alone." She shrugged. "And then there were times when I was allowed in the gardens—depending on the nature of the bailiff here, and Henry's whim." She smiled. "Once, I was even brought to Normandy for Michaelmas—to use my influence on Richard, of course. But I longed for freedom so fervently, I would have promised anything. And at that time . . . I dared believe there was hope that the family could come to peace. Ah, well, that was long ago."

"Yes, all that is the past," Elise agreed quickly. Suddenly she longed to take Eleanor away from the palace that had been a prison. "Where shall we start, Queen Eleanor? I see that you have all your trunks here—"

"I packed several days ago," Eleanor announced with a wry smile and a wave of her long, elegant hand. "I brought you here to look at you at my leisure. Spin about for me, child!"

Elise was not insulted, nor did she feel self-conscious. Eleanor's delight in life was contagious. Obediently, Elise spun about before the queen, who perched regally upon the foot of her small bed.

The queen was smiling when Elise came to a halt before her.

"You know, Elise de Bois, that I bear you no rancor."

"You are generous, ma'am."

"Nay—not generous. Just old. And very realistic! You have a great deal of your father in you, but . . . you are lovely anyway! Ah, don't lower your eyes, child. There was a time when I adored Henry Plantagenet! He was the sun to my eyes. He was almost twelve years younger than I, but when we married we were a perfect match. We were ambitious, ready to found an empire and a dynasty. Henry was a wonderful knight, a gallant king. Ah, but he drove his nobles crazy! He seldom even sat to eat, and therefore, they were obliged to stand through their meals! None could quite touch him for vitality or passion, or statesmanship. But let's be honest with each other, Elise. He was proud, he couldn't bear to part with his power, and, at times, he was stupid. He never knew how to deal with his sons, and therefore he placed their loyalty in my hands. We shall not speak ill of the dead. It is true that I had my reasons to hate him. But never forget that I loved him, too. Just as I never forget that it was often my own nature that came between us. Pride does not mingle well with love." Eleanor was silent for a moment, a moment in which the light that seemed to radiate about her dimmed. Elise felt her heart go out to the exquisite queen, who had for decades been an enigma and a legend; a woman to defy the world. And in that moment, she saw the queen's age, and her wisdom. Eleanor had learned that life was a combination of joy—and pain.

"So much to be done . . ." Eleanor murmured. She gazed at Elise again, and once more the light seemed to radiate from her. "It is all a game of power and intrigue—one that we must play very carefully! Always remember, Elise, that the clever players, the fighters, are the ones who win in the end! Sometimes it is impossible to slay a dragon by the sword; at those times, the dragon must be slain by wits!"

Elise smiled, and if she felt bitterness in her heart, she kept it from betraying her through her eyes. Eleanor was a fighter—and a survivor.

So would she be.

Elise felt strangely as if her plans for the future had been sanctified. If it was impossible to slay a dragon by the sword, then she would surely do so by wits. It was working out so well. Eleanor was obviously very fond of Bryan Stede, but she felt her sense of responsibility to Elise keenly.

Elise had found a friend in the queen. If she bided her time, she could surely manage the eloquent words to bring down her dragon.

Opportunity came along far before she had expected it.

Will Marshal left them the next morning, bound to meet and marry his heiress, Isabel de Clare.

Bryan, Eleanor, and Elise set out for the towns that were scattered about the English countryside.

It was not so difficult as Elise had imagined. Since the night of their arrival at Dover, when she and Bryan had argued over her behavior, she had barely had to speak to him. Will Marshal had become the buffer then, and now, with Will gone, Eleanor had been the force to come between them.

It was, Elise mused, as if Bryan Stede had indeed washed his hands of her.

I would be better off to do the same, she often warned herself.

As accustomed as she had come to knowing that he was near in her days of travel, there were still times when she would see him that he touched a deep, inner core of her, and frightened her. She had never been wrong in her assessment of him; he was a hard man, and if crossed, he would be a ruthless man. In his black armor, riding the midnight destrier, he was the very image of power and might. The people made way for him, and bowed down to him, even before they saw the queen. And not once, with Bryan Stede leading the party, was the queen ever accosted in any way.

Bryan and Elise had both expected Eleanor to travel in a litter—she was, no matter what her strength, an old woman. But when she had been the Queen of France, she had once been forcefully abducted by her husband in a litter, and even now she would not enter one again. She and Elise rode side by side.

Elise loved seeing the country in summer. The weather now remained bright and beautiful for them, and she could clearly see the occasional windmills in the fields, the oxen and horses hitched to plows, the profusion of summer wildflowers. The towns fascinated her with their very narrow streets, and the upper floors that often seemed about to collide with one another over the pathways. Even the smallest village offered some entertainment: jugglers, harpists, flutists, minstrels, and balladeers. Often, once Eleanor was seen, the minstrels would come to her, regaling her, and offering up the love ballads that had been composed in her honor through the years.

In a small valley called Smithwick, they came upon a freeman who commandeered a pair of trained bears. Elise was fascinated by their act, and Eleanor watched her tolerantly.

"Henry loved bears, too," she told Elise. "He traveled with them frequently. Did you know that?"

"No, no I didn't," Elise admitted, and Eleanor smiled. Elise knew then that she would never be able to believe anything wicked about the queen; she was coming to know Eleanor too well herself. She would say nothing malicious about Henry to Elise, although she didn't pretend to deny his shortcomings. She knew that Elise had loved him.

Elise could have been extremely happy—if it weren't for Bryan's constant presence, always making her feel as if she burned hot, then fell into chills, only to burn again.

Of course, she still spent long hours trying to ponder just what she would say to bring him down, and see that he lost Gwyneth as she had lost Percy.

A week after their departure from Winchester, they were on

the outskirts of London. Eleanor had spent the day speaking to the people, cheering on the reign of Richard the Lion-Heart.

As usual, they dined early, then retired for the night.

There had been no more dirty taverns; Eleanor could avail herself of the hospitality of any manor. Tonight they were in the home of Sir Matthew Surrey, and the old gentleman was thrilled to greet the dowager queen. Elise and Eleanor had been given a lovely chamber that overlooked a field of summer daisies, and a host of servants had run about to cater cheerfully to any whim. Elise had enjoyed a long, delightfully scented bath, and sipped a goblet of mulled wine as she and Eleanor stretched out upon clean sheets, chatting idly to wind down from the excitement of the day. She and Eleanor shared one vast and fatly mattressed bed, which was of no discomfort to either of them; to travel, women learned quickly that accommodations must frequently be shared.

Serving Eleanor, Elise had learned, was no task at all. The queen was independent. She allowed Elise to comb her hair, and to lay out her clothing, but other than those tasks, Eleanor cared for herself. But Elise never felt useless, for the queen enjoyed her companionship. Sometimes Elise was certain that the queen merely thought aloud, but she was nevertheless glad to listen, and never afraid to offer comments.

This night, Eleanor was once again on the subject of England's empty coffers.

"Richard," Eleanor told Elise as she climbed into the high, goosedown-filled bed, "needs money badly." She sighed. "It is a pity that Richard formed an alliance with Philip Augustus against Henry. Now Richard must pay Philip the twenty-thousand ducats that Henry swore to pay just before his death. That will detract heavily from the sums he might have used for the Crusade. And to go on crusade! Ah, fighting a holy war is a dear proposition indeed! But one quickly learns to miss the comfort of clean sheets and two soft pillows . . ." Eleanor's voice drifted as she closed her eyes and luxuriated in the softness of their bed. She opened one eye. "Elise, would you mind closing the shutter, please? The night is taking on a chill."

Elise sprang from the bed and hurried to the shutter. But before she could close it, she noticed movement in the courtyard below and paused.

A man was mounting a horse. It was dark below, as the moon was at an ebb, but Elise stiffened. She recognized Stede. There were few men of his lean and powerful height, or who possessed his breadth of shoulder. He was not dressed in armor, but in his mantle alone, and his dark head was bare. Even in the meager light, the ebony black of his hair glistened as if caught by the few stars speckling the heavens.

"What is it?" Eleanor asked.

Elise hesitated, sensing that her moment had come to begin her careful attack upon Bryan Stede.

"Nothing, Eleanor," she said quickly—too quickly, and with full intent to do so.

"Nonsense, Elise. What have you seen?"

"Just a man—riding from the manor."

"Oh," Eleanor said complacently. "Then it is just Stede."

Surprised by the reply, Elise closed the shutter and spun about. The chamber was lit only by the one candle on the trunk on her side of the bed. Eleanor's expression was lost in shadow.

Elise exhaled carefully. "Yes, Your Majesty, it was Stede. I did not wish to tell you so because . . . because he should not leave you! It is his responsibility to guard you!"

Eleanor's dark eyes opened and touched upon Elise with fondness. "You remind me of Richard—a little lioness in behalf of your beliefs! But you needn't be so protective of me, child. Nor do you need to lie about Stede, or be angry with him. I suggested that he leave this evening."

"Oh?"

"Gwyneth is in London. A short ride will bring Stede to her. He has been a gallant knight, caring so carefully for his aging queen. He deserves an evening of leisure—and pleasure. I'm really rather annoyed that Richard didn't arrange for Stede's marriage now, as he did for Will Marshal."

Elise bit into her lip in the darkness. *He deserves to have his bloody head whacked off!* she thought furiously. So Stede was riding to the woman he intended to marry. His prize! Wonderful, brave Stede, being awarded for the fruits of his brawn!

Elise remained silent and still in the darkness, trying to think how to phrase her words properly. As it happened, her silence became her best move.

"You don't care for Bryan, do you, Elise?" Eleanor asked curiously.

"I—"

Eleanor chuckled softly. "Don't deny it, Elise. There are benefits to my age. I have watched the two of you often in the past days. You avoid each other. You do not speak, you do not touch. But each time your eyes meet, one can feel it, as if God had suddenly filled the sky with storm clouds and fire."

"You are right, Your Majesty," Elise agreed quietly. "I do not care for Bryan Stede."

"Why?" Elise could see the queen's amused smile as her eyes grew accustomed to the darkness. "If I were young," Eleanor continued with dry, good humor, "I think I could easily be in love. But since I am far past the days of such painful foolishness, I can sit back and admire such men as Bryan Stede. So tell me, Elise, what could this man have done to you to cause you to hate him so?"

This was her moment at last, she thought, and Elise felt a tempest of emotions shiver through her body. She would be taking a step of no return, and she had to weigh her every word with the greatest of care.

"Eleanor, it is something of which I would rather not speak."

"Nonsense!" Eleanor exclaimed with determination.

"But I—"

"Elise, I am ordering you as the Queen Regent of England!" Elise lowered her head quickly, determined that the crafty old queen not see her smile, for the queen was playing perfectly into her hands.

"Your Majesty, since you order me to speak, I shall. But I also beg that you keep every word I say entirely confidential."

"You needn't beg. Whatever you say shall be kept strictly between the two of us."

Elise let out a long sigh, and carefully kept her lashes low over her eyes, shielding them. The riot of tingling hot and cold that had seized her kept her shivering, for here she was going to lie, or at least twist the truth, and on all accounts it was a frightening and reckless thing to do.

"Stede did nothing to me, Eleanor. It is what he has done to others that makes me abhor him so."

"Pray, continue," Eleanor said firmly. She patted the bed. "Lie down, child; don't stand so nervously at a distance. I am not a crazed murderess, although they did call me so when that wretched Rosamund Clifford died! I am not an old bat to be feared!"

Elise slid beneath the cover on her side of the bed and prayed that her features would be hidden by darkness as she snuffed out the last candle.

"I want to hear this story," Eleanor reminded her with a warning note in her tone.

Elise sighed carefully again. "I'm afraid, Your Majesty, that your gallant Stede is not always so chivalrous. He came upon a friend of mine, a lady of some note, when she was in an awkward circumstance and very frightened. He threw her about as if she were refuse, and forced her into . . ."

"Bed?" Eleanor supplied incredulously.

"Yes," Elise agreed sadly.

To her astonishment, Eleanor began to laugh. "Stede *forced* himself on a young lady!"

"Your Majesty!" Elise cried out indignantly. "I assure you, it was no laughing matter for the young lady involved."

"I do apologize, Elise," Eleanor said quickly. "It's just so . . . absurd. Bryan Stede is a man who tends to have women—those who are titled, and those who are not—flocking around him. They are drawn to him, as flowers to the sun."

"The story is true," Elise said quietly.

Eleanor was silent, and thoughtful, for several moments. "If your story is true, Elise, then you must give me the lady's name. And if she has been wronged, then Bryan must forget Gwyneth, and right that wrong."

"He cannot right—"

"He can marry the lady."

"No!" Elise protested quickly. "She has no wish to marry him, Your Majesty. She intends to marry elsewhere, and is happy with her choice. It is just . . . it is hard to watch such a man rewarded by marriage to one of the richest heiresses in England!"

Eleanor sighed softly. "If the woman does not wish to marry him, then there is nothing that can be done. And to a woman, yes, perhaps such a thing is distressing. But I tell you as a queen, with politics in mind, as it would be to a man—I am afraid it would all be of little or no consequence. Bryan Stede served Henry well. His loyalty to the Crown is unquestionable. He will be as invaluable to Richard as he was to Henry, and any king with sense would reward such character. And not only character," Eleanor added wryly. "Bryan Stede offers England one of the best sword arms in existence. The only way Stede could be brought to charge for his actions would be to arrange his marriage to the injured woman—as long as she was of the right class. But since she doesn't wish marriage, there is no reason to stop a marriage that is entirely suitable. Gwyneth has tremendous lands and wealth; Bryan has the power to rule them and keep them."

Brawn, Elise thought bitterly as she lay in the darkness, did seem to be the mightiest weapon. She had struck her blow of words, and it appeared that she had done no damage. Truly, she had lived in a sheltered world. Yes, she was the titled one. And she was the daughter of a king, if only a king's bastard. Still, Stede was the one with the power.

He was the one with the sword arm.

"Perhaps . . ." Eleanor murmured.

"Your pardon, Your Majesty?"

Eleanor yawned. "Nothing, Elise, nothing at all. I was just wondering . . . what shall you do after Richard is crowned?"

"Go back to Montoui," Elise said softly. "It is my duchy." She smiled. "There, I am in command."

"Of course," Eleanor murmured. "Of course . . ."

Moments of silence followed. Elise became convinced that Eleanor slept, and the words the queen had said turned around and around in her mind.

He can marry the lady . . . he can marry the lady . . . he can marry the lady . . .

She did have power—if she chose to use it.

She simply couldn't use it, because . . .

The only way to stop Bryan Stede from receiving everything his heart desired was to place herself in his path. She could hurt him. Oh, yes, she could hurt him. She wasn't Gwyneth, whom he so obviously enjoyed, nor did she have a quarter of Gwyneth's vast lands and great wealth. Her duchy was small; it wasn't even in England, and Bryan Stede was an Englishman.

But she would be saddled with a dark beast of Satan for life. A knight who—she admitted in the deepest recesses of her heart—terrified her still.

No, she would not be saddled with him, she thought with sudden excitement. She could speak—and force Bryan Stede into a betrothal. And then she could stall. Keep putting the marriage off. She could claim that she had made a vow to make pilgrimages to various shrines. Time would pass, and more time would pass—and then Bryan would be forced to ride with Richard on the Crusade. It could be done—Richard had done it himself! He had been betrothed to Philip's half sister for over a decade—but no marriage had ever taken place!

What if Richard insisted on a wedding? she asked herself. But she refused to consider seriously such a possibility. And if he did—well, she could still escape Bryan before the marriage could be consummated, return to Montoui and fortify the castle—and set about the task of finding grounds to present to the Pope for an annulment. She would probably have years in which to manage the feat—the Holy Land was far away . . .

And by the time it had all come about, Gwyneth would certainly have been given to some other deserving knight.

Dear God, yes, it could be done.

He would kill her, she thought, shivering suddenly. But only if he managed to get his hands on her out of Eleanor's sight. And she would never allow that to happen.

"Elise?"

Eleanor's soft query, coming from the darkness when Elise had been certain that the queen slept, was so startling that Elise jumped.

"Yes?" she said nervously in return.

"Are you this 'lady'?"

Elise knotted her fingers into the sheet. If she said yes . . .

She might well be risking her life, or, at least, the safety of her flesh and limbs. But the sweet and beautiful waters of revenge would begin to flow.

She squeezed her eyes tightly together. She had to be crazy!

"Elise?"

She opened her mouth, still not sure of her answer. But she never uttered a word, for a thunderous knocking pounded upon the door and a servant began to scream anxiously for the queen.

"Your Majesty! Your Majesty! Word has just come! He's landed! Richard has landed! The Lion-Heart is in England!"

Eleanor was out of bed with the speed of a winter wind; she sprinted across the room with the agility of a young girl and threw open the door. "Is this true?"

The young serving wench fell to her knees, clasping her hands with excitement.

"Oh, aye, Your Majesty! He came ashore with hundreds of men-at-arms, so they say. The King—our Lion of England!"

"And the people?"

"The people cheered him, and threw flowers of welcome!"

"Blessed be to God!" Eleanor exclaimed, looking upward, as if she could see heaven, and was thanking the Creator with her smile. Then she was glancing back to the girl, and her tone was tense. "And John? Prince John. Has he been seen?"

"Aye, Your Majesty! Aye! He came on the arm of his brother!"

Eleanor glanced upward again, her appeal to heaven mute this time. "Thank you, girl! Thank you!"

"Oh, my greatest pleasure, Your Majesty!"

The wench bowed herself away, and Eleanor spun back into the room, lithe and beautiful in her happiness. Her eyes fell upon Elise, and Elise realized that the queen had forgotten all about her in the joy of knowing that Richard had arrived, and been received well.

It was for the best. All for the best. Surely she had been struck with madness even to contemplate forcing Stede into a marriage with her . . .

It was her only hope . . .

It was insanity . . .

"Ah, Elise!" She laughed happily. "So very much to do! I'm so glad that Richard has John under his wing, but . . . Henry spoiled John so! Richard is going to have to be so wary of his brother. . . . Come, Elise! Up! We must dress! We must be ready!"

Eleanor lit the bedside candle; in her excitement she hugged Elise. "How I have waited and prayed for this moment! Richard—the King of England. The season for lions has come!"

Lions . . .

Yes, Elise thought, *it is a season for lions.* And the head of the pride was her brother.

It was the lioness who was known to be deadly. The lioness . . . who went for the kill.

Richard would soon be crowned King.

He would not allow his half sister to be humiliated, not even for the finest sword arm in his kingdom.

What was she thinking? she asked herself with dismay. But her mind was playing a terrible tug-of-war.

She could allow it all to drop; she could salvage the strands of her own life. But part of her still cried out for revenge, and that reckless portion of her nature tried to ignore the horror of what she could bring down upon herself.

Marriage to Stede; it was unthinkable.

And yet . . .

It was all like a game of chess, Henry had told her.

And now, it was her move.

XII

Elise had little to do the first few days following Richard's arrival. Eleanor and Richard spent their time closeted together, and it was not until the third morning that even his closest advisors were invited to be part of any discussions or plans.

On that third night, Sir Matthew Surrey, who continued to host the royal family and their immediate entourage, threw open his doors for a small, welcoming banquet. Elise was flattered that Eleanor demanded she sit at the high table, and she was touched by Richard's boisterous greeting. But that, she thought dryly, was part of the Lion-Heart's charisma. Richard was a fine, dramatic performer. When she was about, he would hug and kiss her and offer fine, flowery phrases. When he turned his back, he would have forgotten everything that he had said, and would give full rein to his one, all-consuming dream: the Crusade.

Prince John was with Richard. A brother totally different from the Lion-Heart. John was short, dark, and surly, yet his eyes held a bright cunning that Richard's lacked. The prince was pleasant to Elise, and she found herself wondering uneasily about this other half brother of hers. Richard had been betrothed to Alys, Philip of France's sister, for so many years that most people had lost count. It was widely believed that Henry had seduced Alys years and years before, and so had procrastinated until marriage between Richard and Alys had become the joke of the English isle and the European continent. But Eleanor had often spoken to Elise of the truth; Richard had no taste for women.

Prince John was therefore Richard's heir, until such time when the Lion-Heart might bear an heir, if that event ever occurred.

The idea of John upon the throne of England was frightening. Very frightening, because of his irresponsibility and his cruel nature. One could only hope that Richard would live a long and hale life.

And Geoffrey and I are both Henry's brood, Elise mused, *but neither of us could ever touch the Crown. Eleanor, as much as she loves us, would see to that.*

Not that she or Geoffrey would ever scramble for the Crown. They were both too intelligent to do so.

Geoffrey Fitzroy was there that night, too. He stopped to speak warmly with Elise before taking his position on the other side of the table, next to Prince John.

Glancing down the high table, Elise saw that it was an interesting assembly. Hadwisa of Gloucester, John's intended bride, was at the far end, seated beside Geoffrey, who was next to John. John, the second most important individual in the kingdom, was seated next to Richard. Beside Richard, of course, sat Eleanor. And then there was Elise herself. Beside her, at the moment, was an empty place, and beyond it, three more seats. Who were they for? she wondered.

The wonder was not to last long. At first Elise thought that Richard had risen and stood behind her; the shadow on the wall created by a flickering candle could only belong to a very tall man. Then she heard his voice, light and sardonic.

"It seems we shall share a goblet this evening. How pleasant. I shall do the gallant thing, of course, and allow you, good Duchess, to drink first. I shall then drink free of the worry of poison."

Blood rushed heatedly to her breast, her neck, and into her cheeks. As was the custom of the day, one goblet had been placed between every other place setting; she was to share hers with Bryan Stede.

She gazed up at him, her eyes narrowing, but her lips curving into a too-sweet smile. "Dear Sir Stede! I wouldn't drink too recklessly, were I you! If I am truly a 'bitch of Satan'—which you have been wont to call me—I can surely drink deeply of poison myself with little harm befalling me."

His brow raised as he scraped back his chair and took his seat, his thigh brushing hers. "Nay, Duchess, I labeled you incorrectly. You are nothing but flesh and blood, equipped with long nails and a scathing tongue. Ah . . . ah!" he warned suddenly when she would have retorted. "Speak gently, Duchess. Break no illusions. Here comes your intended."

Dismay, like a pool of black liquid, quickly filled Elise's heart as her eyes followed Bryan Stede's line of vision.

Percy was indeed coming toward them.

Tears stung her eyes as she saw him; he looked wonderful: so slim and stately, his features so finely hewn, his changeable hazel eyes soulful and intense as they met hers.

She could not forget the things he had said and done . . .

But neither could she forget that she had loved him . . . perhaps loved him still, since her heart could not always obey her pride.

He did not come to her first; he greeted the royal family. Richard introduced him warmly to Eleanor. But then he was before Elise, and he was bowing low over her hand. She felt the touch of his lips on her flesh, heard his soft whispered query as to her welfare.

And she knew that Stede was watching her, staring at her. Smiling that sardonic, mocking grin of his as he watched the interplay of courtesies between them . . .

Then it was over. Percy was straightening. But he was turning to Bryan . . .

"Stede." Percy acknowledged Bryan with a curt nod.

"Montagu," Bryan returned, nodding in kind.

There was a friction between the two men, some indefinable thing that lurked and hovered in the air.

Then that, too, was gone. Percy moved on. Elise realized that Will Marshal had come to the head table, escorting a lovely young woman, and that he was introducing her to Percy as his new bride.

She felt Bryan Stede's eyes upon her again and she reached convulsively for the wine goblet, only to find his long-fingered grip there before hers. She raised her eyes to his.

"I'm surprised that you did not ask for your betrothed to be seated near you, Duchess."

Elise ignored the comment and said, "Sir Stede, if you wish to assure yourself that your wine is not poisoned, may I suggest that you let go of the goblet and allow me a drink?"

He did so, but he continued to stare at her. She took a long sip of wine, not relinquishing the goblet to him.

"Where is your betrothed this evening, Sir Stede?"

"Alas, still in London. And alas, she is not my betrothed as of yet. Richard intends to allow me no time until after he is crowned."

"Ah, what a pity!" Elise commiserated sarcastically. "Our soon-to-be-crowned king keeps you on pins and needles! And so I still outrank you, sir! How that must frustrate you! Land and wealth . . . so close . . . within your grasp!"

"Land—and sweet beauty!" he reminded her with his grin unaltered.

"It would indeed be a pity if it all slipped through your fingers," Elise murmured sweetly.

He leaned closer to her. "But it will not. And with each day that passes, I come nearer my goals. Take heart!"

"Me? Whatever for?"

"Because each day we come closer to that day when we can part our ways. To a day when I shall not be tempted to strangle you because I will not be close enough to do so . . ."

Elise smiled sweetly and drained the wine goblet. "Oh, yes, Sir Stede, I do take heart. I do."

There was to be no more conversation between them then. Marshal—a changed and radiantly smiling Marshal—greeted them both. His young bride, Isabel de Clare, was a soft-spoken and gentle beauty. She appeared to be happy with her warrior husband, and Elise felt a touch of wistful envy sweep through her.

Isabel was young and very attractive. But though her marriage had been arranged, she had been granted one of the kindest and most considerate men ever to draw brave steel for his king. While she . . .

She could only pray that Percy kept his own counsel—at least until her own plans were complete.

The trouble did not begin until the meal was long over, until the musicians had played, until the assembled guests had applauded and cheered.

Elise had paused to talk longer with Isabel and Will Marshal. They had been married a little more than a week ago, and both were pleased to speak of their London wedding. Elise instinctively liked Isabel. She was an intelligent and quiet woman, perfect for Elise's dear Will. And when Elise listened to the happy chatter about the wedding, she could truly forget her own situation and be warmed by the pleasure she felt for the newly wed pair.

It was when she exited the hall into the courtyard, poised and relaxed, that she was startled into instant alarm by the sound of a surly voice, arguing too loudly from the shade of a far arbor.

" 'Twas you, Stede! And you'd no right to take what was mine. You owe me a debt—"

"What I took belonged to no one but the lady involved. And that was little enough, Percy, for her heart remained steadfast to you."

Elise cringed inwardly, looking anxiously about herself. Percy's voice was rising with each word. But even as dread filled her like something horribly alive, she realized that only she, Will, and Isabel stood within the courtyard to hear the exchange between the two formally dressed knights.

"You raped her—"

Hoarse laughter interrupted Percy. "Is that what she said? Perhaps she forgot to explain the circumstances. I tell you this; I acted as I did with no knowledge of your concern with the lady. The situation was . . . unique."

"You will apologize! You will beg my pardon, and you will pay me a compensation for what—"

"I will beg your pardon for nothing, Percy Montagu!" Bryan suddenly raged with impatience.

Percy has drunk far too much, Elise thought with alarm as she watched him swing wildly at Stede. Bryan Stede stepped back, and Percy fell to the ground. But he was up quickly, wielding a dagger this time.

They were in full view now, free from the shadow of the arbor. Stede knocked Percy's arm away when the dagger would have torn into his arm. Then he stepped forward with his fingers wound into a fist and took steady aim at Percy's chin. Percy crumpled to the floor.

Elise forgot all about Will and Isabel; she even forgot about Stede. As Percy fell to the hard stone of the courtyard, she raced to him, dropping to her knees. Cradling his head in her lap, she stared furiously up to Stede.

"Beast!"

It was one of those times that his eyes appeared black: deep, dark, and fathomless. He started to speak, then shrugged his shoulders.

"You do owe him!" Elise charged. "You had no right to . . . to . . ."

"I did not begin the quarrel."

"You could have had the decency—"

"To allow him to stab me? My apologies, Duchess. Perhaps I am a beast. My instinct to survive is too strong for me to act the gallant in such a situation."

Elise glanced back to Percy as he groaned. She smoothed his

hair from his forehead, biting her lip as she anxiously ran her fingers over his flesh, searching out serious injury. "You did defend me," she murmured tenderly, barely aware that she had spoken aloud.

Stede laughed, a sound that was harsh and bitter.

"Defended you? Duchess, the 'apology' he wanted was a monetary one."

Elise glanced up quickly. "You're lying!" she charged, but her voice was a weak whisper; she had already learned ideals and truths often did not mesh.

Stede never answered. Percy's eyes opened and stared at her, numbed with wine and pain.

"Stede . . . has the rewards. The prize is always his . . ."

"I'm *not* his, Percy," Elise said softly. "And I'm not a prize."

"But you were . . ." His voice faded away as his eyes met Stede's, far above him. "He is always first. And he never seeks to rectify."

"What would you have me rectify, Percy?" Bryan demanded in exasperation, throwing his hands up.

"Elise . . ."

"Elise?" Bryan's arms crossed over his chest and he stared at her, his dark eyes narrowed, but his stance patient, his tone polite. Elise found herself unable to speak under his scrutiny, and Bryan returned his gaze to Percy. "Perhaps she should explain what happened to you in greater detail. I did not ride to Montoui and snatch her away. Indeed, the duchess presented herself to me with a most intriguing lie upon her lips." His piercing gaze was riveted on Elise once again. "Do you deny this, my lady? If so, please speak. I am open to debate on any point."

"Elise?" Percy queried painfully.

She did not answer Percy; she spoke to Stede. "Before God, how I loathe you!"

He shrugged. "Duchess, you have not exactly endeared yourself to my heart. I make no accusations; you and I both know to what I refer." His eyes turned back to Percy, and Elise hated the pity she saw within them. "But on that, I can say nothing more. It is her affair if she wishes to speak of it. Quite frankly, I am still in the dark myself. But every move I made that night was rational; I will offer no apologies. But take heart, Sir Percy. She despises me. And she is apparently deeply in love with you."

"In love!" Percy choked, and the bitterness spilled from him like wine from an overful cup. "Stede—"

A throat was suddenly cleared, intentionally loud. Elise gazed quickly back toward Will Marshal, and realized that the sound had indeed been a warning.

Richard Plantagenet was striding into the courtyard, his bearing, his swagger, that of the truly irritated ruler.

"God's teeth! I would know what goes on here!"

No one spoke. Richard's sharp gaze lit upon Percy, down upon the ground, upon Elise, and upon Bryan. Bryan compressed his lips in a tight line. Will Marshal, seeing that the debacle was reaching a dangerously explosive level, stepped forward.

"Your Grace, it is nothing. A personal quarrel that sirs Stede and Montagu must settle between themselves."

"Damn you both!" Richard roared. He had a voice to fill the courtyard, and he enjoyed the pageantry of using it. "We seek to bring a peaceful transition to England—and two of my most valued knights tear at each other's throats. Whose quarrel is this?"

Stede remained silent. Percy spoke up sullenly. " 'Tis my quarrel, Your Grace."

"Do you wish to challenge Sir Stede to a joust, or perhaps to swordplay?"

Elise, so close to Percy, both heard and felt the grind of his teeth. He stood, helping her rise to her feet. For a moment, he gazed bitterly at Stede. Then he turned to Richard.

"No, Your Grace. You will need us both in the days to come."

Richard graced them all with his angry lion's stare. "Then we will hear no more of this. Sir Percy, I commend your good sense. If I hear of further trouble, you will both enjoy a taste of a cold London dungeon until you can learn to cool your tempers. Am I well understood?"

"Aye, Your Grace," Percy mumbled.

"Stede!" Richard barked.

" 'Twas never my quarrel, Your Grace." He stared at Elise for a moment, then returned his attention to Richard. "I bear Sir Percy no grudge."

Richard had nothing else to say. With a final, heated stare at the group of them, he swung about, his mantle flying majestically, to return to the manor.

Will, fearing more trouble despite Richard's stern warnings, came hurriedly to Bryan Stede's side. "Bryan—"

"I'm coming, Will." He inclined his head to Elise, and then to Percy. "Duchess . . . Sir Montagu . . ."

Will began to breathe a sigh of relief. But before he and Bryan had taken two steps, Percy was railing against Bryan again.

"I'll kill you yet, Stede."

Will felt his friend's muscle-hewn form stiffen; Bryan stopped in his tracks and turned back, but mercifully did not lose his temper.

"You and the duchess have much in common, Percy—a penchant for threats, and a fondness for murder. I wish you every happiness, and yet I pity you if you plan to spend your lives in pursuit of my downfall. Life should offer more than such a paltry quest."

Bryan Stede swept them a deep bow, turned about, and started to follow in Richard's footsteps with Will Marshal now at his heels. Isabel glanced uncertainly at her new husband's back, hesitated, then came to Elise.

"Please . . . don't worry. Will and I shall take none of this further than the courtyard in which we stand." She smiled, then swirled gracefully to follow Will.

Then Elise was alone with Percy. He rubbed his jaw, and his eyes met hers ruefully. "I'm sorry, Elise," he murmured, and she wondered what he meant. Was he sorry for the scene that humiliated them all before the king? Was he, perhaps, sorry that he hadn't the nerve to challenge Stede to a joust? Or was he sorry because he had wanted to love her, and had simply discovered he could not?

He grasped her hand and drew it to his lips. "I'm so very, very sorry."

But she was never to understand him, because he turned then, not for the manor, but for the emptiness of the black night.

She wanted to call him back, to say something, to do something; to reach out in some way and try to understand all that she had lost—and why. But, like the night, her heart seemed empty and dark, and she could neither move nor speak.

She could only watch him walk away.

"Lord, how I would love to confront that whey-faced Norman in a joust!" Bryan swore loudly, his boots pounding in staccato progression as he paced the floor in the London town house lent to Will and Isabel by friends. "The man looks and acts like a peacock! He accosts me—but refuses to challenge me!"

Will glanced at Isabel, who grimaced sedately and poured another cup of wine for their guest. Will sighed and, as Bryan's longtime companion, ventured his truthful opinion.

"Bryan, you can hardly blame Percy for his animosity!"

Bryan stopped his pacing and stared at Will, his hands on his hips. "Maybe I don't blame Percy. At least I don't blame him for anything other than cowardice! I blame the bitch he calls his betrothed! Were she capable of a single word of truth! Or were she capable of a discussion! But no—she poisons my wine! I swear to you, Will, the night we met, she tried with all her might to slit my throat. Then she comes to me, on her knees, no less . . . God in heaven! What did I ever do to get involved with that woman!"

Will had the audacity to laugh. "Well, my friend, I would say that at one point it must have surely been your desire to . . . get involved with that woman!"

Bryan glared balefully at Will. "I begin to hunger for the Crusade—and a thousand screaming Moslems with their swords waving at me."

"Perhaps," Isabel spoke up, her tone soft and soothing, but her words a knife that twisted and goaded his anger, "you should have asked to marry the Duchess of Montoui."

"Marry her!" Bryan exploded. "Dear God, that the devil should suffer such a fate!" But then he sighed. "Isabel, I am no more a monster than Will, here. When I knew what I had done, the thought did cross my mind. But 'tis true she vehemently wishes me dead, and 'tis equally true—as you saw this evening—that she is in love with Sir Percy. I kept silent about that night, as did she—or so I had believed. I meant her no further harm. She is betrothed to Percy, and I . . . I hope that Gwyneth and I will soon say our vows. If I truly owe a woman, it is Gwyneth I owe, for we have known each other for many years now."

Isabel listened to Bryan, offered him the cup of wine, then spoke serenely again. "I don't know, Bryan. Your anger is curious to me, as was your expression when you watched the Lady Elise give tender concern to Sir Percy." She gazed at Will, her features set in a soft smile that enhanced her young beauty. "I have come to know that expression well, Will. Do you know of what I speak?"

Will grinned broadly at his wife, then glanced slyly at Bryan. "Aye, Isabel, I know of what you speak."

"Well, I'll be damned if I understand either of you!" Bryan exclaimed.

Isabel laughed delightedly, and Bryan discovered that he envied his friend his newfound happiness. Marriage, yes, this was what marriage was meant to be. This pleasant understanding, this wonder of knowing each other. This marriage had been arranged, yet it might not have been, for the stalwart warrior and the young heiress were truly well matched.

"Bryan, if I am any judge of men and women, you do not so much despise Percy Montagu as covet what is his—or will be his."

"What?"

" 'Tis my belief you yet desire the duchess."

"Lady Isabel," Bryan said with a long sigh, "I fear that marriage has caused you to take leave of your senses." He shook his head, then chuckled. "Perhaps not. She is a creature of beauty and allure. But she touches the senses, and not the heart, for she is hard and proud. Yes, maybe I desire her—as man was meant to desire woman. But I assure you, I do mean her no harm. I pray that she and Percy marry and live happily as long as they both shall live."

Isabel shrugged. "Think on this, Sir Stede. What you wish for them may not be possible. I believe that Sir Percy is very jealous of you. You both fought, but you and Will were Henry's favorites. Already Richard draws you to him, and relies upon you. Now you have taken something else from Percy."

"What? A single night with a woman? Then Percy is an idiot, for life is composed of many nights."

"You heard him," Isabel said softly. "You were first. To Percy, this means something. And you know well, Bryan Stede, that most men would feel the same. Men may wander where they will, but they expect their brides to come to their marital bed as virgins."

Bryan listened to Isabel's words and smiled thoughtfully at her. He stepped forward, took her hands in his, and kissed each palm lightly. "Truly," he told her, "had Will scoured the earth, he could have found no woman more lovely, or more wise. Will, my heartiest congratulations to you both."

He embraced Will, then turned to leave them.

"Bryan!" Will called after him. " 'Tis late! Stay the night here!"

"Nay, I cannot stay." Bryan grinned. "Your happiness would haunt me to insanity. And I must return to the manor. Richard has demanded that I meet with him in Sir Matthew's study at the crack of dawn."

"Godspeed!" Isabel called after him.

Bryan waved, then departed. Will and Isabel soon heard the pounding hooves of his destrier as he rode away, his horse's gallop as wild as the anger in his heart.

Will sighed. "It is painful . . ." he murmured.

"Because they are both your dear friends," Isabel said.

"Yes."

"My lord, they are both proud, and both are possessed of tempestuous natures. They are fighters, and therefore they must wage their own battles."

"You are right, wife," Will murmured, taking her into his arms. The feel of her soft, curved body against his made his thoughts of worry and concern begin to fade. He had been blessed with this woman, beautiful, caring, wise . . .

And passionate.

And he was so new to marriage . . .

His lips touched hers with wonder, and when he looked into her eyes again, his own were dazed.

"We cannot interfere," he murmured. But already he had forgotten what it was he spoke of. He lifted her into his arms and began to blow out the candles.

But there was someone who did intend to interfere—fully.

Eleanor was up and gone when Elise awoke. She rose, still weary despite her night's sleep, and poured water from a pitcher into a bowl. She had barely washed her face before a knock sounded on the door, and a serving girl entered, bobbing a curtsy.

"Good morning, Lady Elise. His Grace, Richard Plantagenet . . ." The girl hesitated, and Elise frowned curiously, then realized that the girl was having trouble repeating Richard's words. The girl sighed, then continued. "His Majesty *commands* you to come to Sir Matthew's study, beyond the banqueting hall."

Elise stiffened, wondering what was afoot. Commands . . . commands! This was not an invitation, but a royal summons.

"I shall be down immediately," Elise promised the girl with a composure that belied her quaking heart. The serving girl bobbed her way out, apparently relieved that her message had been well taken.

What have I done? Elise wondered, worry furrowing into her brow as soon as the girl was gone. Nothing, she had done nothing. And Richard was her half brother! He was fond of her . . .

He was Richard—"Coeur de Lion." He was stretching his arms, flexing the muscles of power. He had battled his own father for years and years . . .

And he was about to be crowned King.

He was power, the supreme power . . .

With dread filling her heart, Elise dressed quickly, then hurried downstairs. The banqueting hall was empty; despite the early hour, the servants had long ago cleaned away the mess of the previous evening.

Double, heavy wood doors framed the study off the side of the hall. Elise hesitated before them, trying to still her pounding heart. She was the Duchess of Montoui. She had done nothing wrong. She was Richard's own blood . . .

She forced herself to knock soundly.

"Enter!"

It was the Lion-Heart's voice. He was in a rare mood for roaring. Elise held her head high, then entered the room.

Richard was seated behind Sir Surrey's worktable, a score of ledgers and parchments before him. He glanced at her, and his gaze was impersonal, sending new shivers to plague her spine. Elise noted that Eleanor was ensconced in an elaborately carved, high-backed chair near the table. Eleanor smiled vaguely at her. Elise approached the desk as Richard shuffled and arranged the parchments upon his desk.

What was this? Elise wondered fleetingly. Whatever, at least
it would involve only herself, Richard, and Eleanor.

Or so she was lulled into believing at first. But then she heard
a faint sound behind her, the soft shuffle of a boot. She spun
about to see that they were not, after all, alone.

Bryan Stede stood by the mantel, an elbow casually leaning
against it, his stance that of the knight who could relax, and yet
always be alert. He was dressed formally; his fine linen tunic
was a deep blue; his mantle was a shade darker, and flowed
over a single shoulder. The rigidity drawn into his handsome
features was severe; his expression was anything but casual.
And his eyes seemed neither blue nor black; they appeared to
burn with all the fires of hell.

XIII

"I am a busy man," Richard began without rising, or without seeming to pay attention to anyone in the room. His eyes were focused on the parchments before him. Elise realized curiously that the parchments he studied were land deeds.

At last Richard looked up; his eyes slid over Elise, then focused beyond her on Bryan Stede. "I have come to England to claim my crown, but I have never been unaware that there are those who believe that I hounded my father to the grave. I have matters of great importance stretching before me. When the crown sits indisputably upon my head, I will have to turn my concentration to finances. When I solve my financial difficulties, I will have to plan for God's glorious battle and forge forward to recapture the Holy Land."

Richard went on to emphasize the trials and tribulations of a young monarch. Elise chanced a glance at Eleanor, but the queen merely nodded and continued to watch Richard.

". . . therefore," Richard was continuing, "I find it expedient to settle the petty matters of quarrels, titles, lands, and marriages—now. Stede!"

"Yes, Your Grace."

Elise could not see Bryan Stede, but she knew that he did not flinch at Richard's tone.

"Rumors concerning you and the Lady Elise have reached my attention. What have you to say?"

Only seconds elapsed before Bryan answered, but those seconds seemed a lifetime to Elise. She could feel Bryan's eyes upon her back as if they emanated true heat and burned her with the force of his anger. She wanted to shrink before Richard because it was all so humiliating. She didn't want other people to know, especially Richard. Then there was the knowledge that she had brought this all about, that her carefully planned words to Eleanor had been absurd and foolish . . .

"Tell me the rumor, Your Grace, and I will tell you if it is true or false."

"Did you rape her?"

Elise held perfectly still, wishing that she could melt away and die rather than endure the heavy echo of Richard's words, which seemed to ricochet about the room. Again, Stede hesitated, a slight pause, but one that seemed to compel her. She did not want to turn around and face him, but she did turn, and his eyes were upon her.

"That, Your Grace, is something I believe the lady in question must answer." He gazed at her, coldly, politely. Expectantly. "Duchess?"

She wanted to leave—to leave the chamber, to leave the manor, to leave England. She wanted to go back in time, to pretend that she had never seen Bryan Stede's handsome features, had never known his name.

"Elise!" Richard thundered out.

She wanted to lower her head; she wanted to strike the Lion-Heart for humiliating her so. She could not allow her head to fall; she had to hold fast to her pride.

"Truly, Your Grace . . ." she began, stalling as she prayed for an answer to come to mind. She could say yes, and to her heart it would be the truth. But yes would demand explanations, and Richard, being a man, might well feel Stede's actions justified. "This matter is not one that should consume your precious time—"

"Then let's not allow it to consume more time than it needs!" Richard snapped.

"It can be of little importance—"

"Elise, it is surely of importance to you, else my mother would never have been involved. Now, I would like an answer."

So Eleanor had been the one. Dear God, she thought, Richard had just condemned her in Bryan's eyes, and she had never made the final decision to hang him. But she had set the wheels turning, and now the decision had been taken from her. Or had it? Was this a court of inquiry? Were she and Bryan both on trial? Or had the sentences already been passed down.

Elise felt Bryan step forward. Heat seemed to fill the air about him, and she was tempted to move away, as if her flesh feared the scorching of a fire.

For a terrible moment she wanted to scream. She wanted to cast herself down to Eleanor's knees and beg that she only be allowed to go home. She had wanted revenge. And, ruled by that savage obsession, what had she done?

"The Duchess of Montoui seems to have difficulty speaking this morning, which is most rare for her, Your Grace," Bryan said easily. "But, therefore, I shall do my best to answer the question. Did I rape her? It was never my intent. She said things that led me to believe she was other than innocent. Did I compromise her value as a titled and landed duchess? Yes, Your Grace. But not with evil intent. The night upon which we met was heavy with heartache and confusion, and the duchess, I believe, felt herself prevailed upon to play a role that led me to think her . . . not adverse to a liaison."

It was true. She had gone to him on her knees; she had told him that she had been Henry's mistress. Not a word that he had said had been a lie . . .

"God's blood, Bryan!" Richard said irritably, but Elise could tell that he was not angry with Bryan Stede, merely perplexed by the situation created. "The countryside is laden with eager peasant women, and you . . . never mind. Bryan, you deserved to have been rewarded royally for your never-failing loyalty to the Crown. You held fast to my father; you have proven yourself to me." Richard paused in his tirade for a moment and scratched his golden beard. " 'Tis known that you and Gwyneth have long been lovers, but Gwyneth was no innocent lass when you met. Tell me, when you knew of this situation"—Richard indicated Elise in a way that made her long to crack the bull heads of the two men together—"did it not occur to you that you should have offered marriage to the duchess?"

Bryan laughed, and Elise thought angrily that they might have been enjoying idle banter about the "fair" sex while they awaited a call to the battlefield.

"Your Grace, the thought did enter my mind. But by her own word, the duchess was determined to marry where she would. I felt I had no right to stop her."

"Had you not thought of issue from the alliance?"

"Yes; she assured me there would be none."

They were talking about her as if she were a horse one might think of buying. Elise had to keep reminding herself that Richard was the supreme power in the land, and that if he so chose, he could take everything from her. One did not throw things at the Lion-Heart or fly with flashing nails at his face to attempt to gouge out his eyes. Not if one wanted to continue living with one's limbs, health, and property.

Richard's eyes fell upon her, and Elise faced him squarely. She tried to remind him with her aquamarine gaze that she was his sister, that she was his blood, that he had no right to treat her as property as he did now.

But Richard's eyes remained impassive. "Stede, you leave me in a quandary, for you have bedded both women. But I do not believe that, as of this date, the Lady Elise can guarantee either of us that no issue could result from your time together. Gwyneth . . . is a more worldly woman. And with her wealth, she will be eagerly accepted by any man. I am afraid that I can no longer give her to you, Bryan."

Richard gazed back to his parchments. Elise felt one wild, triumphant moment; she *had* taken something from Stede—something inestimably dear.

But at what price?

Richard looked up once again, at Elise and at Bryan. "Sir Bryan Stede, it is my decision that you and the Lady Elise will be married. I shall set the date as . . . the night before the coronation. I shall need you that night, and, of course, for the coronation, but then I shall give you time, as I did with Marshal, to acquaint yourselves with marriage."

Water, like the great rush of a flooding stream, seemed to gush coldly about Elise. The rushing pounded in her ears. Hadn't she thought of this? Almost planned it herself? It had never seemed so horrible until this moment. Until Stede stood behind her, and she felt his anger, boiling into that cascading stream of water that threatened to send her to her knees . . .

"Here, Stede, come about!" Richard demanded, tapping on the parchment upon his table. "I shall not allow you to lose by this marriage. Elise already had Montoui, but see here. These lands . . . they stretch out beside those that belong to Gwyneth. The territory is even larger, if I have been advised correctly. Once they belonged to old Sir Harold, but Harold died that last week of battle in Normandy. I had scholars check the records carefully so that none be offended, and the records proved that Harold and Sir William—Elise's father—were distant cousins, from the time of William the Conqueror. Possession of these lands, Bryan, will make you not only the Duke of Montoui, but the Earl of Saxonby, and Lord of the lower coastal counties." Richard glanced up at Stede, pride and boyish pleasure etched clearly into his features. "I believe, Sir Stede, that you shall be more greatly rewarded than it might have otherwise been."

Elise could barely remain standing. Tremors that could rattle the earth seemed to grow within her; it was all too ironic, too unjust! Stede was still to be rewarded—through *her!*

Bryan was bent over the parchment, but he raised his head then, and his eyes met Elise's.

There were so many things in that indigo gaze. Triumph. Anger. Mockery. Laughter . . .

Elise stepped forward, bowing before Richard. "Your Grace, this is not necessary. Sir Stede and I are hardly compatible, and since his relationship with the Lady Gwyneth has been one long established—"

Richard stood, towering to his full height. He glanced at Eleanor, smiled, then turned to Elise. "I find my resolution to this matter completely satisfactory."

"Montoui is mine!" Elise snapped out recklessly. "And I despise Sir Bryan Stede!"

Perhaps she had, at last, reminded Richard that she was his father's daughter. His features, though impatient, gentled. "I do not take Montoui from you, Elise. I merely give a husband with whom to share the responsibility. And women are blessed with fickle natures. Surely you will reconcile yourself quickly. This marriage, Duchess, is of your own making."

"No!" Elise protested, "Richard, I shall never reconcile myself!'' she continued, not caring that she spoke to Richard, or that Bryan stood before her, hearing her every word. "What of Gwyneth?" she demanded. "She has a far greater claim upon this man than I!" An hour ago, she would have been pleased to see "poor Gwyneth" go hang—as long as it was without Stede.

"Gwyneth shall have Percy Montagu. He is young, deserving, and in need of land. I think they shall be quite compatible. The matter is settled. Now may I return to my damnable and eternal quest for coinage!"

Elise, not bothering to ask Richard's leave, spun about sharply on her heels and strode toward the door.

"Elise!" Richard thundered after her.

She turned slowly and dropped a grudging curtsy to him. "Your Grace?"

"You will remember that I am the king!"

"I have not forgotten."

Elise's gaze fell to Eleanor, who remained silently watching the scene, her sharp, dark eyes fathomless. *What have you done to me!* she wanted to shout.

But Eleanor's gaze was upon Richard, and Elise realized that she had pushed the fledgling king far enough. The Lion-Heart could not allow himself to be humiliated by a woman. If she didn't control her temper until she was no longer in his audience, he could strip her completely of lands. The slender thread of her relationship to him was good only so long as she obeyed him; kings had been known to kill when bloodlines interfered with their absolute dominion.

I did this myself, she reminded herself. *Yes! So that Stede might lose . . .*

"I beg your pardon, Your Grace," Elise said with a bow. And with a dignity she clung to tenaciously, she exited the chamber.

The country surrounding Sir Matthew's manor was beautiful. Summer blanketed the land with rich greenery and a profusion of colors as wildflowers bloomed over the sloping hills and within the thickets and forests.

Elise saddled her own horse despite the offers of assistance from Sir Matthew's anxious grooms. She knew there was consternation among them because she chose to ride out alone, but she could not be stopped. In part, because she did not care what happened to her. And in part because she simply could not bear to remain at the manor when she was so furious, her spirit torn, her last illusion at an end.

The morning sun touched down upon her and the wind ripped through her hair. Far beyond the pastureland where sheep bleated and grazed, a stream quivered beneath the golden rays of morning, and it was to this compelling ribbon of silver that Elise found herself riding.

Her mare was interested in nothing but the long, damp grasses that grew in thick swatches by the water's edge. Elise allowed her to wander where she would.

Careless of her fine linen tunic, Elise cast off her shoes and inched out into the water. A boulder made flat by centuries of the running water beckoned her, and she waded out to it, stretching herself out upon its length and allowing the sun to ripple over her, and warm her.

What a fool she had been. Her title . . . her relationship to Richard—all meant nothing. Castles were prizes; lands were prizes—women were prizes. She was no different from any other woman.

I did speak to Eleanor, I did play with this idea as a means of cutting Stede to the quick . . .

Vengeance is mine, sayeth the Lord, she reminded herself bitterly. How ironic, how very true. She had committed herself to a living hell because she had been fool enough to believe in herself.

Now it was done. Stede would not have Gwyneth. But he would have half of Cornwall because of some distant relative of her own adoptive father . . .

It was a travesty, a travesty of all that Henry had taught her.

Elise closed her eyes tightly against the sun. What did she do now? Appeal to the Pope—and risk Richard's wrath. Richard would soon be gone on his Crusade, and, surely, nothing else would matter to him. Richard didn't really care for anything but his Crusade. Once he was gone . . .

When he was gone, Stede would be gone. Perhaps to meet a Saracen blade and die. Did she really wish his death?

No. Chinon had taught her about death. About blood and broken bodies. For all the hate that she had harbored within her, she suddenly wanted peace. She had lost Percy. More than Percy, she had lost the dream of love. But it was done; nothing could be changed. By seeking to fight the world, she had done herself nothing but harm.

"I want to go home . . ." she heard herself whisper aloud. She had entered an arena believing she knew how to play the game; she now realized sadly that she had known nothing. Youth and pain had caused her to fight, and she had lost. Now she could only pray that the passing years brought her more wisdom, and a greater temperance.

Was there no way out of this? She could refuse to take her

vows. To what end? Eleanor had defied Henry—and spent sixteen years of life imprisoned. Could Richard be so callous?

Elise became so lost in dismal thoughts that she didn't hear the destrier draw near, nor did she hear anything at all until some slight movement warned her of a presence. She opened her eyes and discovered Bryan Stede staring down at her.

The water of the stream came to his calf-high boots; as was so often his custom, he stood with his hands on his hips, as if he were ever ready to draw his sword.

But he appeared speculative rather than angry now, and she was far too wretched to fear him.

Elise gazed into his eyes, then closed her own wearily once again. "Why are you here?" she asked him tonelessly.

"Why?"

She could not see him, but she knew by instinct that one dark brow had arched. "Duchess, that should be obvious. It seems to me that we have a great deal to discuss."

"There is little I can think of to say to you," Elise murmured flatly. She started as the calloused tip of his thumb grazed over her cheek, and her eyes flew open once again.

"Elise, this is your doing."

"No—"

"Duchess, I am not hard of hearing. You went to Eleanor—and God alone knows what you told her."

"I did not intend this," Elise said uneasily. The temptation was strong to flinch from his touch; it was not a sense of bravado, but rather one of exhaustion, that kept her from doing so.

He smiled, but the curve of his lip was bitter. "For once, I believe you. You intended merely to darken my image before Eleanor—and deprive me of a future."

"You do not deserve a rich future."

"But, alas! It seems I am to have one."

Moments ago, she had wanted peace. But Sir Bryan Stede had a remarkable talent for irritating her.

"It is still in the future," she said coolly, smoothly sliding her legs beneath her so that she cast off his touch and sat an arm's distance from him. "So much in this world is uncertain! Lightning can strike at any time. We speak of a date three weeks away! I could well drop dead in that time, and I'm quite sure I've more distant cousins in Normandy willing to make a claim to my estates—"

She broke off with a startled gasp as he gripped her shoulders, not painfully, but forcefully firm. His eyes held hers with an indigo intensity that startled and frightened.

"You're not thinking of anything foolish?" he demanded harshly.

"Foolish?" Elise repeated, confused and unnerved. Then she laughed dryly. "Do you mean as in taking my own life, Sir Stede? You flatter yourself. You are not worth dying for—or because of!"

"Then," he said softly, "do as Richard told you—reconcile yourself to the future."

"Are you reconciled, Stede?" she demanded.

He smiled at her, but once more the look upon his face was chilling. "Reconciled, Duchess? How could I not be? You bring to me a greater wealth than I had ever imagined."

"Wealth!" Elise exclaimed angrily, wrenching her shoulders from his grasp. "Do you care for nothing else? What of Gwyneth? Just two nights ago you went to her! To be with her. You had planned your life with her, yet today Richard says jump, and you discard her! What of life, Stede? What of the years, the days and the nights, that go on and on as those years unfold? Tell me, Stede. What of Gwyneth?"

A tic had begun in the faint blue line of a vein within the strong column of his neck. She was sorely testing a temper that was as explosive as fire, but she didn't care.

"Gwyneth," he said, with his voice remarkably controlled, "is going to marry Sir Percy. And you tell me, Duchess—what happened to this great love affair between the two of you? Where did he fit in with your plans for revenge?"

Elise lowered her eyes, but she did not hide her eyes quickly enough, for he began to laugh. "This is wonderful! You decided to take me because the great and noble Percy turned his back on you! And you talk to me of love! What an affair yours must have been!"

"Once—before you—it was a wonderful affair. Full of dreams and belief in the years to follow! I never decided I wanted you, Stede! I don't want you. I don't want anything to do with you—"

"You have a remarkable way of showing such things. But despite all of the things you've done to me—"

"The things I've done to you!"

"Poison, to name one," he reminded her drolly.

"I did not—oh, never mind! This is a useless conversation."

"I do mind. I mind very much. This is not going to be a useless conversation because you're going to get a few things straight."

"I am?" Elise queried coldly.

"You do try my tolerance, Elise," he warned her softly, and despite the heat of the sun, she felt suddenly cold from the touch of the stream that washed about her toes. She gazed longingly at the shoreline, and thought of standing to wade quickly there—away from him. Would he dare accost her here, with the manor so close that it could be seen?

"Had you but come to me," she heard him tell her, "I would have wed you without a royal command—and this travesty of an appearance before Richard and Eleanor. I think that's what angers me the most. You railed to me about how you despised me, and I tried to let you be. Then, behind my back, you cozen the queen and cry out to her as if you had been nothing but a sweet, totally innocent victim."

"I was an innocent victim!"

He raised his brows politely. "Henry's mistress? Hardly innocent, my dear duchess. You neglected to tell Eleanor that you were running from Chinon, and that you had Henry's ring in your possession. I'm quite sure you refrained from telling her that you had aimed a dagger at my throat and, in your own castle, poisoned the wine given a guest."

"I'm telling you for the last time, Stede, that I did not poison your wine! But since you feel that you must constantly fear for your life in my presence, wouldn't it be wise to go to Richard? If we both refuse to marry—"

He started to laugh again, casting a foot upon the boulder beside her and leaning an elbow upon his knee. "Duchess, I was angry. Very angry. I don't like to be forced to do anything. But this is your marital bed, and you will lie in it!"

The shore beckoned her with an ever greater charisma. Elise gazed at Stede with a black rage filling her heart. They were discussing their lives, and he found it all amusing. His stance was relaxed and casual and the idea of marriage didn't bother him at all; he might despise her, but as long as she came with a title, wealth, and land, his opinion of her was of no importance.

Elise smiled suddenly, seeing that his position was a little too relaxed. "My marital bed, Sir Stede? I assure you, I shall never lie in it." With those positive words, she stood and planted her palms sweetly against the breadth of his chest. Before his eyes had fully narrowed with suspicion, she pushed him with all her strength, and received the satisfaction of seeing him flounder, almost catch his balance, but then topple backward into the stream.

And she was ready. She made a wild spurt for the shoreline, careless of her bare feet over the pebble-strewn bed of the stream. She knew that she could move like mercury when she chose.

But she had underestimated Stede—a mistake she had made once too often, she reminded herself woefully as she felt the strength of his fingers wind around her ankle. She had almost touched upon the mossy bank when a gasp tore itself from her throat and she found herself falling, wrenched cleanly into the air, and then crashing down hard into the shallow stream. She sputtered as the water filled her mouth and trickled into her lungs, and at first she could think only of the need to breathe.

His fingers tangled into the wings of her hair, bringing her face above the surface, but even as she coughed and wheezed for breath, he straddled over her in the water.

"Let's get back to the conversation, Duchess. I had other plans for my life; you changed them. We will be married the day before the coronation. You are young, and I can forgive what has happened in the past. I am willing to make an effort at this thing, even though it angers me how you have gone about it. I swear to you that I'll hold no malice for what has been, but I'll also warn you that if you use violence or trickery against me in any form again, I'll retaliate in kind. You will be my wife, and it is quite within the law for a husband to flay his wife within an inch of her life. Heed my warning, and we shall get along fine. Doubt it, and—"

"I have never doubted your capability for violence," Elise said, shivering miserably within his grasp.

He muttered an impatient oath, but something in her eyes held him from further speech. They were wide and unfaltering upon his, and as beautifully crystal clear as the aquamarine water of the rushing stream that sparkled all about them. He felt her shaking, and he saw the pain that strained her fragile features. What was she? he wondered suddenly. The sweet and sheltered beauty Marshal seemed to think her? Torn and twisted by loss and the events about her? Or was she truly a witch by nature, clever enough to use her face and form to her advantage when the need arose. She continued to deny that she had poisoned him. . . . But, by God! He had been poisoned . . . in her home.

He sighed, suddenly very weary himself. So often one little wrong led to another that a tree became a forest filled with the webs of deceit and misunderstanding. She had loved—and apparently still did love—Percy Montagu. And the bastard had hurt her royally with his admission of his priorities. Which was truly ironic now, since Percy would still be wedding a woman who had already been Bryan's. But when Percy had refused to wed Elise, she had been nowhere near as wealthy as she was now that Richard had taken a hand in things. Being a natural cynic, Bryan was certain that Percy would have little difficulty accepting Gwyneth. Next to Isabel de Clare, and now Elise, Gwyneth was the richest heiress in the land.

Briefly, Bryan closed his eyes. It was true. Just two nights ago he had been with Gwyneth. Felt her enveloping warmth, enjoyed her laughter and her love of life. And of him . . .

Pain . . . regret . . . remorse—all tugged upon his conscience and his heart. He had imagined a pleasurable life. As a knight he would ride to battle; but there would have been a home to return to. A welcoming hearth, and the sweeter heat of a loving wife. Eager and pleased to greet him each time he returned to his home . . .

But instead of Gwyneth, he was to have this virago. He would never know what she was up to behind his back; he would never be able to eat or drink in his own home without wondering . . .

She is bringing me not only Montoui, but half of Cornwall, he reminded himself. And despite himself, he could not forget the night that had brought about all the events since. The night during which she had bewitched him. Like a haunting perfume, that memory had lingered with him, beckoned to him, made him long for more, as a boy who had tasted a sweet nectar, and he craved that taste again . . .

It was a pity that nine out of ten, he'd also be longing to gag her before taking her to bed.

Bryan opened his eyes and sighed again as he saw that she was still staring at him with hostility and rebellion in her gaze.

"Elise, Richard has issued his decrees. It is for us to decide if life is to be a heaven or hell."

His voice had been so soft. Gentle. There was even a gentleness in the touch of his indigo eyes as they met hers. A cloud passed over the sun and a sudden dizziness swept through Elise. She found herself wondering what this man would be like when he chose to be tender. What he was like when he touched

Gwenyth. Did he stroke her with tenderness? Smile with no mockery when she whispered to him?

The dizziness became a heat that swept along her spine, taking the chill from the water that rushed around her. Was he always stern and forbidding? Or did he laugh with pleasure and whisper sweet words of whimsy when he . . . touched Gwyneth? Was he always as hard as steel and as sharp as his blade, or was he sometimes vulnerable, trusting, tender . . . ?

Elise swallowed, dispelling her thoughts. She could never expect gentleness, tenderness—or even kind and respectable treatment—from this man. He would remain a distant enigma to her, as she was to him. But perhaps . . . perhaps having heard these words that carried no hostility, she could seek to right some of the disaster she had been instrumental in causing.

"Bryan . . . please. If we both went to Richard—"

"I will not go to him, Elise."

"But why?" she began, and then bitterness rose like bile to her throat. "The land. The land and the titles. That is all you care for!" she spat out.

His jaw seemed to tighten, but he replied with no hostility. "Don't be so quick to belittle a longing for land, and a place in the world. I have spent my life fighting for the land—always for another man. You were born with wealth, Duchess. Don't begrudge the fact that I have labored long and hard for mine."

"I do begrudge it! Montoui is mine."

He chuckled softly. "And now, Duchess, so is half of Cornwall. Because of me. Aren't you a little grateful?"

"Grateful! No! I have no desire for 'half of Cornwall'!" She gazed searchingly into his eyes for a moment, wishing that she were not imprisoned in his grasp in the water that was becoming cool again in every spot where he did not touch her. Those spots felt as if they were afire.

"Bryan . . ." she began softly again, thinking that perhaps something might be salvaged. And her words would be reasonable. "Bryan, the titles and land in Cornwall—they are worth far more than Montoui. And you are welcome to them! We can obey Richard. We can marry, but then amicably part ways. I will return to Montoui, and you may go and inspect the estates in Cornwall! We are both well aware that we can never be anything but the most bitter of enemies, and there is no reason to spend our lives in eternal misery—"

"Forget it!"

Her excited words froze in her throat. There was no gentleness, no trace of tenderness remaining in his eyes. The blue had gone terribly dark; indigo to black. His bronze flesh was clenched tightly over his strong features, and his jaw had hardened to a determined square. The heat of his tense touch contrasted sharply with the coolness of the stream.

"Why?" Elise whispered.

"Duchess, just as I crave land, I crave legal heirs to whom I may leave all that I forge. A man may only beget legal heirs with his legal wife."

Elise closed her eyes, unable to contain the shudder that shook her form beneath his.

"That you find me so repulsive, I am sorry," he told her coldly. "I have no wish myself to spend my nights upon a battleground. But if that is what you choose to make it, Elise, that is what it shall be."

She kept her eyes tightly clenched together. *No, it will not be,* she decided. This time, her thoughts were not of malice or of vengeance, just of determination, and of a deep-rooted fear. She could not lead the life he intended. She could not be his property, kept locked away in the manor as a possession, there to greet him when he chose, silent and *reconciled* when he shouted out his orders and departed, for battle—or for a more willing woman.

She could not do it for any man . . .

And especially not Stede. She hated him for not believing a word that she said; she hated him for what he had done to her; and she hated him for what he thought of her.

He was willing to forgive. And she wanted peace, but not at his price.

"Aren't you afraid to marry me?" she queried coolly.

"Afraid?"

"You say that I poisoned you once—"

"Aye," he replied, equally polite and cool. "But I said that I would forgive you your youth, and your past mistakes. I believe I can make you understand that a similar attempt would truly cast you into misery."

The tone was polite; the threat was unmistakable.

Elise maintained what poise she could within the ignominy of her position beneath him in the stream. She made no effort to fight his hold, but kept her voice even.

"Doesn't it bother you to know that you will be marrying a woman deeply in love with another man? That I will be longing for him, for his arms about—"

"What you long for, Duchess, does not concern me. What you do, of course, will. So 'long' to your heart's content, Elise, but as of this moment, consider me your keeper. And remember that you do not at all doubt my capabilities for violence."

"And what of you, Sir Stede?" Elise spat out, losing control of her temper. "What of you—and Gwyneth?"

A sardonic smile curved one corner of his lip, but an opaque cloud seemed suddenly to shield his eyes.

"Gwyneth has just been given to Percy."

"He'll refuse to marry her!" Elise exclaimed impetuously.

"Another theory for us to test. So far, you are the loser."

"You are not my superior yet, if that 'theory' is what you refer to."

"Husbands are always their wives' superiors," Bryan said lightly.

"The bloody hell—"

"By law, Elise, that is true."

Why was she fighting him now, from this absurd position that proved she was under his dominance?

"Do you understand all that I say to you, Elise?"

"Please," she said flatly, giving no answer to his words. "The stream is cold, and you are hurting me."

He must have decided that she had capitulated to his will, for a touch of pity crossed his eyes, and he rolled quickly away to release her. Elise rose with natural grace and met his eyes once more. "You'll understand if I choose to avoid you until the wedding?" she asked distantly.

"As you wish." She felt strangely detached as she watched him rise before her. He *was* taller than Richard, she thought very distantly. And from her great distance, she could admit that he was the perfect knight. Hard-muscled, but honed to a trim agility. Ruthless, determined, powerful, and rugged.

Yes, he made the perfect knight. He would fit the part of landed noble as well as Richard fit the role of king.

But all that he was made her hate him more, because it made her fear him more. She knew that he intended to crush her fully to his will. Therefore, he would set her out of his way. His life would hardly be affected; he would go on as before, only he would be richer.

Elise managed to smile vaguely at him as she turned about and called to her mare. Because her mind was so very distant, and it was so distant because her plans were spinning within it.

She would marry him. She would be just as docile as he or Richard could wish.

And she would attend the coronation. She would duly see Richard crowned King of England. She would go to the great banquet upon Bryan Stede's arm . . .

But once the festivities began, she would be gone. She would start making discreet arrangements now, and as soon as possible she would slip away.

Montoui was hers. If she could reach it alone, it would take an army for anyone to dispute that fact.

And Richard would have no armies to spare. He would need all his forces to hold England, and to go forth with his own passion—the Crusade for the Holy Land. Bryan Stede would accompany Richard and they would be gone for two—perhaps three?—years.

And in three years, she could build an unbreachable fortress—and find the way *out* of marriage.

AFFIX
STAMP
HERE

KENSINGTON CHOICE
Zebra Home Subscription Service, Inc.
120 Brighton Road
P.O.Box 5214
Clifton, NJ 07015-5214

4 FREE
Historical
Romances
are waiting
for you to
claim them!

(worth up to
$24.96)

See details
inside.....

FREE BOOK CERTIFICATE

Yes! Please send me 4 Kensington Choice (the best of Zebra and Pinnacle Books) Historical Romances without cost or obligation (worth up to $24.96). As a Kensington Choice subscriber, I will then receive 4 brand-new romances to preview each month for 10 days FREE. I can return any books I decide not to keep and owe nothing. The publisher's prices for Kensington Choice romances range from $4.99-$6.99, but as a preferred subscriber I will get these books for only $4.20 per book or $16.80 for all four titles. There is no minimum number of books to buy and I may cancel my subscription at any time. A $1.50 postage and handling charge is added to each shipment. No matter what I decide to do, my first 4 books are mine to keep, absolutely FREE!

Name _____

Address _____ Apt. _____

City _____ State _____ Zip _____

Telephone (___) _____

Signature _____

(If under 18, parent or guardian must sign)

Subscription subject to acceptance. Terms and prices subject to change.

KCHM97

We have 4 FREE BOOKS for you
as your introduction to
KENSINGTON CHOICE!
To get your FREE BOOKS, worth
up to $24.96, mail the card below.

4 BESTSELLING HISTORICAL ROMANCES BY YOUR FAVORITE AUTHORS CAN BE YOURS, FREE!

Kensington Choice brings you historical romances by your favorite bestselling authors including Janelle Taylor, Shannon Drake, Rosanne Bittner, Jo Beverley, and Georgina Gentry, just to name a few! Each book is filled with passion, adventure and the excitement of bygone times!

To introduce you to this great club which is part of Zebra Home Subscription Service, we'd like to send you your first 4 bestselling historical romances, absolutely free! And once you get these 4 free books to savor at home, we'll rush you the next 4 brand-new books at the lowest prices available, as soon as they are published.

The way the club works is that after your initial FREE shipment, you will get our 4 newest bestselling historical romances delivered to your doorstep each month at the preferred subscriber's rate of only $4.20 per book, a savings of up to $8.16 per month (since these titles sell in bookstores for $4.99-$6.99)! All books are sent on a 10-day free examination basis and there is no minimum number of books to buy. (A postage and handling charge of $1.50 is added to each shipment.) Plus as a regular subscriber, you'll receive our FREE monthly newsletter, *Zebra/Pinnacle Romance News*, which features author profiles, subscriber benefits, book previews and more!

So start today by returning the FREE BOOK CERTIFICATE provided. We'll send you 4 FREE BOOKS with no further obligation: A FREE gift offering you hours of reading pleasure with no obligation...how can you lose?

XIV

September, 1189
London

Elise stared out from her window to the street below. The people were so plentiful that if she half closed her eyes, they seemed to combine in a great and colorful wave.

Priests, monks, peasants, merchants, and nobles all scurried about. Richard Plantagenet would be crowned king tomorrow and the spectacle could easily be a once-in-a-lifetime affair.

The last month had been spent in preparation for the event. Holy fathers had rehearsed their chants for hours; seamstresses and tailors had sewn garments until their fingers were raw but their purses were full; and the nobility had flocked in from all over England, as well as neighboring Scotland and the Continent. Richard had inherited vast provinces on the Continent, but even those who owed their allegiance elsewhere had come for the pageantry—and for the sake of curiosity. The Lion-Heart was about to be duly crowned King of England.

Donkey carts mingled along with the fine, polished coaches of the landed and titled aristocracy. Occasionally a cry of fury erupted as a chamberpot was emptied from a town house window, but for the most part, priest, peasant, soldier, merchant, and lady moved through the street with little difficulty. The sheriff of London had things well in hand; armed knights were stationed throughout the town, and there were few willing to create a disturbance on this, Richard's most holy day. Richard,

with his flare for the dramatic, wanted the streets to overflow
with people hoping for just a sight of him. There were but two
guiding lights in the eyes of the average man, and those lights
were God and King. The only people *un*welcome at the event
would be those who did not love and embrace Christ, and that
meant London's Jews.

Elise knew that Richard meant to protect his Jewish community, for its people were, on the whole, educated and indus-
trious. They kept together, and they were necessary, for they
were moneylenders. And when a man defaulted to a moneylender, or should that moneylender die, the debt was owed
threefold to the king.

In Henry's day, the king and the Jewish community had maintained a relationship that was distant, but peaceful. Richard intended to carry on that tradition.

But as Elise stared down at the colors of the street, she noted
that she saw no yellow, the color worn by the Jews. The Christian population was too easily whipped to a frenzy these days
against anyone who was not Christ's disciple. God's knights had
been fighting the disbelievers in the Holy Land for many years
now, warring against the Saracens, Arabs, and Turks, and now,
if one was not a Christian, one was an enemy.

"Milady?"

Elise turned from the window as she heard Jeanne's voice
querying her softly. Jeanne had been with her for three weeks
now, and she still seemed nervous—about London, about the
events that were taking place. She knew Elise, and although
Elise had confided her well-laid plans to no one, she felt that
Jeanne sensed she was up to something.

"Is it time?" Elise asked blandly.

"Aye, Elise, it is time. Will Marshal waits to escort you to
the chapel. He asks that you make haste since His Grace, Richard Plantagenet, takes time from this busiest of days to stand
as sponsor for you before your bridegroom."

"I am ready," Elise said smoothly. She was ready. She had
been dressed for hours. Since she had not dared insult either

Richard or Bryan with a flagrant lack of concern for her own wedding, she had donned the stunning gown of ice blue made especially for the occasion. Her mirror of hammered metal had assured her that she appeared the perfect bride—or offering. The shift she wore beneath the gown was of the softest white silk; the tunic had flowing, angled sleeves that were trimmed with elegant white fox. Her headdress was delicate, combining gauze silks of both blue and white, and crowned with a row of gleaming sapphires and gold fleur-de-lis.

It mattered not, Elise decided, that the bride herself was as pale as snow, or that her eyes were huge sheets of turquoise, and seemed far too large for her face. She had pretended to no one that she entered into marriage happily; the artificial trappings, those that designated her obedience to her king despite her own wishes, were all that was important.

"Your cloak, Elise," Jeanne said.

The protecting garment was swept around her, and then she was moving down the stairs to meet Will and Isabel, who spoke with her current hostess, Mistress Wells, a plump, childless widow who had been only too happy to welcome a ward of the Lion-Heart into her home.

"Ah, Lady Elise! You are lovely!" Mistress Wells cried, her radiant smile sincere. "Pippa!" she called to her maid. "We must have a toast to the Lady Elise."

Wine, served in elegant red glass chalices that were reserved for only the most special occasions, appeared. Elise drained hers quickly. She knew that both Will and Isabel were watching her closely, their expressions a mixture of pity and fear.

Fear—that she would act rashly and cast them all into a state of turmoil the day before Richard's greatest moment.

Elise thanked Mistress Wells for the wine, then turned to Will. "Let's get on with it, shall we?" she queried.

The chapel where she was to be married was but a street away; with the crowds, however, Will had decided that they should ride. He was very awkward and uncomfortable himself, and, therefore, he rode in front of the ladies, his ear attuned to whatever advice his own bride might have for the reluctant duchess.

Isabel was doing her best to ignore cheerfully the fact that Elise despised her husband-to-be. " 'Tis strange, isn't it?" she inquired of Elise. "I'd heard so much of Will, yet never met him! All I knew was that a knight reputed to be fierce was coming to be my groom. I cannot tell you all the horrible things I imagined, knowing that he was twice my age. But then he was before me, and he was not fierce at all, but gentle and well mannered. I hated the thought of marriage, yet it has brought me nothing but happiness."

That is because you married Will Marshal, and not Bryan Stede, Elise thought. But she replied to Isabel with a vague smile. Will and Isabel had offered her nothing but kindness; she could not make them any more miserable about their task as escorts than they already were. And she remembered poignantly that it had been Isabel who had come to spend the day with her—conversing nonstop about flowers, laces, meat, anything to keep her mind occupied—on that morning several weeks past when she had heard that Sir Percy Montagu had willingly—no, eagerly—married the heiress Gwyneth of Cornwall.

Elise knew that they had reached the chapel; Richard had come in secret, but men-at-arms lined the street and guarded the doorway. Will helped her dismount from her horse, and the guards gave way.

The chapel was dim, lit by no more than twenty candles. Elise saw the friar standing at the altar; she saw Richard, royal and formidable in a rich violet cape. She felt Isabel, squeezing her arm reassuringly. "What a splendid groom!" she whispered. "Surely all the women in the land would envy you such a magnificent man!" she added with a soft sigh of envy.

Elise allowed her eyes to fall on Bryan. He stood beyond the Lion-Heart, and was every bit as formidable. His shirt, like hers, was white, and trimmed with Spanish lace. His tunic was red velvet; his legs, sheathed in white hose, gave evidence of the sinewed strength of his hard, lean, muscled frame. His mantle, pinned at one shoulder by a silver broach, was the black for which he had become known, and its angle enhanced the knightly breadth of his shoulders.

Embroidered into the back of the mantle, Elise noted bitterly, was the new coat-of-arms that now belonged to him: a shield, comprised of four sections. The falcon—an insignia bestowed upon him by Henry; the crossed swords of Montoui; the flying hawk that indicated his new holdings, which spread along the Welsh border; and the charging stallion of his counties in Cornwall.

He watched her in return. She had taken great care to avoid him until this day, and now she wished that she hadn't. She had forgotten how his eyes could fall upon her, so deeply blue that they seemed to match the black of his mantle; fathomless and compelling, piercing into her as if they could possess her soul . . . warning . . . threatening.

"Elise?" It was Richard who spoke; all else seemed suspended in motionless time. His hand stretched out to her. The candles, the incense, the silence of those around her seemed to envelop her. It was a misty dream, she convinced herself—one that must be endured so that she might awaken elsewhere . . .

She stepped forward and accepted Richard's hand. He nodded to the monk and pressed her hand in Bryan Stede's.

She wanted to wrench free, to disclaim the possession she felt in his firm touch. Her eyes met his and found them blue again, filled with mockery and triumph. The monk began speaking; Elise did not hear him. She felt the force of Bryan's hand as he pulled her down beside him so that they were on their knees together, facing the monk. Still, she didn't hear the words. She watched Bryan's chest as it rose and fell with the easy rhythm of his breathing; she felt the warmth of his body emanating about her. He was newly shaven, and a fresh scent of soap lingered about him, and something else, something very faint, and masculine. A pleasant scent that was his alone as a man: clean, but as unique as he. A halting reminder that although time had taken them apart so that they met now almost as strangers, she had known him, and would never forget the night in which they had met.

"Elise de Bois?"

The monk was uncomfortably prodding her with his stern voice. She was supposed to speak. He told her the words again, and she forced her lips to move, to repeat them.

And then Bryan was speaking. His words did not falter, as did hers; they were strong and clear.

The glowing light of the candles seemed to mesh together; it was too hot. She was being engulfed by a swirling darkness that threatened to plunge her into a senseless void. The heat and the powerful, innate tension that belonged to the man beside her became oppressive.

Elise clenched her teeth tightly together. She would not pass out; she would not give way to either fear or hatred . . .

The monk was speaking quickly, very quickly, relieved that his task was almost done. He offered mass with nervously trembling fingers, then muttered a last blessing in Latin, and sighed loudly.

Stede was pulling her to her feet. Then his hand was upon the small of her back; the touch was firm; as calculated and coolly victorious as the narrowed indigo eyes that turned to her.

" 'Tis done!" Richard cried jovially. But his impatience was apparent. He stepped forward, clapped Bryan upon the back, and kissed Elise upon the cheek. "We've time for no more than to raise a cup to this union, so let it be done! Elise, my mother awaits the assistance of yourself and Lady Isabel at Westchester Palace. Bryan, I am sorry to offer you such a bride and demand that you leave her, but there is still much to be done before tomorrow."

"Such is life, Your Grace," Bryan replied cordially, his tone belying the unease he was feeling. The wedding ceremony had gone too smoothly; it was true that she had faltered and whispered her vows, but Elise had spoken them without a knife at her throat. When he looked into her eyes, he knew that she was anything but reconciled to the situation. *She is my wife now,* he reminded himself. As Richard had said, it was done. Elise was his, as were all the titles, lands, and wealth that she brought him.

Still, he did not like the look in her wide, turquoise eyes. They were calmly defiant when they met his. The hostility he expected to find within them was tempered, as if . . .

As if she didn't at all accept what had happened.

Richard was leading them out to the portico of the chapel, where one of his retainers had appeared to offer them wine; there should have been a feast for a wedding, but the soon-to-be monarch had warned them previously that they should have to dispense with the customary meal. Bryan knew that Richard was already chaffing with impatience, determined to be back at work planning the morrow and his reign to follow. " 'Tis to Trefallen Castle I suggest you give the most care," Richard told Bryan as they drank the wine. "I cannot allow you leave to go until things are settled here, but it is your wealthiest holding, and falling to disrepair since the death of the old lord."

Bryan nodded. He had inspected the deeds and ledgers of all his new holdings since Richard had given him the complete list, and he knew that his wealth lay at Trefallen. Elise, he was certain, assumed that Montoui would be their main residence. She would have to accept the fact that she was to live in Cornwall. It was better, he decided. Kinder, in the long run, to her. At Montoui, she would feel her own power, and try to fight him. Taken from her home and those who thronged to serve her, she would better accept her role as wife.

"I shall make Trefallen my first concern, as soon as it is convenient," Bryan promised Richard.

Richard finished his wine. "We must leave, and adhere to business," he said, beckoning a guard to dispose of his cup. Bryan made a pretense of finishing his wine while he watched Elise. She was speaking with Isabel as she sipped her wine, but as if she felt his eyes upon her, she turned to him.

It was almost as if she smiled.

He didn't like it.

She had taken the proper pains with her appearance for the day; indeed, he had never seen her look more beautiful. The youth and perfection of her form were accented by the soft material of her clinging gown; the sapphires that crowned her golden head-dress caught the gemstone quality of her eyes and made them dazzling. Her hair was loose beneath the headdress, flowing in thick, lustrous waves that beguiled a man's fingers to caress those tresses. A straying tendril swept and curled over the provocative fullness of her breasts, and he found himself imagining her disrobed, allowing his hands to entangle freely in that lock of hair, and cup around the feminine softness beneath.

Would she fight him still? he wondered bitterly. Or, as she had warned, would she endure him, and dream of Percy with his every touch upon her?

A flash of heat as intense as a blacksmith's fire swept through him; he wanted to take her *now.* He did not trust her, and he railed silently against Richard for arranging his wedding this way. An hour would have been enough—enough to take that secretive smile from her lips, and convince her that what had been done was real. She was his wife, his property—his to possess. Perhaps it would take time to wipe all thoughts of Percy Montagu from her heart and mind, but in just an hour, he could have made a damned good beginning. He did not want to hurt her, just teach her that he was all the male she ever possibly could hope to handle, and exhaust her so with his imprint that she would tire of her hostility and bow to the inevitable.

Bryan compressed his lips. He did not dare to dream yet of a future when she would greet him with pleasure and curve her lips into a winning smile that was meant to welcome and seduce. But he was older and wiser than she was, and aware that, whether she begrudged him or not, she was blessed with youth, vibrant health—and an inherent sensuality. She might well revile him; but, by God, she would accept him, and she would not be able to deny herself.

"Bryan," Richard repeated impatiently. "The lords from Normandy await my council, and the sheriff of London is eager to finalize the guard arrangements for tomorrow night's banquet." He lowered his voice to a comradely whisper. "You may leave the banquet early, and claim your bride then, and I shall give you a royal promise not to disturb your privacy for three full days. Enough time, I should warrant, for any man to satisfy his lust!"

It is the now *that is so important,* Bryan thought fleetingly, noting again that calmly defiant look in his bride's eyes. But Richard had granted him great wealth, greater than he had ever imagined. He had bestowed upon him a high place within the nobility. He had no right to dispute the Lion-Heart. What, after all, was one more day? He had upheld his agreement and stayed away from Elise until this day. Tomorrow night, Richard would be indisputably king, and he could give his full attention to his private affairs.

Still . . .

"One minute more, Your Grace," Bryan said to Richard. "I've yet to kiss my bride."

Elise, pretending an interest in Isabel's conversation, yet longing to be away, could not hide her alarm when Bryan took a sudden, and very deliberate, step toward her. She saw the cool determination in his eyes, and she almost panicked, stepping away from him when he stood near her, towering over her, forcing her chin to tilt back to continue to meet his eyes. He smiled as his arms came sweeping around her, and she felt the hardness of his body. He bent low, enfolding her full against him, and claiming her lips with a slow deliberation. Something, as always, filled her with his touch. Something that was sweet, seeping to stain her soul as wine spread its stain over cloth. Something that was fire, invading her, enveloping her. Something that stunned her against her will, and left her bereft of all reason to fight . . .

Fight. She could not fight. she was standing before Richard, and she was Bryan's wife. So the kiss went on; her mouth gave way to Bryan's, her lips molded pliantly to his. She felt his tongue upon her teeth, finding hers, ensweeping it, caressing it. Strength seemed to fail her; the muted glow of the candles spun and dimmed and began to mist again. His left hand was strong upon the small of her back; his right cupped and supported her head. She could barely breathe; and she became aware of only his dizzying scent, and the sweet taste of the wine that lingered upon his tongue.

A ribald jolt of laughter at last interrupted the kiss. "Come, Stede, the girl is yours for a lifetime!" Richard exclaimed impatiently.

Bryan drew away from Elise; he smiled as he saw that he needed to steady her. But his smile faded as he saw the seething anger fill her eyes again, and he bowed low to her, mocking her with his own gaze.

Richard stepped forward to kiss her quickly on the cheek once again, and at that moment, Elise hated him as thoroughly as she did Stede. "Girl," he had called her. She was his blood, and he might care for her, but only when it was convenient. It had been convenient to fulfill propriety, and still richly reward Bryan Stede with her. But Bryan was the more important individual to Richard; Elise saw that clearly now. Brother, king—traitor . . . was all that she could think and feel.

She was still steadying her wobbling knees as Bryan gave her a final glance—as full of promise and warning as his kiss—and followed the bellowing Richard out of the chapel.

Tears sprang to Elise's eyes; she blinked them away impatiently as she instinctively raised her fingers to her mouth, as if she could brush away the taste of Bryan's lips. She caught Will Marshal's eyes upon her, and they were pitying. Was it because he knew the man who had married her? But Will was Bryan's friend. Maybe it was because he knew how the man who had married her felt about her . . .

She straightened her back, fighting to regain the strength Bryan had somehow managed to rob from her. She smiled at Isabel, and then Will. "Shall we go ourselves? We mustn't keep the queen waiting."

Will exhaled as if he had been holding his breath for a long time; he slipped one arm around his wife, and one around Elise, then proceeded to escort them to the street, where guards flanked around them. He delivered the two women to Westminster Palace, where they would attend Eleanor, and then hurried off to join Richard.

Elise endured the queen's congratulations and good wishes, and sat to discuss the proprieties for the next day's coronation. She listened carefully to the queen's words regarding her obligations in greeting the guests, and noted with great relief that she had planned well; she would be free in plenty of time to make good her disappearance. Bryan Stede would never rob her of her strength and reason again. The marriage kiss was the last he would take from her.

As dusk fell, she was relieved of service, and allowed to return to Mistress Wells's town house. Her hostess—who had generously offered the town house to the young couple for "those days of bliss following a wedding!"—had already departed for a sister's residence.

Elise, feeling a bit guilty since she had grown extremely fond of Mistress Wells, was nevertheless relieved that she was gone. She was alone with only a houseful of discreet servants, and, of course, Jeanne.

The latter was to cause Elise more difficulty than Elise had expected.

"I'm sure," Jeanne told her as she carefully helped her out of the elegant blue gown, "that you haven't eaten a thing all day. I'm going to the kitchen myself to see to a full meal, and then I'm going to put you to bed. You'll have need of a good night's sleep before the ceremonies tomorrow, and then tomorrow night . . ."

Elise clenched her jaw tightly as Jeanne's voice trailed away uncertainly. She spoke impatiently. "I'm not at all hungry, Jeanne. Nor am I ready for bed. I've a letter to write, and then we must sit down together to talk."

Jeanne's eyes narrowed with suspicion. "Milady, what are you about? I know how you felt about this knight, Stede, but things have surely been righted by this wedding—at Richard's command. I was so pleased to watch you accept what was surely the best solution under God; and now you are his wife and sworn to obedience—"

The use of the word "obedience" was the final element that caused Elise's temper to flare. "Jeanne! I can bear no more!"

Elise swept her nightgown from the servant's hands and slipped it impatiently over her head. "I need parchment and a quill," she said firmly, her voice brooking no interference.

Jeanne pursed her lips together, but supplied the requested items with no further word. Elise sat on her bed and leaned over a trunk of her clothing with the parchment laid upon it and the quill in her hand. She had mentally composed the note many times; it took her only a second now to refresh the words in her mind.

"Stede," she addressed it, purposely withholding any of his titles, and most certainly not referring to him as her husband. She began to move the quill quickly over the parchment:

> I have recently heard of a problem in my Duchy of Montoui. As not to ruin Richard's day, or press your mind with further worry, I leave this note, rather than bother you with a discussion. I wish you my best with your Cornish holdings, and I pray God keep you when you depart on the most noble Crusade.

She did not affix her signature to the note; when he found it upon the bed the next night, he would know whom it was from, just as surely as he would know its meaning. Montoui was hers, and she would rule it alone. If he contested such a claim, she would use all her forces against him. He was welcome to everything else that the marriage had brought him.

She was studying her words when Jeanne challenged her again. "Milady, what are—"

"Sit down, Jeanne," Elise said. She waited until her disgruntled maid sat uneasily upon the foot of the bed, then continued.

"I have no intent of becoming nothing more than a useful vassal to Bryan Stede. I—"

"You're his wife!" Jeanne gasped out.

"As Richard ordered. I did nothing to fight that. But I will not live with him, or be ordered about by him. I have sent messages home, Jeanne, arranging for an escort to meet us at Bruges, and take us safely on to Montoui."

"You plan to travel through England to the crossing alone? That is madness, Elise!"

"Jeanne, I'll remind you that I am your duchess," Elise said primly. "I do not plan on traveling through England—or even to make the crossing—alone. Tomorrow night at ten we are to meet a party of holy sisters at the river Thames. They have come for the coronation, but plan to leave London tomorrow night. We will travel with them, and be entirely safe from wayfarers."

"Milady, this is foolhardy. I cannot allow you to walk out on your husband, and to so flagrantly defy Richard!"

"Jeanne—" Elise leaned over and firmly grasped Jeanne about the wrist to draw her full attention. "This is what I will do. And so help me, by Christ, I will see that your tongue is sliced from your mouth if you betray me! If you choose not to come, that is your affair. But I will leave."

Jeanne was silent for several minutes, meeting Elise's glare. The girl was dead-fast determined. Jeanne allowed her eyes to fall with a soft sigh. There had been a time when she understood; when she had hated Bryan Stede as much as she loved Elise. But that had been when her lady had been dishonored; she had even taken secret pains to see that Elise's honor had been avenged. But now, with marriage, honor had been returned. Most ladies of breeding were wed without choice or consent; it was the way of the world. Elise was creating a road of deeper misery for herself to desert and humiliate the man she had married—a man who was not, Jeanne was certain, the type to forget and forgive such treachery.

"Milady," Jeanne began again, but she saw the stubborn set to Elise's jaw, and knew that nothing would change her mind.

She loved Elise as she might have her own child. She would
never leave her.

"What of the banquet?" Jeanne asked.

Elise smiled brilliantly, and laughed with a sound more sweet
than Jeanne had heard come from her mistress in a long time.
"You shall await me at the rear door of the banqueting hall.
You'll be quite safe; Richard has men stationed all about. You'll
have a cart; I've already purchased it; it will be here tomorrow.
I'll leave the banquet as soon as it's safe to do so, cover myself
with the simple wool cloak that you'll bring, and we'll be on
our way."

"I don't like it," Jeanne murmured.

"We must pack," Elise said, ignoring the words. "And then
it's true; we will need a good night's sleep."

The streets were filled like an overfull cup; the crowd hustled
and shoved, and the Lion-Heart's men were hard put to hold
back the cheering throng. But the pageantry was magnificent.
Cloth covered the ground from the palace to the abbey, and first
the highest clergymen, and then the most powerful nobles,
would precede Richard along the path to his coronation.

Summer flowers were thrown; the monks raised their trained
voices high in chant. And then, Richard was before them, ac-
knowledging his people with nods, absorbing their idolization.
He was wonderful to the people: a beautiful, muscled soldier
of God; a king who would make them proud and England great.

Elise was not a part of the procession, but she had a special
place reserved for her along with Queen Eleanor, Isabel de
Clare, and John's new bride. She watched the proceedings, feeling every bit as awed as any spectator. The clergy and the nobles
were all decked out in their finest dress; gold, silks, furs and
jewels abounded, and she felt the sense of excitement as a child
would . . .

Until Bryan Stede passed.

He walked with Will Marshal and Prince John, and the

crowds went wild when the three passed. Bryan and Will had long been famed as "England's" champions, and John, well, John was Richard's brother; his boyish sins could be forgotten for today.

Elise barely noticed John; her eyes were upon the man who stood a head taller than he. Bryan was dressed in crimson today, and with his dark eyes serving as a sharp contrast of color, he was arrestingly handsome. He nodded to the crowds, as did Will, accepting their homage gracefully. Like Richard, he was a man to give them pride. A proven soldier, stately, masculine, and heartachingly handsome to boot.

If only they knew him! Elise thought bitterly. Then she paled suddenly, for he was before her, and his eyes were upon her. He bowed low to her; Eleanor laughed delightedly and cheered, and the crowd took up the cheer. Such a knight should have a young and lovely lady, and just as the crowd loved pageantry, it loved a good romance. Elise saw that Bryan's eyes were filled with sardonic mockery; the crowd did not. There was little she could do but smile graciously, and wish that the day would end so that she could make good her escape.

The procession went on into the abbey; here Elise had a place. She watched Richard humble himself before his people, swear to protect and defend them, and then be crowned King of England. The crowd went wild, welcoming him to their hearts. If there were any dissenters, Richard's guards had seen that they had no voice.

The parade and the religious ceremony took most of the day; it was dusk when Richard made his last appearance before the crowd, then ducked into the banqueting hall. There was still a crowd about him, for hundreds of guests had been invited. But these guests were the nobility. Silks and furs and jewels filled the hall.

Even entering with Eleanor, Elise found herself jostled about and brushed and bruised as she followed the queen to the head table. Drink was already flowing freely—mead, ale, and wine— and it quickly appeared to Elise that England's nobility was pleased for any occasion to behave as drunks, the ladies no less than the lords.

She tensed as she felt a hand upon her shoulder, and spun about to see that Bryan had at last caught up with her. "Good evening, wife," he said softly.

He was not among those who had been imbibing freely, she noted instantly. He was dead sober, which made his grim smile all the more difficult to tolerate. Elise did not resist his grip, but neither did she reply to his greeting.

"We are, I believe, at the head table, seated to the left of Eleanor. I understand that we will be by Percy and Gwyneth. It should lead to an interesting evening."

Bryan saw the blood drain from her features, leaving her face pale and strained. *So she still craves Percy!* he thought, and he fought desperately to control the fury that rose within him with reason, reminding himself that she had been deeply in love with the man—happenstance had worked against her. Bryan grated his jaws hard together and swallowed to keep his voice even. Tonight was his; he might have to watch his wife adore Percy with her eyes, but he would be the one to take her home, and if he left a dozen candles burning throughout the night, she would know that it was not Percy Montagu who held her.

"Come," he said more kindly, "let's take our seats." She still did not speak to him, and as he led her through the crowd, he wondered at his fury, and his emotion. Marriage . . . it was a legal matter, meant for the procreation of legal heirs. It was a contract. He had always considered it so. He had cared for Gwyneth, enjoyed her sweet spirit and willing embrace. Yet he had accepted her marriage to Percy easily. Regret, yes, he had felt a tug of regret. But nothing like this . . . fury . . . that consumed him senselessly over a woman he had touched but once, and would need to watch like a hawk just to assure himself that she wasn't ready to take a blade to his back.

Possession, he told himself dryly. A man was always ready to fight for his possessions. He would fight readily for the land so recently given to him; with equal fervor he would protect his horse, his castles, his crops—and his wife.

"Bryan!" His name was called with cheerful delight as they reached the head table. He saw Gwyneth, and smiled in return, then extended his greeting to the scowling Percy, who rose beside her.

"Sir Percy," he said with a nod, trying to ignore the fact that Percy's eyes were upon Elise, and that Elise was returning his stare. "Gwyneth, I don't believe that you and Elise have met as yet."

"No, and 'tis a great pity, for we are to be neighbors!" Gwyneth exclaimed enthusiastically.

Elise tried to return the smile offered to her by the dazzling Gwyneth, but the awkward situation was not so easy for her to handle. *How can you smile at me so when it is I who am wed to this man who you . . . loved? And bedded.* She wanted to shriek.

Gwyneth's smile seemed to be sincere. She was a beautiful woman with snapping dark eyes, beautifully translucent, fair skin, and thick, midnight hair that enhanced the beauty of her pale features. Elise could not resist a glance at Bryan. Was he looking at Gwyneth and seeing her as she was? Or did he, in his mind, strip her of her finery and imagine the times that they had shared together in sweet and eager passion?

Suddenly, she hated Bryan all the more fiercely. He had slept with Gwyneth, and with her. And Gwyneth had slept with Bryan, and now, with her husband, Percy. Elise felt a sudden fury that the situation was not twofold. She wished fervently that she had fallen into bed with Percy that long-ago night at Montoui just so that now she might force Bryan to wonder whether she was remembering another man's touch, just as she wondered about him.

"Neighbors?" she heard herself query.

"Oh, yes!" Gwyneth said, her smile broadening with pleasure. "Our main manors are but an hour's ride apart. I so look forward to becoming friends, Elise."

Elise managed to mutter something polite in return. Whether Gwyneth was glad that she was to be her neighbor—or merely pleased that Bryan, her old lover, would be near—Elise wasn't sure. But she convinced herself that her own feelings were immaterial; she would never be Gwyneth's neighbor because she was leaving—this night. Gwyneth and Bryan were welcome to each other. And Percy! Percy deserved whatever fell his way. He had turned from her because of Bryan, but had pliantly taken Gwyneth when so offered . . .

And tonight! How could he stare at her with such longing and reproach! It was his doing. His! Yet she could not hate him, for the hurt lurked so strongly in his eyes. He looked wonderful. Lean and slender, handsome with his fine-boned features and dark-fringed, light eyes. She wanted to reach out and touch his cheek, soothe the pain that tightened his brow . . .

"You'll enjoy Cornwall, I'm sure of it!" Gwyneth said, turning to Percy. The hurt instantly left his eyes, and Elise realized that he was not at all dismayed with his marriage. "Don't you think that Elise will enjoy the countryside? It is so beautiful."

"Yes . . . I've seen it so briefly, but it is beautiful," Percy responded to her.

Elise became aware of Bryan's hand, encircling her waist. She didn't want him touching her, and she didn't want to endure any more of their polite farce. "Excuse me. I see the queen, and I promised to help her oversee the seating arrangements . . ." She managed to elude Bryan's grip easily and to move with graceful dignity toward the queen.

Bryan watched her go speculatively, then took his seat beside Gwyneth. Percy's behavior was circumspect, and the three enjoyed a surprisingly civil conversation about animal husbandry and the benefits of having a trustworthy steward to govern a fief in the owner's absence.

A stalwart knight who had apparently imbibed freely of ale hailed Percy. Percy, too, excused himself, and Bryan found that he and Gwyneth were alone. He smiled at her with the comfort of a long friendship. "How does married life go with you, Gwyneth."

She chuckled huskily. "Well enough, Bryan. He is young, gentle, and can be very charming. But I miss you," she added with a soft insinuation. "But . . . we will be neighbors."

Bryan took her hand with a tender smile. "Gwyneth, I have wronged your husband once. I cannot, in good conscience, do so again."

Gwyneth's eyes traveled down the hall. Bryan saw that she watched Elise, who was helping Eleanor to placate a knight who had been given a position at the far rear of the hall.

"She is lovely," Gwyneth said with no rancor.

"Yes."

"But not at all pleased with the situation."

"Not at all."

"Well, remember, if life becomes too bitter, I can still be your friend."

Bryan took her hand in his and squeezed it gently, then placed a tender kiss upon it. "A good friend," he told her. "And I'll always remember."

Elise could not hear the words exchanged; she did see the chivalrous gesture, and she felt a burning of fury deep within her. She shouldn't care that he was still entranced by his old mistress; she was leaving him. But she did care. She cared because . . . because he intended to have her . . . imprison her and keep his alliance with Gwyneth all the same. Well, he could have Gwyneth this very night if he wished; she would be gone.

Elise frowned suddenly, forgetting the disturbing picture of Bryan Stede tenderly touching Gwyneth. An armored guard had just jostled his way through the drunken revelers to Stede's side. She watched Bryan's features tense and harden. He nodded to the guard, then rose and followed him out.

Elise nervously moistened her lips. If Bryan were outside, he could waylay her plans to escape.

She hesitated only a minute, then rushed through the crowd

to follow Bryan at a discreet distance. But when she at last cleared the hall and reached the street, she stopped in horror.

Bodies littered the steps; men were screaming with pain, and she saw the harried sheriff of London thundering above the chaos to bring order.

"Go no further, lady!" a guard cried, stopping her.

"What has happened?" Elise cried out.

"The Jews!" the young guard exclaimed breathlessly. "They sought to honor Richard with the gifts, but the rabble went crazy. They called them the enemies of Christ, and a riot broke out. Get back inside; no one is safe here . . ."

"Oh, dear God!" Elise caught her breath as the body nearest her moved, reaching out a bony hand. The man's yellow cloak was stained with a brilliant spot of red. Blood. "He needs help!"

"His own will help him," the guard told her. "Feeling runs high against the Jews tonight; a man risks his life and reputation to give them succor. The best we can do is stop the slaughter. God Almighty! The priests are urging the people on to murder!"

"Go home! Disperse! God does not ask us to be murderers of innocent, unarmed men and women!"

The stern, deeply thundering shout at last stilled the noise of the crowd. Elise saw that it was not the sheriff who spoke, but Bryan. He was moving through the crowd, not brandishing his sword, but walking with such a vengeful fury that all gave way. "Go, I say! And seek no blood. God has given you a king this day; do not sully the gift with the spilling of blood."

The people murmured beneath their breath, but they began to move away. Tears and cries of anguish rose then, as women and children ran about to find their dead and wounded.

As Elise continued to stare with horror, she saw Bryan stop and kneel down before one of the yellow-clad bodies. He ripped a length of fabric from his mantle to bind the wound of an old man. Then, from the corner of her eye, she noted a furtive movement near Bryan. A man, who by his size and bulk and tattered, sooted clothing might well have been a smith, was moving upon Bryan with a wooden beam held high in his hand to strike—not at all ready to forget his vendetta against the Jews at the say-so of a well-clad knight.

"Bryan!" Elise heard herself shriek out. He spun about in the nick of time, wrenched the club from his would-be attacker, and broke it over his knee. "Go home, man!" he charged furiously.

The large man backed off in fear, then lowered his head in shame. He met Bryan's eyes, nodded, and departed.

Elise started, swallowing as her husband's eyes came to rest upon her once again. His look was different . . . curious. She didn't mean to walk toward him, but her feet carried her to his side nevertheless. Once there, she knelt down by the injured man.

"Go back into the hall, Elise," Bryan told her.

"This man . . . is . . . hurt," she said miserably. Her teeth were chattering.

"I'll tend to him until his family comes. Get back inside."

She met his eyes. In the darkness of the night she could read nothing in them, nor could she find anything in his voice except for a weary acceptance that the night had brought him more to handle.

"Elise, go in. I'll join you soon."

"I . . . I . . . was told that the nobility should not involve itself . . . that a man could risk his reputation . . . or his life, by helping these people. The crowd is surly and dangerous . . ."

"You did your part to save me from the crowd," Bryan said quietly. "And I will leave no unarmed, innocent man to die merely because he tried to honor his king. I care not for the temperament of the people; my reputation must stand alone. Now, please, Elise, go back inside. There are many dead out here, and many wounded. And there are still those about who are frenzied with the scent of blood. Go inside; I do not wish to have to worry about your safety."

She rose, her movements lacking their usual grace. *I am not going inside, Bryan,* she thought, *I am running away.*

But she did begin to walk. Toward the entrance to the hall.

She moved like a puppet, following her plans. Jeanne would be around the corner, waiting for her—if nothing had happened to her during the riot.

Tears that she could not begin to understand stung Elise's eyes. She skirted by the entrance to the hall, and saw that Jeanne was, indeed, waiting for her. Jeanne was safe; this eastern street had not succumbed to the violence at the entrance to the hall . . .

Elise paused before hurrying toward the cart. She glanced back to try and catch a glimpse of Bryan, but Richard's guards had already thronged around him to take charge.

A tear slid down her cheek and she impatiently brushed it away. She was doing what was right, what she had to do. It was her only chance to escape Bryan Stede, to escape the plight of finding herself his wife in truth. . . . It was just a pity that to-night, of all nights, had to be the occasion when she had seen in him something that she had to . . . respect, and admire.

XV

September 15, 1189
Montoui

Elise had never been so glad to see the stalwart ramparts of her castle rise against the blue morning sky.

Traveling with the sisters had indeed been safe, but it had also been painstakingly slow. A journey that should have taken her no more than seven or eight days had taken two full weeks. Sister Agnes Maria had suffered from severe corns, and Sister Anna Theresa had become the victim of painful blisters—upon her posterior, no less—and so the party had stopped many times, unable either to walk or ride.

The nights had been misery, spent in crowded hostels that were more often than not stale, dank, and dirty. But it had been more than the poor conditions that had kept Elise awake; as the others found the peace of sleep, her mind haunted her with battle. She could not forget the last moments she had spent with Bryan. But even as the picture rose of his stalwart concern for the injured, a new one replaced it. Bryan . . . and his fury on the night they had met. Bryan . . . with the taunt of triumph in his eyes when they had stood in the chapel.

Bending low over Gwyneth's hand, a tenderness that he had never directed at her softening the severity of his features.

Sometimes, when she had lain between the snoring nuns, she had found herself digging her nails into the bedding, touched by a strange bolt of heat that was followed by shivers that threatened to rattle her teeth. Heat caused by memory of his kiss that day in the chapel, a memory that combined with another hazy image, that of the night in the hunting lodge, and she would feel again as if she were swept by the maelstrom of the storm, and seared by the warmth of the fire.

When morning would come and she would awaken from broken and restless sleep, she would be more tired than when she had lain down the night before. Irritability would become the smoldering anger that was ever ready to rise, and she would be more than ever determined that she would best Bryan Stede.

The night before last had finally brought them across the Channel and to the Continent. Fine armored men, decked in the colors and emblems of Montoui, had been there to meet them. She and Jeanne had parted company with the sisters, after seeing that their cloister would be well endowed.

And now . . .

Now she could see the parapets, towers, and ramparts of home, so proud and beautiful against the rolling green landscape. Elise began to laugh with the sheer pleasure of at long last returning to the land that was hers, and she spun her mare about to accost her maid cheerfully.

"Jeanne! We're almost there! Ah, for a long bath and a night's sleep without the sound of snoring and being elbowed off the bed by Sister Anna Theresa!"

Jeanne smiled vaguely, but made no reply. Elise frowned at Jeanne's lack of enthusiasm, then shrugged and turned about to spur her mare forward once again. Jeanne had been behaving more and more peculiarly since they had reached the Continent. Which was strange, because Elise had been the nervous one in England, always looking over her shoulder to assure herself that no one was in pursuit.

She wondered if Jeanne was nervous because they did not know the guards who had come. Elise had been surprised herself that Michael had not sent men she knew well—Michael was always so anxious about her welfare and comfort. But unless Montoui had been burned to the ground and Michael de la

Pole along with it, no one would be wearing the specially crafted armor of Montoui without his consent. And the young men sent to escort and guide them had proven themselves efficient and cordial beyond fault. It was absurd for Jeanne to be nervous now. Unless she was fearing the wrath of Bryan Stede.

But now . . . now Montoui was before them. Once they were beyond the sturdy walls of the town, nothing could touch them, except for the King of England himself, and Elise knew full well that Richard would not let such a petty matter take his time when he had the affairs of England to settle and a Crusade to launch. And the day of their homecoming could not have been more beautiful. Soft white clouds lightly powdered a brilliant sky, and the fields and forests were alive in verdant green.

She laughed again and gave her mare free reign. It felt wonderful to race with the breeze across the land. Uplifting, exhilarating . . . and free. So very, very free! It seemed as if it had been forever since she felt this wonderful sense of freedom, as if she was once again the mistress of her own fate.

At last she came to the town gate, and waved once more to the men-at-arms who saw her, and allowed her entry. She swept by the smithy and the market, and over the bridge, past the stones of the castle and into the keep. Only then did she pause her reckless ride and swing from the mare's saddle, too jubilant to care that she raced like a child into the entryway, then on to the great hall.

"Michael!" she cried, stripping off her riding gloves. "Michael!" She could see that a fire was burning in the hearth, and she strode to it. The day was not cold, but the castle was always damp, and the warmth of the fire seemed to welcome her home. She began to practice mentally what she would say when her steward congratulated her on her marriage, and thought about how she would explain that she intended to fortify her castle against her new husband.

Then she froze slowly, for she realized that she noted something that wasn't quite right . . .

Elise felt herself turn as if she were in a dream, for what she had seen from the corner of her eye could not be. It had been a trick of the light, and nothing more.

She stood deathly still as she stared down the hall to the head of the banquet table; it seemed that even her heart had ceased to beat.

He was there. Bryan Stede. Sitting in Duke William's elaborately carved chair. His legs were stretched out upon the table, one booted foot crossed over the other. One set of long fingers strummed idly upon the table; the other held a silver chalice. He took a sip from it as he stared at Elise, one raven's brow raised slightly, a sardonic smile slashing a grim line against his jaw.

"Home at last!" he murmured, making no effort to move. "The journey took you long enough."

She could not accept what she was seeing: Stede, here, ensconced in Duke William's chair, *her* chair. It was too bitter an irony to accept . . .

"What are you doing here?" she asked, her voice heavy and too slow. Her mind was spinning, and she felt as if she could not breathe.

"What am I doing here?" he repeated politely. But then she heard the hard edge to his voice, and ruthless tension swept the smile from his lips. "You wrote of a problem in Montoui. It was surely . . . noble . . . of you to take the responsibility upon yourself, but you need not have done so. Indeed, you might have traveled here far more swiftly in my company." He set the chalice down and swung his feet to the floor, rising. "But do you know, wife, upon arriving I discovered something strange? Your steward assured me that there had been no problem. In fact, Michael was quite offended. He is a competent man, adept at handling the affairs of the duchy in your absence. He was quite surprised to see me; he had assumed that I would be arriving with you. Apparently, when you wrote asking him to send an escort to the crossing, you neglected to tell him that you were rushing home alone."

Instinctively, Elise backed away from him, although he had as yet to take a step toward her.

"Where is Michael?" she heard herself ask, and then she wondered what difference it made. Aging Michael could not possibly protect her against Bryan Stede.

"Seeing to a feast to welcome you home, Duchess," Bryan replied evenly. "The north tower guard saw your party arriving some time ago."

Elise found her lips too dry to form words; she moistened them with the tip of her tongue, then spoke quickly, way too quickly. "This conversation is a farce, and we both know it. You cannot stay here; I will not allow it. You may leave in peace, or I shall call my captain of the guard and see that you are expelled by force. I do not wish to humiliate you so, but if you leave me no choice—"

She stopped speaking suddenly, because he was laughing. But his laughter was dry, and the husky timbre held a threat more chilling than the loudest shout. "Elise, a wife with no wish to humiliate her husband does not desert him hours before the marriage is to be consummated. You are welcome to call the captain of the guard, but I am afraid that you will not know him, nor will he be willing to remove me by force."

Floodwaters of dismay waved all around her, but she fought them. "Stede, you're a fool! You may have replaced a few men, but my garrison is five hundred strong, and my people are loyal—"

"Oh, very loyal. But when you wrote to inform Michael that you were coming home, you also neglected to warn him that you had decided to go to war against your husband. And you underestimated our king. Richard sent out his own letters— among them, one to Montoui to inform your steward of your marriage, and of my status. Michael was pleased to welcome a new duke. Your young captain of the guard . . . well, he was most anxious to accept an offer to journey to London to serve King Richard. You'll find that a number of the men—among them the five who escorted you here—are mine. Old friends who fought with me long and hard at Henry's side. Those men who are not my own . . . well, not even your most loyal servants would dare defy orders written by Richard himself, claiming me to be the Duke of Montoui."

"You . . . cannot . . . stay . . . here!" Elise lashed out.

He smiled. "I do not intend to stay here. But neither shall you."

"What?"

"We leave tonight. Your antics have dearly cost me time. Richard gave me two months, and no more, in which to settle my affairs. I must go to Cornwall."

"So go to Cornwall!" Elise whispered. "But I am not going. This is my home. Where I belong. I am not going anywhere."

He stared at her a long moment. She was trembling so that she feared she would stagger and fall at any second; it appeared that he had outplayed her every move, and now she was cornered, with no move left to make.

He strode to the fire and reached his hands out toward it, staring into the flames. "Milady, I'm afraid that you leave me with no choice but to threaten you in return. We leave tonight. As soon as you have had time to dine, bathe, and rest. You may come with me peacefully, or by force. I do not wish to humiliate you, but if you leave me no choice . . ."

His sentence dangled mockingly, then faded away.

For once, she sensed that he was about to move before he actually did. "I am not leaving Montoui!" she snapped out determinedly. And then she tore swiftly for the stairs, racing along their length to the door to her chamber. Once inside, she slammed the door and drew the heavy wooden bolt firmly into place. She slumped against it, shaking.

No force on earth would make her open that bolt.

He watched her run up the stairs as swiftly as if she floated, and he locked his jaw as he heard the slam of the door and the thud of the bolt. Then he stared at the fire again, his hands clasped behind his back.

It had gone as he had expected.

Well, so be it, Bryan thought with angry impatience. He had been worried sick when he hadn't been able to find her the night of Richard's banquet. Eleanor had calmed him by suggesting that Will and Isabel had seen her home, since trouble had promised to plague the streets through the night.

But then he had arrived at the town house to find her note, and all the worrying had knotted into a hard fury in his stomach. She had duped him. Cleanly and precisely. No wonder she had waited so obediently for their wedding and walked so calmly through the ceremony; it had given her time to plan. Once she reached Montoui, it would take a war to drag her out . . .

Even now his stomach knotted again with the sick fury that had assailed him with the knowledge that she had taken him completely.

But there had been another note left him; it had taken him a long while to cool his mind enough to see it.

The second note was from Elise's maid, a woman he had scantly noticed before. It began with a confession, and a plea. She, Jeanne, had been the one to poison his wine—but not enough to kill; by the Virgin Mary, she swore it. Only in retribution for what he had done. But now, since he had righted his wrong before God, Jeanne wanted to right hers before him.

And so he knew that Elise would travel slowly with the holy sisters. And he knew that she had decided not to order her castle armed against him until she could do so in person.

He had gone to Will that very night, enduring his friend's laughter with a scowl in order to gain his support.

"What will you do?" Will had demanded. "Richard wants you here to help assure him that he leaves England in good hands—and comes up with the money to pay Philip and finance the Crusade."

"I cannot let her get to Montoui ahead of me! She will fortify the castle, and then, by God, Will, it would take bloodshed to get her out."

"Bryan—"

"Don't tell me, Will Marshal, that you would allow your wife to desert you, and bar you from your own lands!"

"Her lands," Will had reminded him softly. "Elise was born the lady to inherit—"

"She is my wife."

"All right," Will promised at last. "I will help you present your case to Richard. But Bryan . . ."

"What?"

"Promise me one thing."

"What?"

"That you will go gently with her. Let her know you for the man you are. She is a woman. Let her come to you. Remember that she is young, her heart is tender—"

"As tender as stone."

"Promise me that you'll be gentle."

"For the love of God, Will! I'm not a cruel or vicious man! I promise that I shall try."

Now, Bryan's gaze traveled up the stairway to the bolted door and he sighed. He already knew that there was going to be no way to remove Elise gently from Montoui.

A movement in the hall arrested his attention and he turned to see a slender, graying woman enter, then stop short, color flooding her cheeks as she saw him.

"Jeanne?" he asked.

She nodded wordlessly, and he knitted his brows, perplexed by her apparent fear of him. Then he realized that she must surely be wondering if he meant vengeance against her for his painful bout with the poison. He offered her a disarming and rueful smile.

"I'm taking the duchess with me tonight. We will travel to Cornwall alone, but I am leaving men to escort you and Michael to the new residence. I'm sure I'll need your able assistance to set matters right; God knows what condition we'll find the estate in."

Jeanne's face brightened. "Thank you, milord."

He grimaced, then walked up to her. "The Duchess is not

enthused at the prospect of leaving; nevertheless, we shall. She needs a meal, and a long, hot bath. Since I'm afraid she would bar the door to you if she believed me near, I will be out in the keep with my men, in full view of her window."

"Yes, milord," Jeanne murmured with a little bob. Bryan smiled again, then walked on past her.

When he was gone, Jeanne felt her old knees tremble with weakness. She thought of the beautiful sparkle in his eyes—they were the deepest blue she had ever seen!—when he smiled. And that smile! Perfect, even teeth, God bless them! Dimples in his bronzed cheeks. He had spoken to her so pleasantly, and she had been in mortal terror of him. Her belief in the sanctity of marriage had compelled her to leave the note, but her love for Elise had compelled her to admit that it had been she who sought revenge against him. For what she had done, many a man would have had her back flogged to ribbons, at the very least . . .

He was far more of a man than Percy, Jeanne decided, at peace at last with what she had done. He was young, honorable, strong—and handsome enough with his indigo eyes and pitch-black hair to make even her old heart flutter.

If only Elise would realize what she had!

Jeanne sighed as she started up the stairs.

And Bryan, carefully situating himself before Elise's window as he drew a stableboy into conversation, was unaware that he had just acquired a most devoted and loyal servant.

Elise still slumped against the door when the soft rapping sounded upon it, startling her so that she stood and bolted halfway across the room before responding.

"What?"

" 'Tis Jeanne, milady. I've . . . brought a tray of food."

"I'm not hungry."

"Michael saw carefully to the preparation of this meal. All the things you like, Elise. Lamb simmered in wine and seasoned with herbs. Swimming with summer vegetables. Fresh, hot bread, milady, the likes of which you did not see in England, I'll swear it."

"Where is the . . ." Elise hesitated a long time about whether to call Bryan by his title. Others might have plainly accepted him as the Duke of Montoui, but in her own mind, as long as *she* didn't, he was not. But their marriage had given him all his titles, and he was all those things. Only a fool would say otherwise. "Where is the duke?" she asked Jeanne wearily through the closed door.

"Out in the keep—"

"Don't lie to me, Jeanne! I swear that I can be far more the tyrant than he if—"

"Milady! I would not lie to you!"

Elise hesitated, closing her eyes. She could smell the lamb; the delicious aroma wafted through the thick door. It was true; no meal in England could begin to compare with one prepared by her cooks. She was terribly hungry, as last night's meal had been at a tavern where the meat had been too fatty to stomach. Breakfast had been a piece of hard bread . . .

"If he is in the keep, Jeanne, then I shall see him," Elise announced with menace. She walked firmly to the window so that her footsteps could be heard. She did not at all expect to see Stede; she was certain he had a knife to Jeanne's back, entreating her at pain of death to betray her mistress.

But Bryan was in the keep. A smile lurked upon his features as he apparently discussed horseflesh with Wat, her stableboy. To Elise's irritation, she noted that Bryan looked very noble in his flowing red mantle, and that he also looked very much at home. Comfortable, and confident.

She left the window and drew back the bolt. She did not allow Jeanne to enter, but deftly plucked the tray from her servant's hands.

"Wait! Elise!" Jeanne cried out. Elise paused and Jeanne continued hurriedly. "I'll have your bath brought while he remains in the keep."

Elise hesitated only a second; she longed dearly to submerge herself in fragrant oils and steaming water. "Hurry! And, Jeanne, bring me several pitchers of fresh, cold drinking water . . . and whatever bread and cheese you can find." Her order to Jeanne was unintentionally snapped out, but it was imperative that the bath be delivered quickly—and she be prepared to hold out in her chamber.

Jeanne nodded. Elise heard her calling for assistance as she rushed down the stairs. She moved back to the window and breathed more easily as she saw that Stede was still talking with Wat, and was now busy examining the teeth of one of the heavy plow horses.

Jeanne had whipped the servants into quick action; when Elise opened the door again, they sped into her with her tub and with a multitude of misting buckets, balanced two at a time by beams across their shoulders. The house servants all greeted her warmly after her absence, and Elise had to remind herself to be gently cordial in return, as she was so anxious to bolt the door again that she barely heard a word issued by the strong young peasant girls.

"Where are the water and food, Jeanne?"

"Elise, I just brought you a tray—"

"And I want the other, too. Now! Quickly!"

Jeanne called to one of the girls; she waited silently alongside Elise until several pitchers of water, two loaves of thick-crusted bread, and a wedge of sweet white cheese had been brought.

"Milady—"

Jeanne tried to remain with her; Elise firmly pressed her out of the door.

"I wish to be alone, Jeanne." She closed the door firmly, then slid the bolt into place, checking the strength of its bracket. It was secure, she assured herself before turning back into the chamber to decide if she would rather enjoy the comfortable luxury of the meal first, or that of the bath.

In the end, she drew a trunk near the wooden tub and set her tray upon it. Before casting off her traveling clothes, she lit a fire in the chamber's grate, building it to a cozy warmth with the ample supply of wood stacked before it. She frowned as she did so, curious that the pile of logs should be so high and neatly stacked when she had been absent so long. But then she clenched her teeth together with a rush of anger. The answer was obvious. She didn't know how long Stede had been at Montoui, but it was apparent that he had been using her chamber as his own.

No more, she told herself impatiently. She was not coming out, and he would have to tire of his vigil and make haste toward his Cornish estates before too much time passed.

Weary from the tension that tormented her since her arrival, Elise at last shrugged out of her travel-stained clothing, poured attar of roses into the water, twisted the length of her hair into a high knot, and sank into the tub. The water was wonderful. She leaned her head against the rim of the tub and allowed herself a moment just to enjoy the comfort. Then she lifted her meal tray from the trunk, set it across the tub, and lit into her food with a healthy appetite. The lamb was delicious; she savored it until the final mouthful had been consumed. It was, she decided, despite all else, a delightful way to dine, and she would remember it in the future.

She poured herself some wine from the silver carafe that was set upon the tray, then rested her head comfortably against the rim of the tub once more as she sipped at it slowly. Was it possible that she could still win this war? Yes, by God, it was!

She smiled as she continued to sip her wine. So . . . he had proven himself the Duke of Montoui. For the next few days, he was welcome to wield his power. He would soon tire of the game. His English possessions were the more valuable ones—to an Englishman, that is.

The mesmerizing fire in the grate, the sweet taste of the vintage wine, the soothing heat of the soft, oiled water—all combined to ease the strain from her body and the tempest from her soul. Her lids began to flutter, and half close. She heard a soft clanging sound and jumped, then laughed at herself as she realized that she had dropped her wine goblet. She closed her eyes again and allowed a light doze to enwrap her pleasantly.

"Milord?"

He was standing before the fire again, hands clasped behind his back as he stared at the flames. He turned politely to Jeanne as she approached him.

"I have had provisions packed as you ordered, and the horses are ready, awaiting your leisure. But . . ."

"But what, Jeanne?"

"I can assure you that the Lady Elise will not come out."

"I will wait. She'll have to come out—when she grows hungry or thirsty enough."

Jeanne shook her head, nervous despite her new admiration for him; she had also heard his voice rage when he was in a temper, and she did not care to have his temper directed at her.

She moistened her lips. "She demanded that several pitchers of water be brought to her. And bread and cheese. She can easily remain within her chamber for perhaps three . . . or four days."

He didn't move, and he didn't speak, and it took Jeanne many long seconds to realize how angry her words had made him. His emotions were only visible in the tightening of the bronze flesh across the strong bones of his face, and in the slight narrowing of his eyes.

"I see," he said quietly, turning back to the fire again. When he spoke, it was with his back to her. "Jeanne, ask Michael to see that the servants are kept busy in the kitchen or elsewhere."

Jeanne edged quickly away to do as told. When she was gone, Bryan slammed his fist hard against the mantel, then regretted the action as his hand immediately began to ache.

"Be gentle!" he muttered dryly beneath his breath. Casting his eyes up the long stairway, he sighed, then resolutely and resignedly squared his shoulders. Silently he began to tread up the stairs.

Elise jolted from her dozing the second time with confusion; the sound she had heard was not the soft clattering of light silver against stone. It had been a shuddering thud, and she shook her head briskly, trying to dispel the sweet mist of her sleep. She frowned tensely, waiting for the sound to come again so that she might ascertain what it was.

It came again, and there was nothing left to ascertain, for with the sound, both the heavy wooden door and the stalwart bolt seemed to shiver, then dissolve into splinters. She was so stunned that the door had been broken that she didn't think to be alarmed as it groaned on its hinges, then limped uselessly inward.

Elise stared from the fractured door to the man within its frame. Only then did she realize her position, and she floundered with horror from the tub, her eyes still upon him as she groped about on the trunk for her towel. He assessed her with a cool contempt as he approached her, and no matter how she longed to stand straight before him without betraying her dismay and fear, she scurried across the room—and succeeded only in cornering herself against the wall beyond the bed. She could only stare at him then, clutching the towel to her breast.

But he stopped when he reached her trunk, haphazardly removing the remains of her wine and meal to delve into it. He dug out a dark woolen tunic, a linen shift, and a pair of sturdy hose, knit for service rather than elegance.

Then he tossed the lot at her.

"Get dressed."

Elise swallowed and nervously moistened her lips, glancing longingly at her clothing. Her heart was thundering, and she was desperately trying to assimilate the fact that he had not broken down her door to attack her.

"Get dressed!" he snapped again. "We are leaving."

"No . . ." Despite herself, she mouthed the protest.

"You can dress yourself, or I can help you. Either way—as long as the task is accomplished quickly."

From the look in his eyes she knew he meant his words, and she edged to the spot where her clothing had landed upon the floor. Her fingers were shaking so badly that her every movement was awkward. The towel slipped from her grasp before she could pull the shift over her head, and she knew that her entire naked body stained with color before his hard, dispassionate scrutiny. His eyes upon her made her fingers all the more leaden. He cursed softly, and a step brought him before her. He reached down and jerked her to her feet, pulling the shift over her head, then repeating the action with the tunic before she could protest. His brusque touch slid along her torso, grazing her breasts and her hips, and she cried out softly when he shoved her negligently toward the bed so that he could slip her hose over her feet.

"I'll do it!" she swore fervently. He allowed the hose to fall into her lap, but continued to tower over her. Elise clenched her chattering teeth together and concentrated solely on easing the soft knitted wool over her toes.

At last he turned, scouring the room. "You need your heaviest boots." His eyes fell upon another trunk, and he was quickly delving into it, satisfied as he pulled out a pair of doe-skin boots. They were more delicate than he would have liked, but they would do. He brought them to her and dropped them in front of her. Elise bit into her lip as she slid her feet into the boots, then gasped again as she felt his fingers grip firmly about her arm, wrenching her to her feet once more.

They reached the broken door to her chamber and panic imbued her with a renewed and frenzied energy. She twisted furiously from his grasp and sought wildly to fight him, sending frantic blows flying across his chest and face. He allowed her to flail against him, then warned sharply, "Elise!"

She did not register the fury in his tone. Oaths were being sworn out in a high-pitched shrill; she knew only vaguely that they were coming from her.

Then she knew nothing, because he turned on her at last, clipping her jaw with the brunt of his fist. She recognized the taste of blood in her mouth, then nothing more. Consciousness deserted her in a burst of starlight. As limp and pliant as a bundle of rags, she fell into his arms.

Bryan hoisted her over his shoulder and left the chamber to start down the stairs without a backward glance. He left the hall for the keep, where the horses were waiting. Wat and Michael were there, looking keenly uncomfortable.

Bryan smiled at them. "It seems that the duchess will be riding with me," he said smoothly. "Give me a lead for her mare, Wat. And see that the packhorse is tied securely behind her."

Wat scurried to do as he was told. Bryan whistled softly as he stood with old Michael de la Pole. "Well, it's a fine night for travel, isn't it, Michael?" Bryan queried, still smiling, as if it were perfectly natural for him to be carrying his duchess over his shoulder like a sack of wheat ready for the mill.

"Aye, sir," Michael responded, trying, in turn, not to stare at this new overlord of his, or at the limp form of the duchess strewn over his shoulder.

Wat returned and secured the leads. Draping Elise over his destrier's shoulder, Bryan mounted behind her. He nodded to Michael and Wat. "Michael, I will see you soon in Cornwall. God knows, I shall have need of your administrative talents. And Wat, you are to come along, too. My squire died of a lung disease while I still fought with the old king; I have not acquired one since. I think you would do well for the job, if you've a mind to follow me to battle."

"Aye!" Wat cried out, dazzled by the offer. "Aye, milord! Thank you, Duke Bryan, God bless you, sire—"

Bryan saluted the young boy and the old man, then urged his horse onward. The gates of Montoui swung open, and he rode out into the night.

XVI

Elise became aware that the night was very dark, and that she was miserably uncomfortable. Her side ached, and she realized that the pain was caused by the constant chaff of her body against the pommel of Bryan's saddle, and she felt a tenderness at the spot where his knuckles had caught her.

From the moment she opened her eyes, she had known exactly where she was. Beneath her she could see the massive hooves of the destrier, plodding along at a brisk walk. Because she saw those hooves, she shifted carefully. Twisting about only brought her nose in contact with Bryan's knee, so she turned to hang limply again, despair overriding the misery of her body.

Apparently he had felt her movement, for he reined the destrier to a halt, dismounted from the horse, and was there to steady her when she slid limply from its shoulders, her legs too cramped to hold her. Elise kept her face hidden against the stallion's neck and asked tonelessly, "How long have we been riding?"

"Three hours, perhaps four," he answered her, his tone equally bland. Elise stiffened against his supporting hold. "I can stand now," she told him coolly.

She felt his shrug, and he released her. She proceeded to slide to the road, unable to convince her tingling muscles that they must hold her up.

"You can stand!" Bryan muttered irritably, stooping to pluck her into his arms. She was too drained to protest his hold, and she allowed her head to lie against his shoulder. She still felt so tired, so very tired.

He set her down against the trunk of an old oak, then swung about immediately to return to the stallion. She heard him as he led the horses to the side of the road, but she was too drained to pay much attention to his actions. Everything seemed to ache. Her throat was dry and parched, her flesh felt bruised from head to toe. She didn't even have the energy to care that she had lost the final battle.

At last, when she heard his footsteps crackle on the nearby leaves, she looked up. He had unsaddled his destrier and her mare, and relieved the packhorse of its burden. And he had cleared the ground to form a hollow of earth over which he now bent low, kindling a small fire. A flash of red appeared, and then a strong glow of yellow and orange. He watched his fire, feeding it kindling until the larger logs scorched and caught the glow. Hunched back on his heels, he looked at her again.

"What are you doing?" she asked him nervously. She knew the countryside, and yet she didn't know where they were. There seemed to be nothing beyond them; they were completely alone with the fire.

"Building a fire," he replied with the obvious.

She swallowed painfully, aware then that he had decided to stop here for the night. Why was it so terrible? she wondered bleakly. Whether they rode all night or not, she was his wife—and his prisoner. Did it matter when she was finally forced to accept it?

"We're staying here . . . for the night?" she asked him, dismayed to note the weak flutter in her voice.

"Yes. The service is limited, but the bedding will be clean."

She could not appreciate the gentle humor in his voice. She closed her eyes and waited miserably for the inevitable.

But he didn't come near her. When tension and curiosity at last forced her to open her eyes again, she saw that he had taken blankets from the pack, plus a drinking gourd and a tanned skin of bread and cheese to set between them. He offered her the gourd, and she knew that her fingers continued to tremble as she accepted it. "It's water," he told her. "I'm sure you need it."

She did. The cool and clear water was delicious, if a bit too reviving. Bryan was stretched out upon the blanket drawn by the tree; his dark head was bent low as he cut hunks from the loaf of bread with his hunting knife. The firelight was playing upon the darkness of his hair, making it appear almost blue, then black again. She found herself noticing the individual strands, and studying the way a stray lock persistently fell over his forehead.

He glanced up suddenly, and she averted her eyes, turning her attention to the gourd in her hand, and offering it silently back to him.

"Bread?" he asked her.

She shook her head, not meeting his eyes, but staring past the spidery leaves of the tree above her to the stars in the heavens. They might have been at the ends of the earth. If he had wanted to find an absolute place of privacy in which to assert his rights, in case she screamed and fought like a lunatic, he had done well. There was none to witness them except the darkness of the night.

If she crawled away into a secret place within her heart, he could do anything and it wouldn't matter, because she wouldn't really be there. She must stay calm. Distant. And . . . immune.

To do so, she couldn't watch him. And she couldn't allow her panic to rise with every passing moment. She had fought him; she had lost. She could barely sit straight, much less run, and even if she were to run, he would catch her. The only dignity left her was the pride with which she could accept defeat, and she meant to accept it well. But these moments . . . these moments in which she waited! They were cruelly wearing upon her nerves.

"You should eat something," he told her.

"I'm not hungry."

She sensed his shrug, then was stunned when he cast a second blanket toward her. "Get some sleep, then. I'd like to reach the Channel by tomorrow night."

Her heart seemed to spiral within her chest, and then unwind slowly. She clutched the blanket nervously for a minute, then hurriedly wrapped it around herself and tried to shift very silently until she was lying comfortably on the ground. But then she was afraid to breathe, afraid that the sound would be too loud and would bring attention to herself, and thus end this unexpected reprieve.

Eventually, she had to breathe. Half opening her eyes, she noted that Bryan was staring out into the night, not watching her at all, as he ate.

She closed her eyes again. In time she heard him wrap the remaining food, then lie down upon the earth himself. She waited, but he did not move. The fire burned lower and lower. She slept.

Birds were trilling when she next opened her eyes; the darkness was gone, and the morning was beautiful. The sun, brilliant as it rose high in the sky, was almost blinding.

Elise could not help but feel revitalized. As she lay quietly against the earth, she could feel the warmth of the sun seeping into her, giving her strength. She was not so foolish as to forget that she was with Bryan Stede, but the sparkle of the morning gave new leeway to daydreams. Morning meant promise.

"There's a stream down the slope. I'll take you."

A chill was cast over the radiance of the sun when she heard Bryan speak. She did not try to pretend that she still slept, and her eyes fell upon him. The morning was cool, but it appeared that a nip in the air had not kept him from stripping down and plunging into the stream himself. He was clad in his tight-fitting hose, but his hair was glistening with water, and his bare chest remained damp. Elise started inwardly, realizing she had never seen his naked chest before. The expanse of his shoulders was somewhat awesome, and she reflected ironically that it was not now so surprising that he had managed to shatter her door. Crisp, dark hair grew in abundance across his breast, slimming triangularly to his waist, and helping to hide the numerous scars that gave credence to his years upon the field of battle. His belly was lean and flat, yet even there she saw the taut ripple of muscle, and she closed her eyes once more, trying to still the tremor of fear that seized her. He was her husband; she did not ever want to find herself at his mercy again . . .

"Elise, we should be under way."

She rose silently and folded her blanket, then faced him. "I'd like to go to the stream alone."

"I'm sorry," he told her, his hands casually upon his hips. "I don't trust you."

"If I were going to run, I would have done so last night while you slept—"

"Would you have, now? It would have been difficult, lady, since you slept soundly long before I did. No, I don't think that you would have run last night. You were very tired; I would have caught you before you had taken the first step. Shall we go to the stream?"

"Bryan, I beg of you!" Elise pleaded. "Give me a moment's privacy!"

He hesitated a minute, then shrugged. He plucked his shirt from a branch of the tree. "Be back quickly, Elise," he warned her.

The urge to keep going when she reached the stream was so strong that she could barely subdue it. But she knew that he would be upon her like lightning drawn to metal, so she quickly enjoyed a refreshing wash in the cold water, then hurried back. Bryan was fully dressed when she returned, with his sword securely in its scabbard, and his mantle pinned about his shoulder. He had laid out the bread and cheese once more, and Elise silently knelt down to eat. He did not join her, and she assumed he had already eaten, for he was impatiently standing by the horses. She took as long as she could to eat, and knew it was time to stop goading him when he drawled out, "My horse, Duchess? Or your own?"

They rode in silence until well into the afternoon, at which time they came to a cluster of cottages that seemed to be a small village. Bryan came to a halt before one of the wattle-and-daub homes and dismounted from his horse, tossing the reins to Elise.

"I'll see who's about—and if we can't get something decently cooked to eat."

Elise nodded with all appearance of docility, but even as she did so, a fever of excitement swept through her. She watched him walk up the dirt pathway to the door, waging silent battle within her mind.

He had been decent. She had deserted him; he had bested her, and reclaimed her, but he had been decent.

But only since he had slammed her senseless and dragged her out of her home. This could be her last opportunity—*ever*—to escape him. Her mare was spirited and fast, but could not outrun the destrier at any distance. Now might be the only chance she would ever have to change horses and run . . .

There wasn't time to think or reason further—or even to contemplate the small twinges of guilt that tugged at her conscience. Elise slipped quickly from her mare. She waited until Bryan's broad back disappeared behind the door of the cottage, and then she leaped onto the destrier, spurring him into a reckless bolt, without a single backward glance.

Earth and grass flew in her wake; the sky, gold and blue, swirled around her. She sped through the low valley they had just plodded across in a matter of seconds, and then the gold brilliance of the sun was dispersed between the dark, thick greenery of tall forest pines. She ducked, hanging low against the destrier's neck to avoid the heavy branches that snapped and broke at the onslaught of the stallion's power.

How far, she wondered, before she could safely slow the beast? Not yet, not yet. Nor should she simply retrace the route home that they had taken out. He could too easily come upon her. If she followed the sun, she couldn't get lost. All she had to do was to keep riding south, southeast.

Elise broke through the forest. Two paths awaited her: the one they had taken earlier, circling the mountains; and a second, one that followed the slope of the mountain.

She hesitated only a second, then followed the trail that led up the slope.

While the footing was good, Elise kept the destrier's pace at a gallop. But soon, the path became overgrown and strewn with hard rocks, and she slowed the massive horse, aware that she had run him cruelly. As well as the path being a dangerous one, the destrier was heaving with exertion; his black coat was slick with sweat.

She allowed the horse to cool at a trot, then brought him down to a walk, and at last twisted in the saddle to look back. There was nothing behind her except the forest. Exhaling a long breath, Elise looked forward. Again, a twinge of conscience that she didn't really understand tugged at her. She had at last eluded him. She had the more powerful mount. In another night, she could be home, and this time she could prepare against him. She owed him nothing, she told herself. Elise twisted uneasily in the saddle once again, but there was no sign of Bryan. She hoped he would not realize that she had chosen to take a different path. She had left a trail of broken branches as clear as day through the forest, but the mountain path had been sand and rock, and it was possible that the destrier had left no betraying hoofprints.

Still . . .

She urged the animal into a trot once again, and it was not until dusk fell that she stopped looking back.

When darkness, complete except for a sliver of moonglow, surrounded her, Elise regretted her decision not to have found a place to camp for the night. She was desperately tired, hungry, and thirsty. Since the packhorse had carried their supplies, Elise had nothing. Guilt at how hard she had driven the destrier plagued her, and she began to worry that if she didn't find water soon, she would kill the animal.

"Can you smell out water, boy?" she asked the horse, patting his sleek flank now and watching the twitch of his ears as he heard her speak. Elise realized that with all she had done and intended to do, Bryan would surely despise her the worst for killing his horse. And why not? she wondered morosely. The horse was a beautiful creature that had served his master well; he did not deserve to die because of her quarrel with a man.

"Whoa, boy!" Elise called aloud softly to the horse. Water had to be her main concern at the moment; she couldn't allow her mind to drift.

Especially into such a region of envisioning Bryan with Gwyneth. Bryan, tender laughter in his eyes as he bent low to kiss the hand of his mistress . . .

I hate him, she reminded herself. But she didn't really, not anymore. She had stopped hating him the night of Richard's coronation, the night she had seen him ready to defend a man because his principles—and not popular belief—demanded that he do so.

"Water," she murmured aloud again, watching the black, twitching ears of the destrier. "There has to be a stream nearby, boy. I wonder if I give you your own lead if you could manage to find it . . ."

Her voice trailed away, and the sounds of the night flooded around her. Crickets chirping, the occasional screech of an owl. The foliage about her, which had appeared warm and green with the day's light, now seemed dark and foreboding, mysterious and dangerous. Elise promised herself that she would find water, and then find some kind of shelter until the dawn came. Bryan had seen to it that she was dressed roughly for hard travel, but there still might be highwaymen about. The horse she rode would be well worth stealing.

The destrier stopped suddenly, flattening its ears back, snorting, and nervously pawing the ground. Elise was confused, until she narrowed her eyes, straining to see in the darkness. She had reached a plateau; she could hear the soft sound of running water, and more. There was a sound of voices, of children laughing, of a woman humming.

Cautiously, she edged the destrier forward.

There were perhaps ten houses built on the plateau; and the dim glow from ten hearth fires surrounded them. She could hear sheep bleating, and then the fervent barking of a dog. Elise hesitated, then noticed something glitter golden in the moonlight. It was a cross, a gold cross nailed to what could only be a chapel.

This would be a small village of Christian peasants, she told herself firmly. Richard, King of England, was also the duke of these provinces. She could ask for shelter here, in the name of Richard, Coeur de Lion.

Elise nudged the destrier forward, thinking rapidly. She would not identify herself as Elise, Duchess of Montoui. She would say only that she had been a pilgrim, journeying to pray at the holy shrines in England. Then she could come and go, with as little bother as possible.

The hound that had been barking was joined by several others. The door to the first house was thrown open suddenly, and a woman began to chastise the dogs, wringing her hands as she did so. She looked up and saw Elise, and ordered the dogs to be still.

She was a squat, sturdy woman with graying hair, an ample chest, and warm, sparkling brown eyes. "What have we here?" she called out to Elise. "It's not many travelers we see here upon the plateau!"

Elise slid from the destrier's back, wondering belatedly how she would explain such a magnificent beast as the destrier. "My name is Elise, good woman," she said softly. "I am homeward bound for Montoui after a pilgrimage to England. I need water for my mount, and for myself, and . . . I—"

"You are surely hungry, I daresay!" the woman finished for her. "Well, come, come, child!" she encouraged Elise. "I can hardly feed you if you insist upon standing in the dark! George! George! Come care for this girl's horse. I am Marie, wife of Renage. Come in, come in!"

Elise smiled as the woman slipped a friendly arm about her to escort her into the cottage. An awkward boy of about fifteen came running out of the house, ogling Elise, and then the horse. "Ma!" he called, whistling softly. "Will you look at this beast! I've never seen such horseflesh—no never!"

"He needs water," Elise said softly.

Young George stared at her again, sweeping her a long gaze from head to toe that judged her as surely as he had judged the horse. The boy couldn't have been more than sixteen, Elise decided, but his gaze made her very uncomfortable.

"See to the horse, George!" Marie said firmly. She began to lead Elise toward her house again.

" 'Tis a lonely place where we live," Marie said, excusing her son with the words.

The cottage was small, but clean and very warm with its crackling fire. Marie directed Elise to a bench and hurried to the fire. "My stew is just done simmering," she told Elise, spooning some of the delicious-smelling preparation into a wooden bowl. "My man and boys come in late; they wait till dusk to bring the sheep down from the mountain slopes."

"Thank you," Elise said as Marie placed the stew down before her, smiled, and drew a cup of water from a cistern.

"Eat!" Marie encouraged. "Does my heart good to see food enjoyed."

Elise drank the water, then bit into the stew. It was as good as its aroma had promised. The food, the fire, and stout Marie all made her feel safe and content. And it was nice to hear her own language again, although the dialect here was the northern style, not the soft, melodic slur of Montoui. Bryan slipped easily from language to language—she assumed that he had been on the Continent with Henry so long that it was second nature to him. But he always spoke English to her, and now . . . now it was nice to hear a tongue closer to her own. She felt very close to home. She consumed the bowl of food without a word beneath Marie's benign eyes, but refused when Marie would have filled her bowl again.

"I've nothing to pay you with," she said softly. Bryan had dragged her away so quickly that she had worn no jewelry; she didn't even have a decent mantle pin to offer the woman. Then her eyes brightened. "My saddle is a fine one. Perhaps—"

"What I should like more than your saddle," Marie said cheerfully, sitting before Elise as she sliced huge chunks of fresh bread, "is news! Tell me, did you see His Grace Richard crowned King of England?"

Elise answered carefully. "Yes . . . I was among thousands, of course, but I did see our Lord Richard crowned King of England."

Marie was hungry for gossip; Elise ate bread with fresh sweet butter and cheerfully told Marie about London and Richard's coronation, avoiding any mention of herself as she described the gowns of the ladies and the elaborate procession.

Elise was startled in mid-sentence when the door suddenly banged inward. She stared that way to see a heavy-jowled and barrel-chested man breeze in, followed by George and two older boys, all bearing a resemblance to their fleshy-faced peasant father.

"So this is our pilgrim!" the man muttered, eyeing Elise suspiciously. "Where did you get the horse, girl?"

"Renage!" Marie chastised swiftly.

"Out of my way, woman!" Renage demanded, striding toward Elise and the table. He straddled over the bench to stare at her more thoroughly. "That's a knight's horse, girl. I've seen such— oh, aye, I have. In the stables of Sir Bresnay, our overlord. Did you steal the horse, girl?"

Elise finished swallowing a piece of the bread. It stuck in her throat, and she choked and coughed, watching Renage through watery eyes. She didn't like the look of him. His eyes were dark and too small in the fleshy folds of his face. And as much as she had liked Marie, she didn't much like the look of the boys, either. They were all staring at her as their father accused her, with that same look George had given her outside. A look that made her feel as if she wanted to squirm uncomfortably away.

They were good, Christian peasants, she told herself.

She would lie. Carefully.

"Aye, Renage," she said. She quickly added, "I was traveling with a party of sisters when I lost my way. A knight came upon me—an Englishman—and he . . . tried to steal my honor. I was desperate. I had a chance to escape him by stealing his horse, and so . . . aye!" She tilted her head proudly and conjured a mist of tears to her eyes. "I stole the horse." She held her breath. Most men of the Continent, peasants and beggars included, considered Englishmen to be little better than barbarians. Richard might be the duke of the territory, but the English King had been sired by Henry Plantagenet—an Angevin—and Eleanor of Aquitaine.

Renage let out a long breath. "Where do you go, girl?"

"To my home. Montoui. A day's ride to the south."

Renage scratched his head. The boys, still staring at Elise, scuffled with one another as they jostled to be the first to have their stew bowls filled by their mother.

"It's not safe these days for a *good* woman to travel alone," Renage said suspiciously.

"I was not alone. I was with a party of holy sisters—"

"A story I've heard before!" Renage said, laughing boisterously and slapping Elise upon the thigh. His laughter faded. "I want your horse."

Elise tried to keep smiling as she pushed his hand from her thigh. She decided quickly to give him the destrier—in exchange for another mount.

"He is yours—if you will but give me an animal in return that I may use to journey onward."

"Marie! My food."

Marie silently set a bowl of the stew before her husband. Renage kept his small eyes narrowed upon Elise.

"Have you no husband, girl?"

She hoped that a flush did not steal to her cheeks. "No," she lied.

"I've three sons," he said bluntly.

"And a handsome lot they are," she lied once again. "But I was betrothed at birth to marry Roger the Smith by . . . by the Duke of Montoui to wed another. Please, good Renage, see me safe on the road again by morning!"

Renage grunted and began sloppily spooning up his soup. The boys took seats upon the plank, too close to Elise for her comfort. Marie came to her rescue.

"Come now, girl. I'll take you up to the loft to sleep—with me," she added vehemently, turning around to offer her husband a harsh glare. Renage kept chewing, unmindful of his wife.

"Perhaps," Marie said loudly, "you can ride a ways with our priest, Father Thomas. He cares for several small villages in the mountains."

Elise bowed her head and smiled. She would be safe. Marie and Father Thomas would see to her well-being.

"What's that, now?" Renage said impatiently, lifting his chin and halting Marie before she could lead Elise up a rickety ladder.

Elise frowned, confused. She hadn't heard a thing. But then she did hear the noise—the dogs were beginning to howl and bay again.

"A man can't have a decent dinner," Renage complained, rising, and shooting Elise a hostile gaze, as if she were responsible for this new interruption. He threw open the door. "Stop—you curs!" he bellowed at the dogs, leaving the doorway behind as he walked out into the night.

With her heart rising to her throat, Elise swept past Marie to the door.

She was responsible for the new interruption. In the glow from the cottage light she could see him. Stede. Leading the mare along, towering over Renage as he walked beside him.

Elise felt the blood drain from her face; it was over. Always the hope; always the despair. Always . . . he won.

She felt the color return to her cheeks as she cried out determinedly, "Dear Lord! It's him! Oh, please! Let me run to the church. Where is this Father Thomas? Help me!"

She swirled around and dropped to her knees at Marie's feet.

"Poor child!" Marie swore softly just as Renage came into the doorway and Bryan ducked beneath the frame to follow him.

Elise risked a glance at Bryan. His brows were knit with confusion as he stared at her upon the floor, but his eyes darkened quickly to a merciless blue fire as he ascertained her game.

"Mistress, your 'poor child' is my wife."

"Your wife!" Elise cried out. "These English lords think we are nothing but their playthings! No female is safe—and they swear to fight for Christendom!"

Renage looked from Bryan, with his deadly stare, to Elise, with her pleading eyes. He cleared his throat.

"I've no wish to make an enemy of such a worthy knight, milord, but the girl claims you've done nothing but try to steal her honor."

"Her honor?" Bryan inquired with an insulting snort. He threw a gold coin upon the table, and Elise felt dismay clutch at her stomach as she watched Renage's small eyes widen and brighten.

She started to rise, then paused, stunned, as Bryan started to speak casually.

"If she chooses not to come to me, that is her concern. She is, I feel, my responsibility, and so I will pay you for her care. But don't be deceived, my friend. She is no sweet innocent."

Bryan gazed at Elise once more; she could not tell if his indigo eyes glittered with anger, or with amusement. Then he spun about, exiting the chamber and slamming the door behind him.

Renage burst into laughter. Elise stopped staring after Bryan to turn her eyes to Renage.

"Ah, wife! What a night. We lost the destrier; the knight claimed the animal to be his. But he left us a fine young mare with fancy trappings in its place and"—Renage turned his eyes upon Elise—"I think we've acquired another fine piece of flesh! The girl is in good health and she's quite a beauty. She may not come untarnished to her marriage bed, but I've never been one to think a bit of experience ruined a woman. She'll do quite well for one of our boys, Marie. Where else would we find such a girl? She'll breed us fine grandchildren. Now, as to which son . . ."

"I saw her first—" George began.

"I'm the oldest." He was interrupted by the son most resembling his rodent-eyed father.

The second one laughed. "If she's been used already, Pa, shouldn't we all get something?"

"We're Christians!" Marie snapped out.

"Christian duty is to beget sons!" Renage told his wife gleefully. He took a step toward Elise and drew her to her feet, lifting her chin. "Maybe we'll let the girl pick her own mate, eh, Marie?"

Elise found herself shoved into the middle of the room. George grabbed her and pulled her to him, smacking her lips with a slobbering and repulsive kiss. She clawed at him, but he laughed along with a howl of pain as he pushed her to another brother. The older, pockmarked boy made a licentious grab for her breast, laughing merrily along with his brother and father.

Fear was rushing up to engulf Elise even as she desperately fended them off. Damn Bryan! Damn him to a fiery hell! How could he have left her to this—

She heard her bodice rip, and furiously brought her knee hard against the peasant's groin. He yelped with real pain, buckling over. Elise gave him a shove, then raced wildly for the door, throwing it open and tearing out into the night.

She stopped short suddenly, seeing Bryan leaning against his destrier. "You son-of-a-bitch!" she railed.

He lifted a brow politely. "You told me once that you would rather have ten toothless peasants than me. There are only four in there—and they all seem to have their teeth . . ."

He broke off as Renage came running out with his sons, all armed with pitchforks.

Bryan reached out and grasped Elise, throwing her atop the mare, leaping upon the destrier himself. "Go!" he warned her. "They're an awkward lot and I've my sword, but I'd hate to take their poor lives for the paltry fact that they were dragged into our quarrel."

A grunt of pain escaped him as he finished speaking; Elise saw him clenching down on his jaw as his features paled.

"Go!" he screamed, clawing at his back. Elise was frightened and confused; her heart thundered in her chest, but she dared not disobey him.

She nudged her heels against the mare's flanks. A second later Bryan was rushing past her, leading her through the darkness. The night, the moon, the stars whipped by. The glow from the cottages faded. Again, it was like that first night; they might have been alone in the world, racing the wind.

At last he slowed the destrier, sliding off the horse rather than leaping, as he was accustomed.

"Bryan?" Elise queried hesitantly, her voice seeming to echo in the darkness about them.

He didn't answer her; she saw that he was leading the destrier through a narrow, overgrown path amid the trees. Silently, she followed him, again feeling danger in the night, in the black that surrounded them in the forest. "Bryan!" she called softly, unable to see him. But she could follow the destrier, and she did. The path led to a copse by a stream.

The moon played upon the water here; Elise saw that he had torn off his red mantle, and his tunic. She picked them up. Both were stained with blood. She hadn't seen the blood before because the mantle was the same shade.

"Bryan!" she called out, alarm rising in her voice. And then she heard him, at the water's edge. She saw his broad back, the bronzed flesh gleaming in the moonlight . . .

And the blood. "Bryan!"

Elise raced to his side; he spun about, raising a hand to her. She swallowed. "Bryan . . . I want to help you—"

"Why?" he demanded with dry bitterness. "Just get away from me."

"But you're wounded—"

"Not badly. I'm not going to die."

Tears stung her eyes. "I don't want you to die. I just wanted you to leave me alone, Bryan. Please . . . let me help you."

He stared at her a moment, eyes raking over her, their emotion shadowed by the night.

"No," he said bluntly.

He turned back to his task, wetting a torn strip of his mantle, then cleansing the wound in his back. "Damn!" he muttered, grimacing as he rose.

"Bryan, I never meant for something like this—"

"Then what *did* you mean!" he shouted with sudden fury, stalking to her in two swift steps that took a painful toll upon him, evident as the strain riddled his eyes. He wrenched her arm and she gasped, but his words thundered out, bleak and weary, before she could speak. "What do you mean to happen? Do you intend to go to war against me—against Richard? Will it satisfy your sense of honor to see men battle and die? You claim you hate me because I raped you. I'm a brutal man. Duchess, you don't begin to understand what violence is—what rape is! I should have left you. I should have left you to those double-chinned brothers and then you could have learned—"

"Bryan!" Her teeth were chattering as he shook her, tears were springing to her eyes, and she was sorry, very sorry, but also terrified and about to scream with the pain of his tense fingers biting into her arm. "Bryan . . . let . . . go . . . of . . . me . . ."

He did, pushing her from himself so vehemently that she fell against the pine-softened bed of the forest.

And he was quickly on top of her, straddling over her, pinning her wrists to the ground. His voice was still swift, harsh thunder in the night. "Let you go? Never, Duchess! Don't you understand that yet? Be gentle! Marshal tells me. Have patience! And for my pains, I take a dagger in the back. Milady, perhaps it's time for me to be guilty of all that I am accused!"

His face was so tensed and strained; his eyes were so cold and hard and laced with pain. She felt the ripple of his muscles as he leaned closer to her, the terrible, shuddering power of his enraged body.

His hands, moving, releasing her only to touch her once more; his thumb was rough as it grazed over her cheek; his palm was shaking. He was so angry.

Her tears started sliding down her cheeks. "Bryan," she whispered, "please . . ." She couldn't find the words to tell him that she knew her attempts to escape him were at an end—that she was resigned to being his wife. That she was just begging he not take her in such awful anger.

He paused. His eyes closed briefly, then opened. He took a deep breath, then jerked away from her, standing quickly over her, then walking away. It took her a moment to realize that he was gone.

She was suddenly very, very cold, and she didn't think she had ever felt so empty, so totally void, in her life.

Slowly, she roused herself. He was standing by the stream again, winding strips of his mantle around his torso. Elise stood, shivering for a minute, then finding that she was compelled to walk to his side again. She spoke to the breadth of his back, swallowing hard at the silent dignity of his stance.

"Bryan . . . I swear, I had no wish for you to be harmed. I . . . behaved recklessly and foolishly and I brought on your injury—and I am truly, truly sorry."

He didn't reply to her. Not for a long while. She stood tensely, miserably behind him. Then she saw his dark head lower as he stared into the water of the stream; he issued a soft sigh.

"Elise, you are my wife. You have to come with me." He paused. "I, too, have been guilty—of condemning you unjustly at times. I know now that you didn't poison my wine." He lifted his head again but still did not turn to face her. "Jeanne put the poison in my wine. She admitted the deed to me."

"Jeanne!" Horror swept through Elise, and a new fear. Fear for Jeanne. "Please, Bryan!" she whispered with soft vehemence. "Jeanne is aging—her real crime was her love for me. The fault was mine, if she sought to injure you. You must not deal harshly with her. I . . . I beg you."

"She will not be punished."

Elise stood still, dizzy with relief. He might have done many things. Jeanne was a villein of Montoui; Bryan could even have ordered her executed for such a crime. Or flogged so cruelly that a woman of her age could not survive the ordeal. And yet, he was stating that Jeanne would not be punished. She owed him for that mercy.

"Bryan, I . . ." she began softly, but her throat tightened, and she had to begin again. "I swear by the blessed Virgin that I will not try to escape you again."

He turned to her then, curiosity touching his eyes, along with a cool skepticism. "You needn't be so frightened or humble, Elise. My decision about Jeanne has nothing to do with promises from you. Whether you tried to run a thousand times, I could never bring vengeance against an old woman who had risked her own life for love of her mistress. Don't make a vow you don't intend to keep."

"I . . . intend to keep it," Elise said softly.

He did not reply. Elise winced as she saw blood escaping the bandage of fabric strips he had wound about it.

"Bryan, your wound—I wish to help you."

"Bind it more tightly," he said with a sigh. "The *lout* could not throw his dagger hard or with a decent aim, but it is a scratch that bleeds like rain."

Elise picked up the remnants of his mantle and ripped it into broader, wider strips. With her eyes lowered, she approached him. She tore away his efforts at a bandage, and carefully wound the strips about him again, putting padding upon the wound.

She noticed the tense, sporadic ripple of his taut abdomen as she touched his torn flesh, but he didn't emit a word, a sigh, or even a grunt.

She could not look at his face when she finished. He stepped away, and she heard him with the horses. A moment later, he was back beside her, carrying his saddle and blanket. "This is all we have for the night," he said curtly. "I left the packhorse with the old woman at the cottage we came to this morning. I could travel more swiftly without it. Let's get some sleep."

Elise nodded numbly. She was shivering again. Not with cold; not with fear.

Moments before, she had pushed him to his limit of endurance. She had felt his touch; the sinewed heat of his body pulsing against hers. She had cried out, and found reprieve . . .

Yet had been stunned by the cold when he left her.

How long, she wondered, feeling dizzy, how long before he did insist . . . ?

"We've only one blanket. Come here; if you don't sleep beside me, you could have a chill by morning."

Nervously, she tucked at the ripped material of her bodice, but he wasn't paying any attention to her. He was laying the blanket upon the ground, positioning the saddlebags as cushions for their heads.

He lay down, staring up at the night sky.

Elise walked over silently and lay down beside him. He pulled the blanket around her, but the warmth that she felt came from him.

She would never sleep so, she thought. Feeling the even keel of his breathing, the movement of muscle, the heat . . .

She closed her eyes. He made no move to touch her, and she wondered in misted confusion if she were relieved . . .

Or bereft.

XVII

He felt her movement as she twisted slowly from his grasp, but Bryan made no move to stop her. He opened his eyes, barely, allowing his jet-black lashes to shield them as he watched her.

Dawn was breaking; sunlight, gold and crimson, streaked against the gray of the dying night. The clear water of the brook was reflected in its glow like thousands of sapphires glittering to greet the day.

As Bryan watched, Elise cast off her boots and tunic and waded into the stream dressed only in her thin linen shift. She gasped slightly at the shock of the cold, then bent, heedless of her clothing, to cup the clear water in her hands and splash it over her face. Just as the sunlight caught the water in magic, it touched upon her hair, making the tangled strands appear like silken webs of purest gold and copper.

She stood, shivering slightly, then began to unwind the coil of her hair, allowing it to fall about her. The tips of the longest tendrils swept over the water. She combed through it with her fingers, and when she released it, it was like a cloak of sunlight itself streaming about her with a rich and radiant glory.

Bryan opened his eyes fully and leaned upon an elbow, and drew in his breath. She turned around suddenly and stared at him, her eyes startled and wide, crystal blue today, along with the color of the stream.

The water in which she had recklessly played dampened her shift and molded it to her form. The linen had become taut, enhancing the full rise of her breasts, the dip of her belly, the swell of her hips. He smiled suddenly, thinking of how capable she usually was of appearing aloof and . . . regal. A duchess born: proud, distant, judicial. Beautiful, but untouchable.

But now . . . with her hair in silken disarray, fluttering softly to her knees in tangled splendor, her eyes so wide, her young figure so clearly outlined, she looked like . . .

A magical, legendary creature. A child of legend. Some sweet creature created for the delight and reward of a man. A "Melusine," to haunt and possess the soul . . .

She wouldn't much like the description, he thought dryly.

His smile began to fade, although his eyes remained riveted to hers. The morning was cool; he felt uncomfortably hot. His limbs were tense, his muscles coiled and tightened—and damn if he didn't feel his breath coming hard and fast from lungs that seemed to burn! His desire for her was painful, tearing at his gut like a gnawing hunger, tightening him, hardening him, when he hadn't even touched her except with his eyes.

Be patient, Marshal had told him. *Be gentle. Let her come to you . . .*

But Marshal did not live with a constant longing that was never abated. She was his wife. And now, she had sworn not to leave him again.

He lifted a hand to her, palm up and open. "Come here," he said softly.

She hesitated, and in those moments he prayed silently that she would not refuse him. His pride would demand that he go to her, and magic would fade to battle once again.

He stood, unwilling to let it come to that. She was proud, too, he knew. And he could not forget the broken way she had cried out to him when he had lost his temper and thrown her down.

He walked to her slowly, ignoring the water that soaked his hose and boots. Not once did he stop gazing at her eyes; it was imperative that he hold her so; he did not want her to run.

She did not run.

She watched him come, shivering against the morning cold.

He stopped before her. Her arms were bare, glistening with water. He set his hands upon them. His eyes at last left hers as he watched the gentle movement of his fingers as they caressed the soft flesh of her shoulders.

Was it the cold that she shivered from? Or did she shrink from his touch?

His eyes met hers again. "It is inevitable that you come to me," he told her quietly.

She did not answer him, but neither did her eyes waver from his.

"I hurt you once," he continued, not pleading, but speaking truthfully. "For that, I am sorry. The union of a man and woman should not be a hurtful thing." He offered her a crooked smile. "It should be a . . . touch of heaven, for the lady as well the lord."

Such a dubious glitter touched her eyes that he laughed. "I swear by my sword, it is true, Duchess!"

She sighed softly, casting her lashes over her eyes. "I have learned that it is futile to fight the . . . inevitable."

Bryan's lip continued to curl with a secret amusement. No, she wasn't going to fight him. But neither was she going to offer a simple acquiescence. Coming from her, the words were as close to a willing consent as he was ever going to get.

"You're injured," she reminded him a little breathlessly. "You must be in pain."

"A nick in the flesh, nothing more. I am, indeed, in pain—but the pain has nothing to do with a minor wound to the flesh. And," he murmured, "it seems rather ridiculous to put off until tomorrow what is going to happen anyway . . ."

He moved his fingers to the straps of her shift, peeling them from her shoulders, then slowly tugging the sodden garment lower. A flush rose throughout her when her breasts, their peaks rosy and hard from the cold, were bared. The material abetted his effort at that point, falling free to wind about her ankles in the water.

She was like the dawn, flame and pastels. Shrouded in innocence, yet not innocent.

"I'm going to freeze," she told him nervously, and he knew that it embarrassed her to stand naked before him. He took her into his arms, freeing her from the look of ardent hunger in his eyes.

"I will make you warm," he assured her, and his mouth was hot with that promise as he took hers in a deep, thirsting kiss. Instantly, she thought of that kiss in the chapel. His lips seemed to meld with hers, widen, taking the whole of her mouth. Moist . . . velvet . . .

She felt the same sensations. The weakness. The sweetness. Invading her bones, her blood. Her breasts were hard against his chest. The coarse hair there teased her. His chest was so hard . . . she pressed her palms against it, not to push him away, but to feel him with her fingertips . . .

He stepped away. Elise was afraid that she would waver and fall. She did not, and he reached out a sun-browned hand to cup the fullness of her breast. She lowered her lashes, unable to meet his eyes.

It was so like that distant day at a different stream. She was cold; where he touched her she was hot. Fire and water, heat and cold, and that feeling . . .

The promise that if she just reached out, something infinitely fine and sweet would tumble into her hands.

How long had she been fighting him? Since that black, rain-swept night when they had met. Even then she had felt the promise, but then she had been dreaming of Percy, and now . . .

She couldn't even summon a likeness of Percy's face to her mind's eye. The name was a confusion. Memory of him was nothing more than a misted haze.

Someone moaned softly; it was Elise. She had stepped toward him, burying her face against his shoulder, slipping her arms around his neck. She stumbled in the tangle about her ankles that was her shift, and she didn't mind at all when he slipped his arms around her, carrying her from the stream. Elise closed her eyes and rested pliantly against him. She didn't know how to reach out and seize that elusive promise, but she felt drugged by the beauty of the morning, and the tenderness of his touch. A dazzling mist of magic seemed to encompass her; if she allowed the mists to swirl, the sweetness that rendered her limbs so very weak could grow and . . .

Her shift was discarded upon the bank, and she found herself lying upon the bed of blanket and earth that was still warm from the hours they had slept. She opened her eyes. Far above her, the leaves of the old oak spattered across the soft, glowing, now crimson morning sky. A breeze wafted through the leaves, creating dappled patterns of light shadow upon her flesh. She closed her eyes. She could hear him removing his boots . . . his heavy wool hose. She felt him stretch out beside her, but still she did not open her eyes. She knew that he was propped upon an elbow on his side; his naked flesh brushed against hers.

His fingertips, light and feathery, touched her cheek, caressed and outlined her jaw. That soft touch followed along her throat, and long before he did so, she was craving that he touch her breasts. Still, it was that feathery touch, circling, as elusive as the breeze. She tried so hard to remain still.

Lazily . . . leisurely . . . that gossamer touch moved along her. She felt him with each rib . . . drawing idle patterns along her waist . . . making her burn deep within as the strokes crossed low over her belly. She heard his whisper, close to her ear.

"Am I hurting you?"

"No . . ."

Bryan smiled, watching her mouth form the word. Until that moment, he had been almost afraid to touch her. Stretched beneath the tree, one long leg angled slightly at the knee, her nakedness entirely free of blemish, she had appeared so pure and innocent that he had felt it almost irreverent to touch her. Surrounded by the golden haze of her hair, cast into shadow and then clarity by the ever-drifting leaves above them, she seemed ever more untouchable: a virgin nymph of the forest; some creature of a distant Camelot.

It was now that he felt the despoiler; not on that night when he had taken her so unknowingly. Perhaps, because although he had touched her physically that night, the woman had eluded him, and therefore he had, in a way, left her innocent. Today he meant to take more. He had to have more; the obsession that had stirred within him that night remained with him. It grew like the winds of the storm that night, and he would know no peace until he had grasped her elusive quality and held it in his hands.

Now, the scarce-heard whisper of a single word had changed her. The beauty was still there; the innocent perfection. But her mouth remained slightly parted; she moistened it with the tip of her tongue, and the soft, rising mounds of her ivory breasts heaved slightly with the quickened intake of her breath. He bent over her, nuzzling against the valley between her breasts, teasing the flesh with his tongue. He traced a wet path to a nipple that crested with a crimson challenge to the dawn. He felt her shudder, and he knew that he shuddered himself as he savored the sweet succulence of her flesh, swathing her with his tongue, then nipping gently with his teeth, then drawing her hard into his mouth.

Soft sounds were coming from her parted lips. Whispers . . . moans . . . whimpers—or maybe it was just the breeze, rustling and seeming to whirl like a tempest about him, within him. His hands tangled in her hair as they splayed over her midriff, holding her to him. He rolled onto his back, bringing her with him, groaning softly as he felt that silken web swath all about him, each tendril, each strand, a burning caress to his flesh.

Her eyes were open now; she gazed at him, startled by the movement. He slipped a hand around her neck and drew her face to his, kissing her forehead, the tip of her nose, and then her lips. Again his kiss was long and passionate. His left hand cupped her head, his right moved along her back, caressing her with the teasing strands of her own hair that so enchanted him.

He explored the length of her spine, grazed the curve of her waist, and enjoyed the firm, swelling rise of her buttocks. Then he rolled again, pinning her beneath him. His touch was no longer feather-light, nor slow. He needed to feel her, to soothe the fever in his palms with the soft femininity of her flesh. His hands were rugged and calloused; yet where they touched upon her roughly, he soothed her with the gentle healing of his kiss, with the soft stroke of his tongue. He wanted to arouse her, but more than that, he was fascinated by her scent; she was like the sunshine; like the verdant beauty of the forest. She tasted as sweet.

She no longer lay still; she writhed and arched to the play of his hands and lips. He gloried in her motion, and felt the strength of his desire thunder within him. He moved lower against her, driven by some demon of the wind to know that she would welcome him. She started, gasping as she shuddered. But she didn't fight him, and he savored the triumph as he savored her tender intimacy, knowing that he had taken from her all will to resist, and given her the crystal beauty that was nature's gift.

He rose above her, laughing as her eyes met his, then fell as a rose flush touched her cheeks. He caught her with his kiss again, and she tasted the fervor of his passion. She did not remember wanting him there, yet he was between her thighs, and she had wrapped her limbs around him. The sweetness had invaded her completely; it burned, it raged. It was so wonderful that it was a strange agony, yet she did not want it to end. Her fingers dug into his arms, and she was awed by the hardness and power of them. She returned his kiss with a fervor that also awed her; she wanted to taste him, to feel him against her. Even now he teased her, moving against her, hard and potent, yet not coming into her, not soothing that center of the burning sweetness . . .

She ran her fingers over his back and faltered at the bandage. She trod tenderly there, touched flesh once more, and found his buttocks. They, too, were hard and firm and rock-muscled. She pressed against them, and at last he moved. The essence of pleasure itself could be heard in her shudder, her gasp.

She had welcomed him, wanted him, craved him. A liquid, warm, embracing shield. He wanted to go slowly, to assure himself further that she would know the exquisite joy they could reach together. But his own need, held in careful abatement for so long, rose to engulf him. Desire drove him to a hell-bent rhythm, with shuddering strokes that invaded and sought. But it didn't matter, for she was ready to meet him. He knew with a satisfaction that was ambrosial that her hips writhed and undulated beneath his. Her soft cries were the loveliest melody; her hands, so uninhibited upon him, were the closest thing to heaven that he had ever known.

And then he felt her tense beneath him; shudder after shudder gripped her. Her cry was almost startled, yet it was a gasp that tapered to a soft moan. He allowed all that was within to explode like burning oil, and then the guttural groan of replete satisfaction that he heard was his own.

She was curled quickly to herself with her back against him, but not away from him. He lay staring up at the leaves again, glad that she was not looking at him, for he could not wipe the grin of smug pleasure from his face.

Elise shivered slightly; the breeze had suddenly become cool. She could feel things again, things other than the flesh and substance of the man beside her. She needed the breeze to cool her, yet she did not want it to sweep away the lingering sensation.

Sweet, sweet promise had been fulfilled. The wonder was awesome; it was the most delicious thing she had ever known. It had left her exhausted, and so contrarily feeling wonderful, powerful, complete in a way she had never even imagined. She felt drunk with it, drunk with the pleasure and satiation. He had been the wine, the nectar. Magnificent to touch, to feel. She had forgotten their quarrel, forsaken her resentment. That he was Bryan Stede and she his unwilling bride had lost all truth. She had only known that he was beautiful as only a man could be, and he had been totally hers to enjoy and admire and hold; all of him with all of herself.

It was only now that she could begin to feel regret. Now that the magical colors of dawn had faded to the cool, clear brilliance of naked day. Nothing had changed; he was still the king's hardened warrior, a knight eager for battle, taking time out to assuage his lust for lands and wealth.

It was little more than a pleasant boon that he could assuage his lust for his rebellious wife at the same time.

She was wrong, she thought bitterly. Things had changed. She could no longer call herself his "unwilling" bride. She couldn't have fought him any further, but she might have been "resigned" rather than been torridly eager.

Yet she knew even then, deep in her heart, that it was not the easy conquest of her senses that plagued her. She loved the new feeling and the new knowledge; that sense of promise had teased her for so very long. What hurt, what grazed so roughly against the fabric of her heart, was jealousy. They would go on to Cornwall. Bryan would see to his affairs with stern determination. And then he would be gone. Being with God only knew how many women, just as he had been with her. Then, of course, there was Gwyneth. Gwyneth . . . who had shared an affair with Bryan that had never been a secret. An affair which, it appeared, neither of them saw any sense in ending . . .

Elise closed her eyes in sudden misery. She didn't want to think of Gwyneth and Bryan. Not the way that they had been. Not sharing intimacies that she had never even imagined . . .

She swallowed, forcing herself to open her eyes to the day. She was not a timid fool; she was a duchess in her own right, and she would not tolerate an affair conducted before her eyes. The future seemed to loom ahead with new misery, but she would take it a day at a time, and she would never allow Bryan to know her feelings. If he had found her stubborn and difficult so far, he would learn that she could be even more so.

The sun began to burn into his flesh. Bryan idly touched the lock of hair that waved over the rounded curve of her hip, then stroked the flesh beneath it. He wanted to pull her around to face him, but then thought better of it.

"Elise?" he said quietly. She either murmured or grunted an acknowledgment, and he continued with the question that had never ceased to haunt him. "Why did you steal Henry's ring and tell me all those absurd lies?"

He felt her freeze against him, and then she laughed softly, the sound barely hinting of her bitterness. "Do you know, Stede, that the truth wouldn't matter in the least now?"

"Then tell me," he urged.

"Stede," she replied to him in a tone so low it was a whisper, "you have everything: land, titles, wealth. You . . . even have me. Submissive, quiet. Montoui . . . all that was mine, mine to give, you have taken. But the answer to that secret . . . it is something that you cannot take. It is still mine; it is a secret that I intend to keep, which I must keep."

He was still and silent for a long moment. Then she felt him roll away. She closed her eyes, wondering how she could have known a pleasure beyond imagination one minute, then find herself cast into despair the next. She felt numb. She heard the sounds of his movement as he dressed and went to the horses, yet they did not touch her mind . . .

Until he returned to her, planting one booted foot on either side of her hip as he stared down at her, his eyes blank. She started, staring up at him, wishing that she could hide more of her nudity with the cloak of her hair.

He dropped something before her. Stunned and uneasy, she followed its fall.

It was the ring. Henry's sapphire ring.

"You bartered a lot for it," he told her bluntly. "You might as well wear it."

"Where—" she began, but he cut her off curtly.

"I found it in one of your trunks before you returned to Montoui."

"How dare you go through my things!"

He shrugged indifferently. "I felt I needed to know more about you—and I wasn't expecting a pleasant conversation."

Elise clenched her jaw tightly and stared up with her silent hostility burning brilliantly in her eyes. Remorse set in again. How could she have allowed this . . . cold, arrogant—ruthless!—warrior to touch her as he had! At that moment, she wanted desperately to crawl away with shame. She hadn't allowed him, she had invited him, giving way to his every intimacy.

"Wear the ring," he repeated.

"I can't wear the ring!" she snapped. "Have you forgotten? There are others who know it belonged to Henry."

He laughed with no humor. "You can wear the ring, Elise. When you so hastily departed London, I felt obliged to explain our first meeting to Richard. Our king had a rather strange reaction. He was totally silent, quite unlike Richard. Then he bade me to go with Godspeed—after telling me when I must return to his service, of course—and he said something rather peculiar. He said that you should wear the ring; if anyone should ask you about it, you are to say that it was a wedding gift from him."

She tore her eyes from Bryan's and stared at the ring. She picked it up and slipped it on her finger.

"Get dressed," he told her curtly. "We've lost half the morning."

"Not by my choosing," she bit out in return. "And if you want me up, I suggest that you move."

He stepped over her and walked back to saddle the horses.

Elise rose and hurried to her shift. It was sopping wet, and without the packhorse, she had no other. She sighed, rang it out, and donned her tunic. The rough wool chafed her skin, flesh that seemed especially tender and sensitive now.

She would endure the discomfort, she decided wryly. She was going to learn to endure a lot, and somehow she was going to come out of it with her dignity and pride restored.

Her hair was badly tangled. She tried to smooth it with her

fingers and braid it, but the tendrils kept escaping. She felt him behind her, and she stiffened, but did not protest against his touch. In a matter of minutes he had tamed the unruly mass and she wondered at his proficiency with a woman's hair. "Let's be on our way," he told her. "We will stop to eat after we've traveled a distance."

"I am not hungry," she said tonelessly, and stepping away from him, she mounted her mare and gazed down at him coolly, waiting.

They did not stop until they reached the cottage where Elise had mounted his destrier to escape, and Elise marveled at the difference in herself between then and now. Then . . . she had made her last, desperate bid for freedom, and learned that worse things could happen to her than her marriage. And now she was resigned.

The old crone who owned the cottage fed them a meal of wild hare roasted over her fire. The meat was tough and stringy, but it was hot, and Elise discovered then that she was very hungry. But they did not tarry long; Bryan paid the old woman for the meal and for her care of the packhorse, and they were on their way once again.

They stayed that night in an inn by the Channel at Barfleur. The room was a small, stuffy cubicle in the loft, but it was all that was available. Elise fell upon the lumpy straw bed, utterly exhausted. She was asleep before Bryan had doused the single candle allotted them. When she awoke, he was gone from the chamber. He returned to tell her that their passage was arranged.

The Channel was calm that day. Dead calm, and silent. They crossed in a matter of hours. Bryan was anxious to move onward, so they did not linger at all, but started riding the northeastern trail. That night they were welcomed into the manor home of Sir Denholm Ellis. Sir Denholm was nearing his eightieth year; he had ridden on a Crusade with Eleanor of Aquitaine when she had been the Queen of France, and he enlivened their evening meal with stories of Eleanor's courage.

The manor was small, but well kept, and staffed with efficient servants. Elise was able to indulge in a long bath and wash the leaves and forest dust from her hair. " 'Tis good you've come here, milady," Mathilde, Sir Denholm's young housekeeper, told her. "Ye'll not be enjoying much luxury in the days to come."

"Why do you say that?" Elise queried.

Mathilde chuckled. "The lands in Cornwall be vast, milady, and rich, but . . . the old lord has been dead a long time now, and his steward was a lazy chap to begin with. You won't find much of a welcome awaiting you."

Elise silently digested Mathilde's words, easing herself more deeply into the water. What were they coming to?

She was still in the bath when Bryan entered the room, his presence filling it. Apparently he had bathed elsewhere, for he was dressed in a fresh white tunic, and nothing more. Mathilde blushed and chuckled and made a hasty exit.

"We leave early," Bryan told Elise. She heard him doff the tunic and climb into the large bed that awaited them. Elise hesitated, but heard no sound from him. She rose from the bath and wrapped herself in a linen towel, then dragged a chair by the fire, where she combed her hair, allowing the warmth to dry it. She stayed at the task, becoming involved with it, until she jumped, hearing Bryan's voice.

"Come to bed, Elise!"

She did, and when his arms reached out for her, she had no wish to turn away. The room darkened as the fire burned lower and lower in the grate, and in the darkness she gave way to temptation to touch him in return. Their lovemaking was all the sweeter, yet when he held her close in the aftermath, she again knew a feeling of dismay.

She found comfort in the strength of his hands upon her. It was good to lie beside him, to feel his hair-roughened legs entwined with hers.

She was going to be empty when he left her.

* * *

It was well past midnight, the witching hour, Elise thought when they came upon Firth Manor. Elise didn't think she had ever been so tired in the whole of her life; they had been riding since dawn. With their land in reach, Bryan had been loath to stop, and Elise, determined to match at any endeavor, had stubbornly refused to ask that they stop and rest. The rain, a slow, miserable drizzle, had begun at about dusk, and now, as they came upon the home he had so persistently dragged her to, she did not know if she longed to laugh or cry.

The moon—when it broke through the drizzle and clouds—was full. The house rose out of wild and overgrown shrubbery like a dark monster, empty and lifeless. It was a Norman edifice, built of stone, half castle, half manor, and in daylight it might boast a pleasant architectural grace with its high arches and jutting towers.

But now, it appeared nothing less than harsh and forbidding, a reminder of the time more than a century ago when the Normans under William the Conqueror had battled hard to quell the Saxons.

Bryan began to swear softly beneath his breath. He stopped at the gatehouse, but no one answered his knock, and when he barged inside, he found nothing but a filthy hovel. He came back outside to his bride, waiting upon her horse, sodden and weary.

"We'll go up to the main house," he told her with a scowl.

They rode in silence. The path was overgrown with weeds. The door hung open. Bryan entered and worked in the darkness while Elise leaned wearily against the door. At least here she was out of the never-ending drizzle.

The kindling was as damp and dreary as the night, but Bryan at last managed to get a sooty fire going. Acrid smoke filled the hall with a dismal glow.

Once . . . once the manor had been grand. The hall was large; the fireplace had been sculpted of stone. Many glass-paned windows, some in beautifully stained colors, still remained.

But many had been stolen or broken. The floor was littered

with stale and dank rushes. No furniture remained; it appeared that what had not been part of the structure itself had been carried away.

Elise at last began to laugh. She walked into the hall, sweeping her arms about as if to encompass it. "Here we are! The great home of that magnificent warrior, King Henry's champion, King Richard's right hand—Bryan Stede! The earl, the duke—the mighty lord! For this! For this you cast aside Montoui! My God, but it is amusing!"

Had he not sensed the beginning of a weary hysteria in her voice, he would have been tempted to slap her.

"Shut up!" he told her harshly instead. He stood slowly, staring at the fire while anger filled him. The wound that had not pained him at all during the day suddenly ached. He noticed absently that Elise had moved to the built-in window seat. Once, he assumed, it had overlooked a fine garden. He was certain that, now, the darkness concealed nothing but weeds. He slammed his fist hard against the mantel and muttered to himself rather than to her.

"By the blessed Virgin, these lazy serfs shall pay! I've the time to tear a good number apart, limb by limb! By the rood, they will know the extent of my wrath!"

He had all but forgotten Elise. He started when she spoke, her voice soft and weary.

"If you deal with the situation as you say, milord, you will find yourself with nothing but dead serfs. You are a warrior, Stede, trained to do battle. But you cannot joust with undisciplined serfs. That will not bring you the prosperity you desire."

"Oh? And what will, madame?"

"Nothing at the moment," she told him. " 'Twould be best to sleep as well as possible through the remainder of the night. Morning can better bring order to chaos."

He rested his head against the mantel. She was right. What was he going to do? Run like a lunatic to the village, rousing the peasants from sleep and earning nothing but their hostility?

He didn't know how much time passed before he lifted his

head to tell her that he would bring in their blankets and their packs.

She was gone. But as he turned around, he saw that she was already bringing in their travel blankets, arranging them before the fire. She gazed at him, a little uncertainly.

"If you would like me to tend to your wound—"

"My wound is fine. Go to sleep."

She curled up before the fire.

Bryan stood by the mantel, listening to the damp kindling crackle as it fought to stay ablaze. At last he walked outside and discovered that Elise had already relieved the horses of their trappings. They were tethered beneath the overhang. The overhang leaked no worse than the manor. The saddles and the packs were drawn as tight to the building as possible.

Bryan carried the packs inside. He delved into their supplies until he found a skin of ale, which he proceeded to drain as he sat and stared morosely at the fire.

XVIII

Alaric, the steward, was sleeping soundly. He had drunk heavily the night before, and sleep was bliss. He started, nearly jumping from his cot, when his door burst open with a tremendous shudder.

He blinked in wild and panicked confusion. Then his eyes focused on an apparition in the doorway.

She was tall and slim. A haze of gold seemed to surround her head, and he thought for one shuddering moment that the blessed Virgin had come to strike him down.

"Dear God in heaven, forgive me my sins!" he cried out, falling to his knees.

His apparition frowned and took a step into the gatehouse, distaste filling her features. He saw that the gold about her head was not a crown, but neatly bound hair of the same color.

" 'Tis likely God might forgive you your sins, but I'm afraid that I am not sure about my husband. This is disgraceful! You are living no better than a swine! And I had heard that Cornish men were a breed apart. Fine men, stalwart and proud!"

Alaric crawled up from his knees, trying in vain to smooth back his ruffled hair. "There's been no one here to care, milady. No one to care for so very long. Aye, we've grown slack and lazy."

"That will have to change," Elise said quietly. "And very quickly, I believe. Have you heard of my husband? He is Bryan Stede, our good King Richard's champion, and his temper is fierce! He is a just man, oh, aye, quite just, but when he comes to claim an estate such as this . . ." Elise allowed her voice to trail off with abject dismay. Then she gazed at the steward with her eyes brightening. "But he still sleeps! Rouse the peasants, bring the servants quickly. With God's grace, we can get much accomplished before he awakens!"

Alaric began to nod profusely, bowing at her all the while he edged around her. *Hurry! hurry!* he urged himself silently. It was still possible to salvage his scrawny neck.

Alaric looked back as he ran toward the village. She had followed him out to the sunlight, and now seemed shrouded in gold once more. So elegant, so beautiful. Her words were firm, but soft-spoken. Perhaps God had sent her, after all; she had come as a warning, a blessing.

Alaric would forever confuse Elise with something mystical and holy. And he knew from that morning on that he would serve her with the greatest enthusiasm, and the utmost loyalty.

The pounding awoke him; a sound that echoed irritatingly all around his temple. Bryan opened his eyes slowly. They felt swollen. Just as his tongue felt thick, as if he had grown hair on it over night. How much had he drunk? Enough to give him a splitting headache, apparently. A headache compounded by the confounded hammering.

He groaned slightly and rolled to a sitting position, holding his head between his hands. He had wanted to awaken to realize that it had all been a nightmare, that the great reward he had so coveted had not proven to be nothing but an empty and rotting castle.

But it was no nightmare.

And neither was the pounding he heard an invention of his mind. He continued to hear it, sharp and rhythmic, thudding above his head.

He looked around himself. The dank and filthy rushes of the night before had been swept away; the fire he had nurtured to a sick and sooty flame was now blazing away with a healthy crackle. The only dirty thing remaining in the vast hall was him and the blanket beneath him.

The pounding ceased, then started up again.

"Elise!" he thundered out, wincing at the pain his action caused him. He staggered to his feet and continued to look around. The mantel had received a furious scrubbing; tapestries had been hung between the structural arches, and as well as having been swept, the floor had been polished. The place even smelled clean and fresh.

"Elise!" he started to holler again, but he broke off as a buxom and homely woman in dull gray wool came running in, bobbing a half curtsy every few steps.

"Who are you?" Bryan demanded.

"Maddie, milord," the girl replied nervously, tucking away a straying wisp of dark hair. "I'm to be in charge of your kitchens, or so milady told me, with your approval, sir!"

Bryan quickly blinked, trying to hide his astonishment as he looked around himself again.

" 'Ave I your approval, milord?"

"What? Oh, uh, yes, of course. But, Maddie, where is Lady Elise?"

"Gone on to the village, milord. Alaric has the carpenters going on the roof, and we've 'ad the girls in cleaning and freshening the place, but the smith and the priest long ago moved down to the town. There's a perfectly fine smithy round the back, and the chapel is beautiful, milord, truly beautiful! Milady said that we were going to set things to right as they were in the old days."

Bryan continued to stare at her blankly. Maddie's dark eyes grew wide and she took a step back from him. "We didn't mean to neglect the place so, Lord Stede; truly we didn't. No one came for so very long, you see. . . . If you'll just give us a chance, we'll see that the manor stands grand again and that the crops yield you a bountiful rent. Please, milord—"

Bryan held up a hand to stop her prattle. She was making his head feel worse, and he'd be damned if he knew what to say to her. Last night he'd wanted to hang every serf on the property. This morning he knew that would be unwise, as well as grossly barbaric. This morning he was also forced to admit that for all his cravings, he knew nothing about managing his estates. He needed to say something. But he admitted grudgingly that his wife had already been at work—and doing a splendid job at that. What approach had she taken? Not too harsh, but apparently firm.

"I can see that you're working hard, Maddie. And I can clearly hear the carpenters at work. I've no wish to deal blows against my people. We shall see how things progress."

"Bless you, milord!" Maddie chortled. "Will you be 'avin' something to eat, or would you prefer to bathe first? I've fresh bread ready, with thick butter. Trout from the stream, and kidney pie!"

Her mention of food was making him feel sick. "I want some water, Maddie, only water." He rubbed his stubbled chin. "And a bath and a shave. But—"

"Come, milord, and I'll show you the master tower." She swept up her skirts and headed for the stone-railed stairway. "Lady Elise ordered all the bedding pulled out into the sun this morning, so it will not look proper," Maddie explained, "but there's a spring-fed, built-in bath—they say the original Norman lord had been to Rome and seen such things—with a grate below where wood burns to heat the water. We scrubbed out the bath this morning, too, milord," she told him hastily. "Lady Elise was most insistent that it be done immediately!"

Still a little dazed, Bryan silently followed his new servant up the stairs and along a hall to the left. Maddie threw open a handsome set of double doors.

Two Norman arches separated the chamber into three sections. He could see the bath, an elaborate and tempting creation of small red bricks, set to the far right where the sun streamed in through a mullioned glass window. A wood and rope bed frame rested in the second chamber, and though the mattress had been taken outside to be freshened, the chamber already seemed inviting. Draperies had been hung, and Persian throw rugs littered the floor. Here, too, beneath a carved-stone mantel, a fire burned warmly. The packs with their clothing and supplies had been brought up and rested by the fire.

The third section of the room was empty.

"What was this?" he asked Maddie.

"A nursery, milord. For the first days when a wee babe is born. There's a larger nursery down the hall, of course, and rooms for wet nurses and governesses and the like, but 'tis rumored that the Norman lady who came here first was loath to send her babes to be cared for by others. Lady Elise said that it would make a marvelous spot for wardrobes and trunks. A dressing chamber, I believe she said."

"Did she?" Bryan queried, clenching down on his jaw.

"Aye, milord! She is a whirlwind of energy, your fair lady!"

"Um . . ." Bryan replied dryly. There was an old carved chair before the fire, broad and inviting. He sank into it, pulling off his boots. Maddie started to back away. "I'll send Alaric to you, milord, right away—"

"Who is this Alaric?"

"The steward, sir. But he makes a fine valet, too."

Bryan grunted, and Maddie hurried out of the chamber. He continued stripping off his clothing. He winced as he pulled the bandage from his knife wound; it had been healing well, but yesterday he had ridden too hard. The wound was bleeding again.

With a shrug, he decided the water could only help it. He walked over to the bath and ducked low beside it to see that a fire was burning within an iron grate. He touched the water and found it to be agreeably warm. The bath fascinated him, but at the moment he wanted to crawl into it not explore its marvelous workings. He hoped he could purge his headache away.

Bryan crawled into the tub and sighed in comfort. He ducked his head into the water, running his fingers through his hair. It felt good. He lay back and rested his head on the rim. The thing was so damned big a man could swim it. Or share it . . .

He smiled, thinking of the nights that could come. But then his smile turned to a scowl as he thought of Elise.

Always the duchess, always the lady. She was in her element; she knew how to rule and govern an estate. How to bring unruly serfs to order. How to refurbish a manor in a matter of hours with practically nothing at hand.

He should be grateful. She was his wife; it seemed that he had at last convinced her of that. She was working hard to pull this Cornish estate together, when he had feared that he would have to expend his energies merely to keep her here. Her proficiency at such tasks made him feel ignorant, but he did not resent her talents.

What, then?

He didn't trust her yet. There was a part of her that was still closed to him. He had managed to rouse her to passion, but he had not touched her heart. Or her soul—or her mind.

The third section would make a good "dressing chamber," she had said, apparently dismissing it as a nursery. Did she know something that he did not? Or was it not a matter of planning, rather than knowledge? He remembered how vehemently she had denied the possibility of being with child after their first meeting; she did not want to have his child—and had simply determined that, therefore, she would not. How long had it been since their first meeting? Almost three months. It seemed that she had been right.

He clamped his teeth hard. Did she perhaps plan to spite him by refusing him an heir? Could a woman do such a thing? Surely there were dozens of whores who went year upon year without conceiving.

He wanted children. In the days when he had wandered from tournament to tournament, and even when he had begun to serve Henry, he had come to realize that he lived with an emptiness. Nowhere was really home. It was then that he had begun to crave land, but just as he ached for the land, he longed for sons to whom to leave it, and a family to build with, to grow with. He wanted to teach a lad how to string a bow, how to make an arrow fly straight, how to wield a sword, and how to stand proud, even before a king.

He had his land. And he had a duchess who wanted to turn a nursery into a "dressing chamber."

He closed his eyes and allowed the water to swirl around him. The pounding seemed to ease slowly in his head. When the rapping at the door began, he calmly bade the caller to enter without opening his eyes.

"My lord?"

The words were very hesitantly voiced. Bryan opened one eye and surveyed the slender little man, who was almost tearing apart the cap he held between trembling fingers. A casket had been set beneath him, and the toweling spilling forth from it further portrayed the man's uneasiness, since he had obviously dropped his supplies. His eyes were a sparkling brown; his brown hair was much longer than fashion dictated.

Bryan closed his eyes again. Alaric—his steward. The man who deserved the brunt of his anger. Last night, Bryan would have gladly thrashed his back to ribbons.

"I offer you my humblest apologies, milord. But you see, when no one came, the people began to believe that I ordered them about for my own reward. They thought I took their hard-earned produce and goods. The old lord was not always a just man. He was one of those oafish Normans who called all Saxons swine. I—"

Bryan opened his eyes again as Alaric broke off with horror. Bryan started to laugh as he realized his steward had just assumed he'd cooked his own goose by insulting the Normans.

"Alaric, I come from the old Saxon stock myself, although I admit, Henry surrounded himself with Normans. However, the conquest took place a hundred and twenty something years ago—I will not be plagued by trivial quarrels between races."

He was surprised when the scared little man drew himself up to his full height. "Trivial, milord? Men were slaughtered like sheep; our sisters, mothers, daughters—raped. And still they refer to us as dogs."

"If you're to be my valet, Alaric, I could use a shave."

"Yes, milord."

Bryan wondered with a moment of uneasiness if he should bare his throat to the man, but decided then if he didn't, he would never learn if he would ever be safe when turning his back on these people.

Alaric set himself up, lathering Bryan's cheeks, then sharpening his blade upon a strap. "As to the manor, milord—"

"Yes—as to the manor?"

"Everything can be righted in a matter of days. The ledgers are good. I have counts of every home, and every man, woman, and child. I know the rents; I know the fields; and I know the livestock. Milord, if you will just see fit to forgive me."

Bryan sighed, wincing as Alaric took the blade to his face. "Alaric, I owe Richard ten mounted and armed men from this province for his Crusade. Where the hell am I going to get ten men out of this stock?"

Alaric paused. Bryan could feel the man's indignity. "This stock, milord? You've several score men to choose from! They're descendants of mighty warriors, even if fate cast them into being nothing but serfs of the land. Tom, the smith's son, for one. He's nineteen, tall as a birch, and made of muscle. Then there's young Roger the baker. And Raul, although he's a farmer born and bred. And then—"

"Whoa, Alaric!" Bryan laughed. If he had his ten men for Richard—his due to his king—he could relax. Ten men from Montoui; ten from the Cornish lands. "You know the lot; you choose the ten. Mind you, don't take those who are more valuable here. I've followed a merry trail for the last month; I borrowed men and coin from Richard. He does not part easily with either. Show me that you can be efficient, and the management of the estate shall remain yours. I've a man coming from Montoui, the duchess's steward. Let him handle the household; you will handle the land."

Alaric sighed. Bryan felt the blade slide smoothly over his face. "Aye, that sounds a fine arrangement, and I am grateful."

For several moments, the only sound that could be heard was that of the blade scraping over Bryan's face. Then Alaric stepped away and Bryan ducked beneath the water. Alaric's hand hadn't faltered once; Bryan was pleased to discover he hadn't a nick on his face. Alaric provided him with a towel, and he stepped from the bath.

Bryan vigorously scrubbed his skin and hair and stepped before the fire. He felt Alaric's eyes on him and turned with a brow lifted in query.

"Your back, milord. You've a wound turning nasty. I've a salve for it."

Bryan wrapped the towel around his waist and shrugged. "Do your damage, Alaric."

The steward reached into the casket and produced a small container. He rubbed the ointment into the wound, then came up with a clean binding. He didn't speak again until he delved into the packs and drew out fresh clothing, holding out a white linen shirt so that Bryan might slip his arms into it. "Pardon my boldness, milord, but might I ask you a question?"

Bryan shrugged, hooking the shirt, and plucking his stockings from the man's hands. "Ask what you will. I guarantee no answers."

"How is it that you—a Saxon—rose so high in the king's esteem?"

"I had a good sword arm," Bryan returned dryly, then laughed. "All right, Alaric, I'll tell you. My father was a fine fighter; he earned his knighthood when Henry first came to England. King Henry was an Angevin, remember? William the First's great-grandson through his mother. But Angevin or Norman, he was the rightful heir. My father had a wise philosophy. The Normans, he always said, were here to stay. Better to absorb them into us than to try to pretend we could beat them decades after the fact. I grew up in a very small town house in London. My mother died when I was very young; my father died in service to Henry. I lost the home to taxes, but I had my father's training. I went on to tournaments, then to fight for Henry when his sons joined with Philip of France to fight him. Aye"—he laughed, looking at Alaric's face—"I fought Richard. But our new king is a man who knows loyalty cannot be truly bought or bartered; those of us who defended the Crown to the end found that we were rewarded. And so here I am, Alaric. An Englishman, a Saxon, a great landowner again—that is, if you haven't run my land entirely into the ground!"

Alaric regarded him gravely, then slowly smiled. "Nay, milord! I have not run your land into the ground. You will see!"

"I'd best see soon," Bryan said dryly. "I've got to return to the king soon. With ten men prepared for battle. Do your choosing by this evening; I'll want to see them in the morning. I've not the swords I need for them yet—I pray God that our smith is competent!—but with time my major factor, I must begin to train them now. And, Alaric, you'd best pray to God that I can trust you in the future. I'll be away, but I'd best know that my affairs are well cared for!"

"Where is your concern, milord? Truly, you are a man blessed by God!"

"What are you talking about?" Bryan demanded with confusion.

"Your duchess!" Alaric exclaimed, and a glow settled over his face. "Truly she must be one of the wisest—and most beautiful—women in Christendom! By the cock's crow she had us moving! I believe that by nightfall, she will even know the exact number of chickens in the village!"

"Yes, the duchess is quite efficient. That will be all for now, Alaric. I'll see you in the hall in a few minutes; I want to go over the ledgers."

"Yes, milord."

Alaric left him. Bryan stepped behind the bath to the paned window and looked out.

He could see the village houses, pretty, thatched-roof houses that glimmered white beneath the sun. They settled in a valley that dipped downward from the manor. Hundreds of them, stretching almost to the sea. And the land. Sloping meadows, rich green hills. Grasslands, filled with cattle and sheep. He was overlord of all this.

And it would be brought to order. Not with the lash, but with firm justice. It would be made as strong and proud as Montoui . . .

Montoui again! Montoui . . . and Elise.

Soon Michael would be here, and Jeanne. Then things would run with pristine order.

Whether he was here or not.

Was that what bothered him? he wondered. The knowing that he was to leave? On Richard's great Crusade. Once, the thought had been inviting. But now . . .

This little piece of England was his. Despite last night, he felt that it could be strong, impregnable, and rich. It would be very ironic if he were to catch a Saracen blade with his throat at a time when so much had fallen his way.

And when he had no heir to whom he could leave it all.

Impatiently, he turned from the window and quit the chamber. His boots clattered on the stairs as he hurried down them. Alaric was awaiting at the table, his books and parchments spread before him. "Let's get busy, shall we?"

Alaric nodded, and the two went to work. Maddie brought food and ale. As the afternoon passed Bryan learned that there were several other, smaller manors to the estates. His serfs numbered in the many thousands. All the trades were represented; their wool was considered to be some of the finest in the land.

He was also pleasantly surprised to hear that he did have coffers full of coins. The tenants had paid their rents for a long time before the sloth and lethargy had set in, and Alaric, although he had control, had been an honest man.

When they finished, Bryan was pensive for several minutes. Then he told Alaric, "We must form an army for protection."

"But why, milord? Richard has been crowned and accepted; we are at peace—"

"Who knows how long any peace can last? Richard's reign should be peaceful at home. But . . . I want to train an army. I want defensive walls built to surround the manor. Tell the smith he will need many apprentices; we've blades and armor to forge."

"Aye, milord! The people will be very busy again—but, proud, too, I think!"

Maddie interrupted them to tell them that the smith had returned, and was around back. Bryan and Alaric both went. The smith was a stocky man with gray tingeing his temples. His shoulders and arms were massive, a sign of long years at his trade. Bryan found that the man was bright and eager, and quickly understood all that he wanted. By the time Bryan left the smithy, the fires of creation were already burning, even though night was falling.

Elise was in the hall when he returned, directing Maddie as to how she wanted the table set. Bryan strode to the mantel and leaned idly against it, saying nothing until Maddie had returned to the kitchen again. Her eyes met his across the room; he was not sure if they carried defiance or a plea for recognition.

No, there was never a plea about her. Her hair was neatly combed, her dress was immaculate. She was as always tall and proud . . . and perfect. He could touch her with a blaze of fire, yet when he looked again, she had regained the cool poise of winter's deepest frost.

By God, he didn't know if he loved her—or hated her. She haunted him, day and night. Perhaps it was best that he was leaving. Long months of riding into battle would make him forget the way she seemed to have taken hold of his insides.

He bowed to her.

"You've done quite well, madame."

She shrugged. "I did not care to live in squalor. Now, if you'll excuse me, milord, Maddie will shortly have supper served, and I would like to bathe . . ."

He smiled. "No. We will dine first."

Her eyes contested his, but then she sighed with a show of patience and tolerance. "As you wish." She swept from the hall to an arch at the far right of the room. Moments later she returned. He was already seated at the head of the table. She took her place beside him. Maddie appeared with a young boy in tow, and between them they served an aromatic meal of meat and vegetable pies, September apples, thick cheese, and ale.

The food was good, the ale even better, but Bryan, remembering his overindulgence of the night before, drank sparingly. He was pleased to see that Elise seemed to be drinking much more. He still made her nervous. She was probably yearning for the day when he would leave, and she would be left to reign over these lands alone.

Maddie and the lad hovered in the background, ready to refill their cups or plates, to serve at the lift of a hand. Bryan noted that Elise did not ignore them as the nobility were wont to do; she thanked them with a soft word each time they appeared.

He kept his conversation light, knowing that even the best of servants hung on every word spoken, and that gossip ran riot when they sat in the kitchens alone at night. He commended the smith, and spoke of how a sword must be made with the blade honed just so. Elise did not speak much, but she replied politely to his comments, and seemed to understand his desire to strengthen the lands.

"Montoui," she murmured to him, "was most often at peace. But that is, I believe, because our walls were insurmountable, and our garrison was always strong."

At last there was nothing more to eat. The last juicy apple had been enjoyed, and they hovered over a final cup of ale. Then Elise rose; the lad took away the last of the dishes.

"I'm very tired," Elise murmured, and Maddie was right there again.

"I'll come up and assist you, milady."

Bryan rose. "The duchess needs no assistance, Maddie. I am very weary, too. The meal was fine. I applaud your talents."

Elise made no protest; he knew she would not do so before the servants. He took her arm and was pleased to hear the thunder of her heart. She stepped into the center of the chamber as he closed and bolted the doors and stood still before her.

Bryan noticed that the mattress had been returned to the bed; it was dressed with fresh linen and a heavy fur coverlet. The fire was still burning brightly, and a new one had been built in the iron grate beneath the bath.

"The place holds promise," Bryan said, sitting upon the chair to pull off his boots.

"Yes, it does," Elise agreed stiffly. "Among the villagers are many fine carvers; they are eager to provide our home with their best pieces. Though the fields have been neglected, there is still ample time to pull in the late summer harvest. It is not yet September. We're quite fortunate in the abundance of our sheep. They pay dearly for English wool in Flanders; our revenues can be high once the place is in order again."

She was still standing in the center of the room. Bryan came behind her and started to pull the pins from her hair. He felt her shiver and he breathed in the perfumed fragrance of her hair with the familiar longing building in his groin. He lifted her hair and pressed his lips against her neck. "You have quite a talent for charming men, haven't you, milady?"

"Milord?"

"Our villagers."

"Nay . . . I merely reminded them that their new lord was the king's champion; a formidable knight who was just, but capable of a terrible temper."

"Hmm." He ran his hands along her arm and found the shoulders of her wide-sleeved tunic. It took little effort to tug the material down, and the rich green garment fell to the floor.

He continued to caress her flesh, hampered only by the gossamer material of her thin shift. "And do you consider what you said to be true?"

She answered him flatly, but he heard first the quick intake of her breath.

"You are now Richard's champion, and your temper is certainly . . . hot."

"And yours, milady?" He slipped his fingers beneath the straps of the shift and allowed them to roam suggestively.

"It is hot only when . . . provoked."

The shift fell to the floor. From behind her he swept his arms around her, cupping and cradling her breasts in his hands. She turned and buried her head against him with a soft moan. Bryan slid to his knees before her and removed her shoes and stockings. She silently allowed him.

He stood and cast aside his mantle, and then his tunic and shirt. "Have you tried the bath yet, Duchess?" he inquired politely.

"This morning . . ." she murmured.

" 'Tis large enough for a small army . . . and quite perfect for two."

He laughed, swept her off her feet, and deposited her in the warm water. Discarding his hose, he joined her, sitting opposite her and grasping a cloth from the side. He leaned toward her and kissed her, and while he did, he took the cloth, with its perfumed soap, and used it to massage her throat, and her breasts. Downward he moved, until her laughter made him break the kiss with a scowl.

"You find me amusing?"

"Nay . . . you are tickling me."

He joined her in her laughter, then dropped the cloth to allow his hands freedom to roam her length as he angled above her. "Tickling you, am I?" he demanded, delving into her center with his touch. She gasped, and her lips seared into his shoulders. She reached out to touch him, too. The strong extent of his arousal made her feel giddy, as if the warm water swept through her. She arched against his touch and found a boldness taking hold of her. Her hands roamed beneath the water; her lips explored the expanse of his chest.

His tongue played about her ear, and she started laughing again, holding tight to him. It was then that he stood, dripping and glistening. He reached for her and lifted her and carried her, mindless of the water, to their awaiting bed. The boldness was still with her; she found the play between them exciting and exhilarating. When he lay beside her she began to kiss the water droplets from his bronze flesh. His groans gave her a delicious sense of power, and she continued to tease him like a wraith rubbing her body against his, enjoying the graze of her breasts against his flesh, kissing him until she captured his sex completely, sweetly triumphant with the wild and passionate response she drew.

He caught her shoulders and dragged her lips to his. And when he had slated his desire for that kiss, he stared into her brilliant eyes. He pulled her atop him, and the laughter left her eyes for something darker as he came into her. The fire that gripped them both blazed quickly and completely, and when it had passed, he held her against him, tangling his fingers in her hair. He lifted her so that she still lay over him, her hands pressed against his chest, and when her eyes met his, there was no shame in them, just the soft sparkle of the aftermath of pleasure.

"You are in truth a little vixen," he told her softly. His gaze searched out her eyes. "Yet why do I feel that I . . . never have all of you."

"Because you don't," she told him.

He rolled her to her back and came over her, suddenly grave. "I want all of you," he told her tensely.

Her lashes shielded her eyes against his sudden anger, and the impertinence left her voice. "What is not yours?" she asked him. "I am your wife; I have done well with your home. I come into your arms whenever you choose. What else is it you want?"

"I want to know what is in your mind, what rules your heart, what you are thinking when you answer me politely, but sweep your lashes over your eyes."

She laughed softly, but the sound of it was bitter and she answered him sardonically. "You would have my soul, too, my lord Stede? Never would I be such a fool to lay that at your feet! They are ruthless feet, Stede."

"Is that really it? Or does your soul, perhaps, still belong to another?"

"The soul may be, my lord, the only thing one has that is truly free. It cannot be possessed, as can the body."

His eyes darkened so that she was suddenly frightened. "All that should be rightly yours is yours!" she cried out.

He played deceptively lightly with a lock of her hair. "It had best stay that way," he told her with a voice so low it sent shivers of dread tearing along her spine.

"You question your authority?" she asked him.

"I speak so that there is no misunderstanding between us." He rolled from her and lay on his back.

"You are not with child?" he asked her suddenly.

"We have not been together long—"

" 'Twas plenty long enough ago, the night we first met."

"No," she murmured uncomfortably.

He laughed. "You said then that you would not have my child. And it seems you willed it to be so. Tell me, Duchess, is it still your will not to have my child?"

"Will has little to do with it—"

"Is that true?"

"Of course!" she snapped irritably. "What did you—"

"There are ways. Yet if I were to discover that you used them, Elise, you would find that you have yet to experience how fierce my temper can be."

She turned her back on him. "It is not me, my lord," she said mockingly. "I do not deny you an heir. Perhaps God has decided you are undeserving."

"They say, Elise, that God assists the man who strives for himself."

His arms came around her, pulling her to him again. "I have not much time left to be here, Duchess. So I must strive mightily in that time I do have left."

Her eyes seemed to glitter when they met his, and he fancied that it might be the mist of tears. But as he entangled himself again in the sweet-smelling web of her hair and flesh, she did not protest him.

Here, in his bed, he had her. She had told him as much.

Perhaps if he captured her and recaptured her, he would at last find and claim that something which eluded him.

What was her claim upon him? Her beauty . . . but that was his. He stopped thinking. The night was dark, and the fires of his body were finding the sweetest fuel . . .

At such times, it seemed ridiculous to ponder over what, in passion, came to naught.

XIX

In the span of a few weeks, a remarkable change had come to the manor.

When Jeanne and Michael arrived from the Continent, the place began to take on the ambiance that so graced Montoui. Elise's trained guards arrived, including her experienced captain. Bryan found his ten men for Richard's army, and a hundred more to train as guards and soldiers to protect his Cornish borders. A wall could not be built to encompass the village and the far-spread farms, but Bryan set boundaries around the manor, and in his first few days of labor he was able to see the foundations set. There was no lack of stone, since his property contained the quarry from which the walls of the manor had been dug a hundred years before.

At sunrise each morning, his rough army went through drills. They were ignorant of the way of arms, but eager to learn, and grateful for their new station. As Bryan well knew, a man born with little could expect to gain little in this life—unless he had exceptional wit or strength. It would take months for the army to shape together, just as it would take months for his stone wall to rise, but he could leave knowing that the foundations were well laid for each.

He sat upon his horse on the morning that marked his eighth in Cornwall, watching the captain put the men through drill. Dummies were staked out upon spits, and the men, who so far had swords, practiced tearing their lifeless opponents apart.

He called to a man now and then with a suggestion or comment, and saw that his orders were well taken. He was musing over a number of talented lads when Alaric came running to him, across the rear fields, from the back of the manor.

He was panting when he reached Bryan's horse, and had to take several seconds to catch his breath.

"Milady . . . the duchess . . . asks that you come to the house with all speed! Riders are coming; she's seen them from the west tower!"

"Riders?" Bryan queried.

"Seems she knows them," Alaric replied.

Bryan raised his brow, then turned his horse toward the manor and galloped full speed toward it. Young Wat, who had come with Michael and Jeanne, was ready to care for his destrier, and he was able to jump from the horse and hurry into the hall.

Elise had been supervising the curing of meat to carry the household through the winter ahead. She wore simple gray wool for the task, and her hair was plaited in two loose braids. She looked like a fresh, young peasant girl herself when he strode in and found her calling hurried commands to Maddie.

"What is it?" Bryan asked her.

Her glare at him assured him that, whatever it was, she considered it to be his fault.

"Company!" she snapped, and then she hesitated, lowering her lashes. "Lord and Lady Montagu."

"Gwyneth and Percy? How do you know? If you saw them from the tower, they must still be a distance away."

Elise hesitated again, then said blandly, "I know Percy's standard when I see it. They come with an armed escort of four. I've told Maddie that supper must be exceptional; Michael and she are putting together a meal now. Would you have Alaric bring up whatever wine is in the cellar? I know that it is a poor stock, but please make the best selection you can. I must run up and change my gown."

She was distressed, he saw, and it irritated him because he was not quite sure why.

"I wouldn't overly exert yourself," he told her dryly. "They are both aware, I'm sure, that we've just arrived. And being as close as they are, both surely knew that this place needed a great deal of work. They will not expect us to offer sumptuous hospitality."

"Well they will be offered it!" Elise snapped in return, and then her eyes lowered again. "Please, Bryan. I will not be pitied by either of them."

"Pitied, madame?"

Her eyes raised to his, turquoise, crystaline, and wide. She swept an arm to encompass the hall and the estate. "Please, Bryan?" she asked him softly. "I want no one to know that we . . . struggled."

He sighed. "Go change, Duchess. Alaric and I shall drag out our finest, and if some should starve through the winter for it, so be it."

"No one will starve!" she retorted, hiking her skirts up and scampering for the stairs, since no one but Bryan was about to see her. He watched her go, wondering if she wished to deck herself out because of pride, or because she needed to assure herself that she could still attract her lost love.

Grating his teeth, he spun about. Alaric, still panting, had entered the hall behind him.

"Come, Alaric. You must escort me to whatever wine cellar we have. That which is important must be ceased. The duchess wishes to entertain."

Alaric did not understand his duke's sudden foul temper. He nodded, then proceeded to lead Bryan to the kitchen, and then down to the dampness of the cellar.

In truth he felt he owed Percy Montagu no grudge. He considered his neighbor knight to possess a strange set of priorities and a foolishly quick temper, but he felt sorry for him. Percy had been in love—a fool's quest, at the very least. It had been his own confused sense of honor that had cost Percy Elise, and he had certainly been rewarded handsomely with Gwyneth. But

Bryan had, albeit unknowingly, taken the woman he had loved. Knights felt a keen sense of justice toward one another, and because of that, Bryan still felt that he wronged the man—whether he particularly liked him or not. If he but trusted Elise . . .

There had been a small, cobwebbed supply of Bordeaux wine in the cellar. Bryan had left Alaric to bring it up, and had then come back out, calling to Wat for his horse. Elise wanted to offer hospitality; he would ride out to greet the callers.

It was just minutes before he reached them. Gwyneth waved wildly when she saw him coming, and was ready to greet him with her ever-lovely smile. Percy took his hand in a firm grip with more solemnity, and as their horses pranced, he spoke apologetically.

"Perhaps we shouldn't have come; word is that you have just arrived yourselves. The truth of the matter, Stede, is Gwyneth. I am recalled to London to join Richard, as you are, and I would be happier if Gwyneth and Elise were to keep in close touch with each other." He hesitated a moment. "Gwyneth is expecting a child, and should we be in a distant land when the time comes, I would like to know that she has a friend nearby."

Bryan glanced quickly at Gwyneth, then offered them both his congratulations. "I'm quite pleased, as I'm sure Elise will be, with your good fortune. And you are quite welcome here at any time. It's true that we've just arrived, but we're glad to have you come."

They walked the horses to the manor. Gwyneth spoke about the crops that grew best in their rocky soil; Percy told him that Richard had started on his campaign to raise money. A knight with no desire to go on crusade could honorably "buy" his absence. The King of Scotland had offered several thousand marks rather than his service, and other great barons, dukes, and earls were doing the same. Merchants were being sold concessions; obscure offices and titles were being revived, and for a goodly sum, a man could purchase himself a place in the king's government.

"Of course, he's being careful. And some knights have paid their dues—and then announced they were riding with our king anyway."

Bryan laughed. "I sense Queen Eleanor's fine hand in all this," he told Percy. "She would have warned Richard that he could not remain a popular monarch while taxing his people further! So no taxes—the king becomes a merchant. Brilliant!"

They had reached the manor. Bryan was surprised but pleased to see that Wat and two other—suddenly *uniformed*—boys were standing by to take the horses, and to escort Percy's guards to the freshly refurbished gatehouse.

Elise was waiting for them before the mantel. Although he wasn't sure he didn't prefer the long-braided waif, Bryan had to admire her elegant transformation. Her gown was a deep green velvet, long, gracefully sleeved. The scooped neckline and hem were edged with gold trim; it was a simple dress, yet entirely fluid and lovely upon her curved figure. Her hair had been captured and sleekly coiffed to curl about the gold-and-pearl crown of her headdress. A light train of wafting beige silk flowed from crown as well as plaited lengths of her hair.

She stepped forward to greet them. "Lady Gwyneth, Percy . . . what a pleasure it is to receive you here. Come in, come in. You must be parched from your ride."

Bryan watched her as she addressed the two; she was so cordial and demure that he felt the urge to shake her. He couldn't tell what went on beneath her turquoise eyes when they rested upon Percy, but he wondered if he wouldn't be tempted to slap her if he did know.

She smiled her elusive smile and seemed to float across the room as she approached the table. The burgundy had been brought up and set into a silver decanter; four jewel-crested goblets rested beside it. Bryan hadn't seen the goblets before; he assumed that Michael had brought them from Montoui along with other "niceties."

Gwyneth and Percy followed Elise to the table, and Bryan followed. They took chairs before the fire and conversation continued. Percy expounded on King Richard's affairs; Gwyneth invited Elise to come hunting in their forest acres.

The time passed easily, Bryan noted. A lad appeared in the room, and Elise needed only to lift her hand and he stood ready to refill a glass.

One would never think that she had just left the heat of her own kitchen, sweating along with the others to preserve meat for winter. It appeared that her most difficult task in the world was the selection of the proper gown for the day.

My cap is off to you, Duchess, he thought dryly.

They gave Percy and Gwyneth a tour of the manor, and Bryan smiled as he realized how smoothly Elise avoided the rooms they had not yet cleaned and refurbished. The only awkward moment was in their chamber, when Gwyneth exclaimed with delight and envy over their bath.

"How wonderful!" she cried.

"Yes, it is," Elise told her. "The water escapes constantly through a pipe, and is replenished constantly through a mechanism that dips down to the spring beyond the walls. It was an invention from Rome, or so they tell us."

"Absolutely wonderful!" Gwyneth repeated with awe. "And right in your bedchamber!"

"You must come and make use of it sometime," Elise told her politely. But it was at that moment that an uneasy cold seemed to settle over the group. Bryan glanced at his wife. All of them . . . who was thinking that they would enjoy the bath with whom?

Percy would be leaving when he did, he reminded himself. He did not like the amount of relief that the thought gave him.

Gwyneth laughed and broke the uneasy spell. "Perhaps, when we two are left behind when our husbands enter the king's service, I shall come and stay with you."

"That will be pleasant," Elise murmured. "But, you must be famished by now! We'll go on down and dine . . ."

The meal was wonderful, impeccably served. Bryan wondered how even Elise and her loyal servants had managed such a feast in such short time. There was roasted pork, huge legs of lamb, endless pies, sweetbreads and puddings, fresh fruit in abundance.

We might well be the wealthiest nobility in the land by such a spread . . . he thought. Ah, yes, his wife was efficient.

It was not until the meal was almost over that Gwyneth thought to explain their appearance that day to Elise.

"So you see, though I do apologize for coming so hastily upon you two, I was most anxious to see you! I'm not as young as I should be for a first child, and I confess to being very frightened."

There was a subtle difference in Elise's expression and tone of voice.

"But this is . . . wonderful . . . Percy, Gwyneth . . . I wish you every happiness with your child." She took a sip of her wine. "When . . . is the child due?"

"Late spring, I believe," Gwyneth said enthusiastically. "It sounds so far off, but time can so easily escape us."

"Yes . . ." Elise murmured. "It can. Don't be afraid, Gwyneth. My maid . . . Jeanne . . . was in attendance when I was born. We are both nearby."

The words were cordial, but Bryan thought the warmth had gone from his wife's voice. Why? Because she had longed for Percy's child herself? He wasn't to understand her reasoning until Gwyneth and Percy had been lodged in a guest chamber, and he had at last closed the door to their own.

"What was the matter with you down there?" he demanded. "One would think you wished them ill with their child."

"Their child?" She spun about and he saw that fury burned, vibrant and vital, burned deep within the turquoise depths of her eyes.

"What are you talking about?" he queried, equally tense as he crossed his arms over his chest and surveyed her.

"Can't you count, my lord? The child is due in spring. Is it Percy's child—or yours?"

Bryan narrowed his eyes at her and said evenly, "They were married in August."

"Yes—conveniently close, I would say."

Bryan ignored her and moved into the room. He sat upon the bed and pulled his boots off, then wearily drew his fingers through his hair.

"Well?" Elise demanded in a hiss.

"Well, what?"

"Is it your child?"

Bryan threw off his mantle, not caring that it fell to the floor in a heap. "No," he told her, but he had hesitated just a minute too long.

"You're lying."

"I'm not lying," he snapped impatiently. "I'm doing my best to shut you up without any English barbarism."

"Is it or isn't it your child?"

"All right, Elise. If it comes in March, it is my child. If it comes in April, Percy is the father."

He stood up, ignoring her, as he pulled his tunic over his shoulders. He completed undressing and climbed into bed. She hadn't moved. He cast a glance her way. She stood dead-still with her hands knotted into fists at her side as she stared at him with dark fury burning a lethal tempest in her eyes.

He closed his own, casting a crooked arm over his eyes to shield them from the candlelight.

"We played your game today, Elise. Our company was suitably impressed with our elegance. I am weary; come to bed."

He remained still, opening one eye beneath the shadow of his arm. She swung about suddenly, her footsteps sharp as she headed for the door.

He sprang out of the bed with an agile leap, catching her arm and swinging her about.

"Where are you going?"

"Out."

"Out where?"

"Anywhere. Away from you."

"Why?"

"That is clearly apparent."

He released her and leaned negligently against the door, staring at her. With her chin obstinately raised, she returned his stare.

"I have not been with Gwyneth since the night Richard reached the outskirts of London."

She blinked, but gave no other sign the words meant anything to her. "I would like to walk by," she told him coolly.

He was silent for several seconds. "Because of Gwyneth? Or because you suddenly find it distasteful to sleep with your husband when the gallant Percy rests beneath the same roof?"

"Does it matter?" she queried. Elise was very close to tears, and more than willing to lash out at him and make him feel the hurt that gnawed at her like a hundred tiny knives.

He raised a brow. "In the outcome of anything? No. To me, yes."

"Maybe I feel, my lord husband, that you should be forced to the same doubts as the rest of us. Maybe I should seek Percy out—and allow you to wonder if the heir you crave is your own or not. And maybe knowing that Percy is in this house does make me ache to feel his arms about me—"

It was as far as she got. He never meant to do so, but suddenly he was grasping her to him and shaking her. He realized what he was doing and released her—too quickly. She fell to the floor, stunned, but not beaten. Like a whirlwind she was on her feet, flying at him, fists pounding his chest, nails raking his flesh. He closed his eyes briefly, fighting for control, then caught her and held her hard against him. Her head tilted back; her eyes met his, still blazing a liquid turquoise fire.

"Leave off, Duchess," he said quietly.

"Just let me by," she whispered.

He shook his head slowly. "You'll never shut me out because of Percy Montagu—or any other man."

"Yet you expect me to jump demurely into bed while I accept your mistress and your bastard into my house?"

"Ex-mistress—and it was at your insistence that we offered hospitality. And . . . it is most unlikely that the child is mine."

"Most unlikely!"

"Elise! The past is something I cannot change. I doubt that she carries my child; Gwyneth is wise in the ways of the world, and I have always been careful not to leave a string of bastards across the battlefields or home. What would you have me do? Insult Percy further and demand to know if he is certain he is about to be a father?"

"I would have you leave me alone!"

"You are not going out that door tonight. I'll not have you combing the corridors to snare the unwary Percy, should he wander from his chamber and discover his hostess ready for reckless abandon upon the stone—"

He broke off, ruefully rubbing his jaw as he discovered that she could break his grip and return a slap to rival his for potency. The sharp sound echoed between them.

Perhaps it was deserved.

"You are not leaving, Elise," he told her quietly.

"I am—"

"No, you're not. And if you push me any further, I'm going to forget that I possibly deserved your blow. If we must have a scene before guests, it might as well be that of the brutal husband flogging his sharp-tongued wife."

If she'd had a sword at that moment, he was certain she would have gladly pierced it through him. As it was, she held his eyes with brilliant defiance, then spun about, wrenching from his grasp, and sat in the chair before the fire.

He watched her for several seconds, then sighed. He knew that set of her chin. She was not about to budge.

He walked to her side and grazed her cheek with his knuckles. She flinched at his touch.

"I am sorry, Elise."

She lifted her eyes to his. "Just what, pray tell, milord, is it that you're sorry for? That you railed against me? Or that we were forced into this mockery of a marriage to begin with?"

"You never bend, do you, Elise?"

"I asked you a question."

"I am sorry that you are hurt."

Her eyes dropped from his to her hands. She played idly with the sapphire ring she wore now on her middle finger.

"I must admit, I'm flattered."

"Flattered?"

"I had not thought you would care."

"Then don't flatter yourself, Stede," she told him coolly. "I don't like to be humiliated, and I consider this a humiliating situation."

Bryan stepped away from her. "Get in bed, Elise," he told her tiredly.

"I don't care—"

"I don't give a damn what you do or do not care to do. I can't leave you sitting there fully dressed upon the chair; I know your talent for disappearances."

She remained in the chair, staring absently at the ring, as if she hadn't heard. With a muttered oath of exasperation, he wrenched at her arm, jerking her from the chair. Her eyes fell upon his with surprise and brilliant hostility. "Elise, I did nothing with malice in mind to hurt you. But, by Christ, I will not allow you out of this room, and therefore I will have you by my side to assure myself you do not attempt any of your foolish escapes. I am very tired, and weary of this pointless argument. You have until my count of ten to undress and be in bed—else I'll see you there myself."

She started to laugh. "The valiant man who never stoops to force—"

"And his wife the shrew," Bryan interrupted her. "I won't force anything from you—other than your form where it should, by right, be. But, sweet wife, that I swear I will force with little patience if—"

"Just don't touch me!" Elise hissed, pulling her arm from his hold and turning her back to him. With shaking fingers she doffed her finery, allowing her clothing to fall at her feet. Tears were hotly stinging her eyes; she wanted to pound against him until he was black and blue, pound against him until he understood . . .

What? She didn't know. She didn't understand herself. He thought she wanted to run to Percy; she couldn't even remember what it had been like to love Percy.

She had just wanted to run . . . from Bryan. And yet, if he had let her go, she would have known an even deeper misery.

Her shift fell to the floor. Still shaking, she threw aside her headdress impatiently and unwound her hair, wrenching the pins so that liquid rushed to her eyes with pain. Barely aware of any feeling, she climbed beneath the coolness of the sheets, turning her back to the center of the bed and closing her eyes. It would have been foolish to fight him, because he would have won.

It would have been even more foolish to fight him, because she would have touched him, and perhaps given away the fact that no matter how hurt and angry she was, she still longed to touch him. Maybe more than ever, she wanted to be reassured and held, and she wanted to believe that Gwyneth's child couldn't possibly be his, because Elise did not think she could bear to share Bryan in such a fashion. She would go mad . . .

She dug her fingers into her pillow, forcing herself to keep her eyes closed, her body perfectly still.

He moved about the room, snuffing out the candles. She felt his weight as he lay down beside her.

True to his word, he kept his distance. She heard his breathing in the silence of the night; she fancied she could hear his heartbeat.

It was but her own, pounding mercilessly against her chest.

She waited, tense and miserable, but the seconds ticked by to minutes, and the minutes continued to pass. He did not reach out for her. Elise brought her knuckles to her mouth and bit into them; she needed him . . .

She didn't want to need him.

The conflicting desires created a havoc in her heart that was as painful as it was confused. Her emotions roiled within her, out of control like a wave begun at the ocean floor, and tearing now toward land. She could not stay in the bed, not without screaming, not without exploding like a dry log in a hot fire . . .

Her knuckles grazed against her cheeks and she found that they were damp. She tried to take a deep, steadying breath; instead, a muffled sob escaped her.

"Elise . . ."

At last he rolled to her, his fingers smoothing her hair away lightly, and grazing her throat.

"No!" she groaned out miserably.

"You're crying . . ."

"I'm angry!" she retorted, and her very fragile grasp upon control snapped. She spun on him, entangling herself in the sheets, and pounding brokenly upon his chest. For a long while he allowed her to. Then he crushed her against him, holding her. He touched her cheeks and felt the tears, and he knew a feeling of tenderness to rival the passion she could always arouse. He abruptly rolled her beneath him, and, forgetting his promise, kissed the dampness from her cheeks, and then found her lips. To his surprise, her lips parted hungrily to his, and she clung to him, pressing fervently against him.

Elise discovered that anger could spark desire—dark, fierce, and tempestuous. Her heart had never been more in a tempest, but never had she longed for him more.

Yet suddenly he drew away from her. She had wanted the night to surround them with only the dim embers from the fire to break the blackness; Bryan began lighting the candles about the bed.

He met her eyes as he came to her again, lowering himself slowly over her.

"Tonight . . . tonight we will both see with clarity. You will keep your eyes open when I make love to you. And you will whisper my name to me . . . again . . . and again."

She did not answer him. Their eyes continued to meet in a fiery clash of wills until all was forgotten but sweet urgency.

When it was past, Elise curled against him, and, exhausted in body and mind, slept.

Bryan lay awake a long time, watching the candles burn low and thinking that he should douse them.

And wondering bleakly what had driven his wife to such wild abandon. Could she keep her lashes wide, yet dream in her mind's eye of another man . . . ?

He had to leave so soon. Too soon. He did not believe Gwyneth's child could be his, but only time would tell. Elise . . . her pride was so great. She would never forgive him. It was possible that as soon as he left, she would be gone again. Crossing the Channel for Montoui, more determined than ever to escape.

At last he sighed and rose to pinch out the candles. He paused before snuffing out the last flame. She was beautiful tangled in the silk of her own hair, yet her cheeks seemed strained with pain, and a frown, even in sleep, furrowed her brow. She twisted and whimpered slightly as he watched her.

His fingers moved over the last flame and then he crawled beside her, taking her very tenderly against him and holding her to his heart.

Gwyneth and Percy departed in the morning. Bryan and Elise saw them off together, waving until the horses disappeared over the crest of a hill.

Elise murmured that she had something to do, and hurried away from Bryan. Bryan tightened his lips and went back to the tasks of building his army and his wall.

The days passed by quickly in an uneasy and too silent truce. Food was prepared for winter; the cellar stocks of ale and firewood continued to grow. Bryan spent several days hunting; Elise roused the household to long and tedious hours over the caldron to make candles.

Each night Bryan held his wife and lay awake wondering if he held her at all.

Then came the inevitable day that was to be his last at home. Bryan was satisfied to see that the wall was rising steadily, and that his ragtag army of guards was shaping up well.

The manor had become an elegant and welcoming place; Elise had sent for tapestries and finely crafted furnishings, Belgian laces, and Mideastern rugs. It was a home.

Lacking only the warmth of those who inhabited it.

She came to him eagerly that last night; as always it was amazing that a woman so cool and aloof by day could offer such sweet heat by night. Night . . . his last night.

A despair of leaving seized him, and as soon as thirsts were quenched, they rose again. He was fierce and demanding, inexhaustible and insatiable. She did not murmur a single protest, but met him in a reckless, smoldering fervor of her own.

When dawn came he rose to dress, having never slept.

With his scabbard in place, he knelt down beside her. Shadows played beneath her eyes, and her flesh was pale. The dawn creeping through their windows played upon her hair, and she seemed to be wrapped in silken threads of red and gold.

He picked up her hand and played idly with the sapphire upon her finger. He looked into her eyes, and spoke with deep sincerity.

"Who are you, Duchess? Do I truly have you? Or have you forever locked away your soul in mystery and secret?"

Her eyes glistened, turquoise pools that threatened to spill and drown him. She shook her head.

"Do not hate Gwyneth because of me," he told her softly.

"Another threat, my lord, or merely a warning?"

"A suggestion, not a warning or threat." He smiled, suddenly bitter. "I leave you no threats—Percy rides with me."

"Convenient, isn't it?"

He shrugged. "To my way of thinking, yes."

"And I am to be kind to your mistress!"

"Cordial, merely, to a neighbor. We are isolated here, and she is with child."

"Ah, yes! Aren't you wishing heartily now that she, our fertile neighbor, were your wife?"

"She has by far the better temper," Bryan said lightly. "And I admit, I would feel more secure in the belief that I would return to find a wife. I wonder if you don't intend to forsake this place yourself the moment the dust lies in my wake."

"Run to Montoui?" she queried him. "I wonder what welcome I would find. Your friends, the king's men, have surely taken a strong foothold in *your* duchy by now."

"As that is mine, this is yours."

"Don't fear," she murmured, turning her back on him. "I have no desire to be dragged through the countryside again."

"Or do you merely wait with the hope that the Crusade will take her toll in the lives of men?"

"I do not wish your death."

"Just my absence."

"You have been as eager as Richard to go to battle."

"And you have been as eager to see me go."

"Richard is still in England."

"Yes . . . so I will most likely be back before the forces take leave for the Continent."

"A warning, my lord?"

"A statement. Perhaps of curiosity." He reached out, touching her chin lightly with his thumb and forefinger, yet firmly forcing her eyes to look at his. "I will be intrigued to discover if you really do await me."

"The future does promise to be intriguing, doesn't it?" she murmured, and he knew as always that, as with himself, mockery lurked behind her words.

"Very intriguing. I shall be especially interested in the state of your health before we leave for the Holy Land."

"My health? It is always fine—"

"I am hoping to find you wretchedly ill with sickness each morning."

Her cheeks flooded with color. "You should truly have fought to marry Gwyneth, since 'tis likely she would have surely awaited you—wretchedly ill each morning!"

He stood and walked to the door, having no wish to leave her with the bitterness of a full-scale quarrel between them.

He paused at the door.

"I have no regrets about our marriage, Duchess."

The door closed softly behind him, and in minutes she heard the clatter of hoofbeats as Bryan, with his party of soldiers and squires, rode out to greet the day.

The room grew chill; the manor seemed empty.

Already she knew a terrible void in her heart.

XX

Fall passed quickly to become winter, and by the middle of December the manor sat like an ice palace atop a mountain of snow.

Elise managed well enough. The guards had become proficient at their duties, the household ran smoothly, and the serfs seemed cheerfully resigned to the new order of things. The lord of the manor might be gone, but they had quickly learned that the Lady Elise could be both astute and hard if pressed, judicial and merciful when honestly approached. Disputes were settled each morning in the hall, and when there was no clearcut answer to a problem by the law, Elise selected five men at random to deliberate the case, and so far, all had accepted the verdicts delivered. To her people, even to her closest servants, Elise presented a façade of complete stoicism and calm.

Inwardly, she seethed with a roiling of emotions that threatened to drive her mad. They would make her all the more insane because she didn't in the least understand them.

With each day that passed, she yearned anew for Bryan. When each day came to an end she lay awake long hours in her chamber, alone and cold. She longed for him passionately.

When she awoke each morning, she longed to kill him.

Throttle him, thrash him, tear him apart limb by limb.

No matter how she tried to reason with herself, when Elise thought of Gwyneth and the child she was to bear, she felt an overwhelming cloud of black anger engulf her. She felt ill. And then she wanted to lie down and cry.

It was jealousy, of course, but she could not accept it as such. Nor could she allow herself to believe that she was anything more than resigned to her marriage.

She spent long hours wondering where Bryan was. Gwyneth might have remained behind, but London was filled with women, of the high and low variety, and she knew that, in the past, Bryan had enjoyed a level of entertainment from commoners and nobility alike. He had, after all, been intending to marry Gwyneth on that night when he had first taken her in the woods . . .

Men—from Percy to her father to Bryan (most certainly Bryan!)—were little better than animals. Henry, whom she had loved, had treated Eleanor and his scores of mistresses abominably. Percy, who had filled her with dreams of a different life, had proved himself to be little better than pathetically weak and hopelessly hypocritical. But thoughts of Percy no longer plagued her. Though she wanted Bryan to believe she was still in love with Percy because she sensed it gave her a small edge over all that she had been forced to swallow from him, she truly could not conjure her onetime betrothed's face anymore when he was beyond her view.

While Stede's image haunted her continually.

Angrily, she would remind herself that her husband might be anywhere. He had claimed that he had not seen Gwyneth since Richard had ordered their marriage—but had that been only to soothe ruffled feathers? Men, it seemed, were not expected to be faithful to their wives, especially not in the service of their king, when that service carried them far from their homes. Yet when thoughts of his probable infidelity plagued her, she did not imagine him with vague strangers. She saw him with Gwyneth.

When she closed her eyes at night, the picture could be disparagingly clear. They would stand in a room with only the glimmer of a few pale candles. A frothy bed of down and clean sheets would await them. Bryan's eyes would meet Gwyneth's; they would lock in a heated stare, Gwyneth would

smile, her lips damp and parted, her dark eyes sultry. They
would both begin to shed their clothing in eager haste, and
Bryan would groan deeply. He would toss Gwyneth upon the
bed, but she would rise upon her knees to greet his tall warrior's body; she would touch the tight bronze flesh, press her
face against his chest and hear the pounding of his heart, feel
the ripple of hard muscle as she ran her hands and lips over
him . . .

Elise would awaken with a start, groaning softly herself—and
hating her husband with a fervor to match that of the night they
had met. Why hadn't he left her be? she would wonder savagely.
She hated him because she yearned for him so passionately, and
because she scorned herself for doing so. Her neighbor was
about to bear her husband's bastard, a neighbor who had openly
been her husband's mistress, who might, at a future time, become his mistress again.

Why not? Bryan wanted a child. Gwyneth was about to supply that want. Elise could picture them, meeting in a clandestine
tryst, awed with the life they had produced between them.

But Gwyneth's child could not be Bryan's heir! Only Elise,
his legally wed wife, could give him an heir . . .

But, she told herself to still her misery, hell and the devil
himself would freeze solid if she gave Bryan his heir! Not when
he ran about the country creating bastards.

Was it true, she wondered wistfully, that she could deny
Bryan his heir by willing that she not conceive? Foolish thought,
for even now she was left to wonder if she might not have
conceived. A brief thought consoled her; if she did have a child,
her child would not be a bastard.

As she was.

And that, too, was another thing she still held from her
husband. Not that it mattered now. No one would dare lay
claim to anything owned by Lord Bryan Stede. But the ring
still bothered Bryan; that mystery was something he could not
touch, and she felt it was a wall that protected her from completely . . .

Completely what?

She refused to face the answer. She did not love him, could never love him. She had once given him a wise truth; she would be a fool ever to lay her soul or her heart at his feet.

It was better to hate him. Better to deny him. Ha! she derided herself. She had never managed to deny him; when he had not reached for her, she had turned to him. What had he done to her that she longed for him night and day, and only him?

It was a riddle that would continue to haunt, no matter how serene the appearance she gave the world.

Gwyneth visited Elise in the middle of December.

She came encased in furs against the cold, her dark hair beautiful and lustrous against the white of the fox. Elise had stiffened immediately when informed that a party approached boasting Percy's banners, knowing full well it could only be her rival. Yet when Gwyneth reached the manor, Elise was ready to greet her demurely, telling her that she shouldn't have braved the weather in her condition.

"I was going stark, raving mad all alone!" Gwyneth proclaimed, settling herself before the fire. She still looked trim, Elise thought. Had her child been conceived before her marriage, her girth should have grown more rounded by now!

"I'm afraid there is little diverting here," Elise told her.

"Oh, but we are at least together!" Gwyneth told her.

With the other woman's dark eyes upon her, Elise felt a slight chill. Gwyneth was indeed beautiful. Yet, despite her friendly smile, Elise felt that there was something secretive and smug about the curve of her lips, and the knowing flash in those mahogany eyes, as she narrowed her lashes in appraisal. "I've been so anxious to see you, Elise, as I fear that I must throw myself upon your mercy! I know this might sound terribly silly, but I'd like to beg your hospitality from the month of March onward."

Elise kept her expression immobile and inquired sweetly, "Are you afraid that your child will come early, Gwyneth?"

Gwyneth lifted her hands vaguely and smiled again. "Winter frightens me. My first child . . . I so hope that you can understand."

"Yes, I understand," Elise murmured. But did she? Was Gwyneth seeking companionship—or something else? Did she wish to insinuate to Elise that her child was Bryan's—or was Elise imagining such a thing because of her own turmoil over the question.

"You are welcome to be here whenever you choose, Gwyneth," she told the other woman serenely. "I had thought you would want your heir born on your property."

"Oh . . . well, our all being so close . . . it doesn't really seem to matter, does it?"

"No," Elise replied, smiling, "I don't suppose it matters at all."

Gwyneth stayed the night. Elise, determined not to let Gwyneth believe that there was the slightest chink in the armor of her marriage, was charming and considerate of her guest. She even offered Gwyneth the master chamber, with its fabulous bath, for the night. And she insisted when Gwyneth demurred—and saw beneath Gwyneth's lowered lashes a sparkle of pleasure.

Again, Elise wondered. Was it evident that Gwyneth was imagining herself in the bath . . . in the bed . . . with Elise's husband? Or was Elise putting malicious thought where it was not due?

Elise did not sleep that night. She alternately raged and agonized over Gwyneth's blithe statements.

The child cannot be due in March! she assured herself staunchly. Gwyneth was too small.

But if the child was Bryan's . . .

Then it seemed natural that Gwyneth would want the baby born on Bryan's property rather than her own. But to what end? Elise wondered. Gwyneth was legally wed, as was Bryan. By

Richard's order. They could never be together . . . unless they
determined to wade through the long years it would take them
both to procure annulments through the Pope . . .

Or, Elise thought, with another chill, unless she and Percy
were both to die. And Gwyneth could become a widow again;
men dropped like flies when they rode on crusade . . .

But I am young and healthy, Elise reminded herself. *Very
young, and very healthy.*

She forced herself to turn over and close her eyes. Such
thoughts were truly ridiculous. Gwyneth might possibly be a
troublemaker, but the fragile brunette beauty was hardly a murderess.

Elise sighed, wishing she hadn't been foolish enough to give
up her own chamber. The guest lodging was comfortable, but
Elise was accustomed to her own bed. The bed that she had
shared with her husband.

She began to wonder if Bryan would return to her anytime
soon. Richard was still in England, the last she had heard, still
collecting money and provisioning and organizing the army
that would cross the Channel. In Normandy, he was due to
meet with Philip of France, as the two monarchs were vowed
to ride together. The army was due to travel to the Continent
soon, though, she knew. But Bryan had told her that he would
try to come back before they had left England for the Continent.

She began to agonize all over again, wishing he would come,
wishing he would not. If she possessed the least bit of dignity
or pride, she would deny him. Yet if she did so, she would leave
way for him to seek out another.

Or would he do that anyway?

Gwyneth left in the morning. Alaric stood beside Elise as
Gwyneth, a snow nymph in her furs once more, rode away.

"I don't much care for her," Alaric muttered beneath his
breath.

"Alaric!" Elise chastised, turning around to stare at her steward with surprise. "You shouldn't say that in regard to Lady Gwyneth."

"Lady!" Alaric said with a sniff. He urged Elise back into the warmth of the hall. "Meaning no disrespect, milady," he told Elise, settling before the fire himself to whittle upon a piece of wood, "she may be nobility, but she is no lady."

"She is very beautiful," Elise heard herself begin.

"Beautiful, oh, aye. But not like ye, mistress. She can fool most men, but not a serf who watches her when she does not know it. She is dangerous."

"Nonsense," Elise said briskly. And she turned about, determined to give her attention to a tapestry that would need mending.

Alaric almost spoke again, but he held his peace. Broodingly, he stared into the fire.

The Cornish folk were a superstitious lot; he was Cornish, and knew this. He was a good Christian, and therefore tried not to allow his soul to wander into superstition.

But there was something about the dark-haired beauty who had just left that made him want to cross himself. He did so, looking covertly at his mistress. She did not see him; he almost wished that she had, that she had questioned. He had wanted to warn her that it seemed to his superstitious heart that the Lady Gwyneth held evil in her own—and was very dangerous to the Lady Elise.

Elise was just heartfully glad that Gwyneth had departed. She threw herself into her household, visiting those who had taken ill in the village, along with Jeanne. She was grateful to see that her stonemasons were still working despite the winter weather—and that Bryan's wall was rising high about them.

A week later a guard spotted another party traveling toward Firth manor; he hurried to Michael, and Michael hurried to Elise.

"The queen is coming!" Michael exclaimed.

"Eleanor?" Elise demanded with surprise.

Michael smiled with nervous excitement. "Since our sovereign Richard has yet taken no bride, I can think of no other woman in this realm to call queen!"

"Michael, call Alaric. Call Maddie. Call Jeanne! Chambers must be prepared; we must present her with our finest!"

Elise changed hastily and hurried downstairs. Alaric was busy adding kindling to make the fire especially warming. Maddie was ordering the girls to prepare handsome serving caldrons of mulled cinnamon wine. Jeanne hurried about sweeping the floor and dusting the tapestries.

When Eleanor arrived with her retinue, the household was lined up to greet her. Elise stood upon ceremony, falling to her knees when Eleanor entered, but the queen would have none of it.

"Up, child, and give those cold, old bones a warming hug!"

Elise did so, delighted to be with Eleanor again. The queen was traveling with several women, among them Alys, Philip of France's sister, and Richard's supposed "fiance." Alys was a pleasant and pretty—if slightly fading—young woman, full of melancholy. Alys had long ago resigned herself to the way of kings. Purported to have been seduced by Henry not long after her arrival in England when she was little more than a child, it did not seem she now had much hope of marrying the elusive Richard.

Elise made her as comfortable as possible. The queen and her entire company were made royally welcome, and Elise was proud that her new home had come so far. A banquet amazing for wintertime was spread before Eleanor, and the conversation throughout dinner was so light and pleasant that Elise laughed with real pleasure . . . until she learned that King Richard was not still in England—that he and his company had landed in France two days previous.

Bryan would not come by.

Elise tried to hide her bitterness from her guests, and she believed she did an admirable job of it. She ordered that her chamber be given to the queen since it was the best in the house, but Eleanor, it seemed, was determined to speak with her alone.

"I'll not take your chamber away from you, Elise, but I shall be glad to share it with you. I miss those nights when you were near to talk to and make me feel young again!"

By the time Elise saw to her other guests and came to her chamber, Eleanor had bathed and crawled into bed, donned in a fresh white nightgown. Her graying hair was loose and it spilled about her shoulders, and she was reading a letter with a frown creasing her forehead.

She smiled, however, when she saw Elise, tapping the letter with a finger. "Richard! He is my pride, and my dismay. I am following him about with Alys, determined to get him married, so he hurries off and leaves me a letter stating that God's holy war must first be fought. Dear Lord! Does he not realize that he but leaves his country to John!"

Elise smiled wanly with sympathy. Eleanor was no fool. She knew that her son had carried a love for the wily Philip of France in his heart that could not extend to Philip's sister. "Ah, I will get him married. If not Alys . . . the King of Navarre has a daughter. She saw Richard once and swore she would have no other. . . . But Richard's affairs cannot be settled tonight. And I am very interested in yours."

"In my affairs! But why?"

The queen was always direct. "Why didn't you come when your husband summoned you to London?"

"Bryan never summoned me—" Elise began in confusion.

But the queen interrupted impatiently. "Elise! I had hoped that you would be reconciled once Bryan brought you here. To ignore his call as you did was a stunt as willful and child-ish—"

"I did not!" Elise said sharply, forgetting she was speaking to the queen. "I swear to you, by Christ above us, Eleanor, that I ignored nothing. Bryan sent no one for me."

Eleanor looked at the girl's lovely, puzzled—and, yes, an-guished—features and frowned once more. "I saw the messenger leave myself," she murmured, gazing downward, then to Elise once more. "He reached the Lady Gwyneth, who told us all that she had just seen you and that you were fit and well."

Elise felt her heart sink low within her breast. Gwyneth had been in London; Bryan had been in London. Percy had been in London, too, but . . . "I am confused," she murmured bleakly.

Eleanor sighed. "I believe that you are, child. Richard, once his affairs were settled, was suddenly very eager to reach France. The men knew that once they left London they would not stop. But there were a few days' grace while still assembled in London, and those with wives summoned them. I believe that Bryan was very angry. It is difficult to tell with him, he is so silent. But one could tell by his eyes, by the twist of his jaw . . . He told me only that it was but what he could expect of you."

Elise laughed hollowly. "I don't know that I would have bounded at his beck and call had I had the chance, but I do swear to you, Your Grace, by all that is holy, I never had that chance."

"I believe you," the queen said. "It is my fervent hope that your husband believes you."

A swift and terrible desolation suddenly swept through Elise. She was so young, and all she could see were years ahead with her life nothing but a constant battlefield. She flung herself on her knees at the queen's side, her turmoil bringing bright tears to her eyes.

"Eleanor! Once you swore you would protect me! Why did you do this to me? You gave me to a man who did not want me, who wanted my land. And you gave Montoui to him, too . . ."

Her voice trailed away with a choked sob. Eleanor smoothed back her hair soothingly, as if she were her own daughter, rather than Henry's bastard. "Elise . . ." She sighed deeply and lifted the girl's chin with a bony but still elegant finger. "Elise," she reminded her softly, "you were determined to stop Bryan's marriage to Gwyneth. You must admit that. You would not have told me the tale that you did if you hadn't been determined that something be done. There are those who do call me a meddlesome old woman, but . . . Elise, you two are so right for each other. Percy would never have suited you, Elise. He is a good man, but his backbone twists with the wind. And Montoui . . ."

Eleanor paused a minute, taking a deep breath. "Elise, an inheritance is a curse, not a blessing. I was in love once, when I was very young. But it couldn't be, you see, because I was the Duchess of Aquitaine. They married me off to the King of France—because of my lands. And when Louis and I divorced, I knew I must marry again hurriedly before I was dragged to the altar drugged by some enterprising nobleman intent upon seizing my land. When Henry came to me—I do believe he loved me then—he held Normandy and Anjou. But Poitou and Aquitaine were mine, and the richer lands. He was the heir to the English throne, of course, and when Stephen died, he claimed that throne. I was not English, but I came to love England. I bore Henry eight children. Three of our sons died. And . . . I'm not explaining this very well, am I? Elise, I could have gotten out of my prison once—in seventy-six, when Henry had me summoned to Normandy. If I had agreed to take Aquitaine from Richard, and give it to John after young Henry died and Richard became Henry's heir. Elise, Richard bestowed this land on you, just as he did Montoui on Bryan. To hold jointly. Not yours, not his. Yours *together*. Elise, Richard knew how Henry and I fought over *his* lands and *my* lands, and the dispersal of them. He didn't want that for you. Bryan is young, brave, and strong. You are wise in the ways of nobility and ruling. If you just give it a chance . . ."

The queen's voice had such a wistful, yearning quality to it. Elise knew Eleanor was trying to see that her life did not repeat the travesties of the queen's. Eleanor had tried to give her happiness. She didn't fully understand.

Elise kissed Eleanor's fragile hand. "Sometimes I just wish

for the warmth of Montoui," she said softly. "Sometimes it is just so very . . . cold here."

"Ah . . . I cannot tell you how I missed Aquitaine when I first came to London!" Eleanor explained. "How I longed for the sunny south. But the English . . . they are unique. I love the people, for on the whole, they are just, and they are fond of the law! And England . . . Elise, it is solid. We are upon an island. Distant from the Continent. Distant from the wars that rage. Philip is a far more wily king than old Louis could ever have been. Louis was not a bad man; he had been raised to be a monk, not a king or husband. But I fear . . . if Richard . . . dies, I fear that John will be a weak king. He will lose the holdings on the Continent to Philip. But Elise, this piece of England that you hold, this land in Cornwall, it will be yours, and it will be your children's, and their children's. Hold it dear."

"I will, Eleanor, I will . . ." Elise swore, touched by the queen's heartfelt confession. *I will try,* she added silently to herself.

"Be happy, child," the queen said softly, kissing Elise's forehead. "I will tell Bryan that the messenger never reached you," she added thoughtfully.

She did not add that she doubted Bryan would believe her.

But neither woman slept easily that night, for they were both wondering what had happened to the messenger.

Elise was delighted that the queen and her party stayed to celebrate Christmas with her. She would have been lonely and desolate without then. As it was, the manor sparkled, and Elise found a certain peace in the quiet mass and feast enjoyed by the group of women.

The morning of the queen's departure, Elise realized she would know a keen loneliness once Eleanor was gone. She thought of begging to go along, then remembered how fervently Eleanor had wished her to care for her part of Cornwall. She would stay; she would see that the manor and the lands continued to grow in elegance and wealth.

Eleanor had only a few last words to say to her in private.

"Remember, Elise—and please don't think ill of me that I say this—be loyal to Richard, but do not become John's enemy! I fear for Richard; he can be so reckless . . . and John can be so vicious!"

"Where is Prince John? And . . . Geoffrey?"

Eleanor smiled. "Both have left England. Geoffrey . . . I have seen to it that he has been offered high office in the Church. John . . . They have sworn to Richard that they will not enter England in his absence, so that he not fear that his brothers make an attempt to seize his crown. I daresay, though, that they will both be back in a matter of months—on one pretext or another. I don't believe that Geoffrey covets the crown. I think John would gladly slit his own brother's throat for it. So take care."

"What of England?"

"Ah . . . England! I worry. Richard has given the office of chancellor to a Norman. A man named Longchamp. I don't trust him, but . . . I must see Richard married!"

In the icy courtyard, Elise hugged Eleanor ardently, and wished the hapless Alys the best. She waved long after the queen's party, with its majesty and color, had disappeared.

Then she returned to the hall she had worked so hard to make beautiful and elegant . . . and felt the terrible cold seep into her.

Bryan Stede awoke suddenly in the night. The fire in his chamber in Normandy's Stirgil Castle had gone out and the room was freezing, but a fine sheen of perspiration lay over his bare back.

He had been dreaming.

Elise had been before him, so close that he might have touched her. Her hair had been free; a breeze had lifted it until it spun like fine mists of gold web about her naked, alabaster body. She had been walking, slowly, sinuously, with the elegant grace and sultry ease of a cat. Full breasts high and inviting, curved white hips swaying in a seductive enticement. Her eyes flashed like true gemstones, and she smiled as she reached out her arms . . .

And stepped past him. Into the waiting arms of a mist-enshrouded lover. Another man's hands had reached out to touch her, caressing the silky hollow of her waist, grabbing hard at the firm, rounded flesh of her buttocks and lifting her up, against him . . .

Elise twisted in her arms to stare at Bryan, and her eyes were hard with gloating triumph. "She bears your bastard for Percy, and I shall bear his for you . . ."

The dream had not faded; he had awakened in a piercing agony. His flesh cried out to hold a woman, yet any woman would not do; he had to hold the taunting wench of his dream and take her in such a fashion that she would never stop quivering from his touch, never doubt that she was his and only his.

Damn Gwyneth!

The thought was so sudden and strong that he thought he had spoken it aloud. He turned quickly, but Will Marshal, sleeping soundly beside him, hadn't stirred. Will's dreams were sweet; Isabel was expecting their first child and her letters arrived daily. Will's marriage had brought him wealth—and far more. It had brought him contentment and happiness.

He grated his teeth. If not for Gwyneth, he might not be content, but he might know the fringes of happiness. He had believed that Elise was at least reconciled to their marriage—until Gwyneth had come with the announcement that she was enceinte.

He hadn't been entirely certain that the child wasn't his until Gwyneth had come to London. Now he was certain that the child wasn't his, but he was equally certain that Elise would believe even more fully that the child was his.

When Elise hadn't arrived, Bryan had been too angry to pay much attention to anything else. But then Gwyneth had cornered him in his rooms at the town house, throwing herself into his arms and crying that her child was his: What were they to do?

He had been about to hold her, for her beautiful face had seemed wrenched with anguish when she had first entered.

But even as she leaned against his chest, he felt himself go cold. He did not know what her game was, but she was trying to take him for a fool.

He knew the exact night he had last been with her; the night before Richard's arrival on the outskirts of London. And had she conceived that night, she would have to boast a certain largeness of girth that was obviously missing. Did she think that men were incapable of calculation?

"Touch me, Bryan," she had pleaded, groping to bring his fingers to her belly. "Feel our child. *Our* child, while that grasping little slut who set her claws into you proves to be nothing but barren."

"Percy is your husband, Gwyneth. And that 'grasping little slut,' as you call her, is my wife."

"Wife! She despises you still! She refuses to come to your side! What loyalty can you owe her? Oh, Bryan, we were meant for each other! She wanted Percy, and I know that he lusts for her still. Let them have each other."

Gwyneth was as beautiful as ever. As sweet when she spoke her accusations to him. As soft in his arms. He was tempted for a moment to throw her down hard on the bed and relieve himself of all his pent-up hunger and fury.

He could not. She was, but she also wasn't, the woman he had once wanted.

"Bryan, I love you so!" she whispered brokenly.

"When we met here this summer, you seemed quite pleased with your marriage."

"You were lost to me. I thought I would have to bear it. I cannot."

"Gwyneth, your child is not mine," he said stiffly.

"But it is, Bryan. I know it . . . and Elise knows it."

"Elise!"

"I've been to see her, Bryan. I was so frightened. I want your baby born well, and beneath your roof."

"Gwyneth!" Suddenly he was shaking her fiercely. She didn't seem to care as her head fell back and her dark eyes met his in a vixen's gloat. "What did you say to Elise?"

"Nothing . . . she simply knows."

Gwyneth did not have her victory, for Bryan shoved her aside and quit his own chambers.

The next day they had ridden from London. There had been no time for detours into the Cornish countryside.

But now . . . now it was February. And Richard's champions awaited him, day after day. He and Philip could come to an agreement on nothing, they distrusted one another so. The Crusade had not even begun, and already it dragged on and on.

Bryan stood up. He looked out the slim arrow slit of the old Norman castle. To the north lay the English Channel. Past the Channel, an eternity away, lay home.

Home, yes, it was his home. She was his wife. She must accept that, must accept him, must wait, for him alone . . .

The queen had told him Elise had never received his summons. He didn't believe it. Not when Elise had run the night of Richard's coronation. Not when she had threatened him with infidelity to match what she assumed to be his . . .

A sheen of sweat broke out across his shoulders again. He could not rouse the king now, but in the morning . . .

"God's blood, Bryan! Nay, you haven't my leave to return home! I tell you, I need you when I go to council with that sly French fox Philip—"

"Your Grace, William Marshal is at your side—"

"And good there he is, but I need your wits with me also, Bryan Stede. In three days' time we call upon my Norman barons to give support to the cause and you must rouse the knights."

"Then give me three days' time, my liege!"

"For what? That will give you travel time, no more. Perhaps a few hours at your home—"

"I'll take it," Bryan said quietly.

Richard threw up his well-muscled arms in a blustery display of exasperation. "Three days, Bryan."

Bryan bowed low and left Richard.

He set out by himself, leaving Wat, who had proven to be a fine squire, to serve Will Marshal in his absence. Will scratched his head as he watched Bryan mount his destrier.

"You're half mad," Will told him. "You'll reach Cornwall, and have to turn back."

"I know," Bryan said grimly, looping his reins into his hand as he swung his horse about. He grinned then. "I am half mad, Will. I'm hoping that an hour or two will give me back a little sanity."

Will frowned. "Bryan . . . perhaps what Eleanor said was true. Perhaps the messenger never reached her. Don't go off . . ." He cleared his throat. "Don't go riding off like that in a rage of anger. You'd not gain anything by . . . beating her for this disobedience. It would just—"

Bryan laughed bitterly, wondering at the power Elise possessed to drag him across land and sea just for a few brief hours of her company.

"Will, I assure you, the last thing I have in mind is beating my wife!"

He was to reach the Channel and cross it in record time. And then he was Cornwall bound.

By late the next night, the guard atop the southern turret saw a single rider coming toward the manor at a breakneck speed.

The guard hurried to rouse Alaric.

Alaric watched the horseman approach the manor.

"Shall we awaken Lady Elise?" the guard asked nervously.

Alaric continued to stare at the dark rider, coming closer and closer. His brow knit in consternation.

Then he laughed. "Nay, we needn't awaken Lady Elise. Lord Bryan will be here 'fore we could properly do so!"

* * *

Elise had been deep in an exhausted sleep. The day had been bitterly cold; she had spent endless hours boiling forest moss, packed beneath the snow, into a medicament for the winter cough that so often plagued those weakened by the harsh cold.

She, Maddie, and Jeanne had worked late into the night. When she climbed upstairs to her chamber, she had been touched to find that Michael had seen that her hearth fire burned brightly, and had thoughtfully ordered that the braziers beneath the bath also be lit. She had almost drifted off to sleep in the tub, absurdly grateful to be so tired that she dozed so easily, but frightened that she should solve her problems with the simplicity of drowning.

Climbing from the tub, she had deeply and appreciatively breathed in the clean scent of her bath oil, so much more pleasant than the lingering musk of boiling mold! She had dried herself, briefly untangled her hair with her fingers, and fallen into bed, dragging the sheets and heavy fur coverlet over her. Even before her head had touched the down pillow, she had fallen asleep.

Now, it was hours since. Her dreams had wrapped about her like the soft clouds of spring, beautiful dreams in which she loved, and was loved.

She awoke with a start, jolted from sleep, and yet not at all certain that she had ever awakened.

Because Bryan was standing before her.

Delicate, intricate flakes of snow still dotted his dark woolen mantle and dazzled against the midnight black of his tousled hair. For long moments he stood there, those flakes of snow melting against him, one hand still upon the door he had just opened, the other upon his hip. Elise was unable to believe that he could really be there. She had known he was in Normandy.

At the bang of the door she had half risen, the sheets clutched to her, her eyes wide with the sudden alarm. Now she stared, feeling as if time were as frozen as the ice that captured the winter branches of the trees. She had never seen him look . . . so fierce and formidable, yet never had seen such a wistful yearning in his blue-black eyes. It was a trick of the fire, she told herself, a winter's dream. The look he cast her, both tender and hungry, and the tall warrior himself . . .

She was, he thought, as wild and as sweet, as innocent and sultry, as all his haunted dreams. At his entrance she had started to her knees, defensively clutching the bedclothes. Stunned by his appearance, she had dropped the sheets. Gold and copper tendrils of wispy silk curled in dishevelment over her breasts and fell about the sinuous beauty of her form. The dusky-rose crests of her ivory breasts peaked firm and proud beneath the gold and fire of that tangling hair, and, had he ridden a full week solid, desire would have streaked through him like the onslaught of a summer sun. Her eyes were wide, blue and green crystals upon him, her lips were parted and moist with surprise, and as he had so often dreamed, her arms slowly lifted . . .

Not to another. To him.

With a hoarse cry he came to her, slamming the door closed with a foot. His clothing escaped him with the same simple quality of the dream, and he was beside her, meeting her, melding with her. He could not hold her tightly enough, tenderly enough. His body trembled violently as she met his lips in a passionate kiss, her tongue probing his mouth sweetly, hotly, her nails raking through his hair, over his shoulders, his back, his buttocks. She was warm and vibrant, sweetly, sinuously moving, whispering inarticulate but ardent words. His hands moved over her, his lips thirsted for her. Their mouths met in fiery splendor again, and moans that were like sobs caught and then tore from her throat. He rose above her, then lost himself within her, shaking violently with the intensity of that sweet, embracing ecstasy. The fire in the grate seemed to build around them, burning ever higher, defying even the winter winds.

How many times he had held her so! Yet still he felt that he traveled anew. He climbed through uncharted paths of splendor, and his soul flew with the summer sun while his body learned a peak of pleasure that crested anything he had known before. She quaked beneath him when splendor erupted like the burst of a falling star; summer slowly came to be winter again, but a beautiful winter, swept with the fragile delight of wafting, delicate snowflakes.

He did not speak; he held her. When she would have spoken, he brought his fingers to his lips. She curled sweetly against him, the sultry vixen innocent again, the wild wanton a creature of infinite sweetness. For a time he was content, and he began to doze.

Time was his enemy. He awoke with a start, and kissed his dream sprite, arousing her with the slow play of his fingers upon her flesh. Winter winds blew outside the chamber; neither knew nor cared. The sun blazed within.

When they again lay in the glow of sated contentment, she made no effort to speak, but rested contentedly within the crook of his shoulder.

He let her doze, and then fall deeply into the drugged sleep of her contentment. Her lips, even in that deep sleep, curved into a winsome smile, and he knew then that he loved her. More than any title granted him, more than land, more than life.

He rose and began to dress. His tunic and mantle felt wet, and very, very cold. He gazed upon her, so loath to leave. Her hand was curled to her cheek. The sapphire glared up at him, caught by firelight, and he sighed.

He was the fool. He had lost his soul—and she was determined never to give her own. Never to forgive him. And he must ride by the side of his king . . .

Bryan stopped allowing himself to think. The night was a dream, a spun fairy-tale web of a soaring summer sun against the white-flaked, ice beauty of winter.

He would not have that crystal glory shattered.

The naked face of his love stared upon her then, and her heart would have flown with joy had she but seen it.

With a groan of tearing agony that grew not from his throat, but from his soul, Bryan turned and left.

Dawn was almost upon him.

Alaric awaited him downstairs. He conversed quickly with his steward while he consumed a hastily prepared meal of bread and cold meat. Alaric had heated wine, which warmed him for his journey.

Then he was riding away again, a dark knight upon a midnight destrier, racing over the snow.

XXI

Had not Alaric assured her that, aye, the duke had indeed come home, Elise might have believed that the magical night had been a dream. She had wanted him so desperately that he had appeared.

By the end of March, however, with or without Alaric's assurances, she would have known that her Bryan had come to her in flesh and blood and not illusion. She was going to have a child, and she was delighted. The night that Bryan had returned to Cornwall had changed everything for her for a very simple reason. She was able to admit to herself that she loved him.

The admission did not give her perfect happiness; she did not know when she would see him again. She did not know where the path of battle would take him: to death, or to another woman's arms. But when he did return, she wanted to lay the olive branch of peace before him. Whatever had been before did not matter now.

Because he had come to her. Through frigid waters and fields of ice and snow, he had ridden hard just to come to her.

Elise even felt her anger against Gwyneth fade. Gwyneth, she believed, was lying. Clinging to any bond with Bryan that she could. Gwyneth could cast out insinuations all she liked, and Elise knew that she would only smile, secure for the time in the depth of her feeling. She might well be a fool, but she did love Bryan Stede. He was her husband, and she meant to keep him—if God ever allowed her to have him again.

The baby meant everything to her. Bryan's heir, the child he so dearly wanted. It seemed that she would have to wait forever, but even the thought of motherhood seemed to change her, and she mused that her sex—herself included—was a strange lot. She felt as if she had gentled and matured, and she loved the fragile life inside her with the free intensity with which she now allowed herself to love her husband. She took great pains to eat well, to drink warm goat's milk, and when she went to bed at night she slept easily, with a smile curving her lips, for she could now give Bryan something that would be very precious to them both. Sometimes at night, in the solitude of her chamber, she would touch her still-flat belly and whisper to the child. It would be a boy, she decided, for didn't all men want sons? And so she told him that he would be the son of the greatest knight in Christendom, and that the blood of kings ran in his veins.

She waited until the beginning of April to be certain of her news, then sent a messenger across the Channel to find Richard's troops, wherever they were.

Winter refused to relinquish her hold upon the land. The March winds had barely died before they rose again to meet April. Another snowstorm blanketed the country, and in the midst of that storm, Elise was awakened from a sound sleep by Jeanne, who bade her eagerly to come speak with Alaric.

The steward awaited her by the hearth in the hall, and she learned that Alaric was concerned because a small party was approaching the manor, yet seemed to be staggering along.

"We must go out and aid whoever is in travail!" Elise told Alaric.

"But milady," Alaric protested, "it might be a trick! Thieves and robbers are thick in such a winter, for those freemen and runaway serfs who live in the forests often find their children starving and their own bellies empty."

"I will go to the tower myself," Elise insisted. "If it is a party of starving beggars, then they must be fed. And if a friend or messenger labors to reach me, then he must be helped."

"The wind is bitter—" Alaric protested.

But Elise cut him off with, "I will cloak myself warmly."

From the northern tower Elise narrowed her eyes and stared out across the distant fields of snow. A tiny band struggled along, three people only, on foot. Alaric watched Elise stare out with a frown etched into her forehead. Then she suddenly cried out, "Alaric! Call five men—and have my mare saddled!"

"Milady—"

"Oh, Alaric! Do hurry along! Can't you see? It is Lady Gwyneth, and it appears that she has been tricked by robbers! She comes across this snow on foot, with her child due at any time . . ."

Elise rushed back to her chamber to further cloak herself against the cold and snow, somewhat amazed that she could be so truly concerned for Gwyneth. But she was; her newfound love had opened her heart to all kinds of tenderness. But Gwyneth! How foolishly she had behaved, starting out in such weather . . .

Alaric was still against Elise's going; he continued to scowl his disapproval as she mounted her horse. "Alaric!" Elise assured him. "I am almost disgraced to say that I have the strength of a young bull! I will be fine. But I am most concerned for Lady Gwyneth. See that Jeanne keeps fires burning, and water boiling."

The snow blinded them once they started riding; Elise's escort of five tried to form a shield about her with their horses, but there was little to be done. She was strong, strong and healthy, and despite the ravages of the cold, she would have enjoyed the ride were it not for the fact that she was so puzzled and worried. Without the advantage of the tower, they lost the position of the three struggling to reach the manor.

Elise's guards began to urge that she head back. She began at last to believe that it had been foolhardy for her to come; her own child was too precious to risk. But to head back, she would have to split the party of guards, and she was suddenly afraid to do that. And if those on foot were not quickly found, they would soon perish in the snow.

"We continue together!" Elise ordered.

They traveled another ten minutes, cresting around a small clump of naked trees in the strange, snow-swept night, when suddenly the howl of the wind was interrupted by bloodthirsty cries. Elise started, whirling her horse about, to see that they were being set upon by a small band of mounted men. Men with their swords raised, leaping from their saddles to attack her guards.

"Milady!" shrieked out a man, and she turned again just in time to see a swarthy man bearing down upon her. There was a twisted smile about his lips that brought panic to her heart. She screamed, but instinct forced her to swing the mare around, rearing, and where the man had been about to grapple her, he landed upon the snow instead, and Elise felt the sickening crunch of the mare's hooves as they landed hard upon him.

She could not worry about his fate; he was down, and cries and the mortal gasps of death were still loud about her. She whirled the mare about again; bright pools of blood splashed brilliant color against the purity of the snow. Three of her guards lay dead, yet only one of the four attackers remained alive to give the others battle. "Mordred!" she screamed, staring in fascinated horror as one of the men raised a battle ax against the youngest guard. Mordred heard her warning and bolted from his horse; the animal screamed in pain, and fell to the snow in place of Mordred. The attacker fought to retrieve his ax from the dying horse; Mordred slew him, catching his throat with the blade of his sword.

Elise and Mordred stared at each other, and then at the scene around them. Dead men littered the snow. Her last guard and the last attacker had fallen together, both bleeding mortally, both silent now. The horses had run in the night; only the dead beast and Elise's mare remained.

"Where did they come from?" Mordred whispered in a daze. He looked up at Elise. "Why?"

"I don't know," she whispered, as he had, her voice seeming to mock her as it was whipped about and echoed by the wind.

"We must get back to the manor," Mordred murmured.

"We can't; we must find the Lady Gwyneth."

"We'll freeze to death and perish ourselves, milady."

Elise wanted nothing more than to go back. The sight of all the dead about her and the eerie wind that rose over the blood-stained white winter night were terrifying to the soul. She thought of her child, and knew it would make sense.

She also knew it would be condemning the Lady Gwyneth and her companions to death.

"Just a little farther, Mordred. Then I swear, I'll race you and the wind to return home."

Mordred trudged along beside her. "Horses are traitors!" he suddenly swore. He looked back over his shoulder and shivered visibly.

"We will send for our dead tomorrow," Elise said softly, "and give them burial before God."

"And the others?"

"We will try to discover who they are—and why they attacked us."

She and Mordred struggled along in moments of anguished silence. Then they heard the fading cries for help.

"Right ahead!" Elise shouted to Mordred. She extended a hand to him and he leaped to the saddle behind her. Moments later they came upon the Lady Gwyneth of Cornwall.

She was down in the snow, with only a woolen cloak to guard her from the cold; her furs, it appeared, had been wrenched away. Her flesh had little more color than the snow; her sable hair was a slash of darkness against it. Even her lips were as pale as death. An old woman sat shivering and weeping at her side; it was her cries that had at last summoned Elise and Mordred to her position.

Elise leaped from her horse and fell to her knees at Gwyneth's side. She found a pulse at the base of her throat; she placed a hand over Gwyneth's belly and found it hard and round, shifting slightly beneath her touch.

"She lives, and the child lives!"

"Old woman, what happened?" Mordred demanded.

"Unaware . . . completely unaware . . . they burned the manor. Oh, how it glowed! And I took my Lady Gwyneth . . . but they came upon us . . . stole the horses . . . and left her to die . . . and Sir Percy . . ."

The old woman was suffering severely from shock and exposure. Her lips kept forming words, but no more sounds came forth. "Dear God, what am I to do?" Elise prayed out loud. She had to get Gwyneth to the manor. Could she get her on the mare? Or would she surely kill Gwyneth and the child?

She tried to lift Gwyneth's head to speak to her. Suddenly, the brunette beauty's dark eyes flew open. "Percy! Percy! You must find Percy . . . you must . . ."

"Gwyneth! It is Elise. I must get you back to the manor. Percy is with Richard—"

"No! No!" Gwyneth's eyes cleared; she stared directly at Elise. "Percy came home . . . he was ill. Infection. He was . . ." Her voice began to fade; she drew upon some inner strength and gripped Elise's arm with an amazing strength. "Percy! He is behind us . . . he begged me to go on! How I have wronged him! Elise, go for him. Swear to me by the blessed Virgin that you will go for him!"

"Gwyneth, I must get you to the manor. You and your child will perish—"

"I deserve death!" Gwyneth cried in anguish. "Swear to me, Elise, you loved him once. Go to Percy . . ."

Her eyes closed. Elise gazed at the old woman, who burst into tears and rocked back and forth. Elise shook her vehemently. "Is what she says true? Is Percy back in the snow?"

"Aye!" the woman wailed. "My Lord Percy . . . fell. He could go no farther."

Elise stood up. "Mordred, you must take Gwyneth to the manor on my horse, and immediately send others out for us!"

"Milady, I cannot leave you!"

"If you don't, Mordred, we will both be guilty of murdering the Lady Gwyneth and her child. Her woman and I shall find Sir Percy. I order you to take Gwyneth back."

Mordred swallowed. "The child could come . . . and die."

"It will die anyway if we do not do something. Mordred, for God's sake! Go, and get help for us!"

Mordred climbed from the mare. Together he and Elise lifted Gwyneth to the saddle with all possible care. Elise, wanting to cry, watched them ride away. The old woman was sobbing again; she could not cry herself. She gripped the old woman's shoulders and dragged her to her feet. "We must move, or freeze. And we must find Sir Percy." The old woman kept sobbing. Elise bit her lip in consternation, then slapped her firmly across the cheek. "Stop! What is your name?"

The old woman stared at her, shocked. She shook her own head, but then lifted her chin, her tears having abated. "I am Kate, maid to Lady Gwyneth since her birth."

"Well, Kate, you must lead me to Sir Percy, and we must pray that he lives."

She didn't add that they needed to pray for much more: that no more outlaws lurked about; that Percy could send help for the two of them before they succumbed to the bitter cold.

"I don't believe he's far," Kate mumbled. " 'Twas so hard to keep my lady moving, and then she fell . . ."

"Come, Kate, let's walk."

Elise and Kate huddled together, tramping with difficulty through the snow. At last they came upon Percy; he was a huddled bundle, ashen, near death. Elise cried out in dismay and knelt beside him. She called to him; she patted his freezing cheeks. She could not arouse him, and her heart began to thunder with pity and pain. Even now his features were handsome and classic. The poignancy of lost love touched her, and she became determined to make him live.

But there was so little she could do!

"Kate! We must warm him. We must drag him to the shelter of those trees, and huddle against him."

Kate nodded, but her eyes rolled in a way that showed Elise she thought it impossible for two frozen women to drag an unconscious man. Elise ignored her and bent to the task.

He was heavy, but the task was not impossible. Grunting and straining, Elise and Kate managed to bring him to a thicket of evergreens. And there at least the biting wind could not touch him. "Huddle to his one side!" Elise commanded. She herself sat to his left, trying to make the warmth of her body flood to his.

And as they sat there waiting, old Kate came to her full senses and began to talk. "My Lord Percy reached home just two days ago. He was thrown from his horse in Normandy, and his knee festered with infection. Good King Richard sent him home. He arrived in a litter. Lady Gwyneth decided then to stay at her own manor with Lord Percy to birth their child. She meant to send a messenger to you. But then this evening at dusk . . . armed men swept down upon the manor. My Lord Percy was furious because he was so helpless. He and my lady and I fled . . . but they caught us, and took the horses, leaving us to die."

"Armed men!" Elise repeated. "But who—"

"I don't know!" Kate wailed. "Oh, my Lady Elise! I don't know! Some spoke in English, some spoke in French!"

Elise became exceedingly grateful that Bryan had seen fit to further arm their manor at Montoui. No surprise attack there— in the manor, that was. Attack upon a field had happened . . .

"Rub Sir Percy's hands, Kate," Elise said. "His gloves are soaked and useless. Here, put mine upon him, and keep rubbing them."

It seemed forever that they huddled in the shelter of the evergreens, forever that the night wind whistled and shrieked around them. Elise kept talking, and ordered Kate to talk back to her. In the numbing cold the temptation to sleep was great, but if they fell asleep, they might never be found . . .

At last Elise heard the muffled sound of hoofbeats in the snow and the jangle of horse trappings. She started to jump up and cry out in the darkness, then hesitated, pulling back to the evergreen. Percy and Gwyneth had been attacked in force—only

God knew why. She didn't dare call out until she knew for certain that it was her men who rode through the winter's night.

"Lady Elise!"

She smiled, warmth seeming to fill her along with relief. She turned back to the hopeful Kate. "It's Alaric, Kate! Rescue has come!"

Alaric fell to his knees in the snow, kissing the sodden skirt to her tunic when he saw her safe. Elise dragged him back to his feet and hugged him briefly but fiercely.

"Lord Percy desperately needs warmth, Alaric. You must take him tenderly and carefully, and get him back to the manor."

Ten men had ridden out this time, Elise was relieved to see. As their grim party returned silently through the snow, she began to reflect upon the night with bitter sadness. Her men had been killed, their lives shattered upon the snow. She had known violence before, and perhaps she should have become hardened, but she could not take those lives lightly. Women had become widows this night; children had lost their fathers. *Why?*

At the manor Maddie rushed down the stairs to greet her in the hall. Jeanne was with Lady Gwyneth, Maddie told Elise. A warm chamber had been prepared for Lord Percy; bricks had been heated for his bed. A wine-and-herb concoction that steamed and simmered was ready to be trickled down his throat . . .

Elise hung against the mantel for a moment, feeling dizzy herself as the roaring flames in the hearth began to thaw the numbing cold of her limbs. She rallied with a weak smile as she saw men carefully carry Percy up the stairs. "Someone take Kate to the kitchen; she needs warmth herself. How is Lady Gwyneth?"

"Fitful, but she lives. The child will come any time. 'Tis a miracle it was not born in the saddle!"

"I'm not too cold or too old to go to my lady," Kate said to Elise with dignity. "Have I your leave to do so, Duchess?"

"Of course, Kate . . ." Elise murmured. Maddie stuck a warm cup of something into her hands and she began to sip it, watching as Maddie led Kate to the stairs. "Kate! One moment!" she called out suddenly. Kate paused and Elise said, "Think carefully, Kate. Who could have done all this—and why? Did you recognize no one, Kate? Were there no telltale banners, no words spoken to give a hint of reason for such a thing?"

Kate shook her head sadly, "Nothing, my lady. Nothing."

Elise nodded to Kate to go on. She finished the warm drink Maddie had given her, then agreed to change her clothing when Maddie reminded her that it was wet and cold. She entered the chamber where Gwyneth had been brought, but found Gwyneth slipping in and out of consciousness, and Jeanne and Kate efficiently assisting the lady's labor. Feeling still stunned, confused, and now helpless, Elise went on to see to Percy.

He was conscious, but that did not relieve Elise of her misery. Percy was going to die. Elise wasn't sure how she knew; the fact was simply there to be seen in his ghostly pallor, in the shroudlike quality of the sunken shadows beneath his dulling eyes.

"Elise . . ."

With great effort he lifted a hand to her. Alaric discreetly retreated to a shadowed corner of the room and Elise came to take his hand. "Forgive me," he told her, his voice a slender thread that held tenuously to life.

"Percy, you mustn't try to talk—"

He laughed, a bitter, choking sound. "Nay, Elise, I must talk now, for I will never have the chance again. Who would have thought after all the battles I survived that my horse would leave my leg a pus-ridden mangle, and that the snows of an English winter would join with the infection to kill me! The priest has come to grant me God's mercy, and I crave his gentle hand. But on earth and as this life fades to gray—"

"Percy, you must cling to life. Your wife is about to give you a child."

"I strive to hear the words," Percy said without bitterness. "And to hear you forgive me for the wrong I did you."

"Percy, you did me no wrong—"

"Aye, I did. I wronged us both, for I loved you, and I allowed pride and jealousy to make me cast you away. For that I ask your forgiveness—"

"Percy! If you ask it, I forgive you freely, though there is nothing to forgive. Life takes us where it will. Please, Percy, don't give up without a fight—"

"Elise, a knight knows when he is beaten." He beckoned her closer. "I must warn you . . ."

"Warn me?" Elise leaned closer. His hazel eyes lit like fire for a moment, and for that moment she was transported back. Back to a time when she had been very young, and very much in love, and very certain that she could twist fate in her hands by the force of her will.

"Longchamp . . ." Percy whispered faintly.

Longchamp . . . Elise frowned. Longchamp was a Norman, entrusted with the office of Chancellor of England while King Richard marched to the Crusade.

"Percy, what about Longchamp?"

"I . . . scorned him in London. The manor . . . the burning . . . he is a vicious man. Gloating with power. Ruthless."

"The Chancellor of England! Oh, Percy! Would he dare?"

"Not openly. But . . ."

Percy paused, moistening his lips. Elise looked about for water; Alaric came quickly to supply it. She noticed dimly that the priest had indeed been called for, and stood quietly in the back of the room, his eyes closed in prayer.

"Listen to me, Elise!" Percy pleaded, finding substance for his voice again as he waved the water away. "Bryan bitterly and openly opposed him. He will strike against him somehow. Furtively, as he did tonight."

Percy closed his eyes, exhausted from his effort to speak. Elise heard a commotion in the hall and tried to slip her hand

from his. His eyes opened again, his grip upon her hand tightened. "Wait, you must also be aware that—"

"Percy, shh . . . !" Elise murmured. "I'll come right back."

"You must understand—"

She didn't hear the rest; she had hurried into the hall. Jeanne
stood there, awaiting her, with a bundle wrapped in clean linen
swathing. "A son," Jeanne told her.

Elise bit down hard into her lip, fighting tears as she took
the pink-fleshed newborn carefully into her arms.

"Gwyneth?" Elise asked.

"She is weary and weak, unconscious now. But she is also a
fighter."

Elise nodded. The baby let out a pathetic cry, scrunching his
eyes together. "I'm sorry, little one, but you will have a mother.
And your father . . ."

She hurried back into Percy's chamber. "Percy! See your son!
He is beautiful, and perfect!"

Percy gazed upon the baby. Elise brought the infant to his
bedside; Percy touched him. "A son . . ." he gasped. He kept
the graze of his knuckles upon the squalling child, but his eyes
turned to Elise. "His . . . mother?"

"She does well."

He nodded, as if with great satisfaction. "Tell her I am grateful. But Elise, you must heed my . . . warning . . ."

She thought he had merely closed his eyes again. The lovely,
laughing hazel eyes that had once brought nothing less than
dreams and fascination. "Percy?"

Alaric stepped forward. "He is gone, milady."

Elise choked back a sob; the tears streamed silently down
her face. She hugged the protesting infant to her. "Little one,
he was a fine and honorable man. I will see that you are taught
all about him!" she murmured fervently, her words sincere. For,
yes, Percy had met death bravely. In life he had sometimes been
weak; in death he had been strong.

The baby continued howling. Elise turned blindly to leave
the chamber; Alaric touched her shoulders and led her to the

hall. She heard the drone of the priest's voice as he said God's words over Percy's body.

In the hallway, Elise slumped against the wall, holding the baby tight. Jeanne was forced to wrest him from her arms.

"Milady, you must sleep yourself!"

She had no answer. She could not stop the tears from cascading down her cheeks. How she had fought to keep him alive in that snow! And she had lost him.

"Milady!" Jeanne said firmly. "You must think of your own child."

"My own child . . ." Elise murmured. She knew now that Gwyneth's child was Percy's child. She felt no gladness; the pain had robbed her of envy and jealousy. She could not even think of how dearly she loved Bryan, nor could she remember Percy's words of warning. All she felt was emptiness. Only the distant thought of her own babe broke the numbness of her mind. Maddie arrived at Jeanne's side; the older woman nodded to the younger one, and Elise went docilely as Maddie led her to her bedchamber.

Sleep was a tender mercy that came quickly.

She awoke to find Jeanne in her room, stoking the fire that had burned low during the night. She remembered instantly the events of the night.

"How is Lady Gwyneth?" she asked so abruptly that Jeanne started and bumped her head.

"Well, but very agitated," Jeanne replied, rubbing her temple. She hesitated a moment. "She keeps asking for you."

"Does she know about . . . her husband?"

"She knew before we told her," Jeanne said softly. "She . . . is crying so that I fear she will sour the babe's milk."

Elise hurried out of bed. Jeanne sprinted to her side to help her dress. "Milady, you must learn to be easy with yourself. You might well have caught your own death last night—"

"Jeanne, don't hound me. My health is fine."

Jeanne sighed, but insisted Elise drink a cup of warm goat's milk before leaving the room. Elise did as she was bidden, then hurried to Gwyneth's chamber.

Old Kate sat crooning to the baby. Gwyneth was silent when Elise walked in, but when she walked to the bed, she saw that Gwyneth's beautiful features were strained from the force of the tears she had shed.

"Gwyneth," Elise murmured softly, sitting beside her on the bed, just as she had with Percy the night before. "Please, Gwyneth, I know you have lost your husband, but your son is beautiful; you must calm yourself for him—"

"Ah, Elise!" Gwyneth whispered miserably, her dark eyes haunted and shimmering. " 'Tis not just that Percy is dead; I wronged him so!"

Elise felt her heart begin to hammer, for she knew she was about to receive a confession. She did not want to hear that Gwyneth had been unfaithful to Percy with Bryan . . .

"Gwyneth, Percy said to tell you how grateful he was for his son—"

"It is his son, you know, Elise. That is why I wronged him so. I . . . I don't know if you can understand this or not, Elise. I was raised knowing that I would be told where and when to marry. When I was fifteen, they married me to an eighty-year-old duke. God forgive me, but I could not weep when he died! I met Bryan, you see . . ." She paused, her dark lashes sweeping her cheeks.

"Gwyneth, please—"

Her eyes flew back open. "No, Elise! I want you to understand! I thought that Bryan and I would be married. Henry promised it. Then suddenly Richard was King, and Bryan was marrying you. I was resigned; I had always been taught that marriage was political. But, you see, I loved Bryan. You were the interloper; I could not help but grow to hate you. I knew, too, that Percy still loved you. But he was good, Elise . . . so good to me. There were so many times when we laughed and loved together! I don't know why it couldn't be enough. But

I . . . I wanted Bryan, too. I waylaid the messenger from London when he would have come to you before the king left England. And in London . . . I tried to seduce Bryan. I wanted you both to believe that Percy's child was his. I wanted to drive you as far apart as possible."

Relief swept through Elise; Gwyneth had tried to seduce Bryan; she hadn't succeeded. Guilt filled her as quickly as relief. What right did she have to feel such joy when Percy lay dead?

"Gwyneth, thank you for telling me this. And, please, I know you must mourn Percy, he was your husband, and I believe that you did love each other. But his son lives, Gwyneth! You must get well quickly, and give his child your love."

Gwyneth seemed suddenly tired, having said what she felt she must. She lifted herself with a wistful smile and reached out to Kate, across the room. Kate stood and brought the babe, her wrinkled old face alive with a tender smile.

Elise watched Gwyneth cradle the babe to her breast. Then she felt a piercing envy; the child was beautiful and perfect. Soon, she thought, soon she would have her own child, Bryan's child, to love so sweetly and tenderly . . .

But first, this babe's father needed proper burial. Her men, who had died to protect her, still lay out in the snow. If Percy had been right, Chancellor Longchamp was out for more blood—by whatever devious method he could arrange.

There was so much that needed to be done. She must meet with Michael and Alaric and the Captain of the Guard. Sentries had to be posted; the manor had to become the defensive castle it resembled, and she must prepare for a siege.

Gwyneth's infant was christened on the same morning that his father was buried in the chapel vault. He appeared to be a lusty, healthy boy, but Elise knew that in these times when death came so easily to the very young and very old and even to the strong, priests preferred to baptize infants and bring them to God's grace as quickly as possible.

Gwyneth was too weak to witness either ceremony. But she did seem better since that restless morning when she had made her confession to Elise.

Elise sent a letter to Bryan, telling him of Percy's warning, but she had no idea when—or where—he would receive it. She didn't even know if he had received the letter she had written telling him that she was with child.

Twenty men were sent out to inspect Gwyneth's property. Her serfs, they reported, were returning from the forest to which they had scattered when the attack had started. Gwyneth's manor had also been constructed of stone; Mordred told Elise cheerfully that it could, with sound effort, be restored to its former grandeur.

Elise was up early each morning, nervously watching the guards drill. Thank God the wall had risen high! She prayed that her own manor was as unbreachable as Montoui.

Winter, having done its damage, abated that week. No more snow was to fall; a spring heat arrived with a gentle breeze, and the snows began to melt.

And with the coming of spring came a peddler. A little man with bags full of needles and salt cubes, laces and trinkets. His name was Limon, and he also brought news.

Elise bought several needles, and offered the small, hunched man a warm meal. She had it served to him in the main hall before the hearth, and when he had eaten, he began to speak.

Chancellor Longchamp had replaced Richard's officials with members of his own family. They were all Normans, and they were igniting anew the old rivalry between Saxons and Normans.

Longchamp traveled the countryside with his own army of eight hundred men. He demanded hospitality—the type to starve a province for months!—in the king's name. Will Marshal's wife, young Isabel de Clare, had refused him admittance to one of her manors; and Longchamp had declared to avenge himself against Will just as he had done with Percy Montagu.

The peddler's old eyes turned to Elise. "Best take care, kind

Duchess. The people are applauding Prince John and Geoffrey Fitzroy now, they hate Longchamp so. He is a devious man, powerful and power-hungry. He has declared that Will Marshal shall return from Richard's side to find nothing; he has sworn that Bryan Stede shall be brought so low he would have to crawl miles to reach his own grave."

"Bryan isn't even here—"

"Lord Stede, so the rumors go, is not afraid of Richard's wrath. He openly tells the king that Longchamp is destroying his kingdom."

"Why does Richard do nothing?"

"King Richard does not like criticism, even when he accepts it. He trusts Longchamp from long years in Normandy. He will not believe what is until he is absolutely forced to. Don't worry unduly, milady. This place has become a fine fortress. I tell you what I do just so that you keep your men alert."

Elise did not need such a warning; since the terror in the snow the night of Percy's death, she had doubled drills, watches, and manpower.

She thanked the peddler; he promised to return. Thoughtfully, she started to walk the stairs to her chamber. So Percy had been right. Longchamp—who would deny it to King Richard, of course—had ordered the assault upon Percy Montagu's property. And Percy Montagu had died . . .

Dear Percy. Tears stung her eyes again, as they did so easily when she thought of him. He had wanted to warn her with his last breaths . . .

She paused suddenly, remembering. He had been trying to warn her about something else. But he had died before he could do so.

What? she wondered desperately.

Gwyneth . . .

Had he said his wife's name? Certainly . . . he was dying, and his wife had given him an heir in those final moments. Gwyneth had needed to confess to her, too. She felt no rancor toward Gwyneth now; she kept the woman in her household, protected her, even enjoyed her company and that of the baby.

Then what?

What had Percy tried so hard to say?

Elise sighed, quickening her steps. She wanted to reach her own chamber; she had been so tired lately. Today, she had been dizzy several times; black spots had appeared before her eyes.

Rest . . . she needed more rest. It was difficult to rest when the country might be veering toward civil war; when Bryan was miles and miles away and she alone . . .

Suddenly she stood dead-still, swallowing a gasped scream as a pain pierced through her back. She took a deep breath, stunned. It came again, and then the dizziness started to sweep through her, this time out of control.

She saw the stairs as she started to fall upon them. A long, low sob of anguish escaped her, and then she was catapulting toward the hall. The stairs disappeared. Everything disappeared. The world became a wall of gray.

She heard whispering long before she fully awoke. Jeanne and Maddie, keeping her chamber warm, watching over her. They didn't know she could hear; but she did, and she understood.

When she at last opened her eyes, they were filled with her tears.

She had lost the child she carried. The tiny life that had been so very, very precious. Bryan's babe; the fragile creation of a dream night, the life that had meant everything to her . . .

Everything.

The babe had been their future.

Their chance for peace; their chance for love.

She wept bitterly, and no one could console her.

XXII

By August, even those who feared King Richard's wrath and were well aware that he did not take kindly to criticism were writing letters to their sovereign.

Chancellor Longchamp dismissed Richard's people right and left; he was in control of the White Tower in London, and therefore in control of the city. Isabel de Clare, on Will Marshal's orders, had fortified their Irish holdings and moved into her castle in Wales. Even those who did not directly fear Longchamp distrusted him. In Richard's absence, he had taken over the house.

Elise grew more and more anxious about the situation in Cornwall. The peddler became her friend, and he continued to come to Firth Manor, but he seldom brought cheerful news. Prince John had returned to England—under the pretense of saving the kingdom for his brother; Geoffrey had come, too. Now an archbishop, Geoffrey had taken refuge in a monastery; a member of Longchamp's family had ordered that he be dragged from his refuge—surely a sin against God!

Geoffrey was imprisoned by Longchamp's people, and although he was Henry II's bastard, they began to compare him to Saint Thomas à Becket, slain because of a few choice words muttered by Henry. The people began to hail Geoffrey and John; they hated Longchamp's rule, and were ready to accept John as regent in his stead. If something wasn't done quickly, a full-scale civil war would ensue. Longchamp deserved to be beaten, but many feared that if John went to battle against him, he would also attempt to seize Richard's crown.

And it seemed that Richard was determined to believe that nothing was wrong. He left France with Philip in August; by September, he was further arming troops in Messina.

Elise wrote letters constantly. Not to Richard, but to Bryan. She did not know what to say to him. In stilted words, she had told him that she had lost their child. But she could not confess her love on paper, and she feared that he would be bitterly disappointed with her. He had wanted a child so dearly.

And that child, conceived in a winter's tempest, had been the tenuous link of her love. Bryan had always wanted land, and Bryan had wanted heirs to inherit that land. Their marriage had been arranged by the king. The longer he was away, the easier it became for Elise to slip into desolation. She had learned to love him, just to lose him. For she did feel as if she had lost him; it was September, and Richard's great Crusade truly had yet to get under way. God alone knew when she would see Bryan again. Sometimes his image misted in her dreams, and she would wonder if he remembered her at all. Once, he had wanted her. Perhaps he had never loved her, but he had wanted her. Now he had been gone so long . . .

And she had lost the child. She could have waited, she could have endured, she could have stayed halfway sane—if only she could have had the babe to love in his absence . . .

Gwyneth's son, young Percy, flourished like a spring flower. He was solid and happy, a chubby little child, cooing whenever she picked him up. Gwyneth's manor had been rebuilt by September, but Gwyneth remained at Firth Manor. She was afraid to go home, and with Longchamp still such a threat to the unfortified manors, Elise could not bid her to leave. And she was happy to have young Percy; she felt a responsibility to him. She loved to hold the babe, although doing so also brought her pain. She had wanted her own child so badly. A beautiful, healthy boy to hand proudly to Bryan. His son, her son, something of true worth from the maelstrom of their marriage.

Elise and Gwyneth had formed an uneasy friendship. Elise had to admit that Gwyneth had little temper, and could be consistently charming. On many a lonely night, Elise was glad that she and Gwyneth had been able to consume some of the long hours with idle chatter. If she could only trust Gwyneth completely, she knew that she could have shared her own worries and fears, and perhaps found them alleviated. But she didn't trust Gwyneth, not completely, and she could never admit to Gwyneth that she had found herself suddenly head over heels in love with Bryan, and that she lay in anguish every night, wondering where—and with whom—he might be sleeping.

She knew that Gwyneth wrote to Bryan—as she did—but she could not bring herself to ask what Gwyneth's letters contained. She assumed that they were like hers: letters that stated the deplorable state of affairs in England, and begged that someone do something that would force Richard to act. Elise knew that her letters were always stiff and formal, just like the letters Bryan returned to her. He had offered her no condemnation for losing their child; his words were polite. Too polite. She sensed bitter disappointment in them. Maddie and Jeanne insisted upon telling her that she was young, that she had years ahead of her in which to have children. Such assurances gave Elise little comfort, for as it stood, it seemed that it would be years before she saw her husband again, and already she felt the distance between them. By the time they met again, they would be strangers. The ties of tenderness so recently begun would have withered with the passage of time.

There was little for her to do except cling to the belief that she held their property safe from the devious and grasping hands of Chancellor Longchamp.

By winter, Longchamp had threatened invasion of all properties belonging to William Marshal and Bryan Stede. Elise had tripled the guard; when winter's snows fell again, she had over three hundred trained and armed men ready to defend Firth Manor and the Cornish properties surrounding it.

But Longchamp's army was double the size of hers. Only the harshness of winter—and the fact that he was still busy stealing offices from Richard's men in London—kept Longchamp from attacking.

In the deep midst of winter, they were visited by travelers again. No banners were raised as the party of ten or so approached the manor, and Elise, brought to the ramparts by her alarmed steward, strained her eyes against the elements to ascertain just who would be coming so. Not Longchamp; if he were to make an assault upon the manor, he would come with his army in force. And Longchamp was in London, the last that she had heard.

"Shall we call the alarm?" Alaric asked her.

Elise shook her head slowly. "No, I don't think so. They are knights who approach us, but no more than ten. From wherever it comes, it is a party come at peace."

It was not until the party had almost reached the manor that Elise realized it was Prince John descending upon her. She was glad that she had risen no barriers against him, but she was uneasy. Eleanor did not trust John, and if a man's mother could not trust him, then others had best beware.

John had sworn not to come to England while Richard was away; the king, it seemed, was ready to forgive his little brother almost anything, but Richard was not a fool, and he knew his younger brother coveted the crown. Prince John was, however, far more preferable to the people than the obnoxious Norman Longchamp. So he had been welcomed to Cornwall.

And as Eleanor had once warned her, Elise knew well enough that John might be the king one day. Richard was one of the most powerful knights in the world, one of the most courageous.

Highly likely to get his fool self killed.

And so it was important to tread a careful path with the prince, especially since he was her half brother, just as Richard. The two were as different as their coloring: Richard, the golden king; John, the dark and often sullen prince. No, he must be humored, but never trusted, and so welcoming him was a nerve-wracking task. Elise always had to hope that John had no conception whatever of her identity.

"Lady Elise!"

He greeted her with affectionate propriety, and she noted that he had changed of late. He still wore high heels affixed to his boots—John despised the fact that he had never grown tall—but his dress was more sober than in previous times, and his behavior was much subdued.

Only his eyes were the same. They were as ever dark and alert, and she thought that he was a fine actor. John was shrewd and greedy. He could make use of expediency and opportunity quite well.

A little chill shook her. What would happen if he did become their king?

"Your Grace, what a pleasure to greet you here!" she returned to him.

"Ah, pleasure is not my quest, Lady Elise. I have come to see how you fare the winter with Longchamp on your heels!"

"Quite well, thank you," Elise replied, restraining her tongue. She knew he hadn't come to see to her welfare; he simply wanted to know how strongly aligned she was with him against Longchamp!

"I don't know why my brother the king is so blind to that man!" John exclaimed vehemently. "A man who threatens to demolish your husband's property, while Bryan Stede rides at his side! Still, I have every faith that Richard will see justice done, and so I have returned to these shores to know the heart of the people in this matter. They have cried out to me, you know."

Elise said nothing. John, acting the benign overlord, turned to introduce the members of his party. Only one man held back; he was cowled in a priest's frock, which made Elise curious. She recognized his other company. They were lords known for a fondness of drinking and wenching, and Elise remained uneasy as she welcomed them all to the manor. The priest did not belong with the group. Of course, it was true that there were members of the clergy known for ignoring the rules of the cloth, but . . .

Gwyneth made an appearance in the hall, and Elise was glad, for Gwyneth subtly took over the duties of hostess, calling for food and wine, bringing an unstilted warmth and welcome to the hall.

Elise was left to welcome the last of the guests, the cowled man who hovered in the background. When the others had moved on to the hearth, he called to her softly, lifting his head. She saw a pair of light, blue-gray, sparkling eyes.

"Geoffrey!" she cried with true delight. "I worried about you, but I see that you are free and well!"

"Shh!" he told her. "Yes, I am free, and very well." He grinned ruefully. "I am even a bit of a hero, but I pretend not to ride with this grouping; I would not want Richard to know that I banded with John." He sighed. "I am accused enough of coveting my half brother's crown, and though I continue to say that the throne of England would be crowded with Richard already in it, rumors still spread!"

"But, Geoffrey, you are an archbishop now! Surely no one—"

"Nay, there is no 'surely' when one is of royal blood—no matter which side of the sheets they may have come from." He sobered. "Elise, that is why I am here."

"Why?"

"Be careful with John. Be very careful. He is jealous of Bryan—because Richard respects him so, and bestowed such wealth upon him. He is suspicious of you—because of Richard's interest. And if he had all of England while you lived upon a tiny speck of an island, he would want that tiny speck of an island."

"What am I to do?" Elise cried softly. "Longchamp on one side, John on the other!"

"Do nothing; just take care—and sit tight. If Richard should die by a Saracen sword, John will be king. If he believes that you accept that—that you would be loyal to him—you will be left in peace. Longchamp will doubtlessly be bested; he has played his hand too far. The people went wild when his sister dared to arrest me. Richard will do something now; he must. But Richard respects Longchamp, and it is possible that he could rise to power again. And no matter what, Elise, don't let your feelings give you away. These are dangerous times for royal bastards."

"No one knows, Geoffrey," Elise said softly. "Not even . . . Bryan."

Geoffrey smiled. "Ah . . . so you two still fight your little war! I warned you once not to make an enemy of him, little sister."

"We're not exactly . . . enemies," Elise murmured, flushing.

Geoffrey lifted a brow with a slight smile. "I'm glad, Elise, for your husband is sore set upon by the king. Bryan has begged leave to come home; Richard will not part with him."

Elise laughed bitterly. "Then it all seems to matter little, doesn't it? Were we friends or enemies, we would scarce remember by the time he reaches home."

Geoffrey squeezed her hand. "Perhaps it will not be so long," he told her softly.

She tried to smile, but could not. They both knew that he was lying. She had been pitched into a dangerous game between chancellor and prince, with Geoffrey her only real friend.

"Have you . . . seen Bryan?" she asked him.

"Several months ago, before I decided that, despite my promise, I had to return to England."

"And?"

"Bryan is always well. More moody, silent, than I have known him to be. He mentioned that you had lost a child. I'm sorry."

Elise quickly lowered her lashes so that Geoffrey would not see the tears that sprang to her eyes. Bryan had mentioned the child, with great disappointment, she was sure. Perhaps he believed that she could never bear his heir, that she was too frail.

Perhaps he spent his days berating his marriage, his nights finding consolation for the prison of marriage that bound him to her . . .

If only she could be with him! It seemed that she would never have a chance to prove that . . .

She loved him. That she could be a wonderful wife . . . and mother.

Elise lifted her head. Wherever else she had failed, she had held the manor strong. She had kept his property safe for his return.

"Thank you for coming to me, Geoffrey," she told him. "And I promise you, I'll take great care with John." Geoffrey nodded, watching her. "Come, have some wine—warmed against the cold!" she told him, and she led him to the table, where they began to speak of casual things. Geoffrey at last took his wine to the hearth. He kept his eyes upon the Lady Elise. She was very cordial; she kept carefully at bay John's more lecherous companions, those who might fear the "Black Knight" Bryan Stede, but considered themselves safe with him a continent away.

Elise was a rare beauty: posed, regal, wise. Geoffrey thought for the thousandth time that they, Henry's illegitimate children, would have made the far better heirs to the throne.

He sighed ruefully as he drank his wine. He was far too fond of keeping his head upon his neck ever to make a bid for the crown. Richard was a formidable man. So formidable that he would never dream of fighting his brother.

But if and when John came to the throne, they would all need to shudder.

He smiled as he heard Elise tap upon the table with her chalice. She lifted it high then, and allowed her eyes to rivet to each man in turn. "Let us drink to our sovereign Lord Richard! King of England, Count of Anjou, Duke of Normandy, and Aquitaine."

The knights all raised their glasses.

Prince John repeated her toast. Geoffrey was certain that he was savoring the words, and mentally substituting his own name for Richard's.

Thank the blessed Lord that Richard was strong, and as healthy as an ox!

The prince's party stayed with them for a week. For Elise it was misery; she tried politely to fend off the unwelcome attention of John's rowdy followers.

Then there was John himself. He was, as Geoffrey had warned her, suspicious. He quizzed her about her past, about Bryan, about the manor. She was continuously on edge. John needed her now; she was a bulwark against Longchamp. But he was jealous of Bryan; even when he put on his allotment of the Plantagenet charm, she could read the envy in his tone. Would he ever dare to ride against Bryan? Probably not, she thought. John, were he ever to reach the throne, would need men such as Will Marshal and Bryan Stede.

Still, she would probably need to keep alert of this brother for the rest of her life.

The one real benefit of John's arrival was the change in Gwyneth.

Gwyneth seemed to have come alive. She formed no alliances with any of the knights, but reveled in their attention.

"I am so very bored!" she confided to Elise. "None of these are men whom I would wish to marry, though marry I suppose I must now with Percy gone. Richard will command it."

"Sir Trevor is a handsome man," Elise suggested. "He seems more mature than the others. More trustworthy."

Gwyneth laughed. "Sir Trevor rides with the prince. He is as lecherous and foolish as the rest. But . . . oh, Elise! It does grow weary waiting here, snowbound and held almost at siege by that despicable Longchamp! I fear that I shall fade away and die of the monotony if something doesn't happen soon!"

Elise felt the same, but she said nothing.

"You have Bryan to wait for," Gwyneth reminded Elise softly. "If that were my situation, I could bear this solitude . . ."

"At least you have your son."

"Aye . . . and I do love him. But you must know, as I do, the love of a child is not that of a man. Oh, Elise! I would ride to the devil himself to know a real man again!"

"Gwyneth! That's blasphemy!"

"But it is true."

"Something will happen, Gwyneth. Truly it will."

Things did happen. Longchamp increased his threats against the property of Will Marshal and Bryan Stede. The winter kept him at bay; Elise and Gwyneth remained captives of the snow-bound and heavily fortified manor.

Elise began to grow frantic, but when it seemed that she had reached her darkest hour, fate gave her a strange reprieve by the grace of another party that appeared at the manor.

She had barely awakened—indeed, Gwyneth and half the household still slept—when she heard the distant sound of trumpets. Elise fumbled into her clothing and raced to the southern tower. Alaric stood with the sentries, staring across the field. Elise joined him. They stared at the party of riders coming toward them, trying hard to read the banners that whipped in the wind.

" 'Tis not Longchamp . . ." Alaric murmured tensely. Then, suddenly, he and Elise were staring at each other with joy, for the banners bore the leopards and lilies of England. The emblem of the Plantagenets.

"But it can't be the king!" Elise murmured. "Richard would never leave his crusade. And it isn't John again; John comes too secretively to wave banners!"

"Not the king . . . and not the prince!" Alaric exclaimed. "It's the queen!"

"Eleanor!" Elise cried.

Soon the manor was a hub of activity. And very soon Elise found that she was hugging the queen, and feeling the distance time had brought between them fall away like autumn leaves.

In the hall, Elise begged for news. "Oh, Eleanor! I am ever so happy to see you, but what are you doing here? I thought you meant to follow Richard and see him married—"

"I did see him married, so I am very officially a 'dowager queen.' "

"Alys?"

"No, and I feel much sorrow, for we wronged that girl pathetically. Richard married the princess from Navarre—Berengaria. But I'm afraid I did poor Berengaria no kindness, for the afternoon of the wedding, the bridegroom was off again." Eleanor stared bluntly at Elise. "I have come as Regent of England. If Richard refuses to save it for himself, then I must do it for him. Now, tell me all that you know of this Longchamp mess!"

Elise did, solemnly telling all that had happened last spring, including Percy's death. "We could never prove that it was Longchamp's men—"

"But it was," Eleanor said with dry certainty. "Well, we shall miss Sir Percy in our kingdom. But rest assured, Longchamp will take a precarious fall. I come with Richard's seal, and with a goodly number of armed men. Longchamp's rule is over. If I am not enough, Richard has sent others. William Marshal is on his way to Pembroke Castle at this minute. We will return to the ways of the law."

"Will!" Elise exclaimed excitedly. "Richard sent Will? What of Bryan . . ."

Her voice trailed away as she saw the queen's sad expression. "I'm sorry, child, Bryan is not returning. Richard had already given Will leave to come home; he would not release them both."

"Oh," Elise murmured, trying to hide her disappointment. She barely noticed when Gwyneth came into the room; she hardly heard the queen's sympathetic words to the widow. But then Eleanor was addressing her again, and she forced herself to pay attention.

"I heard that you lost a babe, Elise. I am sorry, but you must not take it too much to heart. You will bear others."

"A difficult feat for a woman alone, Your Grace!" Gwyneth supplied for Elise.

"Aye," Eleanor murmured regretfully. "And not even I could convince Richard to release him . . ." Suddenly Eleanor laughed, her still-young eyes sizzling with the excitement of a girl. "Bryan cannot come to you, my dear, but perhaps you could go to him."

Elise caught her breath. "On crusade?" she asked breathlessly.

"Why not? I led the troops of Aquitaine alongside Louis when I was Queen of France. Several of us ladies, heiresses in our own right, rode to the call. They dubbed us the 'Amazons,' and I must say, we did ourselves quite proud. I designed outfits so that we might ride as the men. We traveled with no more baggage than the men. Louis and I had that dreadful dispute that led to our divorce while we were on crusade, but my destiny was not with Louis—it was with Henry. And still! What a wonder to see the Eastern palaces. How we were entertained. My uncle was the Duke of Antioch then . . . Oh, If I were but young now . . . but I am not. And England needs me. But . . ." Eleanor's eyes continued to sparkle brilliantly, "If England has me, then Cornwall will be safe from the likes of Longchamp! And you, Duchess, will then have a very strong—but worthless—army. Take those men! Lead them on crusade!"

"Will they follow me . . . ?" she murmured.

Gwyneth settled that question with a laugh. "They have followed your orders for a year now! Surely, with a chance of knighthood awaiting them on the field, they will follow you anywhere! And I will come, too, Elise! I couldn't bear to be totally alone. We've learned to face things together—really, I'd feel so much safer moving with you than staying behind, so isolated. Oh, to end these days of eternal boredom!"

Elise raised a skeptical brow to Gwyneth. Then she shrugged and laughed. Suddenly, she felt alive again. Alive as she had not felt since she had watched Percy die, and lost her child before it had even known life. Excitement made her feel as if her blood rushed through her in great torrents, as if she were strong, and invincible.

Bryan . . .

She could ride to Bryan. She had worked with her guards, time and again. They were prepared to fight. She could lead them, because she had led them this far. She had made of Firth Manor a bulwark so strong that none had dared attack her.

And the Crusade! She could ride on God's holy war; she could see distant places, lands of mystery and beauty.

And Bryan . . . she would no longer have to wonder where he slept. She would be beside him, fighting with him, and for him. No more waiting, no more torture, no more boredom. No more wondering if he would ever return.

They had been parted so long. Did he still think about her? Would he want her? Could she ever hope that he might love her, too?

It didn't matter. She could hear the call to battle, and she was going to go. Her eyes met with Gwyneth's. They mirrored her excitement.

For a moment she felt a tremor of uneasiness. Gwyneth would come with her. Gwyneth . . . the friend with whom she had endured so many things.

But were they truly friends? Was Gwyneth anxious to end the horrible boredom of their days? Or was she, like Elise, heedless of all else except for the chance to see Bryan again?

It didn't really matter. Nothing mattered. If it came to that, she was as ready to fight Gwyneth as she was the whole Islam army for a chance to see her husband again.

To see if life could rival the splendor of memory . . .

She leaped from her chair and strenuously hugged the queen. "Your Grace, I intend to do it!"

Eleanor nodded slowly. "Aye, Elise, I think you shall. Prepare yourself, and then wait for word. I'm quite certain that Longchamp will flee England; if not, he will know a taste of prison.

I go to London tomorrow; as soon as I may, I will send word to you that it is safe to set out."

Things were not to be half so simple as they sounded. Richard had sent the elderly Walter Coutance with Eleanor, but though Walter presented Longchamp with Richard's orders, Longchamp proclaimed them to be forgeries. Prince John was in the southwest, and, hating Longchamp, the people rallied to John. Longchamp called John and Geoffrey traitors; the threat of civil war became stronger. But at last enough strength rallied together; Richard sent new orders. Longchamp was not only to be deposed, but he would face trial, and his estates would be confiscated.

Longchamp fled at last. He was caught—disguised as a woman—in Dover. He was almost hanged as a witch, but he was recognized and imprisoned instead; he was still one of Richard's favorites, and only Richard could pass final judgment.

Longchamp bribed a jailer, and managed to escape to the Continent. It didn't really seem to matter, though—his threat to England—and to Elise—was at last over. Eventually, Richard would find him, and then he would have to answer for everything.

It remained to be seen what John would do.

It seemed to Elise that her freedom to leave had taken forever. It was spring again—over a year since she had seen Bryan last—before she was able to take her army and Gwyneth, Jeanne, and old Kate, and start out for the Holy Land.

Elise spent her last evening at the manor staring into the fire in her chamber. She argued with herself that she was mad to be attempting such an undertaking. The route would be long, and dangerous. Of course, she was traveling with an army—an army that she would put into the service of Richard the Lion-Hearted.

But she knew that she was not riding to give assistance to the king. She was doing so because she had to; a fever inside of her seemed to drive her. She was desperate to see Bryan again, to discover if there could be love between them. How she ached for him, needed him, longed for him! And she was so afraid, so very afraid that if she did not see him soon, she would lose him forever.

She paced the room, wondering if she weren't indeed the spawn of the devil breed, for she knew now that neither heaven nor earth could keep her from her quest.

In the morning, they took their leave. Young Percy was left with Maddie. Elise wondered how Gwyneth was able to leave the little boy; seeing his hazel eyes fill with tears on the morning that they left, Elise knew that she would never be able to leave her own offspring—should she and Bryan both live to create any.

It was to be a long journey. From the English coastline they crossed the Channel to Balfleur. Through Normandy, Maine, Poitou, and Aquitaine, they were able to find hospitality at Richard's various castles and holdings. She and Gwyneth and Jeanne shared quarters of varying comfort; the army most frequently camped out in the fields. But it was spring, and the weather, for the most part, remained fair. All throughout the countryside, the planting season was on; farmers tilled their fields; the foliage became more green daily—flowers sprang up everywhere.

From Aquitaine, they traveled into King Philip's domains. Here, too, they found hospitality at the French monarch's holding, since on the Crusade, Philip and Richard were allies. Rugged mountain roads brought them from France into the provinces and principalities of Italy. Every mile brought her closer to Bryan.

They set sail upon merchant ships—bartered from Italian seamen—from Brindisi. The Ionian Sea was calm and beautiful as it brought them to the Mediterranean. They spent a night at anchor near Crete, then set sail again. Storms struck the Mediterranean with a tempestuous ferocity within hours of their sailing. The ship rocked with wild fury. For unending hours of fear she and Gwyneth and Jeanne clung to one another belowdecks, offering up prayers to the Virgin, to all the saints, to Christ, and to God. Elise loved the sea, but never had she seen it so vicious. At last, she left Jeanne and Gwyneth together, and stumbled up on deck, holding fast to the masts and rigging. She stared through the pelting rain up at the iron-gray sky and again prayed fervently that though she might be undeserving, she be allowed to live. And she asked God that her determination not bring about the death of others.

The rain continued, the wind rose. Elise became convinced that God had no care to listen to her.

But as she remained by the mast, huddled against it in cold and fear, the wind began slowly to die. Even more slowly, the sky turned from gray to blue. Elise sank to her knees, whispering her gratitude to heaven out loud.

The daylight showed them that none of the ships had been lost. Only one life had been forfeit, that of a warrior gone overboard in the height of the wind.

A period of peaceful seas brought them to Cyprus.

It was there that they learned King Richard was holding the port town of Acre.

One more journey, only one, Elise told herself, and her quest would be rewarded. She barely slept that night, so anxious was she, so afraid, so nervous. Would Bryan welcome her?

They came at last to Acre.

Beneath a hot and brilliant sun, they first entered the Arab world. Merchants hawked their wares in the streets; veiled women moved hurriedly about. A smell of incense was in the air; braying camels moved their clumsy way along the streets. It was hot and dusty and completely foreign. Western knights walked the same paths as veiled, mysterious women.

Elise looked about herself with wide-eyed fascination.

She was here!

She was exhilarated, exalted . . .

And trembling horribly. Soon, very soon, she would see Bryan.

PART III

LIONS OF THE DESERT

XXIII

August, 1190
The Muzhair Oasis
The Road to Jerusalem

The cry of Islam rose all around him, a chant that began low, then rose high and shrill. It was echoed and reechoed upon the lips of infidels; first the men on foot came running with that cry to clash with the Christians, then came the men on their graceful Arabian mounts, swords gleaming wickedly beneath the sun as hooves thundered across the sands.

"Archers!" Bryan called out, and a hundred trained men stepped forward with their longbows. Bryan lifted his hand, waiting tensely; with the slash of that hand through the air, the arrows began to fly. Up in the smooth arches that were beautiful to behold; then falling to pierce through flesh and bone, and break the chant of Islam as men screamed in mortal agony and fell.

But where the ranks were broken, new men filled the gap. So many . . . fighting for their lands; their way of life.

All his life Bryan had believed in the knight's great code of Christianity. Richard's quest had been his quest: Jerusalem . . . for Christ's followers. He had fought at Henry's side; he had killed time and again in battle. The carnage about him should have been nothing new, and killing infidels should have been easy.

But there was nothing easy about this—the Third Crusade. The followers of Islam were being led by a man named Saladin.

Saladin had brought about the Third Crusade by capturing Jerusalem from the Christians left behind to rule after the First and Second Crusades. The Moslems thought him a saintly hero; Bryan, who had been skirmishing with him since they had at last reached the Holy Land in June, could not help but admire his honesty and courage.

Saladin was not a young man, but somewhere over five decades. As a much younger man, he had entered the service of the Egyptian caliph and had become vizier, or ruler, of that country. He had extended his rule over Damascus, Aleppo, Mosul, and Edessa. His military ability neared genius, and Bryan had learned that he was a great builder; schools and mosques rose beneath his hand, scholars were welcome at his palaces, and the peoples of his dry desert lands were rewarded with canals and irrigation. In battle he was fierce; off of the field, he was quiet-spoken, if firmly determined.

He and Bryan had come face to face once; they had battled fiercely with their swords, and been seen somewhat stunned to discover that neither could best the other.

They had almost smiled at each other as they backed off. But all around them had lain the dead, and their smiles had faded.

"You are Stede," Saladin murmured.

Bryan was surprised once again to know that mighty ruler knew his name. Saladin spoke in accented French, but his words were clear and Bryan had no difficulty understanding him.

"Yes. And you are the great Saladin." Saladin nodded. "My people perish, and yours die upon dry, distant sands."

"Jerusalem is our most holy city. Followers of Christ cry out to come in pilgrimage."

Saladin accepted this, and smiled sadly again. "This land, this desert, belongs to our people; I cannot give up Jerusalem. I would have no objection to pilgrims. Tell this to Richard the Lion-Heart."

"I will tell him," Bryan said. He added with unintentional bitterness, "But he will not listen."

"Then we must fight until he does listen. You will take victories, I will take victories. Men will die. And men, such as yourself, will continue to long for home. For your women, and your children."

Bryan had smiled grimly then. "Woman—only one, great Sultan."

"Only one? She must be very intriguing."

Moslem men, Bryan knew, kept several wives. Those with great wealth also enjoyed harems.

"I am a Christian, Saladin. And, yes . . . my one woman is very intriguing. But I have no children."

Saladin had laughed with a lusty humor. "Nor will you have children—while your wife pines in a distant land and you watch men bleed upon this sand! Or does your wife pine? If she is such a woman as you say, perhaps she finds another in your absence. You should be home. I am a reasonable man. Speak to your king."

With no fear, Saladin turned his back on Bryan and rode away. Infidel or Christian, an honorable man recognized another one. He knew that Bryan would have no more stabbed him in the back than he would have done so to Bryan.

Both men had lived to continue fighting.

Bryan told Richard about the meeting, but as he had expected, Richard gave him scant attention. The word of an "infidel" meant nothing to a Christian king. Richard wanted Jerusalem.

Today, Bryan did not fight Saladin, but his nephew Jalahar. Jalahar was an emir himself, with ancient rights to the oasis at Muzhair. His main residence was called the palace of Muzhair, and stood a few hours' ride past the oasis.

Bryan raised his sword now as the Moslems charged into the Christians. His men were the better trained; they were the more efficient fighters. But the Moslems came in hordes. Bryan shouted out orders; his Christians closed ranks, and fierce, hand-to-hand combat began. Bryan saw Sir Theban, a Montouian knight, draw out the old battle ax for which he was famed. A man fell before him, his head almost severed from his neck. Then Bryan forced his mind to go blank as he drew his sword; a mounted Moslem was screaming out his high chant as he flew, sword swinging, for Bryan.

The sun beat down upon them, making a sickening stench arise from the blood being shed. A wind rose, making the desert sands swirl, blinding men, filling their mouths with dryness. The battle wore on. Bryan's arm was nicked by a Damascan sword; he railed, and his sword pierced through the Moslem's middle.

A chant rose again; the Moslems were retreating. Bryan wiped the sweat and sand from his eyes and followed their retreat.

Mounted upon a faraway dune and silhouetted against the yellow-blue day, Bryan saw the Emir Jalahar. He was unmistakable, for his horse was as pure white as Bryan's was midnight-black.

Jalahar . . . Saladin's nephew, and a fierce, brutal fighter. But he was a young man, no more than two decades plus, and he hadn't yet learned his uncle's wisdom and strategy.

This was one battle that Jalahar had lost.

Bryan believed that he could feel Jalahar's eyes upon him, returning the scrutiny. Jalahar had lost, but it had been a battle well fought. Both men knew it. Jalahar dipped low in his saddle in acknowledgment of "Stede." Bryan lifted a hand in return. The Moslems disappeared over the dune, and Bryan turned to the dismal task of sorting the wounded from the dead. "Make haste!" he ordered his men. "Our wounded will die quickly here, of the heat."

Sir Theban, a massive warrior, stocky but built almost as a square so laden was he with muscle, walked by Bryan's side. He paused by a groaning man, and Bryan shouted back for someone to bring aid. They went on; Sir Theban suddenly knelt.

"The Virgin Mary bless the wretched girl!" he cried.

Curiously, Bryan lowered himself to the balls of his feet. Sir

Theban had turned over a sand-encrusted body. It was that of a woman. A girl, rather. One who had been young and lovely, but now wore a circlet of red death about her throat. "Who is she?" Bryan demanded thickly.

"One of the Frenchmen's whores," Theban answered softly. "She must have followed her knight to the camp last night."

Bryan began to swear vehemently. "Damn those men! I've told them time and again that I will not have women brought to the battle!"

He felt sick; so sick that he was afraid he would shortly humiliate himself by spitting the remains of his last meal over the sand. It was one thing to accustom oneself to dead men. But to see a girl—a lovely young girl, whore or no—as food for the desert carrions, he could not bear.

And this one . . .

Her hair was long and golden. It lay tousled and dirtied over her pale, sand-seared features. It had no touch of copper to it, no hint of fire, yet seeing the girl made Bryan think of Elise.

I live in misery because I long to see her so, he thought of his wife, *but I bless God that she is not here.*

He was certain that the Moslems had not meant to kill the girl; she had simply been in the way. No, they would not have meant to kill her. Blonds were rare here; had the warriors not been immersed in the battle, they would have tried to take her prisoner. She would have been quite a prize.

She would be no man's prize. She was dead. And for some reason, her death gnawed at him—he, Bryan Stede, who had learned to look death in the face long ago.

He stood. "Order a burial detail, Theban. I'm returning to the coastal palace to report to Richard."

Theban nodded. "What about the infidels?"

"Bury them, too!" Bryan thundered. "For the sake of God, Theban, do not look at me so. We shall not be able to claim this small ground if we do not rid it of the stench of death!"

Theban nodded. Bryan called to Wat, and ordered the men

who had last drawn burial duty. They would travel back with him, carrying along the wounded.

He was silent as he started the ride back to the coast where the Christians had gained their foothold. Richard would shower him with praise. He had made a strong blow against Jalahar—and, therefore, against Saladin.

He didn't want to be showered with praise. He wanted to go home.

Long hours had become days, days had stretched into months. It was more than a year since he had been home. Letters . . . always there had been letters reaching him. Letters that were a curse rather than a blessing, for when he read of trouble, he was helpless, thousands of miles away. He and Marshal had argued themselves hoarse over the Longchamp problem; it had taken Richard forever to admit that there was a problem. Marshal had been allowed to return, while Bryan . . .

Bryan had lain awake night after night, praying. Worrying, thinking, agonizing. Over Elise.

It had been so very long.

And he had received the letter telling him that she had lost the child along with the one telling that she had conceived, so even that joy had been wrested from him before he had even been able to savor the taste of it. With what bitterness he had received that news! And Percy . . . dead. Gwyneth and her son alive only because of his foresight to arm Cornwall . . .

And only because of Elise.

Elise. He had been consumed with fear when Percy had left Richard's service due to his injury. Fear—and jealousy. Nights of anguish wondering if she would turn to the man she had intended, by choice, to marry.

And then Percy . . . had died. Bryan was sorry, but guilt also plagued him for the relief he had felt.

Elise would not be with Percy.

But the unwarranted attack that had brought on his death!

It could have been Elise. Elise burned out. Left to the mercy of traitorous cutthroats . . .

Only Eleanor had kept him from openly defying Richard and leaving for home.

Eleanor—who had sworn to keep her maternal eye upon Elise.

Bryan grated his teeth hard together. He no longer believed in this "holy" war. The Moslems cried to Allah just as they cried to God for help. They died—and left widows and orphans—just as the Christians.

But he would continue to fight, and fight with vigor. Only when Richard was satisfied would he ever be able to go home.

His brooding silence carried him to the port town where Richard had set up his quarters in a deposed sheikh's palace. It was a dazzling place of arches and minarets, hung with beautiful tapestries and rugs, laden with ornaments of gold and silver. The massive English King seemed incongruous in the delicate surroundings. Bryan often felt awkward himself, sitting on low silk-covered cushions, drinking from tiny cups—and constantly fearing that he might move too abruptly and destroy one of the fragile ornaments of crystal or glass.

He dismounted from his horse before the palace, and smiled at Wat, whom he had ignored for the long ride back. Wat had grown accustomed to his moods, though, and smiled tiredly in return as he took the destrier's reins from his duke.

Bryan looked up at the graceful lines of the palace and sighed. He was probably a miserable commander to his men, though he tried not to allow his own heartache to influence his temper. Sir Theban had told him once that he was alone too much, that there were many talented women about the town eager for a knight's hold.

Bryan had not been created for celibacy, but many months ago, while they awaited the day when Philip and Richard would quit arguing long enough to get the Crusade under way, he had succumbed to the lures of a pretty peasant girl. When she had left him, he had felt more dissatisfied than ever. The girl had not eased his hunger, nor had she begun to still the yearning in his heart that commanded his body. His wife, he decided with dry humor, had bewitched him. He had never really known her; she had never come to trust him. She kept dark secrets from him, and seemed to revel in taunting him.

But she had bewitched him.

If she were never to give the heir that he thought he so craved, he would not care, if he could be but near her. If he could begin to fathom what lay beneath her fiery pride . . .

He sobered suddenly, thinking of the dead girl who had brought Elise so strongly to his mind. His only comfort was knowing that Elise was now within the protective confines of Eleanor's care.

"Bryan!"

He heard his name called and frowned, knowing that he recognized the feminine voice. Then, from the simply fashioned doorway of the sleek palace, he saw a whirl of color. A woman with long, loose-flowing dark hair was racing toward him. A beauty, with the look of the devil in her dark eyes.

"Gwyneth?" he uttered hoarsely.

She was throwing herself against him, hugging him. "Bryan!" she exclaimed. Instinctively, he embraced her in return. He was glad to see her. She was a link with home.

Home . . .

He held her away, smiling. "Gwyneth! What are you doing here? How do you come to be here? Where is your son? And . . . Elise? How does she fare?"

Gwyneth laughed merrily. "I am here with a new force of men!"

"A force of men?" Bryan demanded, frowning. "God knows, we can use more men. But what men are they?"

Her eyes were truly dazzling. "Men who follow Elise, Duchess of Montoui and Countess of Saxony, and so forth! You two do have so many titles, Bryan! It was the queen's suggestion. She told us about the days when she rode on crusade with Louis of France and—Bryan?"

His bronze skin had taken on a frightening pallor; his eyes had gone from blue to black as they could when he was angry.

"Elise . . . is here?" he demanded, his voice grating.

"Installed in your chamber," Gwyneth answered uneasily, wishing suddenly that she hadn't waylaid him first. He was silent for a moment, staring up at the sculpted windows of the palace.

"Elise was . . . truly efficient and wise, Bryan. When the trouble started in England, she increased the guard. With Longchamp a threat no longer, she had more men-at-arms than she needed. They were eager to come on crusade, Bryan . . . Bryan?"

"What?" He glanced back at her as if he hadn't heard a word she had said. "Your pardon, Gwyneth. I will speak with you later. I'm sorry about Percy . . ."

Distractedly, he walked by her, and walked up the few steps leading to the palace. Then he was running, pushing by the servants as he tore along the white and gleaming corridors to the rear stairway. The door to his chamber was ajar; he flung it open.

She had known he was coming. She still leaned against the window seat that looked over the courtyard. At his brash entrance she started, but she did not rise.

He stopped inside the doorway, staring at her as he had that long-ago April night. But then she believed that night had been part of a dream, for she barely knew the stranger before her.

His skin was darkened past bronze by the sun; the creases about his dark-fire eyes were deeper than she remembered last. He seemed to have grown taller, and broader about the shoulders; his dark hair was longer, curling over the nape of his tunic. He had just come from battle, she thought, and she did not remain sitting because of intentional disrespect, but because she suddenly felt too weak to stand. She had been in love with him forever, it seemed now. But time had swept away all tentative bonds between them. She still loved him; seeing him made her tremble; her body seemed to melt and throb along with her heart. But she could not run to him. She could not throw her arms around him, and she could not say all the things that she had dreamed she might when she saw him again. She did still know him enough, or remember him enough, to realize that he was angry.

He didn't want her there. She had traveled across land and water for endless months to be with him—and he didn't want her there! From the window she had watched a smile like the sun strip the tension from his features when he greeted Gwyneth; she had watched him hug Gwyneth, hold her . . . laugh until Elise had been forced to remember breathlessly how handsome he could be . . .

But his laughter had been for another woman.

Bryan swallowed, wishing he had shut the door so that he might have leaned against it. She was like cool water in the sand-parched desert. Like Gwyneth, she wore her hair loose, the sun-fire locks curled about her in sleek splendor. She wore a costume of some new design: loose trousers beneath a tunic sitting along the legs. The sleeves were a pale aqua, the tunic a darker hue that caught that elusive color of her eyes, which was between blue and green. A spellbinding color—he had lost himself within it long ago, and hadn't known a minute's peace since. Her clothing was concealing, and yet to his mind, it concealed nothing. She was slimmer, but still she curved where he longed to touch her, and even as he stood there wanting to berate her for her presence, he had no control over the inner desire that was already pulling her to him, stripping her until he held her naked to him . . .

"It has been a long time," Elise said, speaking first. She had meant to keep her voice soft, but because of his thunderous look, a note of defiance crept into her voice.

"What is this . . . madness?" he hissed to her.

She shrugged, confused and hurt by his attitude. "Perhaps men are not the only ones to crave to ride to glory. I had an army; I brought it on crusade."

"You're not staying," Bryan said bluntly. His knees were shaking. He turned around to close the door, then noticed that Jeanne was busy in the back corner of the room, shaking clothing out from a travel trunk. Jeanne stopped in her task and looked from Elise to Bryan.

"Out, Jeanne," Bryan commanded softly.

"Bryan! Jeanne, you needn't take orders from—"

"Out, Jeanne," Bryan repeated.

Jeanne glanced at Elise, but obeyed Bryan. Bryan closed the door, and at last leaned against it, praying the solid wood would give him strength.

"Bryan! You've been gone over a year! You've no right to start ordering my servants about!"

"I'm sure she understands," Bryan drawled. "Elise, you're not staying here. I appreciate the men, but you're leaving in the morning."

"I am not!" Elise exclaimed, torn between the pain and anger. "I trained those men! I—"

"Elise! It is dangerous here!"

"Dangerous!" She started to laugh bitterly. "There was danger in Cornwall, Bryan Stede, and I handled it quite nicely without you, thank you."

He lowered his lashes suddenly and his fingers knotted into his palms to form fists. No, he hadn't been there. He had been traveling on this stupid quest that meant nothing! She had every right to berate him, she had been in danger, but he could not stand for her to be in such a position again, while he was helpless. The whore who had died today . . . she had done so almost beneath his eyes . . .

"Bryan," she said quietly, "I did not see you ordering Gwyneth to leave."

"Gwyneth is not my wife. She is a duchess in her own right. I cannot tell her what she must do."

"I am a duchess in my own right, Bryan!"

"You are also my wife."

"I'm staying."

"You're not!"

"We'll ask Richard about that, won't we? I realize that you

are the king's right-hand man, but Richard will want my guard. And they are *my* guard, Bryan!"

"So you would defy me by going to the king!" Bryan said hoarsely, incredulous and angry.

It was Elise who lowered her lashes this time. She longed to cry out the truth. I love you! I cannot leave you again! But he was rejecting her. She had dreamed that he would sweep her into his arms and tell her how he had needed her, envisioned her during all the lonely nights . . .

He hadn't even touched her, and he was coldly demanding that she leave.

She answered him tonelessly. "I won't get in your way, Bryan. But I don't intend to leave."

"All right, Elise," he said. "We will take this domestic dispute to the king. I'll agree to abide by his decision, if you will do the same."

She glanced at him again, with her heart pounding. Surely Richard owed her! She would throw herself upon his mercy, and this time remind him bluntly that she was his blood; she had stood up against his enemies, while he had ruthlessly commandeered her husband away. This time, Richard had to listen to her . . .

She nodded, swallowing. An awkward silence rose between them.

"You look well," she told him.

"I look like a sandpile," he replied. "But you . . . you are too thin. Are you well?"

Elise nodded, miserably wondering how they could be so far apart. "I've been very well since . . . I lost the child. Jeanne said that nothing was wrong with me, that with the night in the snow and Percy dying and the manor needing more fortification . . . that it all just became too much." She gazed at the floor, then at Bryan. "I'm sorry, Bryan!" she said huskily. "I know that . . . I wanted the babe desperately myself. I'm truly sorry!" Tears threatened to fill her eyes. She looked quickly to her hands, then jumped when he at last left the doorway and strode toward her, dropping to his knees at her side and taking her hands into his.

"Elise! I'm not angry about the child! Or maybe I am angry. Angry that I couldn't be there. Angry that it all fell to you, and that you probably did lose the babe because you were forced to take on too much. What I am worried about is now. I don't want you here, Elise."

She offered him a crooked, wistful smile, her fingers aching to reach out and touch his tousled hair.

"Not even for a night?" she whispered.

He heard the whimsy in her voice. It was the sweetest siren's call. He looked into the liquid aqua pools of her eyes and shudders racked his frame. He lifted his hands and allowed his fingers to tangle in her hair as he held her face between his palms and leaned closer to kiss her. Her lips were honey; they parted at his touch and he hungrily ravaged her mouth, feeling his body throb with the promise of an ecstasy he had awaited in his dreams, waking and sleeping.

She fell from the window seat, kneeling against him. Her fingers raked through his hair and bit into his shoulders. Her soft sobs muffled against his lips; she clung to him in a sweet and willful abandon.

He tried to pull away from her.

"I'm filthy," he said ruefully. "Covered with desert sand and the grit of battle."

"I don't care!" she whispered. "Bryan, hold me! Please, hold me!" She buried her face against his chest again, letting her feather-light caresses cover his warrior's frame. He held his breath, straining to hear her as she whispered again. "Love me, Bryan. Please, love me . . ."

He needed no further invitation, nor could he restrain his own desires further. He worked on his scabbard, and found her trembling fingers assisting his. The sword fell to his side. With lowered eyes she tugged upon his tunic. Together they pulled it over his shoulders. He stood, lifting her with him, and they found themselves locked in a fevered embrace once again.

It has been over a year since you held her! Bryan reminded himself. *Be gentle, be tender, take care . . .*

But the fire that surged in his blood was strong, and he found himself ripping her strange costume from her, rather than removing it gently. But she didn't seem to care; her lips were roaming over his chest; she nipped at his flesh, kissed it, teased and swathed it with the tip of her tongue. As he fumbled with her clothing, tearing cloth, she caressed him heedlessly, her nails raking pleasure down his spine. She was suddenly naked in his arms; the hard peaks of her breasts teased him, the arch of her hips sent his mind spiraling to rapture. It had been so long since he had held her breasts in his palms, touched the hard rouge peaks with the ardor of his lips, known the satin taste of her ivory flesh. His palms, rough with calluses, scoured over her, his kisses seared her. But when he laid her down upon the silk sheets of the low cushioned bed, she was up and in his arms again, tearing at his boots, at his hose, until he was as naked as she.

And he found that it was he who was being pressed against the cushioned softness of the low silk-covered bed. She came to him, cloaking him in the spun-gold beauty of her hair, rising above him as the shapely length of her long legs embraced him in a wild and wicked beauty, her thighs straddling his hips. She arched as he reached out to touch her, and as his fingers found her breasts with grazing reverence, he caught his breath with wonder at her perfection. Lithe and slender, curved and sculpted. Her breasts were so high, firm, and full to his hands, her waist so narrow, her hips so fluid and curved and lean . . .

Were he ever to be away from her a hundred years, he knew that he would always dream of her, wait for her, covet her; no woman could ever please him or touch him again, for the greatest beauty would pale in comparison to all that he had found with her. His need for her was deeper than the flesh, a hunger that could be sated, but never completely filled. Hers was a warmth far greater than the heat of passion, yet she touched upon his senses as no other woman ever could.

She made love to him with a wild and reckless abandon. As a warm breeze rustled the gauze of the exotic Arabic bedding, inhibition was lost to splendor. Bryan savored the sweet beauty of her aggressive fever, and tried to pull her back to him when she suddenly went still.

"You're wounded!" she told him, finding the spot where the sword had rent his arm.

"A scratch . . ." he murmured.

"But, Bryan, it must pain you—"

" 'Tis a scratch, nothing more!" He swept his arms around her, dominating now. "I feel no pain except that which you alleviate for me now . . ."

He began to whisper to her, words that made her flush and quiver . . . and die a little more each time with wonder at the sensations that consumed and devoured her. Soon they were a tangle of limbs, kissing, touching, loving, soaring. Never had the fever burned so high, so brilliantly; never did it climax with such sweet, shattering pleasure . . . nor drift so slowly into a gratifying peace, leaving them entwined, murmuring . . . caressing.

But when Elise at last lay completely still, smiling shyly and meeting his indigo gaze, she saw that his eyes were brooding and clouded, somewhat torn, but . . . hard.

He smiled somewhat ruefully. "You still cannot stay," he told her softly.

"Why?" she whispered in despair.

He shrugged uneasily. "We gain a foothold, we lose a foothold. And, by God, Elise, I am heartily sick of the sight of blood! Fever, snakebite, the heat . . . our men die as thick as the cursed flies around us. Those we trust turn traitor. Always, it is a standstill. Saladin is strong, and powerful. He has a nephew whom I fight . . . almost daily. I hold the ground; he holds the ground. What is mine one day may not be the next.

I do not want you here, Elise. I swear that the only way you will ever lead troops is over my dead body."

She swallowed, afraid to ask too much. She wanted to believe that he cared only for her life and welfare. She did not want to wonder if he kept one of the beautiful mixed-blood women of the port as a concubine; she did not want to ask how he filled his nights. Not now. She wanted only to stay.

"Bryan, I just arrived. I beg you to let me remain . . . a while. I will stay where you tell me to stay; I will not venture near the battle. The men I have brought will follow you; if I were to leave, I would need an escort. The strength of those who came beneath our banner could one day make a crucial difference."

He did not look convinced. She lowered her lashes and started to press warm, liquid kisses over the faded scars that marred his chest. She shifted slightly against him, allowing the tips of long tresses to tease over his thighs.

"I've . . . missed you . . ." she told him huskily, thrilling at the way his breath caught and his flesh quivered.

He lifted his hand to her face, smoothing her hair, grazing her cheeks with his knuckles.

"Perhaps you needn't leave right away—" he began, but then they were both startled by a sharp banging at the door.

"What is it?" Bryan thundered out.

A tentative voice followed a small silence. " 'Tis Wat, milord. King Richard rages about the solar, awaiting word about your battle with Jalahar."

Bryan swore softly beneath his breath. "Tell the king I am on my way."

He rolled from the bed, not glancing at Elise as he fumbled back into his clothing, swearing again. "Were I ever to have another chance at life, I would not be favored by a king!"

He paused at the doorway and at last looked back at Elise, scowling for a moment, then allowing a slight grin to tug at his lips.

"For the time being, Elise, I will allow you to stay. But not here. We hold Antioch more firmly. I will take you there. I will not be with you often, as we are most frequently camped in the desert. But if it is your wish, you will stay. For now. You will promise me that you will leave if I do feel it imperative."

"Bryan—"

"Promise me."

She smiled very sweetly. "I promise."

Bryan seemed satisfied. He closed the door behind him, and Elise rested against the pillow while her smile became triumphant laughter.

He would never send her away.

She would see that he could never bear to do so!

XXIV

October, 1190
The Palace of Muzhair
The Coastal Road

He was a man of medium stature, slim, but built wiry and strong. He was a brave man, raised to strength and courage by Saladin, a brilliant strategist. His name was Jalahar, and at twenty-five years of age he ruled over his domains with complete authority beneath Allah. He was known for a swift-rising temper; he was also known for a quick intelligence, and mercy when mercy was warranted. His eyes were a deep and haunting brown; his features were cleanly defined, sharp, but arrestingly pleasant. They bespoke his rugged life in the saddle, besting the elements cast his way at birth, reigning supreme over the desert.

From the scalloped window of his palace at Muzhair, the emir looked broodingly out on the Christian forces encamped far beyond the desert dunes that fringed his stronghold.

They could not take the palace. Of that he was certain. Just as Saladin was certain they would not take Jerusalem.

But this war, brought upon them by Christian interlopers, was costing him dearly—in trade, in the lives of his people. Each time he ventured out beyond his own borders, he drew an even greater toll of death, for the Englishman Stede, beneath the Christian king they called the Lion-Heart, knew how to hold his position.

He was a worthy opponent, Jalahar thought. If Allah willed that a man be cast into battle, it was good to be cast against a man with strength and intelligence.

"Jalahar."

He turned about, his desert capes swirling around him. His third wife, Sonina, a Damascene girl who was gracefully petite and exquisitely lovely, awaited him with her eyes lowered respectfully, her arms outstretched to offer him a bowl of honeyed dates. He smiled and walked to her, taking a date, tossing it about in his hand, then popping it into his mouth, keeping his eyes on the blushing girl all the while.

He took the bowl from her hands and set it on a low Turkish table, then walked across the breeze-swept room with her, pushing aside the gauze insect netting to lie beside her upon a bed of plush and colorful pillows.

He swept her veil away and studied her face, still smiling, for she was a gentle creature, yet wondering why he did not feel the joy in her company that he should. The great Mohammed had decreed that a man might take four wives; he had taken three. Sonina was the loveliest of his wives; she had been taught from birth that her place in life was to please a man. Jalahar could find no fault with her.

But the desire that should have risen when he touched her did not; and so he pulled her against him, and stroked the sleek ebony beauty of her hair.

"You go to battle again soon," she whispered.

"Yes," he said simply. Were he speaking to one of his men, he would have explained that he meant to sneak out of the town in a circuitous route that night; he could not attack the Christians head on and find victory, but his spies had informed him that a small party, led by his nemesis Stede, would travel from town to town that night. His attack would hopefully surprise them completely, and if he did not win a great victory, he would at least cause substantial damage to the Christian forces.

"Will it end soon?" she asked him sweetly.

"As Allah wills it," he replied, and she fell silent. Sonina indeed knew her place. In Jalahar's world, his women were fiercely protected; but they were expected to remain quietly in the background, unless summoned forward. Jalahar would never discuss strategy with her; she was merely a woman.

And as a woman, she at last stirred him once more. He made love to her, noting her expertise and commending himself on the choice he had made when he had taken her as his wife. She was a daughter of a Baghdad caliph, a tenth daughter, and so the caliph had not insisted that she be taken as a number-one wife. She had come with a great dowry and far surpassed her sisters in beauty.

But when he had appeased his appetites, Jalahar kissed her lightly and sent her away. He closed his eyes and felt the warm breeze move around him. He did not feel really satisfied. So much was his . . . the magnificence of the palace, scores of servants, thousands of people who worshipped his name. His older two wives had given him sons and daughters; he fought only beneath the great Saladin; he was a man who seemed to have even the desert wind at his command.

He felt as if he held nothing.

It was this war with the Christians, he told himself. This ceaseless, eternal war . . .

But was it? Something was missing in his life, and he knew not what. He possessed all that could be possessed.

Jalahar sighed and rose, stretching his tight banded muscles. He dressed, turning his mind to the strategy of the night.

"Are you weary?"

Elise glanced at Bryan with a full smile beautifully curving her lips. She shook her head.

"Not weary at all, Bryan. I love the ride. Everything is so splendid to see!"

Bryan looked about. There wasn't much to see but desert, he thought dryly. But the sun was setting over the dunes that waved and undulated like a bronze sea, and the sky, shot full of gold and crimson that reflected over the elegant trappings of the horses, was magnificent. He returned his wife's bedazzled smile. "Sometimes, Duchess," he told her, "you can be easily pleased." He urged his horse closer to hers and leaned in the saddle to whisper softly for her ears alone. "Yet since it seems so easy for you to bring pleasure, it seems only fair that it should also come your way."

She blushed slightly and lowered her lashes so that he wouldn't see her continue to smile. "Bryan! Your men surround us."

"My men are quite pleased, too," he told her with a laugh. "They feel that my temper has made a vast improvement since you have arrived."

"Do they?" she inquired innocently.

"Uh-huh. And do you know," he told her with a conspiratorial glitter to his eyes, "I've heard a rumor that they all intend to ask whatever favors they wish of me tomorrow morning. They know that we have been apart a fortnight, but will be together again tonight."

"Bryan!" she exclaimed, glancing about herself, very grateful for the falling dusk, since she knew her flesh was pinkening with every word. But they rode to the rear of the fifty or so men who accompanied them across the desert, and none was watching them. She turned back to her husband with eyes innocently wide.

"Will you grant many favors?"

"Probably all."

She smiled, but then sighed, staring down at the pommel of her saddle. "But you will leave again tomorrow, too," she said softly.

He was silent a moment, then said, "Elise, you know that is the way it must be."

Over two months had passed since that first day when she had seen Bryan again. And in all that time, they had had, at best, ten full nights together. He was always riding out, and as she had promised, she was always remaining behind.

It seemed that when they were just beginning to become close, they were being torn apart.

The words "I love you" always hovered on her lips; they never had a chance to be spoken.

But Elise was happy. Happier than she could ever remember being. She worried about Bryan constantly, but here, she had the faith that he would return to her. Richard launched campaign after campaign; but Bryan was never so far away that he didn't return to her at least once every two weeks.

She refused to believe that God would allow him to die at the hands of the infidels.

And it was better—so much better—than waiting at home! She and Gwyneth visited the bazaars. They bought trinkets and perfumes, sweet-smelling soaps and exotic incense. The music in the streets was haunting; the sight of barefoot waifs scurrying about to earn a coin touched their hearts and made them laugh at the children's antics.

Oh, yes! This was far better than being at home, wondering and waiting.

The Western men of the First and Second Crusades had left their legacies behind them; many of the people were a blend of East and West, beautiful people, swaying easily with each change of government. They followed Mohammed, but served the Christians. Elise, stationed in whatever palace Richard held that Bryan considered safest, was served lavishly and well. She heard fascinating tales of magic and folklore; she learned that snakes could be "charmed"; she was taught the use of wonderful plants that could make hair shine like the sun, and keep the skin fresh and free from blemish.

She had met Philip Augustus of France, the wily French King. And she liked to believe that she had occasionally kept him and Richard from falling into heated verbal battles. The Western kings, it seemed, were always at odds on how the Crusade should proceed. Richard, who often chose to ignore her, had once confided to her that he was disgusted with Philip; the French King was already prepared to give up the quest. Richard's attitude toward Philip was fierce; before Henry's death, they had become the best of friends.

Bryan told her that now he foresaw war with France in England's future. But that was something that meant little to Elise now; Montoui was far away, and England was even farther.

She was here now, and here Elise felt so very alive. Even when Bryan was leading troops, she felt free and alive.

But it was those nights when they could be together that she lived for.

It hadn't been easy; they had become virtual strangers. And the past was marred with so much bitterness and mistrust. Elise had not been able to bring herself to talk about the child again, nor had she asked him about the countless months when they had been apart.

She kept a close watch on her tongue when Gwyneth was about; she still could not say that she trusted her friend, and she would often seethe in silence when she would see the two talking or laughing together. But to be fair, she hadn't seen Bryan be anything other than polite, nor had Gwyneth behaved toward Bryan as if she were anything other than a close friend.

That "closeness" would always bother Elise, but she did accept now that the past could not be changed. To worry about it or harp upon it would only turn her into a shrew.

And, she thought with a wry smile, she was the one in a better position at the moment to drive Bryan a little wild—when she chose. The Crusade was filled with handsome and powerful knights, men fascinated by women from home, gallant—yet respectful—since all were well aware of Bryan Stede's reputation with a sword.

It had been good. Not enough . . . but good. Perhaps she and Bryan were both afraid to delve beneath the surface, and so they accepted what was. He was her husband; she was his wife. For the time being, that simplicity would suffice.

And if he didn't come to her with wild and reckless proclamations of love, he did take her into his confidence. When he was able to come to her, the pattern was often the same. They would love desperately, fearing the barren time in between. But then they would lie awake, naked and barely touching, allowing the night breeze to cool their fevered flesh. Bryan would talk about the war and she would thrill to the fact that she was certain he said to her what he would say to no one else.

"I cannot help but admire them," he would say of the followers of Mohammed. "They strive for learning, cleanliness and purity of the body and soul. Just as we feel that we are God's warriors, they consider themselves soldiers of Allah. I am a Christian knight, and called to defend the principles of Christ. But Saladin and Jalahar . . . they are both honest men. Sincere, honorable. We are miles and miles away from home, and the only resolution that I can see is a truce. I believe that Saladin is willing to offer safety to Christian pilgrims, if we just leave them in peace."

"But Richard won't do it?"

"Richard is still dreaming of taking Jerusalem."

"Will we ever be able to go home . . . together?"

"Aye . . . one day."

And she would talk, too. She told him about Percy's death, about how frightened she had been over Longchamp's threats. He asked about the child Percy, and she tried to tell him brightly what a wonderful little boy he was.

But the things that weren't said were what always gnawed at Elise. If he had married Gwyneth, his son would await him. And he was strangely silent about Percy. Pensive. Did he believe that she had still loved Percy, and that Percy's death had taken her heart? Did he believe she would have been unfaithful . . . ?

Tonight, Elise didn't care what had been. She felt as if God had at last allowed her to purge the past. The horses couldn't move quickly enough for her liking; even when Bryan teased her and her heart soared, she was anxious to reach the palace at Antioch.

Anxious to be alone with him.

She had it all planned out. When they reached their chambers, she would plead sweetly for a bath. It would be filled with the most erotic oils; a scent both deliciously pleasing and sensual would rise with the steam to engulf them.

She would take her time . . .

So much time that they would both be mad with the torment, but she would have to see that he broke first. And she knew Bryan. He would ignore the fact that she was dripping wet, and impatiently plunge into the water to sweep her from it. She would protest his action with mock fury, and indignantly tell him that he must be courteous and gentle with her at all times. He, of course, would ignore her and toss her to the bed, but when he fell down beside her, his curiosity would rise and he would demand to know why. She would make him wait again, pretending not to hear him as she showered his throat with little kisses.

He would be torn between impatience and desire, and that husky grate would be in his voice when he ordered her to speak again. She would meet his eyes with her own wide and innocent, and then, only then, would she grow serious. She would tell him that she knew for certain that she was going to have a child, and she would promise him fervently that this one she would not lose . . .

"What is going on in your mind?" he suddenly asked her, and she turned guiltily about to find him studying her, his indigo eyes narrowed and pensive. "You smile, and then frown, and then smile so secretively again that I feel like dismissing priority and pulling you from that horse into my arms."

"And galloping into the desert forever?" she asked wistfully.

"Perhaps," he answered, feeling his heart seem to constrict in his throat as he watched her. Her hair was free tonight, a swirling cloak about her. Her eyes were so guileless, so startling in their perfect aquamarine color, so lovely against her ivory-and-rose complexion. She was not the girl he had once taken in such a tempest of mutual pride and anger; time had changed her. She was even lovelier now; her face held the beauty of trial and wisdom, she was still a tempest, and yet she had gentled.

He loved her so very much, and yet he was afraid. She was still as elusive as she had ever been; she still wore the sapphire, and he wondered if she didn't hold herself away from him, just as she held the secret of the ring.

He frowned as he reached across the space between them and broodingly took her hand. "I wonder," he murmured, meeting her eyes in a sudden, probing demand, "if you will ever come to trust me. Once, long ago, Duchess, you told me there were things I could take, and things that I could not. You were right. I took you. I made you my wife. I forced you across the English Channel, and I made you the lady of a new household. Yet always I've missed something. Because it cannot be taken. I wonder if you will ever give it to me."

Her heart seemed to pound like thunder within her chest, and she almost cried out with the beauty, and the fear. *Give!* she thought. *I would give you anything in the world that I could . . .*

She couldn't speak, and so she moistened her lips in an attempt to ease their dryness and make them move.

He smiled at her, crookedly, tenderly. "At least, my wife, I don't believe you're swearing vengeance against me anymore."

"No . . ." she managed to say softly. And then her lips curled into a smile, and her eyes met his brilliantly. "Bryan . . . I have looked forward so to tonight. I have many things to say to you."

His brows lifted in surprise. "Secrets?" he teased.

"Secrets . . ." she replied quietly. "One which I think will mean more to you than any other."

His features seemed to tighten suddenly; the indigo of his eyes was so dark she thought she would lose herself in it. His jaw became hardened and square, and she would have thought that he was angry were it not that he spoke to her so gently.

"Elise . . . Elise . . ."

His destrier was so close that their thighs clashed. She felt the tension in him, in his voice, and she started to shiver, wishing desperately that she could catapult herself into his arms. Never had God created a finer knight, a more magnificent man, and at that moment, she felt he was hers, truly hers, completely hers . . .

"Tell me!" he commanded her, and there was fire in the indigo of his eyes, yearning to his command.

Tell me! she wanted to cry out. *Tell me that you love me, and only me, even if it is a lie.*

But if he didn't, it wouldn't matter. She wanted to tell him about their child; she wanted to lay everything at his feet. The ring . . . the ring that had brought them together . . . she wanted to explain, to make him understand how frightened she had been of others knowing she was the king's bastard.

The picture of her beautiful night came to view: the steaming bath; the wonder of being in his arms; stripping away arms and armor; and, at last, touching.

"When we reach Antioch—" she began to whisper, but her words were broken, shattered, by a long, agonized scream from the front of the ranks.

"What the—"

"Jalahar!" someone screamed. "An ambush!"

Bryan nudged his horse forward. "Stay back!" he thundered to Elise. The destrier galloped forward, spewing desert sand. Elise swallowed in sudden terror of the night as she heard Bryan shouting orders. "Close ranks! Draw your swords! Circle protection! Don't panic! They haven't come in force!"

Perhaps they hadn't come in force, but the shrill chant of the Moslems rose as darkness seemed abruptly to embrace them. Horses were rearing, prancing . . . snorting and screaming. Arrows were flying. And the Moslems were upon them.

Bryan appeared beside her again with Gwyneth, Wat, and Mordred, who had been riding at the front. "Fall back to the dune!" he ordered her. "Hide! No matter what happens, don't come forward! Go!"

Elise stared at him, stunned. "I carry a knife—" she began, but he had slapped her horse sharply on the rump, and it jumped forward.

"Hide!" Bryan yelled to her. "By God, I'm begging you, go!"

She did. But as her horse raced forward, she turned back. The Moslems and the knights were engaged in hand-to-hand combat. Screams ripped through the air. Swords flew, glimmering, ravishing. Elise saw a mélange of clashing men and beasts, blood and death.

"The dune!" Gwyneth called to her. "Elise! Get down!"

Mordred was pulling at her. She was too stunned, too horrified, too frightened for Bryan to dismount from her horse. She kept straining her eyes through the darkness.

She saw Bryan. He was still on his horse, raising his sword, plunging it down. Again . . . again. He fought one man, and the next was upon him.

"Elise!"

The battle, the terror in her heart, had mesmerized her. She didn't hear the pounding behind her until it was too late. Nor had she realized that in the trousers designed for them by Eleanor, she might well appear to be a man in the darkness.

She was unaware of anything except for the battle scene before her until she was suddenly attacked by a flying catapult, a man of gripping strength whose impetus dragged her from the horse and sent her spiraling to the ground.

Desperately she grabbed for her knife and raised it. A futile action. The Moslem was above her, his sword raised high, ready to strike.

But he didn't strike.

He stared at her.

Jalahar had been stunned to find his opponent a woman. In the darkness, he hadn't realized . . .

How could he have been so blinded? He had never seen such a woman. Never had he seen hair that was pure gold, or eyes that matched the beauty of the Aegean Sea. Her flesh was like moonlight, silken, pale.

And even though she might have been about to die, she stared at him defiantly, her knife raised, hate and pride illuminating that rare color of her eyes. Her breasts rose and fell hard as she gasped for breath and met his eyes without a flinch.

Jalahar rose abruptly, his movement lithe and smooth. He kept his eyes upon her as he moved for his horse.

Elise saw Mordred about to move from the dune. "No!" she cried, but her guard rushed forward for the Moslem. The strangely handsome, fine-boned Arab swung about, his sword already swinging. Elise screamed again as she saw Mordred fall, his shoulder spurting blood. She rushed to Mordred, but the Moslem man called her attention to him, speaking in a clear, barely accented French.

"He would be dead had I so desired."

She found herself staring at him again, at the deep, mahogany eyes that seemed both to pierce through her and caress her.

Then he bowed, spun around with his white robes flowing in the breeze, and vaulted onto his horse. Elise wrenched her eyes from him to look to Mordred's shoulder. The blood continued to flow, but Mordred opened his eyes and gave her a weak smile. " 'Tis not mortal . . ."

Gwyneth came quickly to Elise's side, ripping apart her tunic to supply Mordred with a bandage. She spoke tensely to Elise. "We must get out of here. They know that we are here now. And that man . . . will be back for you, Elise."

"What?" Elise demanded, startled.

"It was Jalahar," Mordred murmured. "He will come back."

"Come back! You behave as if they will not be fought off! They will not be able to come back—"

Elise stopped speaking as she saw Gwyneth's eyes sorrowfully upon her. She turned back to stare at the ensuing battle. Thank God! Bryan was still horsed! But there were Moslems everywhere.

"Elise!" Gwyneth's scream awakened her to nearby danger once again. One of the white-clad desert warriors was stalking them, coming over the dune—smiling. His teeth were shockingly white against his swarthy complexion. He laughed, let out a cry, and vaulted down.

Elise had no chance to think. She lifted her dagger; it was too late for the Arab to stop his vault. He tumbled onto the knife, screaming his rage. Together they rolled across the sand. Elise experienced a minute of sinking terror, but relief flooded through her as she realized he had little strength left. If she just kept fighting, he would weaken . . . possibly die.

She fought him furiously, kicking, biting, punching wildly. His fist connected with her jaw, and she staggered, but desperation kept her going. She could hear Gwyneth screaming, and Mordred cursing out his helplessness.

But it was all right. The Arab's arms lost their hold . . . she was almost free.

Freedom came at a high price. Just as she entangled herself, Elise looked up, across the dunes. Bryan was riding furiously toward her. He saw nothing in his way.

And then she began to scream in earnest, for the wickedly shining blade of a Damascene sword was whipping through the night. Bryan at last saw it and tried to veer; he was too late. The blade caught his side, and he toppled from his loyal destrier, spinning across the sand with the momentum.

"Dear sweet Jesus! We are lost!" Gwyneth wailed.

Elise was on her feet, racing across the dune. Bryan's men seemed far away, cut off by the rise of another dune. But just as she had to reach Bryan, she had to rally them.

Tears streamed down her cheeks as she ran to his side, but she screamed out orders. "Center and regroup! Rally, Christian warriors! All is not . . . lost!"

She did not see that they formed ranks again, nor would she ever know that her words had saved them from total defeat, that her golden-haired form, racing gallantly across the sand, gave them the spark of valor that they needed. She reached Bryan's side and fell down beside him, grunting and crying as she tried to twist about his muscle-laden form. His eyes were closed to her; his face, so strong of contour, was ashen. Even the firm mouth, which was harsh in anger and tender in love, had gone white. Elise laid her head against his chest; he breathed! She found his pulse . . . it beat . . . but so weakly! Madly, she began tearing at her tunic and struggled with his dented armor, to find the wound and staunch the flow of blood. At last she found it: a gash the length of her foot. And the blood! So much blood! She pressed at it furiously, ripped more material with which to bind, and prayed fervently that she was managing to stop the flow.

She stopped abruptly in her efforts, stunned, when she saw that the tip of a long blade had been set upon Bryan's throat. With horror she stared up—into the dark, hard, and haunting eyes of the Moslem who had wrested her from her horse.

"No!" she gasped, and only then did she realize that the night had gone silent. Not even the breeze whispered then. She looked around her and saw that the Christians and Moslems were at a standstill: the Moslems separating her and Bryan and the others behind the dune from the rallied knights. The tension was alive and vital, holding them all in a plateau as all nervously awaited the next movement.

The Moslem suddenly knelt down beside her. He touched the pulse at Bryan's throat. Then he looked curiously at Elise. "His wound is bad, but he may live. Stede . . . my very worthy enemy. A man who cannot be felled by ten of my best swordsmen, yet he falls like a fly for a woman."

Pain and panic welled in Elise's throat.

"You will not . . . kill him . . ." she pleaded. "You are Jalahar—a leader, not a murderer."

He rose. "Yes, I am Jalahar. And, no, I would not like to slay such a fierce and noble fighter when he lies upon his back. But as you see . . ."—his sweeping arm encompassed the Christian and Moslem armies who waited, deadlocked— ". . . we have reached an impasse. As for me . . . I am intrigued by the woman with the golden locks for whom this man of steel is so willing to die. You will rise, and you will come with me—ordering your troops not to hamper our escape. Then, golden woman, he will be allowed to live. If he is cared for . . . he will live."

Elise stared at Jalahar with dismay rising in a wave of inner agony that was crippling. She gripped her stomach, fighting her tears as she hovered over Bryan. She could not leave him! She could not do as this Arab was demanding!

"Please!" she murmured, turning tear-filled eyes to Jalahar once again. His face remained impassive; he flicked his sword so that she was reminded of its razor's edge.

The tears ran freely down her cheeks as she buried her face against Bryan's chest, holding his unconscious form with all the love she had always been afraid to offer.

"I am waiting," Jalahar reminded her.

She bit her lip, feeling the pounding of her husband's heart beneath her. At last she raised her head and tenderly kissed his dirt-streaked face. He needed care. Every moment that she tarried cost him more. She loved him so much. It would be like dying to leave him; if she did not, he would surely perish.

Elise forced her tears to stop. She wiped her cheeks with cold defiance as she faced Jalahar again.

"One moment. I would leave him in the care of another."

Yes . . . she thought, *I will leave him in the care of another. Gwyneth. It is Gwyneth's face he shall see when he awakens; it is Gwyneth who will nurse him, care for him . . . Gwyneth, while she . . .*

Again she felt as if she would double over with the pain that razed her insides. But she had to do it . . . she had to. Or he would die.

At the dune she called to Gwyneth. The terrified Gwyneth showed her own courage as she gazed at Elise, then crawled from the dune to meet her, her eyes raking nervously over the Moslems as she approached Elise.

"Bryan . . . lives," Elise said haltingly. "But he will not if he does not reach the best of Richard's physicians . . . quickly. He is losing blood so quickly. It must stay staunched, the wound must remain bound . . ."

Her words started to break and falter. Gwyneth gazed from Elise to the still and silent Jalahar. "Elise . . ." she whispered blankly, and then the tears started to fall from her eyes. She embraced Elise, and both women were crying.

Elise tore from her, knowing that minutes—and Bryan's blood—were draining away in the desert sand. "Go to him!" Elise whispered desperately, and, half blinded by the tears that obstinately remained in her eyes, she began walking toward Jalahar. She was tempted to fall to Bryan's side again. One last kiss upon lips that were ashen and cold . . . but Jalahar caught her arm. Not cruelly; firmly. He directed her toward one of his men. She found herself lifted up on a horse.

"Speak to your men," Jalahar told her quietly.

Elise swallowed, then raised her voice high. "Allow the Moslems to ride!" she shouted. "Else all will be a slaughter. I command you to continue on to the king!"

She heard the Moslems mounting their horses around her. Someone said something in that strange tongue; her horse was whipped; it reared up, then broke into a gallop. Instinct forced her to clutch the pommel, for all thought and feeling had gone dead.

She would only remember forever that wild ride across the sand with a distant vagueness; Jalahar did not stop until they had traveled a great distance, through all of which Elise had felt only as if she were entering a great gaping black pit of hell.

When they did stop, he came to her side. The moon now granted a slender light, enough to see silhouettes against the sand and sky.

"There—they continue to the king."

Elise stared out across the desert. It was true. The knights were obeying her command; they trod slowly toward the northeast. The ever-present tears clouded Elise's eyes; she could see that the pace was slow because two husky men carried the makeshift litter they had made for Bryan Stede.

"You love him very much?" Jalahar asked her curiously.

"Yes."

"You will forget him."

Life and spirit returned to her, and she spun about to spit at him. "Never! Nothing that you do will ever cause me to forget him. I am his wife, Jalahar . . . bound to him by God, bound to him by love. You will never change that."

He smiled at her, flashing white teeth, somehow touching her with eyes that seemed strangely sad. Without anger, he wiped his cheek of her spittle.

"But you will forget him. I can be gentle, and I can be patient. From the moment I saw you, golden one, my heart clouded my mind. You will bear me many children, children of my strength, of your beauty and pride. And when you hold them, you will learn to forget the valiant Stede."

Elise started to laugh. "You will have to be very patient, Jalahar. Very patient. I already carry a child. *Stede's child.*"

His smile didn't falter. "I have already told you that I am patient. I can wait."

"I will kill you if you try to touch me. If not, I shall kill myself."

It was Jalahar's turn to laugh. "You will not kill me, Stede's woman. Nor do I believe that you will care to take your own life. I will force nothing from you . . . until you are ready to be forced. And you needn't fear for your child. I am not a murderer of children."

Elise continued to stare at him, fighting for composure. Dismay and confusion swept through her; despair and desolation gripped her.

She wanted to drop to the sand and cry until she created a pool of water that could drown her and ease the pain in her heart. She wanted to die . . . but she didn't want to die. Because Bryan's child was all that was left to her, and she had to believe that Jalahar would never hurt her child.

"Come . . ." he told her, spurring his horse around. He reached for her reins; she was too dispirited to care.

"What do they call you?" he asked her.

"Elise," she answered tonelessly.

He reached out and touched a tendril of her streaming hair, as fascinated as if he held true gold.

"Don't be afraid, Elise," he said softly, his French smooth and strangely soothing. "I will not hurt you. More likely," he added ruefully, "I will revere you."

They continued plodding along the rolling sands. At last they reached the high white walls outside a towering and exotic palace.

"Muzhair," he told her.

A man shouted for entry. Massive, heavy gates began to open, and they entered a courtyard that was prepared for warfare and siege with catapults, crossbows, and rams. Elise swallowed back the tears she had finally staunched as the heavy gates closed behind her.

Jalahar pointed to a window high in a tower.

"Your chambers," he told her softly.

She said nothing, and there was nothing but silent misery in her beautiful eyes when they met his.

"I will leave you at peace," he promised her. "Until . . . your child is born."

Still she made no reply. "You are my hostage!" he snapped at her suddenly. "My prisoner, my possession. I offer you the finest care, the finest quarters. You say nothing."

She smiled at last. "If you mean that you will leave me at peace, then I am grateful. But if you seek to give me something, give me my freedom. I love my husband. I will never be able to give to any man, for I have given my heart and soul to him. He would understand that, Jalahar. He had learned that there are things that cannot be taken, only received—when given."

Jalahar laughed. "That may be, Elise. That may be. But perhaps I will content myself with what I can take. And time . . . time, lady, changes many things. Perhaps you will forget his face." Jalahar sobered. "And perhaps . . . he will die. What then, Elise?"

She didn't answer; the tears had sprung to her eyes again.

Jalahar clapped his hands; two silk-clad girls appeared, and he muttered something to them in the language that seemed so foreign and strange to her ears.

Jalahar dismounted from his horse and lifted her from hers. "Welcome to Muzhair, Elise." He prodded her toward the girls. "Sleep well. Tonight . . . you may do so at peace."

She made no effort to speak or fight as the girls led her to a high-arched entrance. Jalahar called something out, and Elise turned listlessly back to him.

"I do not believe that Stede will die. I will see that you hear how he fares."

"Thank you," she murmured.

It was ridiculous to thank a man who had abducted her.

But Bryan lived . . .

In the confusion, in the fear, in the despair, she had to cling to that fact. She had done the only thing that she could.

Bryan still lived . . .

XXV

"One . . . two . . . three . . . four!"

Elise knotted the last of her sheets together and stared out to the inner courtyard below her balcony. For a week she had watched the courtyard each night; she had learned that it was empty near the moon's highest peak. She assumed that the Moslems were all at prayer.

And tonight . . . she was ready.

She glanced over the railing one more time and stiffened her shoulders as she convinced herself that no one was about. If she could just get out of the chamber . . . she could hide in one of the supply carts constantly leaving with men and arms.

The space between her window and the ground made her dizzy, and she paused, shaking, afraid that she would lose her nerve. She had to try to escape, or else she would go mad. Elise closed her eyes tightly, then opened them. With renewed vigor, she tied the end of her "rope" to the foot of an iron planter and tossed the remaining length over the balcony. She held her breath for several seconds, but no one came; she couldn't hear a sound in the night.

Steadying herself one last time, Elise carefully gathered up the skirt of her gown—a silk creation given to her by one of Jalahar's women—and balanced her weight over the railing. She held tight to the sheet, praying that the wrought-iron planter was heavy enough to hold her weight. She swayed slightly, then whispered a little prayer of thanksgiving as her sheet-rope held tight. Twining her ankles around the slippery silk, she carefully

began to climb her way down. Euphoria lit her eyes as her slippered feet touched the courtyard. She had done it! All she had
to do was meld against the darkened building, work her way
around to the front, and crawl into a cart . . .

"It is a nice evening for fresh air, yes?"

Elise started violently as she heard Jalahar's voice behind her.
She spun around, ready to fight him, ready to run, but he just
stared at her with his rueful smile and knowing dark eyes.

"Do not run, Elise," he told her softly, "or I shall be forced
to call others to stop you." He lifted his hands fatalistically.
"You will fight . . . you will hurt yourself—and possibly your
child."

Elise exhaled, her shoulders slumping in defeat. She had seen
Jalahar only once since he had brought her here, on her third
morning in the palace. She had flown into a rage and attacked
him, and discovered that his slimness was deceptive. He had
not fought her in return; he had subtly twisted her arm so that
any further movement on her part brought intense pain. Then
he had politely informed her that he would not interrupt her
solitude again until she was more receptive to his presence.

He extended a hand toward her. "Shall we walk back together?"

Elise walked on by him. His hand dropped to his side, but
he followed her, and she could sense him clearly. His scent
was that of sandalwood and musk, his footsteps were silent,
yet he emanated an unnerving warmth. He always spoke to
her quietly, almost sadly. She hated him for keeping her prisoner, but she had discovered that she couldn't hate him completely as a man.

A flight of narrow stairs led to her tower chamber. Elise
climbed them silently, then waited rigidly for him to unbolt the
lock. When the door drifted open, she strode into the chamber
and back out to the balcony. Jalahar followed her. She didn't
look at him, but she knew that he watched her as he sighed and
pulled up her concoction of sheets.

"I do not care to divest you of covering; the nights are sometimes very cool. Rest assured that there will be a man beneath the balcony day and night."

Elise refused to give him an answer, and a smile twitched at the corner of his lips.

"Elise . . . that was a dangerous and foolish attempt at escape—to yourself, and to your child. I give you time because I believe you will come to me, and because of your child. But if you do not care enough to look to the welfare of your belly, I shall begin to wonder why I must. And perhaps I will decide that the only way to have you welcome my attentions is to see that you learn to enjoy them."

She stared at him and spoke at last, well aware that his words were a warning, and sensing that he would not threaten idly. "I will not attempt to leave by the balcony again," she told him stiffly.

Jalahar smiled, and his dark eyes glistened with amusement. "Were you a man, I would ask for your word of honor. Knowing your determination, I don't believe there is any way that I should believe you. I will just say that our future rests in your hands."

She started, swallowing, when he began to walk toward her. He laughed when she flattened herself to the balcony, and stopped walking. But he extended his hand and his eyes followed his fingers as they lit gently upon her hair, brushing disheveled strands from her temple. "Your midnight excursions are rough on your coiffure, Elise. Come, and I will brush it for you."

"I can brush it myself."

"But you would not deny me such a little pleasure, especially not . . . when I have news of your husband."

"Bryan!" she cried out, her telltale emotion flaring brilliantly in her eyes. "Tell me. Does he live? Does his wound heal? What do you know? What was your source?"

Jalahar bowed slightly, indicating that she should move in. Elise hesitated only a moment, then returned to her room from the balcony.

She hated her chamber, but not that she had been given unpleasant rooms to occupy. To the contrary, she was imprisoned in luxury. Her room was vast; the east side was taken up by endless cushions of down, silk-covered and tented in sheerest gauze. The floors were warmed by plush rugs, the windows were covered with floating draperies in blue and green pastels. She had a delicately carved dressing table, brushes and combs of hammered silver, and a carved bath so deep she could almost swim in it. She had been supplied with a number of precious books, painfully, expertly copied by scholars, French translations of works by the famous Greek and Roman poets. Nothing that she could need or want was denied her—except her freedom.

And that was why she hated the chamber so. It was, no matter how luxurious, a prison.

"Sit!" Jalahar commanded her, indicating the stool before her dressing chamber. Nervously she did so, pleading with her eyes as they met his in the finely crafted, hammered-metal mirror. He met her eyes briefly, but he didn't speak as he picked up her brush and haphazardly plucked the pins from the bulk of her hair. It fell about her in a radiant splendor, and Jalahar picked up the tendrils with fascination, watching the gold and copper shimmer in the candlelight as he moved the brush in soothing strokes.

"Jalahar!"

She didn't want to beg him for information, but the threat of a sob was in her voice.

"He holds his own, so I have heard."

"He lives!"

"Yes, but . . ."

"But what?" Elise spun about in the chair, raising her eyes to his with torment and anxiety.

"They say he fights a fever. That is the case so often, you know. . . . It is not the wound that kills the man, but the fever."

Elise lowered her eyes, aware that they were filling with tears.

"He is a strong man," Jalahar told her. "He has the English King's best physicians at his side."

"They shall probably kill him if the fever doesn't!" Elise cried.

Jalahar was quiet for a moment, then murmured, "I will ask that Saladin send a physician from the East, an Egyptian man, one well acquainted with the desert fever."

Later she would find it absurd that the man who had abducted her from her husband was willing to do his best to see to her husband's life and health; at that moment, all that she could think about was Bryan, and it did not matter in the least that she discussed him with Jalahar—and that both men were natural enemies.

"An Egyptian?" she demanded.

"He is the best I know," Jalahar said softly.

"But will Richard accept him? Will he allow him to see Bryan?"

"Even your king respects the honesty of Saladin. Your king is stubborn, with misguided intentions, but he is not a fool. I will see that this man is sent to him."

Tears were blurring her eyes. She stared at her hands. "Will you . . . keep me informed?"

"Yes . . . if you will invite me in, of course."

"Invite you . . ."

He smiled at her through the mirror. "This is your domain, Elise."

She stared at his dark, dark eyes, so expressive against the burned bronze of his strangely refined features. His fingers, long and slender, rested against the gold of her hair. She shivered slightly, wishing he were fat and filthy and ugly. He was not. Even clad in his loose-fitting desert robes, he gave the impression of wired strength and agility. He was soft-spoken and gentle, a strange man indeed.

"This is not my domain. It is a pleasantly appointed . . . prison. You are my warder. Prisoners do not invite their warders anywhere."

"You must think of yourself as a guest. A good host does not enter upon a guest without an invitation."

"You entered freely enough tonight."

"Ah . . . but the circumstances were extenuating, wouldn't you say? I found I needed to be of service as an escort."

Elise stared at the dresser and spoke in a whisper. "You know that I would invite you anywhere . . . to learn about Bryan."

"Then when I have news, I will come back to you."

It was to be another week before she saw him again. She tried to read, tried to find some method to maintain her patience, praying to stay sane. As often as not, though, she paced the chamber.

Two women served her, both Arabs, both handsomely dressed and decked out in jewels. Elise found their costume curious for servants, until she discovered through the elder's smattering of French that they were both wives of Jalahar. She was astounded that he would send his wives to care for another woman whom he had taken in battle, but neither appeared to be offended by the action.

"By the laws of Allah, a man takes four wives." Satima, small and a little stout, told her.

"And Jalahar has . . . ?"

"Three. When the time is right . . . he will make you a wife."

"But I have a husband!"

"Not to the laws of Islam."

The Arab women were disapproving of her lack of enthusiasm; as a captive, she should have been flattered to have the great Jalahar determined to make her a wife when she should have been no better than a concubine.

Elise fell into days of deep depression. Jalahar brought her no information; she worried endlessly about Bryan. It was true that fevers brought down the strongest men, and it seemed so long already. . . . How long could even his toned and sinewed strength hold out against a fever that ravaged relentlessly?

And if he lived . . .

Well, she had left him to Gwyneth's care.

She would roll into her vast bed of cushions and silks and cry. Gwyneth would at last have Bryan; she would be the fourth wife of a desert lord, imprisoned forever in chambers of silk.

There were long, long days and nights for her to think and ponder. She remembered Firth Manor and the day Percy had died; he had died trying to warn her . . . about Gwyneth. And now, she had actually given the woman her blessing to take her husband . . .

If he lived.

He had to live. It was better to think of him with Gwyneth than it was to imagine those indigo eyes closed forever, his heart no longer pulsing with life and vitality.

For two days she didn't eat; Satima finally cajoled her into doing so, reminding her that she would harm her child. Even then it was difficult to care; she had not felt the life within her yet, and it seemed so distant.

One morning, as she stood staring blindly up at the gauze netting over her bed, she heard the door creak open. She thought little of it: Satima or Marin bringing her a tray of breakfast fruit and fresh bread. "Just set the tray down," she murmured distantly.

"Ah . . . no, I will sit with you while you eat! You must eat, you know."

It was a different voice. Elise turned around to see another woman, very petite, fragile, and lovely. Her eyes were dark and enormous, her features were sweetly heart-shaped. She stared at Elise with a smile that made her uneasy.

"Who are you?" Elise asked her.

"Sonina. Come, yes? I have selected the sweetest dates for you . . . bread fresh from the oven. Please? You must eat," Sonina cajoled.

Elise didn't feel at all well. She rolled from the tangle of the cushions and stood, offering Sonina a distracted smile as she walked out to the balcony. What was happening? Why hadn't Jalahar come to tell her about Bryan? He couldn't be—

"You die!"

She spun about as the words were screamed, stunned to see the fragile beauty flying at her like an arrow, her hand raised high in the air, her fingers gripped hard around a jewel-encrusted dagger.

Elise screamed instinctively, ducking and bolting about in time to save herself from a blow. She whirled about again, ready to fight. When Sonina came at her again, she struck the girl's arm hard, forcing the dagger to slide across the floor. When Sonina began to pound on her with fury, she doubled up and caught the Arab woman's wrist, amazed by her own strength.

"Stop it!" she screamed to the panting Sonina, who still tried to claw at her face.

"You should have eaten the dates!" Sonina hissed back.

A ripple of fear slid along Elise's spine. "They were poisoned, weren't they?"

"Yes! Yes! And I will kill you yet!"

"Why?"

"Jalahar! I will not allow you to replace me."

"I have no desire in the world to replace you—and Jalahar already has two other wives!"

"Them!" Sonina twisted her lips into a snarl of scorn. "They are but two old crows! I am the one he comes to! The others care for his children—and his whores."

Elise reddened despite herself. "I'm not his whore, Sonina, nor do I wish to be his wife. I have a husband. If you wish to get rid of me, help me! Help me leave—"

The door burst open. Satima swept in, accompanied by a husky guard. Satima pushed past Elise and grasped Sonina by the hair, railing furiously at her in Arabic. Sonina shouted back, but the guard grasped her about the waist and hauled her, kicking, from the room.

"She will not disturb you again," Satima said.

"Don't eat the dates," Elise said dryly.

Satima glanced at the tray of food, needing no further explanation. "Sonina is in a pique. Jalahar returns tonight, and his message requested that you see him after he has bathed and dined."

Elise lowered her eyes.

"Yes, I will see him," she said.

Jalahar came to her chamber late. She had been pacing the room for hours, and when the door opened, she ran to him.

"Please tell me, have you heard anything?"

Jalahar did not keep her waiting. He watched her as he spoke, and she wondered what he found so intriguing about her face.

"The Egyptian treats Stede. He still fights the fever, but the fever lessens, so we hear. He has come to consciousness once or twice, and the Egyptian says that he will live."

Elise was shaking so badly with relief that she sank to the carpet, as her legs were too weak to hold her. She pressed her palms to her cheeks, as if to hold onto consciousness herself.

Jalahar reached down to her, lifting her up again. "I have brought you good tidings. But now, you are my hostess. You will entertain me."

Panic must have filled her eyes, for he laughed. "I take nothing that you do not give, remember?" He clapped his hands and the door opened. Two servants brought in a low, curious table, and began to set carved pieces upon it. Elise glanced to Jalahar.

"Chess," he told her, walking to the table and picking up one of the pieces to enjoy its beautiful workmanship with the sensitivity of his hands. "Most unusual workmanship. It was a gift to my father from the then King of Jerusalem. A Christian king. Do you play?"

Elise nodded and sat on a cushion. "You will move first," Jalahar told her, and she did so.

Pawns were taken; knights and bishops fell. "You play well," Jalahar told her.

"I will win," she told him.

He smiled. "That is unlikely. For I will play you until I do win."

The game continued. Then he said, "I hear that you had an interesting morning."

Elise shrugged coolly. "Your wife tried to poison me. Then she attempted to stab me."

"She will be punished."

"Why? She doesn't want me here any more than I wish to be here."

"A wife does not go against her husband's will."

"Then you would not want me for a wife, Jalahar; I believe in my own will."

His hand paused upon a game piece and he gazed at her, a twinkle glittering in the depths of his eyes, his lip curving just slightly to a smile.

"I do not remember suggesting that you should be my wife," he said politely.

She didn't know why she flushed. "It is Sonina's fear," she told him.

He shrugged. "You will not worry about Sonina."

"I do not wish you to punish her," Elise said. She moved a piece and looked at him again. "I believe you will find that you have no move left. The game is mine."

Jalahar stood and bowed slightly to her. "This game I concede. We will play again a week from now."

Elise learned to survive through the long days by concentrating on two thoughts. Eleanor, Queen Eleanor, who had given her so much in care and affection, had been a prisoner for sixteen years. She had been treated harshly at times, denied the simplest of pleasures. She had emerged as strong and proud as ever.

She had learned how to wait . . .

The thought of sixteen years almost sent Elise spiraling into despair again; her second thought kept her from doing so.

She had to remain healthy, bright, alert. All that she might ever have of the man she had come to love with every depth of her being was their child. For the babe, she would endure.

Jalahar came every week. She learned that Sonina had been sent back to her father. Elise was indignant, but Jalahar was firm.

"My household is a peaceful one. A woman who would stab or poison another is not one I wish to have in my bed. I fight my battles on the field, against men."

Elise faltered at her game, moving her queen haphazardly as she retorted to him.

"Then you do not want me here, Jalahar, for I would readily kill you for my freedom if I had the chance."

"Would you?"

With the swift move of a pawn, he took her queen, and left her in checkmate. Elise barely noted the game, but she gasped when Jalahar suddenly sent the table and the pieces crashing across the floor. He stood, jerking her from the cushion on which she sat until she pressed against his chest, staring into his eyes.

"I will give you my dagger," he told her, pulling a lethal blade from his belt and pressing it into her hand. "Take it!" He ripped open his robe, exposing the flesh and muscle of his chest.

Elise, stunned by his action, began to back away from him, the pearl-handled dagger clutched tightly in her palm. He kept advancing on her, daring her with his dark eyes flashing.

"Stop, Jalahar!" she cried. "I *will* stab you!"

"Will you?"

He reached out and grabbed her hand, bringing the blade of the dagger against his flesh. He exerted a pressure that forced her hand down, drawing blood in a thin, crimson line.

"Stop!" Elise screamed again, wrenching her hand from him. Hysterical tears rose to her eyes, and she stumbled away from him once more, this time tripping upon the silk cushions and pillows of her bed. She fell upon them, and her eyes widened in panic as he smiled, and lowered himself beside her, resting on an elbow as he watched her.

Elise rolled from him and drew herself against the wall, facing him, meeting his eyes.

"You haven't the instinct for murder," he told her softly. He rolled with a sudden, lithe movement and kneeled before her couch. His knuckles grazed her cheek. "Would it be so very hard to love me?" he asked her. His lips touched hers; she wanted to twist from them but could not, as she was pinned to the wall. But the touch was not cruel, or forceful. His mouth was warm and tasted of mint, gently persuasive upon hers. The kiss was light, scarcely more than a whisper against her lips. And then he was staring at her once more.

Elise trembled, torn and ravaged by the sweep of her emotions. She parted her lips to speak, then remembered that she still gripped his dagger in her hands.

She brought it between her own breasts.

"Perhaps I cannot take your life," she told him, "but I can take my own."

A flash of anger darkened his eyes. He slapped the dagger from her grasp with a blow so stunning she cried out as she watched it spin across the floor.

"Am I so abhorrent to you that you would really kill yourself and your child?" he demanded in a cold fury.

Tears filled her eyes. "No," she whispered to him. "You are not abhorrent to me. But I . . . I love my husband. Can't you understand that?"

He reached out for her and she flinched, not because she feared that he would harm her; she feared his gentleness. "I am not going to harm you, golden girl," he told her softly. "Just hold you. Don't fight me."

He pulled her down to the pillows beside him and held her. She felt the soothing caress of his long fingers across her cheek, through her hair. Elise closed her eyes, and her shivering gradually subsided. His words were true; all he did was hold her.

And as she lay, she smiled bitterly through tears of aching remorse. Once, she would have killed to escape . . . from Bryan. She would have gladly seen him strung and swinging by a rope. Once . . . but she had been a different woman then, or perhaps it was because she had only been a girl until she had come to know him, and to understand the depths of ecstasy and despair that loving could bring. Jalahar . . . was so very different from Bryan. Slim, dark, a Moslem, a desert prince. Born to different ways, a different God.

But she had learned from Bryan that there were many ways to look at a man, and that Jalahar possessed qualities that she could not help but respect. And Bryan had told her once . . . that first night . . . so long ago, another world now, that no meeting of the flesh was worth dying for. She had no desire to die; Jalahar had not forced her to that test.

And, no, she did not abhor him. She would fight him; she would have to fight him if he ever forced her. But she was frightened. Very frightened. Bryan had given her so much of love; he had opened the uncharted path to her senses and her heart, and she was very afraid that loneliness and her fear would leave her vulnerable to the very tenderness Jalahar displayed.

He spoke then, moving his hand with idle fascination over her hair, as if he had read her mind. "Would it be so very hard to love me . . . as you love Stede?"

"I cannot say," she told him, "because I do love him."

Jalahar was silent for several minutes. He leaned back, resting his head upon an elbow as he stared into the misted gauze above them.

"What if he were to die?"

"You promised me that he would not!" Elise cried.

"No man can give that promise. But it is not his injury and fever of which I speak." He looked at her. "He will come after me, you know. It will take time; he will need to regain his strength—unless he comes in a wild temper, in which case he will definitely die. We will meet on the field. One of us must kill the other."

"Why?" Her eyes were as brilliant and liquid as the sea as she stared at him. "If you care for me, Jalahar, let me go."

"I cannot," he told her simply.

He rose, straightening his robes, then bowing to her with a sad and rueful smile twisting his lips.

"I must leave, or else chance breaking my vow. I will see you soon."

He came each Thursday; there were no more outbursts of violence between them; most frequently they played chess. Sometimes he asked that she read to him, and sometimes he would stumble through her attempts to teach him English. Elise began to pick up a few words of Arabic, and when he asked to brush her hair, she no longer attempted to refuse him. It seemed such a small thing, and she would always see his dark and brooding eyes upon her and know that he practiced a great restraint. Sometimes she would feel herself shiver at his touch, and she wondered what would happen if the day came when he lost patience.

The week when she knew that the Christian world would be celebrating Christmas was exceptionally hard for her. She had grown accustomed to the endless days passing so tediously that she looked forward to Jalahar's visits with delight. She had shaken herself from despondency, determined to maintain her health and give birth to a strong, lively child. Jalahar talked to her too little of Bryan, but he had told her that the fever had at last broken, and that Bryan lived. He did not talk to her about the Christian-Moslem war; and, most often, she was afraid to ask. She prayed that Bryan would not ride when he was weak . . . easy prey for death.

And she wondered frequently what he was doing. Was Gwyneth at his side? Did she comfort him? Knowing how Jalahar's touch stirred her, she could not hate Bryan if he accepted whatever comfort Gwyneth could offer. Gwyneth should have been his wife. He had known her long before he had known Elise. No, she could not hate him if he reached for comfort. She could only endure the pain of wondering.

Jalahar himself seemed quiet and somber when he came to her two days before Christmas. He had ordered wine for her—which the Moslems did not drink—as a concession to her Christianity. The chess board was set up, but neither of them gave much attention to the pieces.

Jalahar idly moved a castle, keeping his eyes upon the board. "The Egyptian has returned to service at Saladin's side," he told her. He raised his eyes. "And Stede was seen in the courtyard of the palace at Acre, working with his sword."

Her fingers were shaking so badly that she could not pick up her chess piece. She clenched her hands into fists in her lap and stared at them. "He has completely recovered, then?"

"So it appears. My informant tells me that he is pale and gaunt, but that he walks straight and tall."

Jalahar stood and began idly pacing the floor, picking up a curio here and there. Elise felt him behind her. His fingers touched lightly upon the top of her head.

"There is much controversy over you, golden girl. The English King sends messages constantly to my uncle, Saladin. He demands that Saladin return you to him."

"And what . . ."—Elise moistened her lips—" . . . what does Saladin say to our king?"

She felt his shrug. "Saladin has asked that I give you back. He tells me that you are just a woman, that we fight a war for greater purpose."

"And . . . what do you say to Saladin?"

"That which I say to you . . . that I cannot."

"What does Saladin say then?"

His knuckles brushed over her cheek, and he lifted her chin that he stared down into her eyes.

"This is my domain. My palace. We fight toward the greater

good, but in such a matter, my uncle cannot tell me what I must do."

He did not smile, but studied her features. He released her and walked toward the door. "Tonight," he said quietly, "I tire of the game. It makes me impatient. And I am weary."

He paused, brooding as he stared at her once more. "Your child comes in April?" he asked.

Elise felt color flood to her cheeks. "Yes."

"That is not such a long time," he said. "You must start to think about what you will do."

"Do?" Elise repeated vaguely.

"He will be welcome here," Jalahar said bluntly, "but will he not be Stede's heir? You must decide if you wish to keep your child, or give him to his father."

Elise moistened her lips, wrenched by a new pain . . . and a tearing sense of fatalism.

In all the time . . . the long weeks that had become months . . . she had never accepted that it could be forever. She could not be expected to give up her child! Not the babe who had finally begun to move, to exist so strongly in her heart. But could she keep him from his father? She had wanted a child so badly in part for herself . . . and in part for Bryan. A son was perhaps the one truly worthy thing she could give him.

"Stede is still here . . . in the Holy Land," she whispered.

"Do you think this war will continue forever? Or that the Christians will ever subdue us completely? Already King Philip of France has left—to return to his own lands. Not even the determination of the Lion-Heart can hold out forever. Stede will ride against me, yes. He will demand his wife and child, and if it is your wish, the child will be given to him. But, then, perhaps he will not demand the child. Perhaps he will believe that it is mine. Tell me, Elise, did he know that you were carrying his child?"

Her face had gone a frightening shade of white. "No," she whispered.

Jalahar shrugged. "Then perhaps you will wish to keep the child. He will be loved here, for it will be my wish."

Jalahar at last pushed on the door. Elise leaped to her feet, calling him back.

"You said that you must meet Bryan in battle!"

He paused, smiling. "And you will hope that your knight kills me? He will need more than love and desire to battle my forces. For months they have tried to tear down my walls. They have not succeeded. And . . . if he comes for me now, as I told you, he will die. He is still too weak to fight a fair battle. I would not want to kill him at such a time, but in defense, I should be forced to. If you wish him to live, you must pray that he does not desire you unto death."

Jalahar closed the door behind him.

Elise stared after him, fearing the future as she had never feared it before. She felt too numb to cry, but when she brushed her cheeks with her fingers, she found they were wet with the silent tears of defeat.

XXVI

He lived in a world of shadow, where darkness and nightmares reigned. Sometimes he would be riding, his destrier tearing up great clumps of earth as they thundered along. He did not know why he rode or what place he tried to reach. The trail was laden with forest branches, and it seemed that it yawned before him, offering nothing more than a black chasm, a dark void to fill his life.

Sometimes light would penetrate his dream world. It would be early fall, and he would stand in a lush meadow. Birds would sing a gentle chorus, the breeze would whisk by, delicious and cool.

He would see her. Atop a dune, dressed in white. The sun would envelop her, and her hair would be a golden halo that spun in the breeze as she ran to him, smiling, arms outstretched, eyes as brilliant and beautiful as an azure sea. He would lift his arms to her, and he would start to run. But he was wearing his armor, and it was heavy. Every step became harder until he was groaning and screaming for strength, cursing God for making him useless when he needed to reach her to live.

At other times he would be able to move. He would climb the hill. But where Elise had been, he would find a horse, ready for battle. And when he looked, he would be blinded by a halo of gold, and he would shield his eyes. And his heart would stagger, for it would not be Elise mounted upon the horse whom he so craved, but King Henry, come back from the grave. Henry, before illness had ravaged and killed him. The king when he had still ridden tall and strong, when his features had displayed both his wisdom and his temper; when his eyes had been brilliant with justice and strategy.

Henry would lift a finger and point it at Bryan. His voice would not be that of a living man; it would be a cold and stuttering echo from the grave.

"You have failed me . . . failed me . . ."

He tried to open his eyes. It was no longer Henry he saw, but Henry's son, Richard the Lion-Heart. Richard would not talk to him; he would talk around him, as if he weren't even there.

"He is looking straight at me," Richard said.

"I doubt that he knows, Lion-Heart."

A strange man, very thin, in immaculate robes and turban, was staring down at him. The dark eyes decreed him old; his face, brown as a tree bark, was unmarred by the wrinkles of time.

"Stede! You cannot die! You must not fail me!"

Was it Henry who spoke, or was it Richard?

The shadows swirled around him. Elise was sitting on the horse, calling to him with tears streaming down her cheeks. The shadows threatened to swamp her, to take her away forever. She begged him, implored him, pleaded that he come to her.

And he could not; his legs were too heavily laden.

"Be gentle with her; be patient."

Will Marshal was standing at his side. "I cannot reach her!" he screamed. "Help me, Will! Help me!"

But Will faded into the shadow, and he was alone again. Henry's face, Richard's face . . . Elise's face . . . they passed through his mind until they became one, then faded. He was back in the forest, on his horse, racing toward the dark abyss. But now there was a pinpoint of light within it, a golden streak that drew him. It was a crown, a crown heavily laden with jewels. Then the crown blurred, and it was not a crown at all. It was Elise's hair, caught in sunlight and wind, shimmering copper and gold. And she was calling to him again, stretching out

her arms, her fingers so long and delicate. She wore the sapphire
ring, and that, too, caught the sunlight, forcing it to explode
into a field of blue . . . and then shadow again. Shadows became
the swirling sands of the desert, and the merciless sun with its
burning heat. Elise was there again, but the sands made a wall
around her, and when they cleared, she was gone.

"Elise!" He screamed her name. "Elise!"

"I am here!" she whispered to him. "I am here." And something cool touched his forehead. A hand gripped his, delicate,
but firm.

"Elise!" he called breathlessly. "Don't leave me!"

"I will never leave you," she promised.

She was real; she held him.

He would dream again, and when the cold of the forest froze
him, she would warm him with blankets and lie down beside
him. When the desert sun burned him, she would cool him with
cloths. Always he would call her name; always she would whisper that she was there, and she would hold him.

But then came the morning, when he opened his eyes and
found that he was neither in the desert, nor in the forest. He
blinked. His temple was thudding, and his throat was parched.
He hadn't even the strength to lift his head. But he blinked again
and looked around himself. White wall, sheer, billowing cur-
tains. Cushions beneath him . . .

The palace at Acre, he told himself. Richard's stronghold . . .

He felt horribly confused, as if his head were filled with
cobwebs. He closed his eyes and tried to think.

Then he remembered. Riding alongside his wife, wondering—his heart pounding like a boy's—what secrets she would
whisper to him, barely able to endure the rest of the ride with
the wanting of her. Would she lay her heart and soul at his
feet, hold him and tell him that loved him above all men,
wanted nothing more than to spend the rest of their days together . . . ?

He hadn't heard the Arabs until they were upon them. The

battle had been so evenly met. He had fought, and fought well, until . . .

Until he had seen her. Under attack. Battling, striving, desperate . . . And he had been galloping toward her when the terrible pain had rent his side and he had fallen into blackness . . . and then into the dream world.

Elise!

But she had answered his call; just as he knew now that the dreams had been illusory, he knew that a woman's touch had been real.

Someone moved beside him and his heart filled with gladness. It took all his strength, but he managed to turn.

His heart plummeted, and confusion tore at his mind again.

Gwyneth, fully clothed, was leaning upon an elbow, looking at him with wonder.

"You're awakened, Bryan!" she cried. "Truly awakened."

He tried to speak, but his throat was too dry. She leaped from the bed of soft down cushions and hurried to the water pitcher, quickly pouring a small portion into a goblet, and bringing it to his side. He was horrified to discover that he still couldn't lift his head. She had to hold his neck so that he could drink.

"What has happened?" he managed to croak to her.

She twisted her lip nervously without answering. "I must bring the physician, Bryan."

She hurried from the room. A moment later the sun-browned, old-young Arabic face from his dream was staring down at him pensively.

"You have beaten the infection, Lord Stede," the man told him in a pained, slow English. "But you must still fight for your health. You need sleep—the kind that is peaceful, and restful, and allows the body to heal."

"I want to know what has happened!" Bryan exclaimed. His voice was shaking; he sounded like a peevish and sickly child. The man ignored him, and made him drink more water. "Sleep; when you awaken again, you may talk some."

That was absurd! He would never rest. But his eyelids were so heavy; he was as weak as an old woman. He closed his eyes. And slept.

The Arab was there when he opened his eyes again. "Can you lift your head?"

Bryan nodded. It was difficult; it seemed to take all his strength, but he lifted his head.

"Surely your God smiles upon you," the Arab told him bluntly. "You should be dead."

"Who are you?" Bryan asked him.

"Azfhat Muhzid. Egyptian physician to the great Saladin."

"Saladin!" Stede exclaimed.

Bryan allowed his head to fall back to his pillow. The Egyptian smiled slightly, and spoke neither humbly nor boastfully. "It is to my expertise as well as to your God that you owe your life. Your English physicians—they are little better than butchers! They insisted upon bleeding you, when the blood had already drained from you like water into sand!"

"Then I thank you," Bryan said.

"You owe me no thanks. I was sent."

"By Saladin? Then our war—"

"It continues."

"Then how—"

"You will talk no more now, Stede. Your strength must grow again; you are like a child. With time, you will grow healthy. Tended, you will gain each day."

The Egyptian was leaving him.

"Where is my wife!" Bryan called after him.

Azfhat paused, then turned his head only slightly. "I will send the woman to sit with you."

Bryan allowed himself to close his eyes; his lids still felt preposterously heavy. But he did not allow himself to sleep. A great sense of unease had come over him. When he heard the door open, he forced his eyes to open again.

It was Gwyneth. She stared at him anxiously, then came to his side, sitting by his hip on the cushion.

"Where is Elise?" he asked her.

She moved her lips as if to speak, then hesitated, looking downward so that her dark lashes swept over her cheeks. "Bryan, the Egyptian said that you mustn't—"

"Where is Elise? What has happened to her? I must know! I called her . . . I had thought . . . Gwyneth! Tell me! She did not die! I know that she did not die. Before God, Gwyneth! Tell me what has happened!"

"Bryan . . ." Gwyneth sighed, swallowed nervously, then met his eyes. "Elise is at the Muzhair palace."

His eyes closed in dismay. He knew his wife. She would have fought to the end, and God alone knew what the Arabs would have done . . .

"Blessed Virgin!" he muttered aloud. "She will try to stab someone, and they will—"

"Bryan, no! You mustn't worry. She went willingly—"

"Willingly!"

His eyes opened with such horror and pain that Gwyneth started speaking again, tripping over her words.

"Not in that way, Bryan. Their leader . . . Jalahar . . . held his sword to your throat. Your life . . . if she would come with him. She . . . went to save you."

Pain, far greater than any wound, more debilitating than any fever, swept through him.

"I would rather have died," he whispered.

"We would have all died," Gwyneth murmured.

He tried to lift himself from the bed. "We must mount up. We must take the palace. Perhaps . . . perhaps we can still get there in time—"

"No! Bryan, no!" Gwyneth protested, her lovely eyes laden with sadness as she pressed him back to the pillow. God's blood! He couldn't even fight Gwyneth's strength.

"Bryan!" she cried. "It will do no good. Richard's forces have been pounding at the palace day after day. It has withstood all this time—"

"All this time!" He gasped. "How long have I lain here?"

"Almost two months, Bryan."

"Two months!"

He closed his eyes. Two months. Elise! No nightmare could rival this agony. His mind clouded with images of his wife . . . her pale ivory skin, sleek and soft as silk, beneath the bronzed hands of the desert infidel . . .

His eyes flew open. Gwyneth emitted a small sound of fear at the wildness in them. "Bryan—"

"I . . . must get . . . to her . . ." he said softly.

He managed to stand. But then he fell, crashing hard on the ground. Gwyneth screamed, and suddenly there were many hands to pick him up and set him back upon his invalid's bed.

In the days to come, he learned an unwilling patience. The anguish did not leave his heart or mind, but Gwyneth said one thing that kept him pinned to his bed.

"Bryan, you will never see her again, nor will you be able to help her, if you die yourself."

So he ate broth and drank the physician's disgusting concoctions of ox blood and goat's milk. As the days passed, he could lift his head, and then he could sit up.

Gwyneth remained at his side, and as he strengthened, he started to watch her, grateful for her care.

"It was always you, wasn't it?" he asked her softly one day. "I cried for Elise, and you answered."

"We thought it best. You seemed to believe that I was Elise, and so . . . I held you."

He raised a brow to her. "Held me only, Gwyneth?"

She laughed a little uneasily, then stood and moved around the room, straightening things rather than meeting his eyes.

"You were very sick, Bryan. But once you tried . . ." She stopped her nervous wandering and stared at him, as if she were a little amazed herself. "When you could barely open your fevered eyes, Bryan, you were still lecherous!" She laughed ruefully. "And once I thought . . . I don't know what

I thought. When I came out here with Elise, I didn't know. I didn't know then what I would do if the opportunity ever came about. Even the night when we were attacked . . . Elise came to me. She asked me to look out for you. And she knew, she knew then that she would be taken, and that I would be left with you. I can only imagine what that cost her. But still . . . still there were times when I was glad in my heart, because I had wanted you so badly!" She smiled, pausing ruefully. "Percy and I . . . we didn't have a bad marriage. But he always knew how I felt about you. I'm certain the night he died he tried to warn Elise about me. I lived that night because of Elise. My son . . . Percy's son . . . is alive because she came out to us. I owed her so very much, but I still wanted you. I didn't know until now . . . when I could have had you, that something resembling honor lurked in my breast, after all. I have held you, I have lain beside you. I could have soothed you . . . but no more."

Bryan smiled at her and stretched out his hand. She came to him, taking it, and sat beside him once again. His smile faded and his grip tightened. "I have to get her back, Gwyneth. She is the strongest part of me."

"You have to get well," Gwyneth told him.

"I will."

The Egyptian physician, Azfhat Muhzid, came to see him daily. He was often a cynical man, but polite in the strange way of the Easterner; he was quite pleased with Bryan's progress, even if he preferred not to be questioned.

But Bryan at last became insistent, and Muhzid answered him with a sigh. "I was sent here by Saladin—at the request of his nephew, Jalahar."

"Jalahar?" Bryan demanded quickly. "Why would Jalahar do such a thing?"

The Egyptian hesitated, then shrugged. "I would think because his hostage pines for you; he wished to please her. The best gift he could present to her was the news that you lived."

Bryan clenched his teeth hard together and swallowed. Again! She bargained for his life . . . and he lay here . . . helpless . . .

He said nothing more to Azfhat; to Gwyneth he raged against Jalahar, despairing over the fate that Elise suffered because of him. Gwyneth, who had seen Jalahar, and knew as only a woman could that Jalahar would be a man to stir the blood and inspire devotion, wisely refrained from telling Bryan that she doubted Elise would suffer much at his hands.

Bryan slugged a fist so hard against the wall that she feared he had cracked his bones. He turned to her, pain and confusion lacing his indigo stare. "Why?" he demanded. "Why has he taken her when he has endless women, when he can but snap his fingers and have anything that he wants?"

This Gwyneth felt safe in answering. "Her coloring is very unique to an Easterner, Bryan. You should have seen him the first time he looked at her. He was—" Gwyneth cut herself off uneasily.

"He was what?" Bryan demanded tensely.

"Fascinated," Gwyneth finished weakly. Bryan seemed to accept her word; he began to rant in fury again. But "fascinated" was too tame a description of what she had really meant. There had been something deeper about the Moslem lord that night, something that made the situation far worse. Elise was not just a pretty toy to him; it seemed that in seconds she had captured his heart.

It was a pity that she wasn't blond herself, Gwyneth thought wryly. She wasn't terribly sure she would have minded if Jalahar had swept her up on a horse and raced her across desert sands to be ravaged in an exotic palace.

Yes, it should have been her.

Because Bryan was in love with his wife; nothing would ever change that. And there was no doubting Elise's love for Bryan. Poor Bryan! She had never seen such a powerful man so ravaged by loss.

She tried to speak to him soothingly; she tried to tell him that Jalahar was so fascinated by Elise that he would do nothing to make himself more the enemy in her eyes. She was probably well cared for and left alone.

Gwyneth didn't think that either of them believed it, but they were words that Bryan pounced upon as a dying man grasped at life. She would never fall completely out of love with him, so she was glad that she could soothe him.

Azfhat left the next week. He told Bryan that only his own will could take him forward from there. They parted friends.

In another week Brian could stand. He began to work painstakingly, exercising slowly but tediously. He worked his hand muscles and his toe muscles from the bed; he stretched and flexed his legs. When he could stand and walk again without faltering, he thundered into Richard, striking his fist down on the battle maps that lay before his astounded sovereign.

"You sit here idly, Your Grace, while the enemy holds my wife! I demand that something be done!"

Richard stared at him in astonishment, his Plantagenet temper soaring. "Stede, I am joyed to see you well, and the fact that you have lain at death's door all these weeks keeps me from ordering you into the nearest tower! You forget to whom you are speaking!"

Richard's threats were frequently bluster. Bryan determined to keep that in mind. "I do not forget; you are my king, and I serve you well and with loyalty. But I wish to know what is being done."

Richard looked at Bryan, then waved a hand, dismissing the scribe who sat in the room taking notes. When the little fat man had waddled away, Richard sat back in his chair, studying Bryan as he idly drummed his fingers on the table.

"I have done everything humanly possible," he told Bryan

with a sigh. "We continue to thunder at the gate of Muzhair; I send messages weekly to Saladin. There is nothing else that I, or anyone, can do."

"There must be! Pull in more men—"

"Dammit, Stede! There are no more men! That snake of a monarch Philip has pulled out! The Austrian knights are worthless under Leopold! I'm doing my best to hold what I have—"

"There must be a way, Richard! You are not doing everything possible . . ."

"Stede!" Richard thundered, standing. Bryan was gaunt from his illness, but he still rose an inch over the king, and Richard detested that inch. "Sit down!" he grumbled to his knight. "I despise looking up at you, and you know it. And I made you, Bryan Stede. I gave you your castles and your lands—and your wife. I can break you if I choose. Now sit down, and listen to reason."

Bryan sat, but he leaned across Richard's table. "Grant me this, Your Grace. Allow me to lead the men against the palace again. Allow me to take the knights from Montoui, and the knights from Cornwall. And let me hand-pick the others. We will manage to storm the palace. We will—"

"Bryan!" the king said sadly, shaking his head. "I will be heartily glad to put men beneath your command again. I attended special masses to pray for your recovery—because I need men like you. But I will not put an army into your command until you regain your strength. Until I see the knight who out-jousted all others—who was able to unhorse *me!* When that day comes, Bryan, I will give you all that you need. You have my solemn vow. Christ's blood, man! Don't you think that I would move both heaven and earth to get her back if I could!"

Bryan started, surprised by the tension and sincerity in the king's voice. He had been expecting Richard to tell him that he could not interrupt the great Crusade for the sake of one woman. Richard's knights had a habit of remaining tactfully silent, but anyone close to the king knew that any licentious comments regarding women were for show; he approved of only one female, and that one was his mother.

"You mean that, don't you?" Bryan queried.

"Of course!"

"Why?" Bryan asked, before thinking.

Richard glanced at him, as startled as he. "You don't know?"

Bryan shook his head. Richard smiled, a little ruefully. "She is my sister. Half sister, but Henry's blood as sure as I."

Bryan felt his jaw fall, his mouth gape. He was certain he looked like an idiot sitting there, but he had never been more astounded.

And then it all made sense. The tears she had shed for Henry; the night in the storm. The ring . . . the sapphire ring that had once convinced him that she was a liar and thief.

And her face! The gold and copper hair. My God, but he had been blind. Her hair was like a Plantagenet banner! He should have known, he should have realized. Even the dream tried to tell him so, the dream when he had seen Henry, Richard . . . and Elise.

Even the legend, he thought, a wistful grimace tugging painfully at his mouth. Even the Plantagenet legend, that of Melusine's blood, giving fire and beauty and magic to the race. Magic, oh yes, haunting magic. Not evil. Just a beauty so great that it induced a love to bind a man for all his life. He had touched her once, just as that long ago Viking descendant had touched Melusine. Once . . . and had come to know that it would never be enough. That he would want her, need her, love her all his life . . .

He closed his eyes, filled with belated remorse. He had grappled her from her horse, trussed her about . . . and if he hadn't raped her, he had forcefully seduced her. . . .

And all because she was Henry's daughter, determined that he know anything but the truth. . . .

He should have known! When she lost her temper, she was wild. Just like Henry. Like Richard . . . she would fly into danger, risk her own fool neck when she was furious and determined. So many times he had thought that she reminded him of someone! He had ridden at Henry's side for years, and now he had been at Richard's side. He had been blind.

And that night . . . that dark night of sudden violence and heated passion that had changed his life . . . her life. . . . It might never have been, had she but trusted him . . .

"Why?" he whispered out loud, unaware that he spoke.

"She never told you, eh?" Richard said, then sighed. "Perhaps she felt the secret should die with the few who knew. My father told me about her when we were already at odds with each other. He had made some type of a deathbed vow to her mother that she be raised as legitimate nobility. But Henry never could deny what was his. He told her somewhere along the line. My mother guessed, but God bless my mother! She never felt rancor toward any of Father's bastards. She dotes on Geoffrey . . . but back to the point. Father might have been trying to turn *my* inheritance over to John, but I think that even he knew that John was a young boy, not to be trusted. I am all that stands between John and the crown. If I die . . . and if John knew . . . Elise could pay. John bears bitter grudges. And even Elise was given more than John as she grew up. She had Montoui. It is a secret that should be kept, Stede. If . . ."—Richard paused unhappily, then became brusque—". . . if we are able to get her back. If you were to have children, they might even suffer at John's hands, if you and I were no longer able to protect them."

Bryan stood, wavering slightly. "I will regain my strength, Your Grace. And I will hold you to your vow to see that I lead the men I choose."

Richard watched him leave the room. Bryan teetered back to his bed. He slept for an hour. He ate every bite of the food that Gwyneth brought him, and started exercising again. His toes . . . how absurd it would have once seemed to exercise his toes. But his toes led to his feet, his feet to his legs . . .

And he *would* stand again without wavering, he would walk, and he would wield a sword, and he would fight.

If he could just control the pictures in his mind! But when darkness settled at night, his imagination betrayed him. Jalahar! The Arab was muscled and trim, an exotic, intelligent man. What if Elise had gone with him because she was fascinated by his bronzed and swarthy looks, fascinated by a desert prince . . . ?

He clenched his teeth together. It made him writhe with fury and agony to think of her in the arms of another. He could picture her so clearly. He could reach out and almost touch her image, almost feel the softness of her flesh, the silk of her hair as it spilled about her in glorious disarray . . .

He tried to close his mind to the agony while he allowed the anger to grow. Fury could build strength. And he wanted her back. He was willing to fight for her; he would die rather than lose her.

Every day he worked. Stretched upon the floor, he pushed himself unmercifully, regaining the hardness in his belly. He pressed upon his arms . . . slowly at first, tiring after a matter of minutes. But as time passed, determination won out, and he could push his weight tirelessly from the floor for minutes without end.

He moved out to the courtyard, and started with his sword again. Swinging, plunging, hacking. His destrier was half wild from the idle months; Bryan had to learn to ride him all over again.

There were days when he would grow dizzy, and have to retire, but those days came less and less frequently.

And while Bryan worked, Richard carried on his holy war. He would push along the coastline, always nearing Jerusalem, always being pushed back. Coastal towns fell to the Crusaders; Jerusalem eluded them.

In March Richard came to the courtyard, fresh from battle. He watched Bryan work, and he was glad to see that his knight's broad shoulders were filling out with hard muscle again; his waist was trim and tight, his arms bulging. A new scar stretched around his waist, but already it paled. The wound had not been nearly as serious as the fever it had caused.

"You will try me!" Richard commanded.

Bryan was puzzled, but then he shrugged, and he and Richard entered into swordplay.

On and on around the courtyard they parried, thrusting, swiping . . . gaining, retreating, meeting each other blow by blow. But then the king caught Bryan's sword; it spun in the sky and fell to the dirt.

Richard smiled at Bryan. "You're almost ready," he told him. He stepped closer so that his words could be heard by his knight alone. "We both know that the Lord Stede, at his best, can take a sword even from his king. The day that you take my sword from me, I will know that you are ready."

Richard, pleased with his victory, continued on to the palace. Bryan picked up his sword once more, and went back to work.

It was the first of April when Richard summoned Bryan to his council chamber. Bryan entered, surprised to see a slight Arab standing before the king. Richard had not risen. From his chair he indicated the man contemptuously and spoke to Bryan.

"He comes from Saladin in response to my last message. I wanted you to hear his words."

The small Arab looked from Richard to Bryan, then back again. The towering, muscle-bound warriors made him very nervous, especially since he knew that they would not like his reply.

"Speak up, man!" Richard ordered.

The little Arab shuffled his feet and bowed. "The great Saladin regrets to tell you that he has no authority to order a lesser prince to release a hostage of war."

"Hostage of war?" Bryan snapped derisively.

The little Arab looked his way, deciding that the dark-haired knight was the more dangerous of the men, albeit one was the English King. "Yes, English Lord. The hostage Elise is kept well, in noble surroundings. She is served food prepared by the emir's own chefs, and nothing is denied her." The knight continued to stare at the messenger in a way that made him wet his lips once more. "The physician who attended you, Azfhat Muhzid, is at her side daily—"

He broke off as he saw Bryan's frown, then heard the knight's fury. "Physician! Why? Is she ill? Hurt? What has been done to her?"

He had been wise to have feared the dark knight, for now the man crossed the room in what seemed to be a single step; he picked the little Arab up by the neck of his robe, his fingers closing in around his throat.

"Tell me! What ails her? Is she hurt? *What did he do to her?*"

"Nothing, nothing! You are strangling me! I beg of you, set me down. I am nothing but the emissary!"

Richard clamped his hand on Bryan's shoulder. "Put him down," the king said quietly, responding to the dazed fire in Bryan's eyes. It was apparent Bryan was totally unaware that he was about to kill the man.

Bryan shuddered, the wild light faded from his eyes, and he set the man down. The Arab choked and coughed, and rubbed his neck—but then he began to speak very quickly.

"She is well! Very well! Azfhat attends her only because she is with child."

Bryan stood dead-still, staring at the messenger, longing to reach out and strangle him—merely for the news he had been forced to bring. He could not kill Saladin's messenger; he would risk the life of every Christian held prisoner by the Moslems.

He turned on his heel, feeling as if he had been turned to molten stone. Leaden footsteps carried him back to his chamber—ironically, the same chamber he had shared with her that first night when she had come to him in the Holy Land . . .

He sank down to his knees, pressing his temples with his

palms to try to still the pain. He could no longer deceive himself that Jalahar had let her be. Jalahar had probably taken her night after night, imagining a son born with her golden coloring. . . .

A sound escaped him; something that was not a scream, not a cry, but a wail of man's deepest agony.

Gwyneth came rushing into the chamber; she fell to her knees before him, anxiously grasping his shoulders. "Bryan! What is it? Has the wound reopened? Are you ill? What—"

He looked up into her eyes, laughter flowed from him, hearty and deep. Too hearty; it mocked the anguish that darkened his eyes.

"She carries his child!" he exclaimed to her, and his laughter, self-scorning, rose again. "Blessed God! I have lain these nights in torment, wanting her, needing her . . . and she carried his child!"

Suddenly he saw Gwyneth's beautiful dark eyes filling with tears before him. Gwyneth . . . who had cared for him, loved him. Gwyneth, who he had so easily left for Elise!

He grabbed her, crushing her to him. His lips came down on her savagely, and his hands roughly roamed her body, remembering a path of beauty he had roamed long ago.

She started at the savagery of his kiss; but then she returned it. And suddenly they were both rolling on the floor, tearing the clothing from one another. He felt no subtlety; no finesse. She needed to be loved as badly as he needed to love. . . .

But when he rose over, about to take her like a stableboy would a peasant wench, the anger in him suddenly died. He withdrew, shaking as he sat beside her, holding his head between his hands again. This could not ease the heartache in him. Or cure him of desire and longing. It only wronged this woman who did not merit his anger or his violence. To whom he could not give his love, for it was already taken.

"I'm sorry, Gwyenth. I almost—I'm so sorry. You do not deserve . . . this."

She was silent. Then she began to gather her clothing about her again.

"Bryan, you needn't apologize. I would have willingly seduced you a number of times, had I had your attention. Perhaps . . . perhaps I am a little sorry that I cannot heal the real scar you carry. But . . . Bryan . . ."

"What?" He gazed at her, still feeling wretched. She had loved him; he had wanted only to use her. Revenge against a pain she had not caused. And he had learned the agony of loving . . . he would add to that pain for another.

She took a deep breath, steadying herself. "Did this messenger say that . . . that Elise carried *Jalahar's* child."

"What do you mean?" Bryan asked tensely.

"A physician seldom attends a woman at such a time . . . unless she is near giving birth." Gwyneth laughed dryly. "Seldom even then, but if Jalahar considers her special . . . Bryan . . . hasn't it occurred to you that the child might be yours?"

He stared at her pensively for a minute, then was on his feet, fumbling into his clothing. He raced for the door.

"Where are you going?" Gwyneth queried anxiously.

"To catch the messenger!"

He caught up with the little Arab as the man plodded slowly along on the trail leading from the town. The Arab flinched, cringing in his saddle.

"Don't fear, man of Islam! I've no intent to harm you. I want to know more. When is the Christian woman's child due?"

The Arab remained distrustful and nervous. He shrugged and answered carefully. "I am not exactly sure; I do not see her. But I believe it must be soon, for Azfhat remains at Muzhair."

The little man froze in fear, certain that he had given the wrong answer, terrified that the dark, towering knight truly intended to kill him this time. For Bryan reached for him, but then laughed heartily and astounded the man by kissing him on both cheeks.

Truly the Christians were madmen.

"Thank you, my friend! Thank you!" Bryan cried, and as he rode away, he threw a handful of gold coins into the sand.

The Arab dismounted from his horse in amazement. Then he shrugged again, and grinned broadly as he began to dig the gold out of the sand.

Allah worked in mysterious ways.

In Richard's palace at Acre, Gwyneth had hurriedly repaired her clothing, and was preparing to depart on her own impulse. She gathered a few belongings, then rang for a servant to bring her a quill and parchment.

She quickly began to scratch out a note:

> Bryan,
>   I am going to Muzhair. They will allow me in, for I am a woman alone. This might sound insane, and you might doubt my motive, but I wish to be with Elise. She might well need a friend, and that I intend to be.
>   If God truly sits in heaven, and if things are ever righted, you will have your wife, and your child, again. I will never tell Elise anything. There is nothing to tell her in truth; you love her too dearly to love another. As *your* friend, I beg that you never say anything to her. She will believe that you are lying—but she will want you to lie.
>   I love you, and I love Elise. I pray that I am doing the right thing; I know that I wish to stand beside her and give her whatever aid that I can. Do not worry about me; you know that I always land on my feet.
>
> Gwyneth

She set the note upon his pillow and smiled sadly. Then she hurried from the chamber, determined to catch Saladin's messenger, so that she might find her way to the Moslem leader, and then to the home of his nephew.

Bryan returned to the palace in rare good humor. He strode on light feet to Richard's council chamber, and even awaited the page's announcement before barging in on his king.

When he was allowed entry, he walked determinedly to stand before the king. Richard glanced at him with a brow raised in expectation.

Bryan pulled his sword from his scabbard and laid it before Richard.

"I am ready to best you, Your Grace," he challenged.

Richard stared at him a long while. Then he grinned slowly, and stood.

"I believe we can arrange for an empty courtyard. It wouldn't do, you know, for men to see the Lion-Heart drop his sword. They believe that I am invincible."

Together they went to the courtyard. No one knew what passed there, but the sharp clanging of swords rose high on the air.

XXVII

Elise awoke with the strange feeling that someone was watching her. She opened her eyes to see Gwyneth's dark, sparkling eyes staring down into hers; a small grin curled her lips into a pretty set of amusement.

Elise stared at her blankly for several seconds. "I've died—and we've reached heaven or hell together."

Gwyneth laughed. "Nay, Elise, you're quite alive. And I must say, I do enjoy the sight of you! I'd never thought you could look anything other than the perfect slender sylph, but you do resemble the fattest friar I have ever seen!"

Elise flushed slightly, but laughed along with Gwyneth, still in wonder that Gwyneth could be sitting by her side in Jalahar's palace. She raised herself awkwardly—in the past month it seemed that she had doubled in size—and asked, "How can you be here?"

"Very easily. I found my way to Saladin—who is, I might say, a fascinating and charming man—and thereby arrived here by escort."

"But why?" Elise whispered. "Gwyneth, we may never be freed. Now that you are here, they may never allow you to leave!"

Gwyneth shrugged. "I'm not completely sure myself. Ah, well . . . Percy always did say that I was a bit of an adventuress." She sobered. "I heard of your child, Elise. I thought that you might be in need of a friend."

Elise stared at Gwyneth in wonder. A thousand questions

raced through her mind. A thousand fears, a thousand worries. All about Bryan. Yet if Gwyneth had . . . taken her place with Bryan, why would she have come here?

Gwyneth read the questions in her eyes, and spoke quickly. "He is fine now, Elise. Bryan is fine. He had a long, dreadful bout with the fever, but he came from it, strong as always at last."

She wasn't going to cry, Elise told herself. She had shed so many tears already . . . but moisture stung her eyes.

"You nursed him through it?" she whispered to Gwyneth.

"I—and the Egyptian—yes."

"Thank you," Elise murmured, setting her teeth into her lower lip. Whatever had happened didn't matter, because Gwyneth had helped to keep him alive . . .

But had he survived . . . only to die in battle?

"Gwyneth, what does Bryan think? What is he doing? Surely he knows that I am here. Gwyneth, the child is his, not Jalahar's. Does he know that? Oh, I have been so torn! I thought that if he believed the child to be Jalahar's, he might ride away, and therefore live; yet I do not know if I could bear his not knowing . . . not believing that he would come . . . Oh, Gwyneth! Tell me! Tell me about him—I am starved for the truth!"

Gwyneth hesitated, only a fraction of a second. "He is like all men," she told Elise ruefully. "He was insane with fury to think of you with Jalahar, and when he first heard about the child . . ." She lifted her hands in explanation. "Men can also be as simple as children. His attention was directed to the fact that the child was due very soon . . . so I believe that he is convinced that his son is about to be born in another man's palace."

"What will he do?" Elise whispered.

Gwyneth shrugged. "Richard would allow him to do nothing—until he had completely regained his strength. But soon . . . soon he will gather the cream of the army and bring them against the palace."

Elise fell back to her pillow, thrilling sweetly to the knowledge that he would fight for her, whether it was for love, or possession . . . or his child. But the tremors of delight were combined with darker shivers of fear; Bryan and Jalahar would most certainly seek out each other. One of them would die. Bryan had to win . . . but even that victory would bring pain, because she couldn't help but care for the desert prince who had abducted her, but had shown her nothing but gentleness.

Still, she had to pray for his death. Because it would be Jalahar or Bryan.

"Does Jalahar know that you are here?" she asked Gwyneth. "Does he know that Bryan . . . will ride?"

"Aye, he knows I'm here," Gwyneth said dryly. "No one is allowed near his golden prize without his permission. I am allowed to stay with you—as long as I know to leave the chamber the moment he walks in!"

"Did he . . . say anything when he knew for certain that Bryan would ride here?"

"His attitude seems very fatalistic. That appears to be the way of the Moslems. I think he has known all along that Bryan would come and that they would meet."

"I had hoped that maybe . . . maybe knowing for a certainty that the Christian troops would be concentrated against his palace and domain, he would . . . release me."

Gwyneth sighed. "I think, Elise, that you underestimate the power of a man's pride—and desire."

"I am not . . . worth this!" Elise murmured.

"Probably not," Gwyneth replied cheerfully. She stood and began to amble curiously about the luxurious chamber, picking up the silver brush, glancing at the jeweled goblets on the Moroccan stand. " 'Tis not such a bad prison!" she said softly.

Elise leaned back again. She had felt very tired lately, heavy and lethargic. At times her emotions were intense; at other times, she felt too weary and defeated to care about anything.

" 'Tis a prison just the same," Elise noted.

Gwyneth spun about and returned to her side, the sparkle back in her eyes as she asked, "What is he like, Elise?"

"What is who like?" Elise asked.

"Jalahar! Oh, come, Elise! You are a woman, not a stick! Surely he moves you! He is slim, but so solid! His features are handsomely arranged, and his eyes seem to strip a woman, touch her soul. Any but the blind could see that he knows how to touch . . . to love. To appreciate beauty . . ."

Elise stared at her friend and nemesis with amazement, and then understanding. She had felt the draw to Jalahar herself; only the depth of her love for Bryan had kept her from capitulating to the desert prince.

"There is little I can tell you that you don't already know," she said to Gwyneth. "He has never touched me."

"Never . . . touched you?" Gwyneth repeated incredulously.

"He promised from the first that he would leave me in peace until Bryan's child was born." Elise glanced sadly at Gwyneth. "Bryan will never believe that, will he?"

Gwyneth grimaced, then shrugged. "Perhaps he will. He will want to believe it." She smiled. "Now, get up."

Elise closed her eyes. "For what?"

"Because it isn't good for you or the child to lie about like a slug. You'll make the birth all the more difficult."

"Will that matter?" Elise asked wearily.

"Up!" Gwyneth insisted.

Elise discovered it was easier to give in than to fight.

On the morning of the last day of April, 1192, by the Julian calendar, Elise was awakened by a pain in her lower back that rivaled any she had ever known. She gasped, digging her fingers into the silken sheets, but she did not cry out. It was barely dawn; she stood, and shook as she tried to pour herself a goblet of water. But suddenly she felt as if she had been drowned in water herself; the crippling pain came again, and this time she cried out.

Gwyneth, tousled and heavy-eyed with sleep, came to her side quickly. " 'Tis definitely time!" she said excitedly. "Stay still. I'll find you a new gown, and call for Azfhat."

Shivering, Elise did as she was told. Somehow, she had never quite believed she would actually give birth in the palace. In her dreams she had miraculously been freed, and when she had produced a beautiful and healthy son, Bryan had been at her side. Dreams were not reality; her babe was coming. Jalahar would force her decision; she could keep the child, or allow it to be brought to Bryan . . .

Thankfully, another physical pain swept her to ease the torment in her mind. Nature gave her but one objective; that to give the child birth.

Gwyneth was slipping the wet gown from her head, replacing it with a dry one. Her teeth chattered as she was led back to the bed. She vaguely heard Gwyneth pounding at the door; she heard whispers, and she closed her eyes.

Azfhat was with her when she opened her eyes, as blunt and gravely calm as always. "It will be a long time yet," he told her. "Though not too long since you have lost the waters." He lifted her head for her to drink something, assuring her that it would harm neither her nor the babe, but would take the edge from the pain.

The edge was gone; but misted pain remained. Hours passed.

Azfhat was then called away. Satima and Gwyneth were with her, cooling her forehead with cloths, encouraging her to breath deeply. She heard Gwyneth whisper to Satima in her guttural, English accented French.

"Why has Azfhat gone?"

"Jalahar called him." Satima shrugged with typical Moslem fatality. "He did not linger in the palace when his own sons were born. Today he leaves a battlefield, and he demands to know what takes so long, and why he hears her scream."

Downstairs, in the elegant, fountain-laden inner courtyard, Jalahar paced the tiles and railed against the stoic physician.

"You are the physician—the greatest physician, the Egyptian

scholar! Why is it that you can do nothing? If she dies, you will die! I will see you set amidst a pot of tar . . . boiled slowly!"

Azfhat sighed, unperturbed by the hot temper directed wildly at him. "She will not die, Jalahar. She suffers no more than any woman must. I can do nothing, because life must take its course. She screams because life is a painful process. Neither you nor even the great Saladin can order the child to come before it is ready—whether I am boiled in tar or not!"

Jalahar stared at the physician in pure frustration. Azfhat contained his laughter and refrained from shaking his head in wonder. Both the Christian knight and the desert prince . . . magnificent warriors, leaders of men—they were fools over the blond woman.

Azfhat shrugged mentally. That was the way of the world. He was too old and too cynical himself to fall to the spell of a beautiful face, yet even he had felt hypnotized by the power of those eyes of an azure sea. She could not be blamed for bringing them all to ruin. She was already a legend to Moslems and Christians alike, the golden beauty who had lain over her husband and lover, and bargained for his life while he lay in a pool of blood.

Azfhat saw nothing but misery in the future. He had watched the Christian knight live by the power of his will; he had seen him battle his way to towering strength again by that same force.

And he knew Jalahar. When the two men came together . . .

Azfhat bowed. "If I have your leave, Jalahar, I will return to the woman, and offer the service that you require."

"Go!" Jalahar thundered. Azfhat grimaced, then went to attend to Elise.

Although she was quite convinced she was dying—and that if someone would have offered to end it all with the swift blow of a sword, she would have welcomed that blow—Elise's labor was relatively an easy one; the child was born well before dusk.

And when she heard the first cry, she was filled with such wonder that she would have gladly done it all over again.

" 'Tis done—bear down but one time," Azfhat told her.

"The babe—"

"Do as I say," Azfhat commanded. The cord was cut, and the physician drew the afterbirth from her.

She vaguely saw Gwyneth cleaning and swathing the bundle, and she tried to sit. "Gwyneth! Give him to me, please!"

Gwyneth laughed with delight. "Him! Elise, it is a daughter, and she is beautiful. When it dries . . . yes, she will have an amazing full head of snow-blond hair, and her eyes . . . they are the deepest blue I have ever seen!"

"A daughter!" Elise exclaimed. "I had been so very sure it would be a boy."

Gwyneth handed the babe carefully to Elise. Azfhat moved over to her with interest. "She will be a great beauty—and great trouble, I fear, as her mother!"

Elise glanced sharply at Azfhat, but an uncustomary grin took the sharpness from his words. He told her that he would leave her with her child, that she might hold the babe, but then should sleep.

She was far too overwhelmed with wonder and newfound adoration to sleep. She and Gwyneth—and even Satima—marveled over the infant girl, and Elise fumbled awkwardly through her first attempt to nurse her child. But the tiny, fervent tugs against her breast gave her a feeling of delight unlike anything she could imagine, and she was both ecstatic and dead-weary when she at last allowed Gwyneth to take her child from her.

"She makes me think of young Percy," Gwyneth said.

Elise, exquisitely warmed by the wonder of the experience, smiled at her sadly. "Don't you miss him terribly, Gwyneth? How do you bear being away?"

"I don't know," Gwyneth answered softly, cradling the infant to her. "I love him, I truly do . . . but I had to leave Cornwall when you did. I feel as if I'm searching for something—but I don't know what." She smiled at Elise and chuckled ruefully. "Don't worry about anything, Elise. Rest."

The command was easily obeyed. She didn't think about the future, immediate or distant. She closed her eyes and slept blissfully.

That night she and Gwyneth inspected the baby again, counting her toes, laughing at her length. "She will be tall," Gwyneth said with assurance. And look at her fingers! How long they will be! Long and elegant!"

"She isn't at all scrunched up!" Elise said with maternal pride. "She really is lovely!" she marveled.

The door suddenly swung open. Both women looked up, startled.

Jalahar stood in the doorway, his fine features unfathomable, his eyes upon Elise. He gazed from her to Gwyneth with a slight inclination of his head. "Out," he told her bluntly.

Gwyneth was not a woman to be daunted by any man. She glanced at Elise, shrugged, and walked to the door. But she stopped to tap Jalahar's cheek lightly with her palm. "Your wish is my command," she said with marked sarcasm. Jalahar gripped her wrist and stared at her with eyes that burned with annoyance. "Do not play upon temper, madame—not if you wish to return to this room."

Gwyneth jerked her wrist from his grasp and left the room. Jalahar came to the bed and sat by Elise's thigh. He stretched his arms to her.

"I wish to see the child."

An absurd panic filled her; she was weak, and she had never felt so defenseless, nor had she ever felt such a strong compulsion to protect and defend. She was loath to let the child out of her arms.

Jalahar grated his teeth with an oath of impatience. "Have I ever hurt you?" he demanded angrily. "Do you think I am a butcher to harm an innocent babe?"

Elise swallowed miserably and handed him the child with misgiving. She needn't have feared. He was tender with her precious bundle, supporting the babe's neck with care. He stared at her a long while, parting the swathing to count fingers and toes, as Elise had done herself. The baby shrilled a protest. Jalahar smiled, and returned her to Elise.

"She is a truly beautiful child. What will you call her?"

"I hadn't decided . . . yet," Elise said quietly, keeping her eyes downcast. How could she name the child . . . without Bryan?

"You had best decide. I assumed you would want her baptized in your Christian way. A priest will come tomorrow."

Elise nodded, cuddling the babe to her. "Lenore," she said suddenly. "For the queen," she added.

"Ah . . . yes, Eleanor of Aquitaine. Queen of France, and then of England. I was not born when she came here with the old French king, but the legends have not died. It is fitting that she should be named for such a woman."

Lenore, named for a queen, was unimpressed. She continued to howl, despite her mother's tender caresses.

"She is hungry," Jalahar told her.

Elise did not want to nurse the babe with his eyes upon her. But Jalahar's dark eyes were intense; just as she knew that he would never harm her, she knew he wouldn't leave her chamber.

Her eyes repelled his, but she adjusted her gown and brought the infant to her breast. Jalahar watched her silently, seeming to brood. Elise turned her eyes to her daughter's golden head. Despite Jalahar, she felt the sheer delight of her love once again, and she kissed the little head, caressing it with her cheek.

"I wonder," Jalahar said at last, "if you will love our child so tenderly."

Elise forgot the babe for an instant of alarm. She gazed at Jalahar and discovered that his dark eyes met hers with a brooding intensity that was determined . . . and frightening.

"Even now," she whispered, "Bryan amasses an army to bring against you."

"So I have heard. But the walls of Muzhair might well be impossible to scale."

"He will not stop—"

"Perhaps not. As I have said, it is likely that we shall meet. But time begins to run out like the desert sands . . . for you."

Elise swallowed painfully. "You said that you would never . . . force me."

"Will it be force?" he queried softly, bending near her. His hand brushed hair from her forehead; he opened his palm and cupped her cheek, ever careful of the child, who nursed in oblivion to her mother's racing heart. "Have you not come to care for me a little?"

Elise held her breath, near tears at the tenderness of his touch, the wistful longing in his voice.

"I love Bryan," she told him quietly, holding Bryan's daughter near as a steadfast reminder.

Jalahar smiled sadly. "I have waited a long time," he told her. He stood. "Your time has not yet run out; Azfhat says I must not touch you until the moon rises full again."

Elise shivered. A month. It was a long time . . . and no time at all. She had already been in the palace for seven months, waking daily to wonder if Bryan would ever come . . .

Jalahar interrupted her thoughts.

"The English King has sickened, Elise. The Lion-Heart fights his battles from his bed. He holds a number of the coastal towns, but he will never take Jerusalem. It is unlikely that he will take this palace. Yet neither can we best the Lion-Heart. Advisors on both sides, wise military strategists, tell them that they must come to an agreement, and sign a truce. Your husband is a worthy foe: a great and courageous knight. But not even he can take a fortress such as mine on his own. It is time for you to decide if you wish to keep the child, or send her to her father. Since you have produced a daughter and not a son, Stede will perhaps not care so much if you wish to keep her here. Sons inherit."

"I was a girl!" Elise snapped. "And I inherited!"

Jalahar shrugged. "Then perhaps you will wish the babe to be taken to him. You must make a decision soon."

He left the room before she could reply. Elise looked down at her tiny daughter, sleeping now, the soft, platinum fuzz of her hair teasing Elise's cheek. The babe whimpered slightly and one little fist shook. Elise could feel the small motion as the babe breathed; she could feel the warmth of her daughter, and the complete need and trust of the child nestled to her.

"I cannot send you away!" she whispered. "Never . . . I love you so much. You are all that I have of Bryan . . ."

She closed her eyes, the bliss she had felt at the birth of her daughter gone, torment eclipsing all else.

Jalahar never lied to her. Richard was apparently very sick; only desperate illness could keep him from the field. The Christian knights had been fighting a long and fruitless battle; surely they longed for home.

What would happen? Bryan could not scale the palace walls by himself.

Time . . . was running out.

"Elise! Come to the window!"

Elise, after placing Lenore in the lovely little basket Satima had given her, hurried to the window to join Gwyneth. From the height of the tower, they could see beyond the palace walls.

Just days after Lenore's birth, knights had begun to arrive and to set up camp, carefully out of arrow range from the palace. This morning the activity was even greater. A great catapult had been dragged across the sand during the night; a massive ram sat on wheeled carts. And it seemed as if the tents now stretched out far into the desert.

"Bryan is going to try to take the palace!" Gwyneth exclaimed.

Elise didn't know whether to feel fear or elation. Each day that had passed since Lenore's birth had been torture; Jalahar had presented her with an hourglass, and she had often sat staring at it, watching as the sands of time disappeared. Each day she had watched as the Crusaders built up their offense on the outskirts of the palace; but Jalahar had been to see her frequently, and he had told her that his men went out at night on raids to set the Christians back. Gwyneth told her that Jalahar led the raids himself—perhaps searching for Bryan. So far, the two men had not met.

But how many men had died? It was painful to wonder.

And now, her last days were draining away . . .

"When do you think they will attack?" Elise asked Gwyneth anxiously.

"I don't know," she murmured, "but soon."

"How soon?"

Gwyneth studied Elise's face, noting her friend's worried frown. "I see . . ." Gwyneth said at last. She sighed. "Elise, you are not about to lose your head, you know. You needn't be so afraid."

Elise flashed her an angry glance. "You act as if you don't care! You don't understand; everything will be different—"

Gwyneth's laughter cut her off, and Elise stared at the beautiful brunette in fury.

"What *are* you afraid of—Jalahar, or yourself? Elise, he will be a gentle lover; many women would crave such a man. You will not die if he decides to claim you, nor will you be any different. There is no way out of here—"

"Gwyneth!"

"I am an extremely practical woman, Elise," Gwyneth said with a sigh. "And Jalahar has exhibited remarkable patience for a man. He could have well ignored the fact that you were with child for many months; he could have raped you any time he wished. He could have ordered your infant slain; he could have taken her from you the moment she was born. The man is absurdly in love with you. But even being in love with you, he is a man. He could easily die for you on any day. I should think he would want to have enjoyed something first, should he die. It appears to me that you can fight him, break his patience at last and wind up hurt yourself, or accept him—and enjoy yourself."

Elise turned away from the window. "I cannot accept him! Bryan will . . . never want me again."

Gwyneth burst into laughter, then hugged Elise to atone for it. "You little fool! Bryan loves you! Nothing will change that!"

"Yes! Yes, it will!" Elise cried. "I . . . Percy supposedly loved me once, Gwyneth. And I made the mistake of a confession—"

"Elise! Percy was young—and hurt. But he never did stop loving you, and still I think that he loved me, too, in his way. Bryan Stede is not Percy! He loves you very deeply; you are his wife. It is senseless to make yourself ill with worry over something you can't change! Elise! He was probably certain that Jalahar had you every night while he lay in that fever. But there he is . . . out there somewhere, building an army to rescue you!"

Elise caught the tender flesh of her inner lip between her teeth, longing for reassurance. "Do you . . . really believe that he loves me, Gwyneth?"

Gwyneth was tempted to laugh; a moment's bitterness gripped her. But she saw how terribly serious Elise was, and how very vulnerable. "Yes," she said simply. "I'm quite certain Bryan loves you—very deeply." She sighed. "It is a pity Jalahar isn't nursing this terrible fascination for *me*. I'd be very glad to jump upon his cushions!"

"Gwyneth!"

"It's true," Gwyneth said dryly. Then she became somber. "Elise . . . you must realize the only way you'll ever be with Bryan is if Bryan kills Jalahar."

Elise stared at her. "What are you saying?"

"It could also go the other way," Gwyneth said softly. "If so . . . you had best reconcile yourself to Jalahar."

"No . . ." Elise murmured.

"One way or another, I think it nears the time when you can no longer play the queen, demanding this and that. But if . . .

if Bryan does kill Jalahar after . . . after he has . . . lost his patience, we'll say, you can easily keep the peace."

"How?"

"Lie."

"Bryan would never believe me!"

Gwyneth laughed. "Perhaps not. But as I've told you, men are strange beasts. He may not believe you, but he will not dispute you. He would rather live with the lie."

"You are telling me that Bryan will love me no matter what!" Elise cried. "But then you tell me to lie!"

"I believe we all like to cling to a little delusion," Gwyneth said wryly. She started to speak again, then jumped as a swift rapping sounded from the door. The women glanced at each other, then hurried to it. "Come in," she said in a low voice.

The door was unlocked from outside, and it swung open.

Elise was a little stunned by the sight of the man she saw there; he was of an average size, but he seemed large in his flowing robes. His thick mane of curling gray hair was topped by a red turban; his beard was as iron-gray as his hair, and it curled halfway down his chest. His eyes were extremely sharp; his face was wrinkled and weathered by time and harsh sunlight, but Elise didn't think she had ever seen features more powerful. Both she and Gwyneth stared at him, awestruck.

He bowed to the two of them, assessing them as he moved into the room. He stopped before Elise.

"You are the one . . ." he said, his eyes raking her up and down with no apology. "Elise . . . Christian wife of the knight Bryan Stede, subject of Richard, King of England."

Elise nodded, then found her voice. "Yes, I am Elise, wife of Bryan Stede."

"And the child in the basket . . . she is his?"

"Yes—and who are you?"

The man laughed very pleasantly. "Golden hair and a soaring spirit!" he said then, shaking his head. "If I were but a younger man . . . but I am not, and I have learned that the fancies of the flesh pass quickly. Still, there remains a spark in my blood that recalls such a passion—I am Saladin."

"Saladin!" Elise gasped.

"So you know of me . . ." he answered. "I am glad, since you have become such a fine point of trouble in my life! We fight for an empire—and must take time out for matters such as this!"

Tears that she blinked madly away stung Elise's eyes. "You . . . you are going to send me back? Is that why you have come? It will solve the problem that I create—"

She stopped speaking as she saw that Saladin was shaking his head sadly. "Only Jalahar can send you back. And he is obstinate. I have come to suggest that you send Stede's child out in the morning." At the look of anguish that came to her eyes, he softened his voice. "A battle will take place here, you know. If you love the girl, you will see that she is brought to safety. An innocent need not suffer in this affair. Jalahar's children are being sent out."

Elise lowered her head, fighting her tears. She felt her shoulders fall, and she nodded. If Jalahar was sending his own children away, then even he believed that there was danger.

Saladin lifted her head up by tilting her chin. Strangely, she was not surprised to find his eyes warm, filled with empathy and a little regret. "Ah . . . if I *were* but younger! Perhaps you are a prize for which I would have fought, too!"

He bowed low to her, and then to Gwyneth. With a soft whisper of robes, he was gone.

Elise plucked the baby from her basket. She lay down upon the cushions and cradled Lenore close. Gwyneth could find no words of comfort to offer.

That night Jalahar appeared suddenly in the doorway. He stared pointedly at Gwyneth; Gwyneth sighed and rose, and started to leave the room.

"Wait!" Jalahar commanded, and Elise and Gwyneth glanced uneasily at each other.

Jalahar's eyes were riveted to the sleeping infant, curled to Elise's side. "Take the child," he said softly.

"No!" Elise screamed instantly.

"She will be returned to you for the night," Jalahar said.

Gwyneth hurried to stoop to the cushions. "Elise! Let me take her! He seems . . . tense tonight. Elise! He does not lie to you! I will bring her back!"

Elise released her hold on her daughter and allowed the babe to go with Gwyneth. When the door closed behind Gwyneth, Jalahar still stood, staring at her. Elise jumped uneasily to her feet, tempted to crawl against a wall.

He walked across the room to the window and spoke almost idly. "The troops amass outside our walls. You can see all the camp torches lit—fire beneath the stars. He has done well, your Stede. When it begins, the battle will be fierce."

He turned suddenly to Elise, lifting his arm to the heavens beyond the scalloped window.

"The moon has risen full again," he told her.

She said nothing. Tremors shook her violently; fear and lightning seemed to streak through her limbs. She wanted to back away, but it would be a foolish and futile gesture.

He walked to her, stopping right before her. He touched her cheek, then played his fingers through her hair, staying a breath away from her. "It will begin very soon," he said. "Tomorrow . . . the next day. I would know . . ." His voice constricted tightly and he began again: "I would know what I fight for."

Elise felt frozen by his touch and time; she was rigid, unable to speak, unable to move. Unable to think.

He brought his other hand to her face, then used the slim length of his fingers to slip beneath the fabric on her shoulders. She wore only a gown of cool silk, and it slid beneath his touch like rippling sand, leaving her naked, bared to his eyes . . .

"No!" she cried suddenly, vehemently, but he had swept her into his arms, and she found herself falling . . . as if eternally . . . into the soft cushions of her bed. He was beside her. She fought him desperately, pounding, flailing, scratching . . . but she was no match for him, and in time, he secured her wrists, staring at her sadly with his deep, dark desert eyes. "No!" she cried again brokenly, and she shook her head with the tears sliding from beneath her lashes.

"Be still," he whispered to her, over and over, a soft sound, a soothing sound. He held her prisoner with one hand; with the other he smoothed the tears from her cheeks, caressingly . . . softly . . .

At last she lay still, shivering.

"Open your eyes," he commanded quietly. She did, and in a daze she stared at him. He smiled at her, wistfully, ruefully. Then his eyes left hers, and his fingers trailed a path between the valley of her breasts, heavy and firm with the recent birth of her child. "I wish only to love you . . ." he whispered to her. "Never to hurt you . . ."

Elise had never known such a depth of misery. She wanted so badly to keep fighting him, to hold tight to Bryan's memory. But she could not deny to herself that the tender touch of his fingertips upon her flesh was stirring desire within her. If he persisted, her body, grown accustomed to love and then denied it, would betray her, and in her heart she would have betrayed Bryan.

His mouth came to hers. She wanted to wrench away; he held her too dearly. His kiss was one of slow exploration, so very gentle . . . but firmly compelling.

His lips moved from hers, and he looked deeply into her eyes again. Then his dark head dipped low; he kissed the spiraling pulse at the base of her throat, and his lips drew a gentle pattern over her swollen breasts, down to her navel.

His touch, however it tormented her, was good. How strange! That first time with Bryan had been nothing but anger, pain . . . and a tempest of passion. And yet she had learned to love Bryan, and as inexplicable and elusive as it was, she could never explain now why she loved him so very much when she had once hated him . . .

She closed her eyes again, shaking violently. And she cried out in an anguished plea.

"Jalahar! Please . . . please, let me go, and listen to me!"

His eyes came to hers, somewhat suspicious, but curious. "Yes?"

Elise swallowed hastily and gasped for a deep breath, praying he would care enough to listen to her.

"If you take me now," she said hoarsely, "it will be by force. If . . . if you and Bryan meet in battle, and Bryan is killed, I will . . . I will come to you willingly."

He was still for several seconds, slowly raising a brow. "I will fight you now!" she cried out. "I will fight you again, and again, until I faint from weariness, and you make love to nothing but an empty shell."

"I might lose the battle," he informed her dryly.

"That is your risk. War is always a risk. And yet men always fight." He was silent, still staring at her. "Please, Jalahar! If you win, I swear by our Christ and the blessed Virgin that I will turn my back on the past, and come to you . . . willingly."

He closed his eyes; a shudder racked his form. He slowly released her and rolled from the cushions, landing lithely upon his feet.

He strode to the door and paused at it, allowing his eyes to roam her length freely. Elise reached nervously for a sheet; he made a small sound that stopped her, and she lay beneath his scrutiny, aware that she had been granted incredible mercy. "I would at least know how you look, flesh upon silk," he murmured. Then he reminded her curtly, "Willingly, Elise. It is a vow you will not break."

He left her; she began to shake again, and then she hurried to retrieve her gown.

Gwyneth returned—very curiously—with Lenore. "Well?" she demanded.

"The battle . . . will be the outcome," Elise said weakly. She hugged her infant closely to her and caressed the babe's fine silk hair.

"You . . . bargained with him?" Gwyneth demanded.

"Yes," Elise whispered.

Gwyneth was silent for several seconds. Then she said, "Dear Lord! That I had been born a blond!"

Neither of them slept that night, nor did they speak. In the morning, a kindly Arab matron took the babe very gently from Elise, and although Elise didn't understand the words, she knew that the woman promised to care for the infant with all her love and power until she was turned over to a Christian nurse.

The day passed, with tension seeming to build along with the army outside the wall.

Night came again.

Tense and silent; night.

And then the dawn.

XXVIII

"Jalahar!"

Arrows, burning with pitch, had flown with the first golden streaks of day; catapults had hurtled sand and stone, and rams had battered against the gates.

All morning long, Gwyneth and Elise had listened to the sounds of battle: the shrieks and screams and cacophony.

The Moslems were fighters, defending what was theirs. The battle had been rough, and vicious.

But then the gates had fallen.

The Christians had not ridden in; instead, a silence had followed the crumbling of stone and wood, and when the dust had settled, there had been a horseman in the gateway.

"Jalahar!"

The cry, vibrant and chilling, rose on the air once again. Elise, standing at the window with Gwyneth, began to tremble, and an ashen pallor touched her cheeks. Her knees buckled beneath her, and she sank against the wall.

"It's Bryan!" she gasped out.

"Of course it's Bryan," Gwyneth retorted.

"But what is he doing!" Elise wailed. "There . . . in the gateway, with no cover. Any fool could fly an arrow that would strike him—" She found strength and hopped back to her feet again, pushing Gwyneth rudely from the window. "Oh, Gwyneth! What is he doing?"

The last was a whisper, because she was shivering all over again, and her heart was pounding with both fear and pride.

His destrier pranced, chafing at the bit. But Bryan sat straight, the breeze whisking his mantle about him in a crimson glory. She could not see his face clearly, but she could see his form: broad but trim, towering even in the saddle. He was heedless of the restless horse; his attention was focused upon the palace, and upon the challenge he had offered.

"*Jalahar!*"

Once again his voice rang out. Harsh and demanding, it was yet music to her ears. When she had last seen him, he lay near death. And now . . .

Her attention was torn away from Bryan as another horseman rode out to meet him.

Jalahar.

Twenty paces away, Jalahar stopped.

Both men rode warhorses. Both were clad in armor, and both carried naked swords.

"What is happening?" Gwyneth demanded.

"I don't know!" Elise moaned. Then she added, "Shh! They're saying something . . ."

Bryan had dropped his voice; Elise strained to hear the more quietly spoken words, but she could not. A third man on horseback joined them; it was Saladin.

"What are they doing?" Elise whispered when the horses suddenly swung about, then proceeded out the gate to be followed by the Moslems of Muzhair, chanting something that rippled across the air like heat rippled over the desert sands.

"They're leaving!" Elise exclaimed. "They're going out the gates together!"

Frantically, she swung from the window and raced for the door, throwing herself against it. The outside bolt remained secure. Feverishly, she barged at it again. "Help me, Gwyneth!"

Gwyneth came to her side, and together they charged the door. But the bolt was sturdy and solid, and all they received for their efforts were bruises.

"I can't stand this!" Elise cried, leaning heavily against the door.

Gwyneth gasped, then sighed. "Elise, we cannot break the door. I don't believe that a *horse* could break the door."

"But they're out there . . . and we don't even know what is happening . . . Gwyneth, the last time I saw Bryan he was bloodied and wounded on the ground. Almost dying . . . I can't let it happen again! I can't! And Jalahar . . . it's all so foolish!"

"Whatever they are about to do, you cannot stop them!"

"And I can't stay here!"

She started to catapult herself against the door once again, but then stopped, spinning around in midstride. "Gwyneth! The sheets! Grab the sheets!"

"The sheets!"

"Yes . . . we've got to tie them together and climb down. I did it once before, but Jalahar caught me—and told me he would station one of his men beneath the balcony. But he won't be there now, Gwyneth. No one will be there because they've all filed out . . ."

As she spoke, Elise began industriously to tie sheets together.

"You're going to kill us both!" Gwyneth protested, gazing over the balcony and clutching her stomach uneasily.

"Just help me tie them. I'm going; you can do whatever you like."

Elise secured the tail end of the last sheet to the wrought-iron planter, jerking it hard and testing it. She hiked herself to the railing and knotted her fist tightly around the silk. Then she glanced at Gwyneth, closed her eyes for a moment, smiled nervously, and started over. She slid down the silk too quickly and landed hard upon the tile of the courtyard, but she staggered to her feet, then waved up to Gwyneth in triumph.

"Wait!" Gwyneth called anxiously. She paused, then drew in a deep breath. "I'm coming with you."

"Hold tight!" Elise encouraged her. "I can catch you before you reach the ground—oh!"

Gwyneth, too, slid along the silk—and Elise did try to catch her. They tumbled to the courtyard together, gasping for breath, but unharmed.

"Now what?" Gwyneth demanded.

"We have to get to the main gate."

"But we're in the back—"

"Gwyneth! You've been out of the chamber. Think! Which way? Where do we run?"

Gwyneth paused for a minute, then replied, "This way."

The palace was a labyrinth of sculpted arches and hallways. Silent hallways now. Their footsteps clattered over tile and marble as they ran; they reached a dead end. "Around!" Gwyneth announced, and they started back. "I see the inner courtyard!" Gwyneth exclaimed.

A moment later they were passing through the inner courtyard, with its exotic plants and splashing fountains. Gwyneth paused, staring at one of the fountains.

"Come on!" Elise hissed, pulling her arm.

They raced on through the courtyard, but paused at the main entrance to the palace. A guard remained on duty, although they could see the battered and fallen gate, and, far out on the sand beyond it, the chanting crowd.

Gwyneth pulled Elise back; they both flattened themselves to the wall. "How will we get past him?" Gwyneth demanded.

Elise gnawed her lip, trying to think quickly. "We could both run . . . no, wait!" she whispered. A pair of carved ivory lions was stationed on either side of the first fountain. Elise dashed over to retrieve one, then ducked behind the door. She waved frantically at Gwyneth.

Gwyneth took a deep breath, then sauntered to the entrance, In full view, and just slightly behind Elise.

"Oh!" she screamed out helplessly, falling to the floor. As Elise had hoped, the guard turned, lowering his sword, and hurrying to Gwyneth. Elise moved silently behind him and raised the lion, praying her aim would be true. The lion hit the back of the man's head with a dull thud, and he fell upon Gwyneth, causing her to scream again. "Get him off me!"

Elise helped Gwyneth roll the unconscious body of the guard

to the side. Gwyneth was quickly on her feet, glancing from Elise to the guard.

"Let's go!" Elise pleaded.

The gate seemed to be an endless distance away; swirling sand choked her as she ran, the morning sun blazed cruelly, and the desert chant seemed to rise in a frenzy. At the gate she and Gwyneth struggled to climb atop the rubble, but when she would have started down, Gwyneth stopped her with a startled cry.

She turned to see Gwyneth staring out over the heads of the amassed armies, Christian and Moslem, her hand clutched to her throat.

"What is it?" Elise demanded. Gwyneth didn't answer. "What is it?" Elise screamed then ignored Gwyneth and clutched at a piece of fallen masonry to gain height again herself.

The armies had aligned on either side of a vast sand chasm; Saladin, donned in his full war regalia, sat at the center of the forces, his sword raised high in the air, beaming like a ray of lightning as the sun caught and reflected its steel.

Suddenly his sword flashed in the air, coming down, and from either side of the sand chasm came a sound like roaring thunder.

The horses were racing . . .

To the left, Bryan on his destrier.

To the right, Jalahar on an Arab stallion.

Elise could not move herself, or speak. She could only stare upon the spectacle with horror as the very ground seemed to quake with those clashing hooves, coming closer and closer . . .

It was a desert trial. Man to man. Honed to deadly perfection by the advent of armor.

Both contestants rode with their swords raised high, their bodies hunched low to their horses. It was like a tournament, but it was no game. Death was the cry that rose to the air—the Christians shouting the name of their knight, the Moslems chanting that of their own. The voices and the pounding rose and rose as the horses galloped madly toward each other, spewing dirt and sand in their wake. The swords glittered in the air; the armor cast off a silver sheen.

"No!" Elise screamed, closing her eyes instinctively as the horses met. The sun seemed to burn her, and rob her of strength; she was afraid that she would fall.

A cheer rose high about her and she opened her eyes with amazement. Neither man had been unhorsed. She started to breathe a sigh of relief; then dizziness swept over her again as she saw that they were returning to their fields to ride again.

"Stop it!" she screamed. "Stop it!"

No one heard her; if they had, they wouldn't have cared. Elise started climbing down the rubble again.

"Elise!" Gwyneth called after her. "Come back! You can't go any farther—"

Elise gazed back toward her, not really seeing her. Her eyes were wild with anxiety and horror. "They have to stop . . ."

She turned and raced into the crowd. She jostled and pushed her way through the throng of Arabs. They glanced at her with nothing more than irritation; their attention riveted to the field.

But they did not part easily for her. She heard a roar begin again, and then the thunder of the ground. The horses were racing madly down the sand again, charging toward each other with flaring nostrils and flattened ears; sweat foamed along their sleek bodies.

"Stop!" Elise screamed half hysterically.

The glittering swords rose and fell; the crowd went mad. Elise barged past two fat men to get near the chasm.

Both men were down, rolling in the sand, reaching quickly to retrieve their swords. Their horses wandered from the action as Jalahar and Bryan stumbled to their feet.

She could see neither of their faces, for they both wore faceplates beneath their helmets: Bryan . . . in the coat of arms that proclaimed him Duke of Montoui, Earl of Saxonby, Lord of the Coastal Counties; Jalahar . . . his armor scrolled in the ancient and elaborate carving of his desert peoples.

They were both standing, both fighting for balance, to clear their minds from the clash of unhorsing each other . . .

They raised their swords again, and the battle on foot was under way. Elise watched for a moment, mesmerized as steel clashed with steel. Bryan was the larger man, taller, broader of shoulder; both men were agile. Both could attack with strength, dodge and parry. The battle took them veering toward the crowd, which quickly moved back, giving way. Bryan caught Jalahar with a stunning blow across the helmet; Jalahar's sword skidded past Bryan's chest, denting the armor.

"No!" Elise whispered, aware that the men about her were pleased with the battle. Two worthy opponents fought; warriors to be respected, admired. To die, to become the dust and ash of legend . . .

"No," she whispered again to herself. When she had last seen Bryan, he had lain broken and bleeding. Ashen.

She had been taken away from him. Forced to live without him just when she had learned the wonder of living with him . . . and loving him. If he died, she truly did not think she would have the will to live . . .

But as her eyes twisted to Jalahar, so did her heart. He could have practiced cruelty. He had never been anything but tender. And long ago she had learned how badly it hurt to love someone . . . if that love was not returned.

Jalahar's sword glittered brilliantly in the sun as it made a sudden swipe, sending Bryan's sword flying from his hand. Elise screamed, but the sound was deadened by the crowd.

Jalahar's triumph was short-lived; Bryan retaliated instantly, bringing his elbow down to slash Jalahar's arm, and sending that glittering Moslem sword to lie in the sand beside his own.

A flying leap by Jalahar brought the two men together, grappling bare-handed in the sand under the weight of their armor.

Elise's eyes blurred. Then she saw Saladin again, sitting on his mount and watching the battle as it raged. He did not chant or cheer as the others did; he sat calmly, only his remarkable eyes registering emotion—a calm acceptance.

Elise broke through the crowd, racing to him, throwing herself hard against his leg for his attention, her eyes beseeching his as they turned to her.

"Stop them! Great Saladin! You must stop them! Only you can do anything, only you . . . please, Saladin! I beg you!"

He shook his head at her sadly. "They have chosen to save the blood of others by fighting each other; it has been agreed that all go in peace at the outcome. They fight for their honor, and men such as they are willing to die for that honor. It is their right. I cannot take that right away from them."

"There is no honor in death!" Elise protested.

Saladin reached from the saddle to cup her chin lightly in his hand, and he was touched by the tormented eyes that sought his like twin gems of heaven. "You truly did not wish this, did you, girl?" He sighed. "One might have thought you a witch or a temptress, yet you are innocent of malice. It is no fault of yours; but men must fight, and Allah must rule the outcome."

Elise jerked angrily from his touch. "Allah! God! When men are fools, they must be stopped by other men . . ."

Her voice trailed away as she was turned back to the fighting. The crowd roared.

The men were minus their helmets and faceplates now; they were covered in sand and grime. Blood trickled from Bryan's mouth, and from Jalahar's temple and eye. Jalahar made a sudden dive across the sand for his sword; Bryan did the same.

But when they were standing again, facing each other, they were both panting heavily. Their footsteps wavered; the clashes of sword against sword became weaker. The heat, the armor, the weight of their swords was tearing them down.

Jalahar took a swipe at Bryan's middle. Bryan doubled over, backing away. But then he charged forward, returning the blow. Jalahar staggered then, falling back. Bryan raised his sword in the air; on an elbow, Jalahar lifted his own to meet it.

It was then that Elise screamed again—so loud and shrill and with such horror that the sound rose above the chants, jeers, and cheers. Her feet took flight with no conscious thought; she was running. She was flying, determined that neither God nor Allah would take a toll from her that day. It was a foolish flight, for the battling men had thought of nothing other than themselves at the moment; indeed, as she charged between them, Bryan raised his sword. Jalahar prepared to thrust with his own. She would have been impaled upon it herself had not the Arab's strength given out at that moment, causing him to falter, falling helpless to the sand.

Elise flung herself against Bryan, tears streaming down her cheeks. She had not touched him . . . seen him . . . in so long, and now she sought indigo eyes that were glazed with fatigue, eyes that barely recognized her and saw her as nothing more than an irritating interference to the business at hand. Blood, she saw, streamed from more than his mouth; gashes pierced his arms and his thighs; he was barely standing . . .

"Bryan!" she screamed to him as he started to thrust her away. "Bryan!" Her hands gripped the sun-hot steel of his armor, and she wished desperately that she could touch his flesh, for the man seemed as hard and relentless as the steel. But even beneath the barrier of that armor, she felt his sinewed form shake. He was about to drop. His size had given him the last advantage of power and stamina, but like Jalahar, he was to drop, felled by a dozen wounds.

"Bryan! It's done. Oh, please, Bryan, listen to me. You will kill each other . . . you will both die . . ."

But it was Jalahar who was down then. And the crowd, like ancient Romans at the arena, was screaming for blood. " 'Tis honorably done!" Elise pleaded.

He thrust her aside and she fell, blinded by her tears and the tangle of her hair. She lay beside Jalahar, and his deep eyes, dulled by pain, were upon her. He whispered to her, his voice so tired it carried no substance.

"He must . . . wield the blade. He is the victor. I die with honor; 'tis better than life . . . with defeat."

"No!" Elise cried, and she rolled in the sand, placing herself between Bryan's staggering form and Jalahar's body. She was vaguely aware that Saladin was roaring that she be dragged from the fight. If they were to take her from it, she would have to be dragged.

Men started to come for her. "Bryan!" she screamed in beseechment, throwing herself against his knees.

And at last he gazed down at her, at her tear-stained and mud-streaked face. A crooked smile twisted his lips.

"Elise . . ." he muttered.

"Please, Bryan . . . no more death. Please . . ."

He stared down at her. He heard the roar of the crowd, screaming for blood.

But suddenly, he didn't need to kill any longer. He loosened his grip on his sword. It fell to the sand.

Just as they had screamed for death, the throng of warriors, Moslem and Christian, turned their fickle cheers to a cry of mercy.

Bryan wavered, then buckled to his knees. His eyes suddenly closed, and he collapsed against Elise, pitching her back into the sand again, and leaving her entangled between himself and the already prone body of Jalahar.

Victor and vanquished; both lay unconscious with the woman they had fought for battered and bruised, and caught between them.

Elise struggled against Bryan's heavy shoulder, certain that her own slender limbs would quickly snap. Someone was suddenly helping her; she looked up into Saladin's sparkling eyes.

"Allah works in mysterious ways," he told her. He rolled Bryan from her and lifted her to her feet; an old and graying warrior, but one who held her with a strength that the years could not take away. He lifted a hand, and men rushed forward to care for their wounded knights; two Arabs lifted Jalahar; Wat and Mordred rushed forward to collect Bryan.

Saladin kept staring at Elise. "Men . . ." he said, ". . . are often as boys. Fighting and squabbling over a favorite toy."

"I am not a toy," Elise told him softly. "I am the Duchess of Montoui, and the Countess of Saxonby."

He smiled. "Perhaps you are not a toy. And perhaps you have taught us . . . and these boys . . . that you are not. Go in peace Duchess . . . golden girl."

"In peace?" she whispered.

He placed an arm about her and walked her toward the Christian troops who prepared to depart.

"Your King Richard ails from fever and heat; he has won, I have won. Soon, we will sign a truce. I will keep Jerusalem, but I will open it to your Christian pilgrims."

"The Crusade . . . will really be over?"

"This time . . . yes. Peace will not be everlasting. Our differences are vast. War will come again. But for you, Elise, and for your warrior, it will be over. Go now, tend to your husband."

She smiled at him uncertainly, then continued across the sand where Mordred awaited her with a mount.

"Elise!"

Saladin called her back and she turned to him.

"Thank you," he told her softly.

She lifted a brow in query and he added, "For my nephew. For Jalahar's life."

Tears stung her eyes and she nodded, then continued across the sand to Mordred. She had mounted her horse, anxious for Mordred to lead her to the litter that would carry Bryan, when her eyes suddenly widened and she cried to Mordred, "Wait!"

"Milady—" Mordred began to protest, but she turned to him swiftly and interrupted him.

"The Lady Gwyneth is still somewhere by the gates! I must find her!"

Mordred called another protest after her; she heard his footsteps racing after her own, thudding against the sand. But she eluded him swiftly, horrified that she had forgotten Gwyneth. And she knew no one would waylay her; she had Saladin's protection.

But Gwyneth was nowhere to be seen by the rubble of the

gate; Elise stood upon it, searching, but saw no sign of her friend. She climbed down and ran toward the palace, hurrying through the doors, only to stop dead-still at the fountain.

Jalahar had been brought here. He lay before the bubbling stream of water, stripped down to his robes.

And it was Gwyneth who tended his wounds, cleansing the gash atop his forehead. Elise took a faltering step forward. Jalahar's eyes opened and met hers. He smiled painfully at her, and lifted a hand to her. Gwyneth stepped back, nodding that she could come forward.

She took his hand in hers. "Would it have been so hard to love me?" he whispered. "Or did you, perhaps, just a little bit?"

Elise brought his hand to her lips and kissed the palm. "It would have been very easy to love you," she told him. "It was just that . . . I already loved another man."

He squeezed her hand, still smiling. Then his eyes closed tiredly once more, and he released her.

Elise stared at him a long while, then at last tore her eyes from him and turned to Gwyneth. "You must come now; we're leaving."

Gwyneth shook her head with a rueful grin.

"I'm not coming."

"You're not coming!"

"I'm an excellent nurse. And with you gone . . ." Gwyneth allowed her voice to trail away, and Elise understood. But she was anxious and worried.

"Gwyneth . . . he has two wives, you know. I don't think that you could ever be happy—"

Gwyneth laughed. "Those two stout crones! Elise, don't underestimate me so. I can be a very persuasive woman. And," she added, softly, seriously, "I think that perhaps we both might find what we have searched for. Bryan is yours, Elise. I think home would be only . . . painful for me."

"But . . . your son, Gwyneth. Percy . . ."

"Love him for me, will you, Elise? I know that you and Bryan can give him far more than I. Go on, Elise. You have waited so long; go to Bryan. And to your own babe. I will be happy here, I promise you."

Elise would have argued longer, but Mordred was now at her elbow, and he steered her firmly away.

It seemed amazing that the sun was still shining, and that the desert sands were still shimmering.

It seemed as if a lifetime had passed.

But it hadn't passed.

It had only begun.

There were no dreams this time, just a struggle from darkness, and then awareness.

Something cool soothed his forehead and his cheeks; a light and tender touch was upon him. He smiled before he opened his eyes, because this time he knew.

It was his duchess.

He knew her sweet and fragrant scent, and he knew that distinct touch of her fingertips, so gentle now. He opened his eyes, and they met and locked with hers. Turquoise . . . aqua . . . a tempest; an endless, peaceful sea where a man could drift in bliss eternally. He reached out an arm and captured her head with his hand, drawing it to him. His lips touched hers, trembling, and he savored the kiss as he might a vintage wine, wondering, awed by the taste that was unique nectar, soft and subtle, forever in his heart.

A sudden wail interrupted him, and he released her with a start. He saw that he was once again in their chamber at Richard's stronghold palace, and that the disturbing wail had come from the quickly crafted cradle that gently rocked on the other side of his bed of gauze net and cushions.

"I think our daughter is calling you," he said lightly. Elise glanced at him apologetically and hurried to the cradle. Bryan smiled as he watched the love his wife gave their child add an even greater beauty to her features.

She picked up the babe and came back to his side, gazing

anxiously at him. "Do you . . . like her, Bryan? I know that
men prefer to have a son, but—"

He laughed. "Do I like her? What a question to ask a man
of his firstborn! She is beautiful, and though we've known each
other but a day or two, I love her dearly."

He was surprised to see Elise lower her lashes quickly, and
more surprised to see a tear slide down her cheek. He reached
for her quickly, holding back a groan as the movement caused
his sore muscles and torn flesh a new pain to remind him of
the battle so recently fought. He didn't want her to see him
flinch now; he didn't want her worrying about him when . . .
it had been so long since he had seen her face, had her beside
him. Alone except for their daughter. Together when life had
threatened to rip them apart forever.

"What is it, Elise?" he asked her huskily, careful of the babe
as he brushed her cheek gently with his open palm. "Elise, dear
God, all is well now! I had feared that I would never hold you
again, yet we are here. You are well, and but for a headache and
a mass of cuts and bruises, I am well—"

"Oh, Bryan!" she whispered fervently. "I was so afraid . . .
afraid that you would never accept the child! That you wouldn't
want me back! There was so much distance between us! Oh,
Bryan, I know how hard this will be for you to believe, but . . .
Jalahar never touched me. He promised to wait for the child to
be born . . . and then I promised him that I would abide by the
outcome of the battle . . . and . . . oh, Bryan! I love you! I loved
you for months and months when I was terrified to say so. I
kept loving you when we were apart; it was all that kept me
sane—"

Despite his wounds, Bryan clenched his teeth together and
sat in his bed, tenderly drawing Elise and his daughter to his
chest, threading his fingers through the gold and copper hair
that had long ago entangled his heart.

"Elise!" he whispered ardently, kissing her cheeks, her forehead, her lips. "Elise! I believe whatever you say to me, my
love, but you know, it wouldn't matter. I love you. Nothing could

change that. I was fascinated, bewitched, from that night in the forest when I thought I had caught a thief. From that point on, you nestled your way so thoroughly into my heart that I often thought the loving would make me go mad. Even when I held you, I thought that you had somehow eluded me. You were such a feisty thing, never willing to accept defeat. But didn't you see, my love? I could never let you go. That was why I abducted you from Montoui and dragged you through the countryside." He smiled at her ruefully. "I was so jealous of poor Percy that I wound myself into knots. I think I even hated Gwyneth at one time because you were so angry and so deceived about her child."

Lenore, secure in her mother's arms and warmed by her father's chest, had had enough of confessions. Her tiny fists waved in the air and she began to howl again. Elise glanced from their daughter to Bryan, and she broke into a spurt of merry laughter despite the tears that still dampened her face.

"Bryan!" She laughed over the wail. "I was so jealous that I was furious! I couldn't stand the thought of Gwyneth having your child . . . especially when it seemed then that I couldn't."

"I'll give you lots of children," he promised her wickedly. "But don't you think you should do something about the squalling one that we already have?"

"She's hungry," Elise said.

"If you wish, you can call the nurse—"

Elise objected—adamantly. "She was taken away from me once; I will not let her go again. The time was not so great that I cannot care for her myself."

Bryan patted the silk-and-down cushion at his side. "Lie down with her beside me."

"I shouldn't even sit here so; you're wounded."

"Lie down beside me," Bryan persisted. "I cannot let you away from me again."

She smiled and did as he requested. The baby lay between them as Elise adjusted her clothing to feed her. Now Bryan marveled at their child as Elise had so often done, leaning upon an elbow, touching her cheek, touching the babe. A warm silence surrounded them and dusk's shadows darkened the room as Lenore continued to suck at her mother's breast.

Elise gazed at Bryan in apologetic surprise.

"She's very demanding."

He laughed. "King Henry's granddaughter would be."

Elise's eyes widened to huge orbs, and Bryan laughed again.

"How long have you . . . known?" Elise asked with startled reproach. "How . . . who . . ."

Bryan smiled wryly. "Richard saw fit to tell me when I accused him of not doing enough to get you back. I was glad—since my wife never thought to mention it."

Elise flushed. "I was going to tell you. The night that we were ambushed . . . I was going to tell you about the babe . . . and about my father."

Bryan touched a radiant lock of her hair, and his rueful grin took on broader proportions. "I'm glad that you were going to tell me. I think that I somehow linked the mystery about you with trust; if you had told me, I would have felt that you trusted me . . . and had begun to love me at last. I felt like such a fool . . . because I should have guessed. My God, I think I knew Henry better than any man! You definitely have his temper! And that hair of yours is a Plantagenet banner!" His smile faded and his night-blue eyes fell upon her intensely. "Elise . . . why didn't you tell me that night in the forest? You could have saved yourself . . . from me if you had. I would never have betrayed you."

"I know that now," she told him softly. "But I was afraid. I had been warned . . . by Henry. Montoui was small, but I couldn't afford to be vulnerable. And . . . if John were ever to know . . . Bryan, he could still make trouble for both of us. Or . . . or for Lenore, if anything were ever to happen to us."

"It is a secret that I will keep—and cherish. And I have to say now that I'm glad you were determined to keep that secret from me once—at any cost."

Elise lowered her eyes for a minute. "I was afraid because of . . . of Percy, too. He was so set on propriety. He would never have married a bastard—especially the king's. He considered Henry to be a licentious old man."

"I can only say again," Bryan told her very softly, "that I'm very, very glad." He fell silent for a minute. Lenore, sated at last, had fallen asleep between her parents. He didn't feel his cuts or bruises when he picked her up, his powerful bronzed hands extremely tender as they held his child. "My daughter," he mused reflectively to Elise, "is descended from William the Conqueror. I'm rather proud."

Elise started to smile. Then a frown creased her brow. "I'm not sure I'm pleased with my blood relations. John is a half brother as much as Richard, and . . . Henry was a lecher!"

Bryan heard the babe give off a little burp. He was afraid that he would falter if he stood, so he whispered to Elise, "Take her, she still sleeps."

Elise quickly put Lenore into her cradle. Bryan's arms were stretched out to her, and her heart seemed to pound with a splendid thunder as she came back to him, lying at his side once more. "Elise, I know how much you loved Henry. Don't ever mar that love by thinking that you needn't be proud of him. He was human: temperamental, harsh, and often unjust to his sons—and to Eleanor. But he was a good king, Elise. He gave England law. Good law, and law so strong that it might well last through Richard's absences and—God help us—John's time on the throne."

Elise smiled and reached with wonder to touch his cheek. "Thank you for that, Bryan."

"Thank you," he said softly.

"For what?"

"For Henry's granddaughter. And . . . for his daughter."

Elise lay happily against his chest, then remembered that he was a mass of nicks and bruises. She started to pull away, but he dragged her back. "I missed you . . . incredibly." His voice became tinged with harshness. "I was half insane . . . thinking about Jalahar."

Elise raised herself above him. "He never did touch me or harm me, Bryan." It was only a slight lie. He had touched her . . . but never as Bryan had. "That was why . . . I'm glad you didn't kill him."

Bryan exhaled a long breath. "Then I am glad I didn't kill him, too."

"Gwyneth stayed with him."

"She did?"

"She's says she's an excellent nurse. Is she?"

"Gwyneth was good to me," Bryan told her, reading the unspoken question in her eyes. "Good to me—that was all."

He stared into her eyes, and the happiness that filled them rewarded him for the small extension of the truth. He kissed her very lightly and murmured, "Elise . . . I believe you, and in my heart, I have never been happy to kill a man. But I would as soon not hear about Jalahar's kindness."

"And I," Elise replied, pressing a delicate kiss against an uninjured spot on his throat, "would prefer not to hear about Gwyneth's expertise as a nurse!"

"Agreed. Now, take off your clothes."

"Bryan! You are one mass of blacks and blues and nicks and—"

"I am one mass of ardent yearning—for my wife."

She should have argued with him. He had so recently been carried from battle . . .

But she was also a trembling mass of ardent yearning. His eyes, his touch . . . the beauty of knowing that he loved her . . . really loved her, as deeply as she loved him . . . all increased the hungers that she had leashed in so many dreams.

With only a slight demur of disapproval, she stripped away her tunic and shift, then lay against him once more. "Bryan . . ." She gasped, her mind swirling with delight, as his palms slid with longing over her naked flesh. "Bryan . . . I love you . . ."

"Duchess," he murmured, "I do love you . . ."

Elise rose above him before she could burst into ridiculous tears of happiness. She stared at him with a wicked smile. "I intend to prove, milord, that a wife can far better nurse her husband than any other. . . . Tell me, milord . . . where does it hurt?"

He grinned, restraining himself from flinging her down and easing the torment of need for her that had afflicted his days and nights for so long . . .

"Here . . ." he murmured, pointing to his lips. She kissed, proving a delicious expertise. Then she raised above him again. "Here . . . and here . . . and here . . ."

A warm breeze caressed them with the coming dusk. The sheets were swept from the bed . . . and she eased all his hurts tenderly until they might have been imagined . . .

If not imagined, they didn't matter anymore. In between taunting endearments, she worried about causing him pain, but he would have none of it, and the moment came when he could bear it no more, when he had to enter into her with the sweet rage of desire . . .

He was sore, and he was in pain . . .

But the ecstasy by far exceeded the agony.

In the end, he knew it had been a night he would never forget. The embrace of the night, soft breezes, swirling gauze, his sleeping babe . . .

His wife. Elise. No longer elusive . . .

His love . . . a bastion against the past, against anything the years could bring.

In June, Richard and Saladin signed a truce.

The Third Crusade was over, and Bryan and Elise—and their babe, Lenore—were able to sail for England.

Neither of them really thought of it as sailing home.

They both knew they had already come home.

EPILOGUE

April, 1199
Firth Manor, Cornwall

The rider was gaining upon her. With each thundering moment that passed, she felt the shiver of the earth more thoroughly, heard the relentless pounding of the destrier's sure hoofbeats come closer and closer . . .

Her own mount was sweating, panting, gasping for each tremulous breath that quivered through flank muscles straining to maintain the insane gallop over the mud and through the forest. Elise could feel the sinews of the animal working furiously beneath her, the great shoulders flexing . . . contracting . . .

Elise chanced a backward glance as the wind whipped about her in the darkness of the night, blinding her with loosened strands of her own hair. Her heart suddenly seemed to stop, then to thud more loudly than even the sound of the destrier's hooves behind her . . .

She smiled.

He was almost upon her. The mare hadn't a chance of escaping the pursuit of the experienced warhorse.

And she hadn't a prayer against the dark knight who rode the midnight-black stallion. She had seen him mount the horse. He was even taller than Richard the Lion-Heart, as broad of shoulder, as lean of hip. And, if anything, his agility was greater . . .

She had never had a prayer against him; he had been destined to capture her heart, and it was as securely his now as it had been almost a decade ago when she had discovered herself to be a wife very much in love with her husband . . .

"Minx!" he roared to her, and she knew he had caught her. She slowed the mare, and felt his arms sweep around her as he lifted her from the mare to sit before him on the destrier's large saddle. His eyes were bright in the night as he smiled with warm memory and kissed her . . . lingeringly. He had been away on the Continent again; each time he returned he was awed anew at the depth of the love he felt for her.

His smile faded and he feigned a fierce scowl as he lifted his lips from hers. "What is this behavior on your part, Duchess? A man returns to his home after a month abroad—and his wife races from his manor before he can dismount from his horse!"

Elise chuckled, hooking her arms about his neck and playing with the brooch that pinned his mantle at the shoulder.

"This . . . behavior . . . as you call it, is because your wife longed for minutes with you alone! Had I stood sedately on the doorstep to greet you properly, I would also have been required to entertain Will and the others who rode with you. And the children would have crawled all over you. Neither of us would have had the heart to send them on to bed! As it is, Will shall make himself at home and entertain the others, and Jeanne and Maddie shall supply them with whatever hospitality they require. And you and I . . . can join them shortly."

The last was said with a sultry smile that made his heart seem to quiver like an arrow. After ten years of marriage, and now a houseful of five children—three brothers and a sister for Lenore—she could still merely whisper, or smile in a certain fashion, and his blood would simmer to fire just as it had from the first.

Ten years, by God, yes; September would mark the tenth year of their marriage. Good years, for them, years of building and reaping. It was difficult to remember now that Firth Manor had once greeted them as a place of forlorn decay. They had made it a manor and a fortress; their little corner of the world offered good harvests and plenty, villeins who served with vigor and willingness, for the rewards of their labor, the justice of their Lord and Lady. There was quiet here; serenity and beauty.

Ten years . . . so much time, so much growth.

Time that had brought them ever closer together, yet never robbed them of that first beauty and excitement. Always, to Bryan, Elise would be his Melusine. The magic in his life. Never could he tire of her—only long for her more fully. The blood of kings was in her veins; a lion's pride ruled her heart. She was still golden and beautiful and seductive and he would find her so all the days of his life. She remained his enchantment, eternally.

Ah, but the years!

For England, they had been tense years, years in which a tug-of-war, with neither side gaining or losing, had taken place. After the Crusade, Richard had been taken a prisoner by Leopold of Austria, then turned over to that ruler's overlord, Henry of Germany. England had been bled for an enormous ransom, and Richard's men had fought long and hard to keep John from taking total control of his brother's crown in his absence.

Yet even when he had been freed, Richard, the handsome and mighty king who had been so hailed and revered by his people, had spent little time in England. Inevitably, he had gone to battle against Philip of France.

And now . . .

His scowl had been feigned, but the weary sadness that filled in his eyes was not pretense. She had made him forget in those minutes when he had thundered after his temptress . . . forget that he carried news that was the most disheartening a man could bear.

"What is it, Bryan?" Elise cried, knowing the nuances of his face so very well. Through the years, he had fought to spend his time by her side, and often he had succeeded. But there had also been those times when he had been required to ride at

Richard's side. She had learned to endure those absences, because she had learned that despite the scraps two temperamental people were bound to come to, Bryan's longing for her was as strong as the steel of his sword, as sure as its aim. In a faithless age, he was a faithful man. He always returned to her with gladness, sometimes thundering, usually demanding . . . but always with gladness.

His arms about her, as he walked the destrier through the trees, were as strong and sure as ever; she felt his love and his need in his touch. But she knew him well, and she knew that his heart was heavy, though he had greeted her with a taunting drawl.

"Bryan—?"

"The king is dead; a crossbow at Chaluz brought him down, followed by a fever for which there was no cure," he told her.

"Dear God!" she cried, and for a moment she was silent. She had never been close enough to her great giant of a half brother to feel pain at the news, but a poignant sadness gripped her, for Richard had always cared loyally for her welfare.

The news was astounding . . . and horrifying. For England. For all his absences, Richard, after Longchamp, had left the country in the hands of capable administrators—very capable men, since they had managed to keep John somewhat in check. Yet now . . .

"John will be king," she whispered.

"God help us, yes."

"Oh, Bryan! What will happen?"

He sighed, and she saw the fatigue in his features as the moon shined down upon them. Her beloved warrior was a battle-scarred man, yet time had dealt gently with him. He hadn't gained an ounce of fat on his sinewed body; his shoulders were as broad as ever, and he stood straighter than an arrow. But a trace of gray now silvered his temples, and tiny lines etched his eyes, growing deeper when he was troubled, like now.

"The likes of Will and I shall try very hard to steer him toward a decent rule. But I'm afraid, Elise. In my heart, I'm very afraid. John with a crown upon his head . . . 'tis a frightening thought indeed. There will be hard years before us, my love."

She smiled at him tremulously. "I do not fear the future, Bryan. Nothing shall be so hard that I cannot endure—not when I have you at my side."

He pressed his lips against the golden hair at the top of her head. "You are," he told her tenderly, "my fortress of peace and beauty when all else is havoc."

Elise accepted his words, loving him for them. Then she asked him, "Does Eleanor know?" The queen had so dearly loved Richard.

"She was at his side."

"For that, I'm glad." Poor Eleanor! Nearing eighty, all that she, too, sought was peace. Now . . . now she would be forced to set the best pressure that she could upon John.

"Dear Lord, but I am weary of war and politics," Bryan said.

"The king is dead, long live the king," Elise murmured softly. Yes, Bryan was tired. And the days and months ahead—and possibly the years—would be hard. So hard. He might seek to retire; men would draw him back. Such was the curse of men with character, strong of mind and body.

He had not said so yet, but he was probably not home for long. He would have to report to John. Then he would have to attempt to keep John at bay, or side with Richard's barons and the people against him. It would be a hard time; straining . . . tiring . . .

She touched his cheek impulsively.

She could travel with him . . . but their youngest son—named Henry for a secret past—was but two months old, and she was loath to leave him, or bring him to London. And in London, Bryan would have little time for her. People would be flocking to him for justice. He had served Henry; he had served Richard. The people knew and loved him.

Perhaps she would go to London. If he stayed too long.

But for now . . .

"Bryan, can we not let the future wait until tomorrow?" she asked him wistfully.

He stared down into her beautiful eyes and felt the sultry warmth and hypnotism of their pull. She was soft and pliant in his arms, yet her whisper eluded to a promise of strength, of a tempest of passion that would spur him on to distant shores, and bring him sweetly back to a peaceful harbor.

"Have you been to the cottage as of late?" he inquired huskily.

"Of course." Her eyes dazzled in the moonlight. On their return to Firth Manor from the Holy Land all those years ago, one of their first enterprises was to build a hunter's cottage on a hill in the surrounding woods. It was a place they had often come when the world had seemed too crowded.

"I didn't lead you on a merry chase at the moment of your return without reason!" she informed him indignantly. "There is warm mulled wine heating on a low-burning fire that sheds a soft and glorious glow over the room. The bed is dressed with fresh and fragrant linen sheets, and should the night turn bitterly cold, we've warm wool blankets. Freshly baked bread, should we be hungry. Creamery butter, and venison stew. Bryan, sometimes kings must wait upon men—and women!"

He tossed back his head and laughed, marveling at the way she could ease his mind of even the deepest tensions.

Yes, the will of kings could wait.

"And to think!" he said excitedly. "I once spent a night trying desperately to keep you in a cottage. And it was a night for which you hated me so deeply!"

Elise flushed. "You were a despicable tyrant."

"But I believed you to be a thief of the worst kind. And you did try to seduce me; you simply didn't realize the full portent of your power."

Elise closed her eyes and leaned against his chest. For tonight, he was completely hers. Will Marshal would understand. Will loved his wife dearly, and would understand.

Tonight . . . she would be content.

"Did you say, milord Stede, that I possessed great power . . . of persuasion?"

"Indeed."

"Then shall you mind—if I seduce you?"

"Mind? No. But you shan't have the chance, I'm afraid."

"Oh?"

He gave her a wicked, crooked smile that sent her limbs to quivering.

"For I intend to seduce you without delay."

"Oh."

He suddenly spurred the destrier through the trees, following a well-known trail. And as the destrier flew through the night, a sudden streak of lightning touched the sky, followed by a roar of thunder.

Pellets of rain began to fall upon them.

Elise glanced up at Bryan to find his eyes upon hers.

Together they burst into laughter.

The destrier raced on, galloping toward the distant glow of a fire that burned in a cottage deep in the woods.

ROMANCE FROM JANELLE TAYLOR

ROMANCE FROM FERN MICHAELS

DEAR EMILY   (0-8217-4952-8, $5.99)

WISH LIST   (0-8217-5228-6, $6.99)

AND IN HARDCOVER:

VEGAS RICH   (1-57566-057-1, $25.00)